PARADOX

Also by C.A. Fox
PROPHECY, Book Two
PRAXIS, Book Three - Coming 2025

PARADOX

C.A. FOX

Book One of the Paradox Trilogy

Surrogate Press®

Published in the United States by
Surrogate Press®
an imprint of Faceted Press®
Surrogate Press, LLC
Park City, Utah

SurrogatePress.com

CAFoxBooks.com

ISBN: 978-1-947459-86-1

Library of Congress Control Number: 2023920692

Book Cover design by: Michelle Rayner, Cosmic Design
Interior design by: Katie Mullaly, Surrogate Press®

This is a work of fiction. Any resemblance to actual persons living or dead is simply coincidence.

For Warren and Robbie Fox

"Paradoxes are the only truths."
George Bernard Shaw, *Misalliance*

Character Names, Titles: Relationships

Adgar Allerdale: Doc's spouse

Ahno: slave

Allister Ellswyth, Duke of Aychex: father of Frinz of Aychex

Almac: Midipexian guard

Aric: inn keeper in Hilsen Vale

Axster: slave

Aychex: Duke Allister Ellswyth

Birn: slave in Steppash

Borrel Starrish: Mystic, Florin's twin

Boss Taint: Director Hanter Iron Mines

Broog: Ilyan slave

Bryx Jorvan Sharkin, Sealord: Jax's older brother

Carden Yemmel, Lord of Traik: betrothed to Tallyn of Kordon

Carte Serge, Royal Mystic: Kordon

Cheshir Griffyn, Lady of Deepford: foster sister to Tallyn, Jax and Foby

Chevvain: Duchess Patrice Gracevine

Chora: ferry slave

Clairo: Duke Von Houghlow

Corvyd Cale, Lord of Cale: slave from Ily

Dayne Kora, heir to Rippsmarch: siblings - Foby and Thessaly

"Doc," Mrac Appendel: child of Marith / spouse to Adgar

Dowager Stylla, Dowager Queen: Grandmother of Jax

Dylith: friend in Hilsen Vale

Earl Oklan Kora, Rippsmarch

Earla Stona Swansee, Earla Tarron March

Edeldun: one of Felona's crew

Eleeza St. Clare, Eldar Chieftess: Lexy's sister

Ellica: niece of Earl Kora

Elmore Aethelyn, Earl of Vobury

Emmil Rohan: Tower-tested Mystic

Esmee Choles, Lady of Callisto

Essa de Farsouth, dec. Queen of Farsouth: Klaris's grandmother

Essen, Bricks of Mortar Tutor: Castle Caledra

Fairy Queen: rules the Fae

Father Mallix, Priest to Sageham

Feilor, Weaver: Master of the Mystic

Felona: Head of the kidnappers

Florin Starrish: Borrel's twin

Foby Kora, Lord of Rippsfell: son of Earl Kora, foster brother

Frinz Ellswyth, Lord of Aychex: fostered with Dayne and Bryx

Frola apWestfork: cousin to Tolomund, Herder

Garf: slave broke

Grisham: Ambassador of Baria

Grobber Vloggan, Magistrate Hilsen Vale

Hix Sharkin, Lord Admiral: 2nd cousin to Sealord Rax

Janil Embay: Lord of Phlyx

Jax, see Javix Sharkin, below

Jeress de Farsouth, Queen of Farsouth

Jolira: slave from Ohe

Juna, Oracular Priestess

Kajjon: inkeeper in Steppash

Karric: Captain of King's Guard/Tutor

Keffex: Duke Kevlor Brondon

Kember: one of Felona's "crew"

Kevlor Brondon, Duke of Keffex: cousin to King Kodill

King Kodill, Kodill Brondon

Klaris de Farsouth, Princess of Farsouth: Tower-tested Mystic

Kodill Brondon, King of Kordon: Jax's uncle (mother's brother)

Koralixa Windish, Lady of Jeff

Lad Yob: Saghamite servant to Klaris

Lady Mollish, Priestess to Kree: druid

Lexyl St. Clare, Speaker's Heir: Mystic, sister to Eleeza St. Clare

Lord of Traik: see Carden Yemmel

Marith Appendel, druid in Hilsen Vale: Doc's mother

Midipex: Duke Thorag Addle
Mik: slave
Millicen: minor noble of the Rippsmarch
Moiry: ferry slave
Mother Ayslic, Priestess to Baria
Neben de Rillt, Lord of Rillt: Spouse to Shallyx of Callysto
Nevan: ferry slave
Nyle: slave
Oblek, overmaster
Oklan Kora, Earl of Rippsmarch: kids - Dayne, Foby, Thessaly
Ollie: slave
Oracle, Speaks for the Goddess
Duchess of Chevvain: Patrice Gracevine
Pop Gulligan: friend to Marith in Thequis
Prina: Eleeza's wife
Professor Hiddicot, Dock and Portal Tutor
Professor Lellyn, Tower Tutor
Raggar, Dragon Highlord
Rax Sharkin VII, Sealord of Baria: Bryx and Jax's father
Rippsmarch: Earl Oklan Kora
Shallix of Callisto: preeminent Barian sailor
Shaloh: Foby Kora's favorite dog
Shaman Ashande, Shaman in Arandy
Slave Wrangler: Hanter Iron Mines
Stona Swansea, Earla Tarron March
Stylla Aethelyn, Dowager Queen: grandmother to Jax, Tallyn and Bryx
Tallyn Brondon, Crown Princess: Jax's cousin and foster sibling
The Crone: slave
Thessaly Kora: Foby's younger sister, druid
Thorag Addle, Duke of Midipex: Chancellor of Kordon
Tillish: ferry overmaster
Tolomund apWestbrook: cousin to Frola, Thequis
Valla Brondon, dec., Consort of Baria; child of Stylla; mother of Jax
Viscal Crane: owner Hilsen Mercantile

Vobury: Earl Elmore Aethelyn

Von Houghlow, Duke of Clairo

Widow Keffex, Duchess of Keffex

Wishalore Allowan: Kordish scholar of botany

Yory: ferry slave from Norledge

Expanded biographical information:

Javix Brondon Fellix Sharkin: Prince of Baria, Prince of Kordon, Viscount Norbay. Nephew of King Kodill of Kordon; Son of Sealord Rax Sharkin and Valla Brondon of Kordon; foster siblings, Koby Fora of Rippsfell, Cheshire Griffyn of Deepford and Tallyn Bondon of Kordon. He dislikes the name Javix, especially because it's usually mispronounced in Landish.

Titles and Names:

Thorag Addle, Duke of Midipex, Lord Chancellor:

> Referred to as the Duke of Midipex, Lord Thorag, or simply by his territorial name: Midipex.

> He would be addressed formally as: Lord Thorag, Duke Thorag, or Your Grace.

> Less Formal: my lord. His peers might call him Thorag, as could his wife, but she doesn't (this is explained in book two).

Crown Princess Tallyn Brondon:

> Referred to as Princess Tallyn.

> Addressed formally as your royal highness (because she's heir to the throne), then Ma'am or my lady.

Prince Javix Sharkin:

> Referred to as Prince Javix or Prince Jax.

> Addressed formally as your highness, my lord, or sir.

> Might be referred to as Norbay (his territorial name) but since it's less important than being a Prince of the Blood, he'd more likely be called prince.

Kordish Royal Council:
    King Kodill
    Dowager Stylla (non voting)
    Crown Princess Tallyn
    Lord Chancellor, Duke of Midipex, Thorag Addle
    Duke of Keffex, Kevlor Brondon
    Duchess of Chevvain, Patrice Gracevine
    Duke of Aychex, Allister Ellswyth
    Duke of Clairo, Von Houghlow
    Earl of Rippsmarch, Oklan Kora
    Earl of Vobury, Elmore Aethelyn
    Earla of Tarron March, Stona Sweansea

Floating Islands:
    Helm: Bryx Sharkin
    Jeff: Koralixa Windish
    Rillt: Neben de Rillt
    Callisto: Esmee Choles
    Phlyx: Janil Embay
    Ayx: Villar d'Ayx

THE KNOWNLANDS

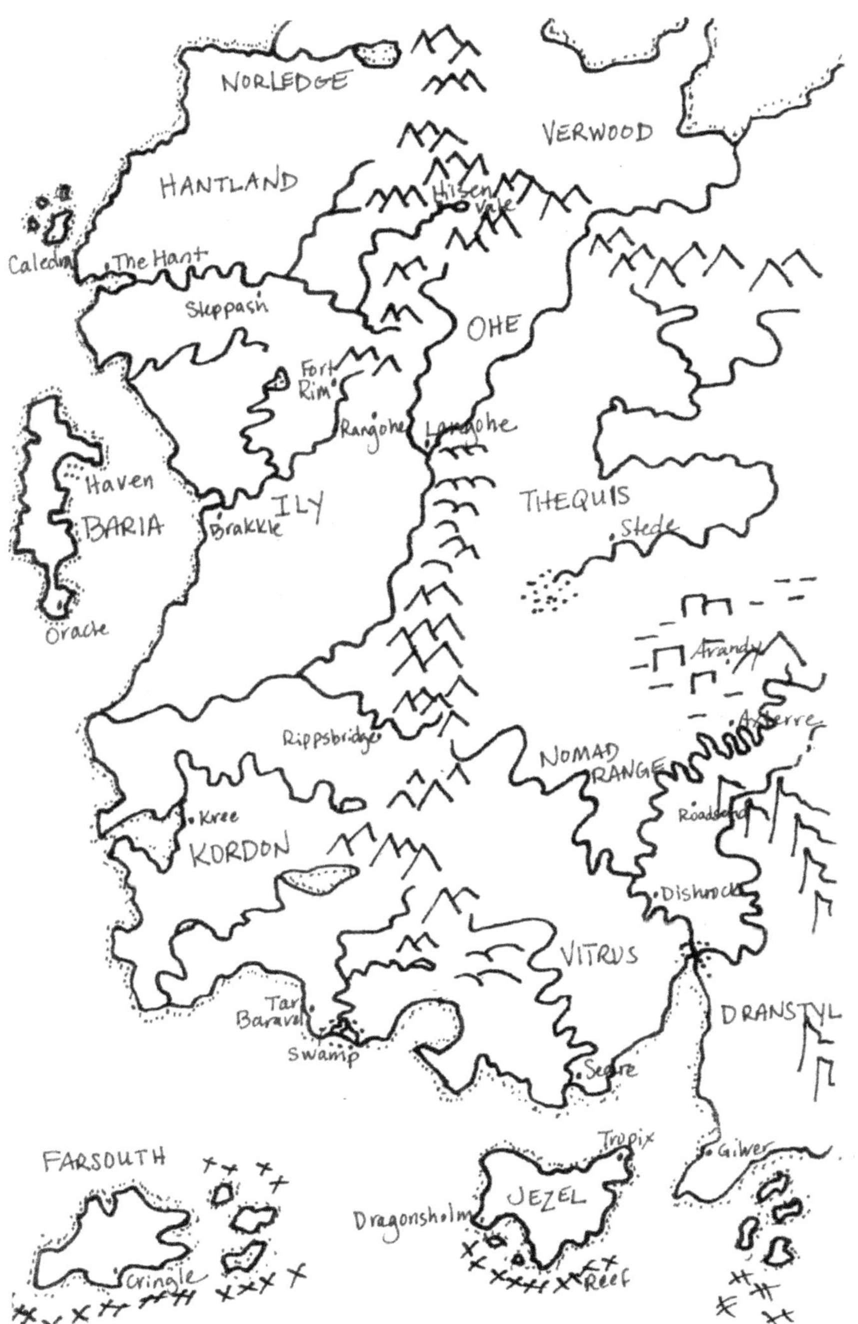

1

Even four against one it took a fight to get him pinned. He had the strength of his youth, the height of his islish father, and he was desperate.

Now, three of them held him, panting and pinioned, on the dirt floor while the leader stood up, wiping blood from her nose. "I've had enough of this," she said,

"Me too," he snapped.

His silk shirt had torn in the scuffle, revealing the small tattoo below his collarbone.

"I ain't never seen one of these up close," Kember said, ripping the shirt back a bit more. "It don't look like much."

"It doesn't make him smarter than us," said the woman, bending over the fire to retrieve a knife that had fallen into the embers.

"Just better educated," the prisoner sneered.

Like a snake, the woman struck with precision, laying the flat of the red-hot knife over the tattoo.

He howled a curse in Islish, his native tongue coming first in the shock of pain.

"Crying in gibberish?" spat the guard working to control the kicking legs.

"Dragons fry you idiots!" he translated, writhing.

Finally, the woman withdrew the knife, leaving a bubbling welt that ruined the tattoo.

The guards released him, and he sat up slowly, breathing heavily. He leaned back against the stone wall, looking warily at the woman.

She stood over him, considering his weird islish eyes. "You're the damned idiot." She wiped bits of gore from the knife. "I'll have no more of your posh and twisty words or your pathetic bit of Dragon force, burning through your tethers. You'll travel along quietly from now on, or I'll let Kember kill you. Is that clear, Half-isle?"

The slur stung. "I have a name."

"Not anymore." She smiled. "We've just erased it."

"It's not the tattoo that makes me a prince."

"Sure, it's the royal blood." She let the knife flash in the red firelight. "But we can drain that from you too." She sheathed her blade. "Edeldun, take him outside. It's time to move."

Edeldun pulled the prisoner to his feet and shoved him out through the blanket that covered the doorframe.

A fortnight ago, Javix Sharkin, Prince of Kordon and Baria, had never experienced such physical abuse or deprivation. He stumbled into the fresh air and noted the surrounding, snow-covered hills, as empty as his stomach. The past ten days had taught Jax some hard lessons about hunger and the simple mathematics of being outnumbered, but he hadn't learned to curb his tongue.

This morning's fight had begun as he considered the others still eating and his own empty bowl.

"I wonder how Midipex plans to murder you," he had said conversationally. "You know he can't afford to let you live as witnesses to his crimes against a Prince of the Blood."

Kember sneered. "The duke can't afford to harm us. We're his best crew, right Felona?"

Felona answered with her mouth full. "You might have thought you were important, Half-isle, but you'll notice that no one has come to take you back. That should tell you something."

The unfortunate lack of rescue had certainly puzzled the prince. The magicians would have scried him days ago. Surely Tallyn or Foby or Ambassador Grisham should have chased down Felona and her thugs and saved him by now.

But no one had. Frustrated by these facts, he threw his empty bowl at Kember's head, sparking the fight that ended with Felona's hot knife branding his skin.

The cold air felt good on the wound and cleared his head. He turned to the guard. Edeldun had been the most respectful of the three men, and the only one who seemed at all troubled by the fact that kidnapping a Prince of the Blood was treason.

"Edeldun, where are you taking me?"

"I ain't supposed to tell you...sir."

"I think we're going to the trolls at The Hant."

Edeldun nodded.

Jax pulled out the golden coin he'd found last night deep in his pocket. His uncle's gilded profile gleamed in the morning sun. "Take this, quickly, and once you're back in Kordon tell a Barian, any Barian, where I am."

"Oh, sir..."

"Take it. And watch your back."

Edeldun shuffled, his eyes never leaving the coin.

The others began to throw their gear out of the blanket-covered doorway.

"Take it," Jax whispered urgently.

Edeldun snatched the gold just as Felona pushed through the blanket. "Move him away," she ordered.

Jax followed willingly to get out of range of the cross-magic he would suffer if he stayed too close while Felona used her Mystic to return the shelter to the earth.

While she was weaving her magic, the guards bound Jax onto a mule, as they had done each day, only now they used chains because

Jax had used his own magic to burn through the all the ropes. Soon they were riding over winter-bare fields and through leafless woods, avoiding roads and villages. Felona had been instructed that the prince must disappear without a trace.

With the mutilated sigil of his birthright still stinging, Jax faced the same grim thoughts that he faced each day. Even after the abuse and terror of the past two weeks, he couldn't quite believe that his father, the Sealord of Baria, was dead, killed in a freak accident at sea.

Tall and fun-loving, Sealord Rax left a big wake as he sailed through life. Now his eldest heir, Prince Bryx, would have to take the Helm of the island nation. Jax knew that his older brother preferred the landish habits of their Kordish mother. He would need help securing his grip on their father's legacy.

But it was their mother's legacy that had put Jax on this mule heading for The Hant.

Nearly two weeks ago he'd woken from dreams of drowning and realized someone had tied a cloth over his head. Hard hands twisted his arms behind his back and bound them. Someone roughly pulled heavy wool pants up his legs and shoved boots on his feet.

"Dragons! I can dress myself."

"Shut up, milord," growled a woman.

"Alright, let's go now," she said. Jax felt himself hefted between several hands.

"All set, Felona?" Jax recognized that fluty voice: Thorag Addle, the Duke of Midipex and Lord Chancellor of Kordon.

"We've got him, your Grace."

They carried him awkwardly down some stairs and came to a sudden stop.

"It's all taken care of, your Majesty," the duke said softly.

"You won't kill him?" This voice belonged to his grandmother. "I don't want him killed."

"No, ma'am," Midipex oozed. "We won't kill him. Felona will take him on a long journey."

"Fine. I don't want to know any more about it. And I don't want to see him ever again."

"Have no fears, your Majesty," said Felona.

A dog began barking somewhere in the castle. "Ma'am," the duke's tone became peremptory, "we must hurry and get him out of the castle and far from Kree before daylight."

"Go."

With rising panic, Jax fought to free himself, but he was bound too tightly. He took a deep breath and pulled on his magic. Flames licked through his captors' clothes.

"Oh, dragons!" They dropped him with a hard thud.

"Pop him on the head," Felona ordered tightly, and Jax's world went dark.

Now, weeks later, Jax squirmed against the chains that bound him to the mule and the heavy dread that lived in his gut. He had studied history. Inconvenient princes had "disappeared" from time to time, but Jax could not understand why the Duke of Midipex had plotted against him. As lord chancellor, Midipex could and did negotiate plumy benefits for his own wealthy duchy, his family, and his personal favorites. By comparison, all Jax had was royal blood.

That blood, however, was the source of his well-understood troubles with his grandmother. Jax's mother, a princess of Kordon, had died at his birth, and his grandmother would not forgive him. Few tutors would or could ignore the opinions of the Dowager Queen of Kordon, no matter how well a student performed. She made no secret of her dislike.

She wasn't the only one. As rare mixed-race children, Jax and his brother had faced constant prejudice and scorn in Kordon and Baria. But Bryx was the heir to the Helm of Baria, and he learned early that no one wanted to insult the future sealord. Without a crown in his future, Jax had to rely on his wits, and a nugget of wisdom he'd learned from his father.

Bryx and Jax were each sent at age six to foster at the royal court of Kordon, as was the Kordish custom. After spending his first six months in Kree, Jax returned home to Baria excited to share what he'd learned while fostering, but also with joyful expectations of being among what he considered his own people. On his first morning back, he went to sail small boats with other Barian children, but he was out of practice, and they taunted him, blaming his ineptitude on the fact that he was only half islish.

Jax had suffered the belittlement of prejudice in Kree, where he had to learn a new language, new foods, new types of clothes, and new activities that often involved horses. Afraid of the large animals, he couldn't get any horse or pony to work with him, and the Kordish had no patience for Jax's left-handedness. To have survived all those indignities in Kree and then find himself ostracized at home, broke his young heart and infuriated him.

He was about to incinerate Orla of Phlyx's little boat, but Nanny Grosmith saw his anger building and hauled him away to his father.

Sealord Rax stepped out of a tense meeting with the captains of Rillt and looked with some exasperation at Nanny Grosmith. Jax, already worked up, poured out his anger at the injustice of the prejudice he faced both in Kordon and on Baria, his voice rising and tears falling.

"Nanny, would you get Prince Jax and me some tea and biscuits?" Rax asked, so that he could have a moment alone with his son. When Nanny left, Rax invited Jax to climb onto his lap. Jax sobbed into his father's chest, comforted by the strong arms and calm heartbeat.

"I can see that it's been hard on you to be in Kree." Rax stroked Jax's Kordish-blond hair. "I forgot that when Bryx went to his fostering, he already knew Landish, so it was easier for him. And he likes his horses."

"I understand Landish now," Jax hiccupped. "Mostly. But I can't always say their words."

Nanny returned with the tea, Jax's favorite biscuits, and a handkerchief. She poured the tea, while Rax wiped Jax's tears away.

"You know what surprises me?" Rax took a sip of his tea. "I don't understand why people think that you are somehow less because you have both Barian and Kordish blood."

"They call me Half-isle," Jax said and repeated the slur in Landish.

"I know," Rax hugged the thin shoulders. "Here, Jax, take a sip of your tea."

Jax did and frowned again. "It's bitter."

Rax dropped a sugar cube into the teacup and used a silver spoon to stir it until the grains dissolved.

Jax took another sip.

"Better?" Rax asked.

Jax nodded.

"So, let's think about someone with only Kordish or only Barian blood as plain tea," Rax said. "When we mix it with sugar it gets a lot better doesn't it?"

Jax took another sip of tea and nodded. He ate a biscuit and sent a calculating look at Nanny. "It would be even better with another sugar cube."

Ever since that day, the taste of tea reminded him that he wasn't just half, but rather a better whole.

But now, bound on the mule in the cold morning, he felt wholly trapped. He wiggled his bound wrists, trying to get some of that mixed royal blood into his frozen fingers. Panic again rose in shivers through his muscles and tangled with the ache in his heart. How was this happening to him? What awaited him in the Hantland?

Jax had been to The Hant once when he served as a midshipman to the lord admiral. He remembered the huge, orange-eyed trolls who ruled there and the miserable figures of the people the trolls enslaved. Jax could not imagine how anyone survived that degradation. Nor could he imagine that a prince would ever be subject to such humiliation. Surely, Felona and her men had other plans for him. Surely.

Cold days followed hard nights as they continued heading north. Jax saw no one but the three guards and Felona. His illustrious names couldn't keep him warm, and his smart mouth just brought further beatings. At night he lay in clanking chains, wondering with increasing anger why no one had saved him. Bryx would be absorbed in assuming the Helm of Baria, but his Kordish foster siblings ought to send help. His cousin Tallyn, Crown Princess of Kordon, had nearly unlimited resources. Lord Foby would have sent out his hounds. And Lady Cheshir, beautiful, artistic Cheshir wouldn't just let him go. Finally, he slept, warmed by a hope that his friends would find a way to rescue him.

But hope fell away as the rolling fields were overwhelmed by the dark Y-Gren forest. Under the trees, the horses stumbled in the heavy snowdrifts, and twice one of the horses slipped into the mule, knocking Jax off in a tangle of chains.

"You are pathetic," Felona told him as he sat in the middle of an ice-bound creek after the second fall. "You can't even stay on when we tie you there."

Bruised and shivering, Jax felt unhinged. "I'm attempting flight," he laughed unsteadily, until the men tackled him and returned him, without humor, to back of the mule.

The next morning, Felona took all the animals, leaving everyone else in the shelter, and returned late in the afternoon with snowshoes and a sled.

"We're all walking now because of you, Half-isle." Kember snarled, as he loaded their gear onto the sled.

"I hope it makes you just as miserable," Jax snapped.

"We'll see about that." Felona smiled and handed Jax the ropes of the sled. "Pull!"

Jax took his time trudging along in the others' tracks. The heavy sled bogged down in the deep snow and caught up on low branches.

"Keep up!" Kember shouted.

"You can yell all you want," Jax answered, "But I can't go any faster."

"He's right," Felona noted. "Edeldun, you pull with the half-isle. Kember, it's your turn next."

For a week they trudged through the shadowed paths of the Y-Gren Forest. Eventually, they emerged from the woods onto the treeless steppes of the Hantland. Travel wasn't any easier here. The unrelenting wind turned their sweat to ice as they continued to wade through drifted snow around the steaming Hanter Lake. By the time they arrived at the walled city of The Hant, Jax was too exhausted and hungry to muster panic, but as Felona left her men at an inn and led Jax into the heart of this city, dread filled his empty stomach.

Felona prodded Jax with her dagger through the slushy street, past a livery stable, and stopped in front of a yellow brick shop. An elegant sign read "Slave Broker."

She pushed Jax before her into the small office. The orange eyes of three trolls turned to look at them.

"Hello Garf," Felona said. "Remember me?"

Garf closed his ledger book and smiled slowly.

"Why Felona, how could I forget? We don't see many southerners here." Garf spoke in a deep voice with a broad northern accent. A grainy yellow powder covered his face, settling more darkly into old pox marks. Two circles of maroon rouge bobbed on the troll's cheekbones. Jax stared at this strange mask, remembering that the trollish oligarchs applied makeup with a heavy hand.

"I've brought you merchandise." Felona smiled and indicated Jax with a wave of her hand.

Garf walked around his desk, considering the unusual combination of features on the "merchandise." It had the slanted blue eyes and pointed ears of the islish, but this one had fair skin and light hair, almost as pale as Felona, herself.

"What is it?" Garf asked finally.

"Half-islish."

"Never had an isle before, much less half of one."

The other two trolls laughed.

Garf screwed up one eye and looked Jax up and down. "How old?"

"I'm nineteen," Jax answered.

"Naught but a boy," said Garf.

"I'm no boy. I'm Javix Sharkin, Prince of—."

"Ha!" Felona's quick fist knocked him to the floor. "That kind of talk is how I got him in the first place. His family got tired of his illusions, you see. His head's not right."

"Now, Felona." Garf answered. "Who am I supposed to believe here? An unscrupulous slave trader or a fancy-dressed islish lad who calls itself Sharkin?"

Felona shrugged. "I suppose you'll believe whatever suits your financial interests."

Garf curled his lips and looked down at Jax. "I don't know..."

He motioned to the trolls lounging by the radiator. "Come take off its clothes, let's have a look at it.... Hey, easy with those rags. Felona here probably thinks I'll pay extra for them."

"You won't get them otherwise." Felona smiled. Business was going well now.

Jax stood naked before the three trolls and Felona. "Do you want to see my teeth too?" he taunted.

The troll frowned at him and poked at the marbled pink scar with lines of purple in it below Jax's left collarbone. "What's this?"

"It was the sigil of my birthright," Jax snapped.

"Birthmark," Felona answered quickly, watching the troll carefully.

"What?" Garf blinked. "I don't understand its accent."

Jax spoke slowly in his aristocratic Landish. "Felona is trying to mislead you. She mutilated the tattoo that proves my Kordish royal blood."

Felona laughed scornfully. "See what I mean, Garf? He's delusional."

Garf considered the way the half-isle held itself. "Nobles don't make good slaves." His orange eyes went from Jax to Felona and back to Jax again. "I'll give you twenty silvers for it."

"Come on, Garf, that won't even cover my costs to get him here."

"It ain't worth more."

"He's worth at least fifty to you. The iron mines always need new slaves."

"Yeah, but they prefer females—they last longer, and they don't have those ugly whiskers." He huffed. "All right. I'll give you twenty-nine silvers, but not an iron more."

"Done." Felona smiled triumphantly.

Garf counted out coins. "Orrg, get it shaved and dressed."

Felona left without a backward glance as Orrg pushed Jax to a chair and roughly scraped six weeks' of beard from his cheeks.

"What the dragons!" Jax protested, trying to squirm away.

"No one will buy a whiskered slave," Orrg explained. "It's disgusting."

A few minutes later, his cheeks stinging, Jax pulled on the cast-off, oversized clothes the troll gave him.

"Sit," Garf barked, when Jax was dressed. "We'll go to the iron mines when I'm done with this accounting."

"Look, Garf." Jax took a step towards the broker's desk. "You know who I am. Ransom me to the Barians. They'll pay whatever you ask."

The troll leaned back in his chair and blinked his orange eyes.

"I thought you said you were Kordish."

"I am half Kordish and half Barian," Jax answered.

"That doesn't help you," Garf said. "Those Barians sail in to The Hant now and again, strut around with their noses in the air, speaking their weird gibberish, and tear out of here once they've made a profit off us poor trolls. Naw. I'm going to sell you to the iron mines and be done with you."

"But—"

"I told you to sit!"

Jax sat, knees drawn up to his chest. He leaned his head back against the wall and, hoping the trolls at the iron mines would be more reasonable, tried to sleep. But hunger gnawed at him. The trolls by the radiator kept throwing bits of trash at him. Jax finally flicked his bit of Dragon force at one of these and the flames leapt to the ceiling.

"That's enough!" In one motion Garf picked up the heavy ledger book and swatted Jax with it. He stood glaring at the goose egg growing on the lad's forehead. After a moment, the sea-blue eyes opened again and blinked at the troll.

"Slaves ain't allowed to use magic," Garf growled.

"I'm not a slave."

"Oh yes, you are, my boy. Yes, you are."

arf returned to his ledger. Jax sat up slowly, his head pounding. He wasn't a slave, yet, so he evaluated the flammable items in the small office: A wooden bookcase held neatly stacked accounts, and a wicker bin overflowed with castoff clothes for slaves. None of this would fuel more than a flash of flame and the trolls' anger. He slumped back against the wall.

Finally, Garf leaned back in his chair, stretching. "Harness it up," he ordered.

The two trolls pulled Jax to his feet, bound his hands behind his back and buckled a thick leather collar around his neck. They attached a worn leash to the collar and handed it to Garf. The troll wrapped himself in a heavy coat and went out, dragging Jax along with him.

"Civilized people use words to communicate," Jax said, his wooden clogs slipping in the slush.

Garf used a fist, which Jax found equally expressive.

Shivering as the freezing air cut through the thin, worn clothes, Jax followed Garf through the crowded streets of The Hant. He noticed eight or nine slaves, marked by the collars around their necks, accompanying warmly dressed trollish masters among the shops and stalls of the streets.

Soon they passed through a gate in the eastern side of the city wall and emerged on the same ice-rutted road Jax had just come down with Felona and her crew. They took a track to the right that led down towards the vast Hanter Lake, which was really a large inland bay. Warmed by the boiling Vrillian River that fed into it, the lake steamed in the icy evening air. About half a mile outside the city walls, they arrived at the windowless gray fortress that enclosed the infamous Hanter Iron Mines.

Jax looked up at the high stone walls as his bit of Dragon force responded to the pull of the old Mystic that had called the building up from the rocky earth. Garf pounded on the heavy wooden door.

A small peephole slid open, and an orange trollish eye looked down upon them.

"Open up, I'm bringing merchandise."

The peephole banged shut, and the door squeaked open.

Jax stood his ground. "I'm not going in there."

Garf just shook his head and hauled hard on the leash. Tall as he was, Jax was no match for the larger troll, who was well practiced in moving unwilling slaves. The heavy door thudded shut behind them.

Low barracks that housed the many administrators and guards of the mine clung to one wall. On the south side of the compound, a tall chimney belched gray smoke. Steam rose from various vents in the ground and walls, seething then dispersing like a ghost. In the center of the courtyard, a gaping hole led down into the earth. A line of dirty mine slaves crawled up out of the hole. On their backs, each carried a large bag of rocks. Hunched beneath the heavy loads, the slaves shuffled to the smoking smelters at the base of the chimney. Jax saw slaves everywhere, lugging, pulling, pounding, digging. Guards stood around with whips and clubs and watched.

Jax cringed as a whistle screeched, signaling the end of the workday.

"Hurry up," Garf growled, leading Jax into one of the barracks. Inside, humid warmth filled the building. Jax had learned that the trolls used steam from Hanter Lake to heat their buildings during the harsh Hantish winters, but he had never felt or smelled the sulfuric, damp reality of this technology.

"Well, if it isn't Garf-the-Parasite." The mine boss' bleary eyes hung halfway down his jowly cheeks, which seemed petrified in a perpetual frown. Two plum-colored blobs of rouge rode the loose skin. These were magnified by the round glass the troll had been using to peer at a cylindrical piece of rock.

"Boss Taint, wait till you see the fine specimen I've brought you today." Garf ignored the mine boss's petulance and gestured grandly towards Jax.

Boss Taint lowered his magnifying glass as he eyed Jax up and down.

"What kind of creature is this?"

"A half-isle!"

"No islish." Boss Taint resumed his inspection of the rock sample.

"You don't want to miss this opportunity, Boss," Garf persisted. "It's young, and it walked all the way here from Kordon. I'll give it to you for a fair price, but only if you buy it right now. You know Glavin Vogglebock has been begging me to find him strong young slaves for his new construction project."

With a grunt Taint pushed his massive, fleshy body up from his desk. Slowly he shuffled towards Jax. Watching the orange eyes, Jax saw the punch coming, but it still doubled him over.

"What'd it do before?"

"Does that matter?"

"I'm a prince of Baria and Kordon." Jax gasped. "That ought to matter."

"Funny accent," Taint growled, bending over to peer into Jax' face.

"You should hear yourself," Jax straightened.

Boss Taint slapped him across the face. "You do not speak." He turned to Garf. "I'll give you forty for it. Guard!"

Another troll entered the chamber. "Take this half-isle thing down to the slave wrangler."

"Wait!" Garf stopped them. "I want my tackle back." Deftly, he pulled the bonds off Jax's hands and unbuckled the leather collar.

The guard took Jax down the hallway to a smaller office. Bookshelves crammed with files lined the walls around a desk strewn with loose papers and small pots spilling red cosmetic powder over everything, but no one was there. The guard rang a bell loudly. Aching from the blows, Jax leaned against the wall.

"What, what, what?" The high voice of a fe-troll rasped against Jax's nerves. "Can't a person eat dinner in peace? Not around *this* place. I'm telling you..." Her words became unintelligible as she stuffed half a loaf of bread into her mouth. Jax watched with fascinated horror as her magenta-tinted lips moved with her jaw while she chewed, ruffling through the papers on her desk, ignoring him and the guard. Finally, she found what she wanted then she had to rummage around some more to dig up a pen. Seating herself at her desk, still chewing on the bread, she peered at Jax, perplexed.

"What are you?"

"What am I?" Jax asked with growing desperation. "I'm hungry; I'm hurt, and frankly, I'm pretty terrified."

The fe-troll blinked, clearly not understanding Jax's crisp accent. "What? Can't you speak plain Landish? Do you even understand what I'm saying?"

"I understand, but I find it incomprehensible."

The fe-troll squinted at him for a moment as she gnawed the already masticated end of her pen.

"What is your name?" She asked very slowly.

"Javix Brondon Fellix Sharkin, Prince of Baria, Vice Admiral of the Barian Fleet, Viscount Norbay, Prince—"

"Half-isle," the guard interrupted.

The fe-troll looked from Jax to the guard and back again. She spoke the words as she wrote them down: "Half-isle."

"No ma'am, it's Javix Sharkin."

She looked up and frowned. "Can't spell that."

"Ma'am, I'm a Barian prince. You can ransom me back to them for far more than you paid."

"Barian prince? Sure!" The fe-troll laughed. "That's one I ain't heard before. A Barian! And a prince, it says!"

"A prince *he* is!" Jax protested. "I am a person, not an *it*, and not just any person. Ask the next Barian ship that makes port here if they know Jax Sharkin."

"Yeah, yeah, yeah." The slave wrangler looked back at her form. "Every new slave has some story. Even if you were a prince, I need laborers more than I need money. Now, what can you do?"

"Do?" He was baffled.

"Aye, do. Are you daft? Have you training as a smith? A farmer, what?"

Jax felt hysterical laughter bubbling from his rumbling stomach. "I rule."

The fe-troll rose from her desk and came around to where Jax still leaned against the wall. She was a head taller and stared down into his face. He stared back, still choking on laughter. She grabbed a fist-full of his shirt and pulled it up to look at his stomach and chest.

"Rule, eh?" She threw down the shirt. "You can't even rule your-self at the moment, can you?" She shuffled back to her desk mutter-ing to herself. "Another sorry creature: beat up, under-fed. And the boss complains to me when they all die of the fever. But it ain't my fault."

Without looking up she spoke to the guard. "Get the smith to put a collar on our new ruler here, then feed it and put it down in Cave Three."

"Him," Jax corrected. "Feed him."

"Yes ma'am." The guard pulled Jax after him out of the dim room.

The smith, having already banked his fires and donned his coat to leave for the night, grumbled and complained about having to start things up again. The guard forced Jax to kneel near the forge. With impatient blows of his hammer, the smith ungently fastened the hot ring around Jax's neck.

Jax gagged at the stench of his own burning skin, and he fought to get away, but the guard held him tightly. After the collar had been hammered into place, the guard stuffed Jax's head and neck into a deep bucket of water. The cold water soothed the burns and washed away Jax's tears of pain. The guard pulled him up by the hair.

"Trying to drown yerself?"

"I'm not going to drown in a bucket," Jax answered, as he shook the water out of his hair and eyes. His neck stung as blisters began to rise where the hot metal had scorched him. The guard clicked a leash into the new collar and pulled him back out into the courtyard.

At this hour the mess hall's rough benches and grease-stained tables stood empty, lit dimly by a couple of sputtering torches. From the kitchen, the guard brought a tepid bowl of thin broth dotted with white globs of grease. Jax gulped it down. It was rancid and awful, but it was something in his stomach, at last.

Once more, the troll led Jax along a corridor, and down a flight of worn stone steps. The reek of sulfur grew worse as they descended. Occasional torches lit the steamy darkness, throwing misshapen shadows along the walls. Wooden doors stood at intervals along the wall, each locked with heavy iron bars.

At the third door, the troll stopped, found the precise key on a jingling ring, opened the padlock, and lifted the bar. The door opened like a mouth into blackness.

The guard shoved Jax in and pulled the door shut. Jax's head started to swim. He put a hand to the wall to steady himself then sank slowly to the floor. His feet knocked against someone.

"Watch yerself," a voice grumbled in a thick northern accent.

"I can't watch if I can't see," Jax said.

"Just lie down and sleep," a woman's tired voice advised.

"Shut up! Shut UP!" a man screamed. Jax flinched.

"Dragons," someone moaned.

"Shut up! Shut UP!" The screamer repeated.

More muffled moans came from around the room. As his eyes adjusted to the gloom, Jax discerned about fifteen people lying on the ground.

"Shut UP! Shut UP!" The screamer again.

Someone started to sob.

"Shut UP! Damn you all! Shut UP!"

Jax folded himself onto the dirt floor and cradled his head on his arms.

This was the end of the road. Even in Baria and faraway Kordon, he had heard of the notorious Hanter Iron Mines. Slaves rarely lasted more than six months here.

"Shut UP! SHUT UP!"

Surely Bryx knew that he had disappeared from Kordon by now. What story had the Duke of Midipex concocted for the king? What had anyone told Tallyn? Would Bryx find him here? Bryx, who was now the sealord. Surely someone had found him in a scry by now, so why hadn't they saved him?

A sob stole his breath and despair locked cold hands around his heart.

"SHUT UP! SHUT UP!"

F elona's feet ached. It was a damn long walk from The Hant to Ily. Tomorrow she'd be in Brakkle, safely across the borderlands between Ily and the Hantland and far enough beyond the reach of trolls, who would snatch unwary travelers and enslave them.

Of course, she was never unwary. That was why she still put up with the sniggering, snoring, stupid trio of guards. But once in the Ilyan capital, she could travel freely on her own.

Kember sidled up to her as she walked. "I'll take Edeldun first," he whispered. "He might be difficult if he has warning."

Felona nodded. "I'll wait for you in that stand of trees on the hill over there."

Kember winked. "Just you and me, Felona. We can celebrate in Brakkle."

Felona's smile was warm and promising. She turned to the two guards behind and played her part. "I'm going to scout that hill up there. I think we're getting close to Brakkle, and I want to look at it before we get to the town gates."

"We'll wait for a signal from you." Kember threw down his pack.
"Good."

She marched up the hill marveling at the arrogance of men. Who, by the goddess, did Kember think he was? Worthy of her? Ha! Indignation fired her climb into the trees. She looked around the grove and chose her location carefully. Kember was quick and strong, but as Prince Jax had noted, he didn't have much for brains.

She turned to watch the men back on the trail. All three of them had brushed snow off some logs and sat down. Kember stood and stretched. Casually he walked behind Edeldun. A knife flashed in the afternoon sun, and Edeldun slumped off the log.

The other guard jumped to his feet.

"Dragons Kember! What'd ye do that for?" He backed away.

Felona could hear the fear in his voice even at this distance. She didn't hear the reply, but she saw the guard trip and Kember followed him down. Kember's burly arm rose and fell sharply two then three times.

She slipped deeper into the shadows of the trees and waited.

"Look what I found in Edeldun's pocket!" Kember called breathlessly as he crested the hill and came under the shadow of the trees. "A gold sovereign."

In one fluid move, Felona drew her bow and fired an arrow deep into Kember's heaving chest.

He fell back. "Hey…?"

This time it was her knife that flashed.

When he was still, Felona turned to the packs, taking just the things she wanted from each. Finally, she pried the gleaming coin from Kember's dead fingers. How had Edeldun come to possess such a treasure? Had that damned prince tried to bribe him? Edeldun had been hesitant about the kidnapping, but he'd been desperate for money. She hoisted her pack and settled it onto her shoulders. Well, Edeldun couldn't save the sweet-faced prince now, and his gold would ease her journey back to Kordon.

Crown Princess Tallyn poured a third cup of tea for her father, the king, and tried to ignore her uneasiness.

She looked up with relief when the door opened, but the relief turned to sharper concern when it was the dowager queen who entered and not her cousin.

The dowager surveyed her son and granddaughter and the decimated breakfast things with icy blue eyes. "Is the lout keeping us all waiting?"

"He must have a number of things to arrange, your Majesty," Tallyn said soothingly. "Would you like some tea?"

"Things to arrange?" The dowager melted into a chair, her skirts billowing around her, waving away the cup of tea. "You should deny him leave, Kodill, for this discourtesy."

King Kodill drained his cup and turned his eyes, pleading, to Tallyn.

"Ma'am," Tallyn smiled at her grandmother. "I'm sure he'll be right up."

A silence as cold as the winter day outside settled into the room. Finally, the door opened again, and again Tallyn's hopes were slugged back into her concern, which was turning to anger despite her better intentions.

The king's chamberlain bowed to the royal family. "I apologize your Majesties, your Highness, but we cannot find Prince Javix anywhere."

"I thought he made this appointment with us last night." Kodill frowned.

"Yes, Sire. He did request an audience with you soon after the ship arrived. He had asked to see you immediately, but as it was so late, and you had retired, the lord chancellor suggested that he wait until this morning."

"But now he's nowhere to be found?" Kodill's pale, almost color-less blue eyes were indignant. "Is his ship still here?"

"Yes." Tallyn glanced out the window. Several ships rested in the calm blue water, their wooden masts looking skeletal against the winter sky. One was Jax's own yacht. Another had arrived yesterday with the bad news from Baria. She turned back to the chamberlain. "This makes no sense. The prince has to be here somewhere."

The dowager smirked. "Perhaps, Tallyn, this display of arro-gance will finally show you the Barian brat's true nature."

Tallyn took a deep breath. Her grandmother's hatred of Jax was nothing new, but to display it now when he was devastated by the news that his father was dead seemed unfair and rather petty.

"I'll go find him." Tallyn curtseyed.

The king, unwilling to be left alone with his mother in such a mood, rose as well. "I'm not going to wait around all day just to give him leave to depart for Baria," he announced. "You can find me after you find him."

"Yes, Sire."

But Tallyn couldn't find Prince Jax either. She organized her ladies in waiting to search the palace, sent Jax's own perplexed squires out to his favorite haunts in the town, and even sent the captain of the King's Guard out to the wharf to see if the Barians on their ships knew where he was. Jax's foster brother, Lord Foby Kora set his prize bloodhounds throughout the palace and the town, only to return to Jax's empty chambers.

At noon Tallyn joined Foby and Lady Cheshir of Deepford in Jax's rooms. These three had fostered with Prince Jax. Abiding by Kordish custom, the four foster siblings had been together since the age of six, learning the arts and traditions of the kingdom. Like most foster groups, they had formed deep friendships.

Now, Cheshir, who had been a more intimate friend than the other two, sat on Jax's tousled bed and pulled a pillow to her chest. Tears gleamed like gems on the lashes that fringed her clear blue eyes. "Something's wrong," she whispered. "You know how much he loved his father. He probably wanted to leave last night."

"I know he'd be worried about Bryx's ascension to the throne, or whatever they call it on Baria." Tallyn, ever the politician, was rifling through the papers on the desk, noting that most of them were written in Islish.

"Maybe he did leave in the night," Foby said, scratching the ears of a bloodhound. "Captain Karric said one of the sentries reported hearing horses galloping away after midnight."

Tallyn turned. "Jax would never leave on a horse. Not with a ship available."

"Besides, he can't ride to the island of Baria," said Cheshir rather foolishly.

"But if he wanted to get out immediately, and not wait to see the king, he could have his ship meet him down the harbor." Foby explained. "This was a theory among Karric's people."

"But his boat is still moored out there." Tallyn shook her head. A few wisps of hair escaped from the elaborate collection of blond braids and floated free.

"Something bad has happened," Cheshir insisted.

Tallyn frowned and rang for Jax's squire. Together Tallyn, Foby and the squire went over the things in Jax's room. Cheshir remained on the bed, crying into the pillow.

"So, all that's missing are some trousers, two cloaks, and a pair of boots?" Foby summarized.

"And Jax." Cheshir added.

The squire nodded. "Aye, my lord. The black cloak and the Barian Blue one."

"And tell us again what he told you last night," Foby asked, fiddling with an ornate dragonpipe his dog had sniffed out from under the bed.

"He bade me goodnight, my lord, and told me to wake him an hour before dawn so he could see the king before breakfast. He said he needed to be on his ship early to ride the tide or catch the tide. You know his odd Barian expressions."

"Did he ask for a druid?"

"No, my lord."

"Oh, if only I'd come to him," Cheshir moaned. "But I met the dowager queen as I came up the stairs, and she told me to leave him alone, that he wanted to be alone, and I should respect his grief."

Tallyn sat in the chair in front of the desk. She remembered the history of Prince Kiffken, who'd disappeared one dark winter night some three hundred years ago, never to be seen again. His younger sister inherited the throne soon after and used Kiffken's disappearance as an excuse to enact a number of policies that consolidated royal power at the expense of the nobles. But Jax wasn't heir to anything, and Tallyn couldn't think of anyone who benefited from his absence.

"Your Highness!" The chamberlain burst into the room. "Your Highness, you are wanted immediately."

She jumped to her feet. "Has Prince Jax been found?"

"No, my lady. But there is an emergency meeting of the royal council. You are wanted now."

Tallyn shared a glance with her foster siblings. Jax, with his left-handed awkwardness, his love for water and his failure to share the Kordish passion for horses, had often been interrogated and censured by the nobles of the Kordish royal council. The council would have his foolish half-islish head for this, and she didn't half blame them. She shrugged at the concern on Foby's face and followed the chamberlain out of the room.

Cheshir closed her aquamarine eyes. Foby watched the tears glisten on her smooth cheeks and worried.

"It's treason!" bellowed the aged Duke of Aychex.

Tallyn kept iron control of her features, if not of her heart, as she listened yet again to the impossible.

"So, these documents are essential to the security of Kordon?" Patrice, Duchess of Chevvain, spoke in a voice of quiet concern.

"Indeed, my lady, they are a detailed account of the royal treasury and its safeguards." Earla Stona Swansea of the Tarron March leaned her elbows on the polished wood of the table. "These reports explain the weakness in our systems in great detail."

"Why?" demanded the king. "Why make such a report?"

"We needed to know how our defenses stood, so that we could undertake improvements." The earla's reflection wavered in the polished table.

"Who is *we*?" Tallyn asked.

"Myself, your Highness." Midipex turned in his chair to look at her. "Myself and the earla. As the lord chancellor, it is my duty to ensure that the treasury is thoroughly protected. Obviously, that means from time to time we must analyze the protections in place. I asked the earla to help me in this undertaking, as I often solicit support for various tasks from the members of this council."

"Indeed," Earl Oklan Kora, Foby's father, leaned forward. "Indeed, my lord, but I fail to see a connection between these treasury documents and Prince Jax."

Earla Stona slammed her hand on the table. "They've both gone missing at the same time."

"But why would Prince Jax take these things?" Earl Kora demanded.

"Well, we really don't know." Midipex picked at a loose thread on the crimson brocade of his jacket. "These Barians sail in and out of here, jabbering amongst themselves in their goddess-curst language, taking our money. We don't know what they may be planning or plotting."

Tallyn thought of the tidy pile of documents written in incomprehensible Islish on Jax's desk.

"But Prince Jax fostered here in Kree!" Earl Kora frowned. "He's a knight of this realm, as well as third in line for *this* throne. Why would he betray Kordon or steal its secrets?"

Midipex smiled sadly. "It's always difficult for good people, like yourself Lord Oklan, to understand the perfidies of less honorable hearts."

"Who else might stand to benefit from the information in these documents?" Patrice of Chevvain asked.

Midipex grimaced. "The Barians, most of all," he said with resignation. "As you know, in the course of their mercantile transactions, they frequently extend credit to the realm and to many Kordish people on behalf of our lands and personally. The treasury documents do reveal the standings of our holdings and could provide the Barians with better leverage over us."

"You should have kept a better eye over such sensitive documents, Thorag," the dowager said with a smirk.

Carte Serge, the Royal Mystic bowed himself into the chamber, a worried look on his face.

"Ah, good," said the king. "Have you found the prince?"

"No, Your Majesty," the magician answered, obviously flustered. "Both I and the Royal Dragon have worked the most powerful scrys we know, but the prince will not appear in them."

"What does that mean?" King Kodill frowned.

"Is he dead?" The dowager asked mildly.

"We don't think so, Your Majesty." The royal mystic shook his head. "The scry just goes black. Dragon force shows the same thing. I've never heard of anything like this."

"Is the half-isle somehow hiding from the magic?" Midipex mused.

"That's suspicious in itself," grumbled Duke Von of Clairo. "Very suspicious."

King Kodill looked around the table at the great lords and ladies of his realm. He had always rather liked his nephew Jax, despite the lad's miserable horsemanship and his silly dislike of dogs. In fact, young Jax was always more fun than the older Sharkin lad, who was rather tedious, though an excellent rider.

More than anything, Kodill hated dissention among his court. "State secrets and Prince Jax have gone missing together," he said finally. "It can't be a coincidence."

"It's treason!" Aychex shouted again.

That evening the young nobles who would likely be the next generation of the royal council gathered around the fire in the princess's apartments. Cheshir's tears had given way to a desolate pallor that heightened her cheekbones and her lovely eyes. Lord Frinz, heir to Aychex, wrapped a careful arm around her slumped shoulders. Lady Dayne, Foby's older sister, sat at a game table absently petting Foby's dog. Carden Yemmel of Traik, the princess's betrothed, held her close on a small sofa. Foby sat next to his sister and shuffled a deck of cards to keep his eyes away from what Carden's hands were doing.

Flip. Flip. One by one, he set out cards on the table, not really seeing them. He was thinking of the many times Jax had gotten himself into trouble with the Kordish authorities who were charged with teaching the noble young. At first, Foby was as wary of the strange half-islish prince as everyone else. The boy didn't speak any Landish when he arrived, was handicapped by being left-handed, and he disliked animals. But Foby soon came to admire Jax's irreverent sense of fun. It wasn't just Tallyn's friendship that made Jax someone to note. Proudly Barian, Jax hadn't bowed to the Kordish assumption of superiority. Foby remembered telling stories to his parents about Jax's arguments with the tutors and his crazy love for the water. Gradually people outside their foster class learned to both fear and appreciate his wicked sense of humor, and his popularity seemed entirely natural, especially when they remembered that his mixed heritage was entirely royal.

The knave appeared among the line of cards that Foby was laying quietly on the table. The lost traveler appeared on the knave's left and the dark goddess on his right.

"I can't believe they convicted him," he said finally. "I can't believe you or my father couldn't talk them out of it."

"It was the lord chancellor who led them," Tallyn said softly. "Midipex is a wonder to watch. I never realized how subtle he is: He never proposes anything; he just makes observations. The others think they're making the decisions, but it's Thorag Addle who lines them up." She disentangled herself from Carden's attentions, rose and went to the window. Outside snowflakes fell through the darkness.

Foby looked at her reflection in the dark glass. "And now Jax faces a traitor's death if we ever find him."

"And so he should!" Carden sprawled alone on the sofa. "He should die slowly and in great pain for betraying Kordon, but mostly for betraying you, Tallyn."

The tableau in the room behind Tallyn was reflected in the dark glass. She felt her own pain at the thought of such betrayal. "No." Her breath steamed against the glass as she leaned on the windowsill. She turned and faced the young nobles in the room. "There must be another answer."

Foby flipped one last card. The dragon. He looked up into Tallyn's pale, almost colorless eyes. "Not a good one."

The door swung hard into Jax's shoulder when the duty troll pushed it open the next morning. Jax sat up and shoved the hair off his face, sticky with tears and sweat. One man slept on a pile of rags that might have been blankets; no one else had any.

"Let's go," grumbled the troll.

Jax joined the others pushing themselves up, noticing that one woman was not moving.

The duty troll noticed too. She walked to the sprawled woman and prodded her with a metal-toed boot. "Get up, you."

The woman just moaned softly.

The duty troll bent to touch the woman's head. "Ach," she sighed.

"Fever?" one of the slaves asked.

The troll nodded. "Baths. All of ye. Go."

Jax heard the slaves groan softly, but he followed the others. "What's the fever?" He asked the man in front of him.

"Fever. Kills ye."

The group of slaves shuffled along the dim tunnel down another flight of stone stairs to a giant stone pool. Mechanically, they all stripped off their clothes and stepped gingerly into the dark, steaming water.

Jax could hardly believe it. Thrilled by the idea of a hot bath, he shed his clothes and sank gratefully into the water, submerging himself to rinse the dirt out of his hair.

"You don't have to do that," a woman next to him said. "You only have to go under twice."

"Just twice?"

She shrugged. "No one likes the water. The trolls think these baths keep us from getting the fever, but it don't do any good that I can see." So saying, she stepped out and went to a pile of raggedy clothes to dress.

"You! Get out!" the duty troll yelled at Jax. The other slaves were getting dressed.

Jax dunked one last time. As he climbed out sulfuric steam rose from his skin. He shook out his hair and found a pair of trousers and a frayed shirt.

"Come along, Fishman," the duty troll growled at Jax. "We're late enough without you dallying."

The slaves climbed the stairs out of the bath. As they went out the door into the courtyard, each person grabbed bread from large baskets that stood there.

"Where's the new one? The half-isle?" The slave wrangler squinted at the line of slaves, eating as they walked through the frigid morning air.

"You mean the Fishman, here?" The duty troll gave Jax a shove.

"Fishman?"

"Couldn't get it out of the bath."

"It wasn't bath day for this group."

"One had the fever."

The slave wrangler scowled. "Fine. Fishman, you go with that digger, Bloof, or whatever its name is."

"I'm Broog," the man mumbled. "Ye'll dig with me."

Jax followed Broog to a pile of equipment, where a troll handed Jax a pickax and a candle that was clasped in a short iron pike. As the slaves filed down into the gaping mouth of the mine, another troll used Dragon force to light their candles.

Orange eyes met blue: "Use yer magic and we'll whip ye till ye can't."

As the mine walls closed around him, Jax found it difficult to breathe. A cold sweat trickled down his back while he, Broog, and ten other slaves stood on a rattling platform that lowered them far below the surface of the earth. When the lift finally stopped, he followed Broog down a tunnel. Hot water dripped from the walls and ran in muddy rivulets along the floor. Despite the humidity, Jax felt clammy. He jumped in panic as a small rock fell on his shoulder.

"We'll dig here for now," Broog said when the tunnel ended abruptly in a rough wall of rock. A pile of wooden beams lay on the floor. "Those will be used as supports once we've dug another ten feet or so," he explained.

Broog stuck the sharp end of his candle-spike into a wooden strut and swung his pickax at the wall of rock. Jax cringed at the loud clanging, which echoed back and back again off the long tunnel walls.

"Come on, Fishman."

"Aren't you afraid the whole thing will come down on top of us?" Jax looked at the roof of the tunnel mere inches from his head.

"Yeah," Broog said. "But then we'll be free."

"Dragons," Jax swore, shoving his own candle next to Broog's. "That's not my idea of freedom."

"It will be." Broog swung his pick at the stone.

Jax shook his head at the horror of this response. With no other choice, he hefted his own pickax and pounded at the earth. Two times during the day, other slaves, laden with packs, came by to collect the rubble that Jax and Broog had produced. Each time, Jax watched them head out of the tunnel, wishing he was going with them.

Hours later, muscles trembling with fatigue, Jax heard a loud whistling echo through the tunnel.

"Eh, finally," grumbled Broog. "Come on."

Like the others, Jax grabbed his equipment and returned to the lift. He felt his chest expand as they finally stepped out into the stinging cold air of the courtyard. They dumped their equipment in a pile then shuffled to the mess hall.

Jax ate the thin gruel and moldy bread and sat contemplating the blisters on his hands. This was not the first time he had had blisters. Captain Karric's rigorous sword practice for would-be knights had given him plenty, and there were always rope burns and water blisters when he was scrambling through the rigging of various Barian ships and his own racing yachts.

His thoughts drifted to the yacht races during the Gather of the Barian Fleet last summer. Goddess, but he loved to feel a boat rise to the waves and fly with the wind. He had won the big regatta, taking the trophy back from Shallyx of Callisto, who had held it for the past two years.

He remembered Sealord Rax's proud smile as he awarded Jax with a Sharkin heirloom: the ring worn by his mother, a ring that by all rights should have gone to Bryx. But Bryx had never won a sailing race in his life, and Rax was both relieved and ecstatic that at least one of his sons could succeed in the ways most important to the Barian people.

Jax put his hands over his face, feeling the heat of the bulbous sores against his cheeks. How, by the goddess, was he going to get out of here?

With the others from Cave Three, Jax followed a duty troll back into the depths of the slave pens. In the few minutes before the door slammed them into darkness, he watched one slave claim all the blankets. No one spoke. The door shut. In the darkness, someone sighed.

"Shut up!"

Silence.

"SHUT UP!

"SHUT UP! SHUT UP! SHUT UP!"

On and on the voice echoed in the cave.

Finally, Jax sat up. "Does he do this every night?"

"Shut UP! Shut UP!"

"Pretty much."

"Shut up shut up."

Jax pushed his hands through his hair. "Can't anyone make him stop?"

"SHUT UP SHUT UP!"

"What would you do?" someone asked from across the room.

Jax was not sure what he would do, but a few more nights of this and he might find out.

"Which of you has all the blankets?" Jax demanded finally.

"Shut up! I do! Shut up!"

"Be quiet, Fishman, or he'll go on all night."

"SHUT UP SHUT UP SHUT UP!"

Exhausted from the labor, the claustrophobia, and the despair, Jax lay down on the gritty floor and closed his eyes. He hated the feeling of dirt in his hair. "My name isn't Fishman."

"SHUT UP SHUT UP SHUT UP!"

Each day, the terror grew worse as he imagined being encased in the wet earth, unable to move, or see, his nostrils clogged with mud. A cold sweat trickled down his back, and bands of fear tightened around his chest as his heart pounded with every clang of a pickax.

"I can't go down there," he told the duty troll one morning, as she directed the slaves towards the mine mouth.

"No?"

"Isn't there something else I can do?"

"Something else, Fishman?"

"I'm claustrophobic," Jax explained. "I can't breathe underground."

The leather crop came so fast that Jax felt it burn through his thin shirt before he had seen it fly. She belted him again before he had moved out of the way.

Stumbling backwards, Jax raised his arm to ward off further blows. She struck his legs.

"Your cluster-thinger don't matter, Fishman. You're assigned to the mine, and that's where you'll go." She pursued him, swatting ruthlessly with the crop.

Jax jumped into the mouth of the mine to escape her.

When he got to the site of the dig at the end of the long, sweating tunnel, he surveyed the welts and cuts the whip had left. He had not bled much, but the stinging was brutal. Shivering despite the sticky heat, Jax forced himself to breathe against the oppressive weight of the ground above him.

"You all right?" Broog asked.

"Splendid."

"Splendid?" Broog mimicked Jax's crisp Kordish accent. With a sad smile he handed Jax a canteen of water. "You get used to the dark after a while. And every time I swing me axe, I imagine hitting the face of one of them damned trolls."

Jax forced himself to fill his lungs again. He hefted his own pickax and smashed away at the earth until he was almost too tired to care where he was. Almost.

"How did you end up here?" Jax asked Broog, as they sat one night in the mess hall.

"Captured."

"How? Where?"

"The trolls hunt for slaves, you know. Along the borders of the Hantland."

"I didn't know that."

"You'd know if you lived in Ily or Ohe."

Jax swallowed the last of the slimy green mush from his bowl. "When did this happen?"

"Last fall."

"Do you have family? Wouldn't they try to get you back?"

Broog drew a blackened fingernail through a coagulated grease spot on the tabletop. "They ain't got the kind of money it takes to buy a slave. Even if they could have found me..." Broog's face closed in upon itself. "What about you, Fishman? You've got a funny way of talking and a fine way of holdin' that spoon too."

Jax placed his wooden spoon in his empty bowl a little self-consciously. "My name's not Fishman."

"What are ye called, then?" asked the old woman sitting next to him.

Jax considered the drawn, exhausted faces turned toward him with honest curiosity. People like this had always called him *my lord,* or *your Highness*, at the very least such people would call him *sir*. He'd been given illustrious names from both Barian and Kordish history. He wasn't the first Javix Sharkin, but famous names and noble titles didn't belong here in this stinking, miserable hole.

The old woman continued when Jax didn't speak: "The trolls will call ye Fishman now. The way they call me the Crone. They can't be bothered to remember we have names."

Jax looked down at the table. Felona had been right. He no longer had a name. In sending him here, the Duke of Midipex and the dowager queen had taken his identity, erased him. But he'd be damned if he let the trolls rename him.

"I'm Jax," he said softly, giving the nickname he'd always preferred. "Jax," he repeated more firmly.

Broog continued to give Jax the little secrets of survival in the pens. He showed him how to hide an extra breakfast bun under his shirt for a midday snack and pointed out which duty trolls were harsh and which were more lenient.

The Ilyian also allayed Jax's fears the first time the trolls called the male slaves out of the mess hall after dinner one night.

"What's happening?" Jax got in line behind Broog.

"They barber us." Broog rubbed the stubble on his cheeks.

The trolls buckled each slaves' wrists to the arms of a chair. Another troll lathered their faces, while a third moved from slave to slave shaving each with rough efficiency.

Jax held a finger to a bleeding nick under his chin as he walked back to Cave Three with the other men. "Next, they'll be dabbing us with their paint."

The other slaves laughed.

"All the cosmetics in The Hant wouldn't make you any prettier, Fishman," snarled the duty troll, which just made the men laugh harder.

About a month after Jax's arrival, a duty troll ordered Broog and three other slaves to dig in a new side tunnel. Jax remained at the site he had been excavating from the beginning. When the rumbling first started, Jax thought he was just hearing the echoes of more hammer falls. Then a hot gust of dirt-choked air blew out the candles and rocks fell from the dripping ceiling. Jax ducked his head under his arms, but stones still pummeled him.

Someone's scream was suddenly muffled.

Jax stopped breathing. It was his nightmare come true. He summoned his Dragon force and relit the candles.

"Who did that?" asked one of the other slaves.

"Who cares?" Jax pulled his candle from the wooden support. "Let's find the lift and get out of here."

He and the two other slaves stumbled through the boulder-strewn tunnels, choking on the thick dust. Voices shouted through the dark. At the landing they found several duty trolls, who snatched the lit candles away from the slaves. The blast of air from collapsing tunnels had extinguished all lights in the mine.

Jax stood in the center of the lift that was overloaded with panicky slaves. Stressed cables screeched as the lift jerked toward the surface. They burst into the courtyard, gasping at the fresh air, blinking in the bright winter sunlight. Duty trolls screamed conflicting orders at the dazed slaves, trying to figure out who was missing and what had happened.

The mess hall was quiet that night. Four slaves and one duty troll had been crushed to death in the cave in, Broog among them. Jax sat, staring at the grease spot that still bore the imprint of Broog's fingernail. He hoped Broog's release into freedom had been better than the horrid images in Jax's mind, but as he looked around at the dazed resignation on the other slaves' faces, he felt more alone than ever, stripped of another human connection.

The mine work went on the next day as if nothing had happened, and a few weeks later, a new woman was shoved into Cave Three. She was an older Ilyian woman who had been a house slave to a wealthy trollish family. Within a month, she was killed by the fever.

As Jax became accustomed to the mine routine, he began looking for ways to escape. But the more he looked, the more his despair deepened. Orange trollish eyes watched every slave's every move.

One morning while the trolls herded the slaves toward the mine mouth, Jax saw a group of over-trolls drag a new slave to a whipping post. Like the other slaves, Jax slowed to watch in horror. The duty trolls, who enjoyed the spectacle of a good whipping and believed the sight to be educational for the other slaves, allowed them to watch.

The whip cracked again and again. The slave screamed horribly until he finally hung unconscious. Still, the whip cracked and cut.

Jax turned away, sickened, and found himself face to face with the troll who lit their candles each morning.

"You remember what I telled ye, Fishman. Use yer magic and we'll beat it right out of ye."

Jax tramped down to his place in the mine with hard eyes. He picked up his axe and smashed it into the rock. Where, by the goddess, was Bryx?

As the weeks passed, Jax's despair darkened to hate. He hated the tunnels; he hated the trolls; he hated the Kordish who had sent him to this goddess-forsaken place; he hated the royal bearing that his tutors had beat into him, which the duty trolls were now pleased to beat out of him. As time went by, Jax even began to hate the Barians who were clearly unable to find him. But mostly he hated the screamer.

He watched the screamer with increasing loathing. A small man with sharp features and feral eyes, the screamer was absolutely silent during the day. Jax had seen him take ore dug by another man and load it as his own. He had watched other slaves from Cave Three give the screamer choice bits of food, such as there were. Jax also knew that several other slaves took turns having sex with the screamer so that the man would quietly fall asleep afterward.

Jax found this tyranny from one of their own to be even more despicable than all the evils of the trolls. As he had told the slave wrangler that first terrible day, he had been raised to rule, taught to understand the responsibility of leadership and the duties of privilege. The petty despotism of the screamer mocked everything he'd been taught and believed.

Twice each year, at the vernal and autumnal equinoxes, the ocean currents of the Knownseas changed direction. Terrible storms raged over all the waters and most of the land for two to three weeks as wind blew from all directions and waves swelled unpredictably. During these Risings, navigation was impossible.

During the centuries that the Barians had floated adrift on the Wider Seas, they had developed a visceral anxiety that started a day or so before the Risings and lasted until the storms abated. Nervous and testy with this Rising Fear, the Barians huddled in port, drank, gambled, and conceived most of their children. Even in the slave pens, Jax felt the Rising Fear that was bred into his Barian blood and found his temper even grimmer than before.

One morning as the slaves staggered through Rising-blown snow in the courtyard, Jax stepped out of line and walked up to the tunnel engineer. Everyone stared at him in amazement.

"I have an idea to make the mines safer," Jax said.

"Why would I care about that, Fishman?" sneered the engineer.

"You lose trolls as well as slaves to accidents and cave-ins."

"Replaceable. All of ye. Now get to work."

"If you shore up the tunnels, you'll save money." Jax ducked as the engineer's crop flew toward him. He had learned this lesson earlier.

"Shut up, Fishman!" The troll chased Jax into the mouth of the mine.

Seething, Jax returned to his spot in the steamy tunnel, the words of the troll and the screamer echoing in his head: shut up shut up shut up.

In the mess hall that night, Jax took his food and sat down purposefully next to the screamer. The man snarled and put his face closer to the gray mush that he was shoving into his mouth.

"Why do you scream every night?" Jax asked evenly.

The man looked up at Jax, loathing in his eyes, gray gruel on his chin. Other slaves slowed their eating to listen to this one-sided conversation.

"We're all miserable here," Jax explained. "Your screaming doesn't help."

The screamer wiped his messy face with his sleeve and sat up straighter. "I hate you," he whispered, is nostrils flaring. "I hate every dragon blasted one of you."

"Why?" Jax was genuinely puzzled.

"Weak, stupid, docile," the screamer snarled. "You all deserve to suffer, and you will. I will make sure you do."

With his eyes still on Jax, he reached across the table and took the bowl of food from the woman sitting there. Still, staring at Jax, he began to eat her rations.

The woman slumped on the bench but made no protest.

The screamer curled the stolen bowl into his chest, shoving globs of mush into his mouth with his fingers.

Jax stood up and swept his eyes around the room at the other slaves and trolls who were watching silently.

The screamer made a noise like a snarling laugh. Food spilled from his mouth onto his shirt. When he spoke, his words were muffled by the mush in his mouth. "Because of you, no one will sleep tonight, Fishman."

Jax shook his head. "My name is not Fishman." He handed his own bowl of mush to the woman who had lost her own and walked to the door where the slaves waited to return to their sleeping caves.

Jax leaned against the wall, thinking about how hate had fueled him through the dark days in the weeping tunnels. The Rising Fear sent electric tingles up his spine, and he fidgeted. The screamer licked his fingers like a cat.

One of the other slaves from Cave Three came up to wait beside Jax. "You've pissed him off good, Fishman. He'll scream all night."

Jax looked hard at the rumpled man next to him and at the other emaciated, bruised people who were slowly gathering in an uneven line. "Why do you put up with it? Why do you let him rule you?"

The man shrugged. "Him, the trolls. No difference."

"We shouldn't be ruled by hate."

"Dragons, Fishman," grumbled one of the women. "You sound like some fancy lord."

"Imagine that." Jax's smile didn't reach his eyes.

After the door to Cave Three swung shut leaving the slaves in darkness, Jax sat on the rough dirt floor, listening to the rustles and groans as the others tried to settle themselves. He could sense everyone waiting. But the long day's work took its toll, and soon the sound of rhythmic breathing indicated that people were falling asleep. He knew the screamer was waiting too, waiting until the others were just dropping off, waiting until his screams would be most painful. It was time, Jax thought, to let go of hatred and try something different.

He spoke quietly into the dark silence. "I'd like a blanket."

Everyone froze. They couldn't see Jax's silent grin, but they could hear something in his voice that they recognized.

"Could someone please toss me a blanket?"

The screamer squealed then, "SHUT UP! SHUT UP! SHUT UP! SHUT UP!"

Jax laughed.

The screamer roared.

The other slaves in the cave lay tense and still.

"SHUT UP SHUT UP SHUT UP!"

"Is that all you can say?"

"SHUT UP, *FISHMAN!*"

Again, Jax laughed. "I told you; my name isn't Fishman." He stood up. Gingerly he moved through the darkness of the cave toward the screamer and his pile of blankets.

"Who are YOU? SHUT UP!"

Everyone could hear the tremor in the screamer's voice, but they were not sure if it came from fear or fury.

"Come on. Let's share those blankets." Jax's voice was quiet as he stood above the screamer.

"I will kill you, Fishman!" The screamer howled.

"Why bother?" Jax asked. "The trolls will do it soon enough. And my name is Jax."

"NO! NO!" The screamer curled himself around the mound of blankets.

Jax bent down to pull at the pile. In the dark he felt the others join him, felt their hands tear the fabric free from the screamer's clutches. The man's inarticulate howls echoed off the walls. Someone grabbed the screamer and held his arms so that the other slaves could pick up blankets.

Jax knelt in front of the screamer who spit at him.

"We're not putting up with this anymore," Jax said firmly. "We'll each have a blanket; we'll each eat our own ration; we will have sex when it feels right, but not to appease you. And you will let us sleep in whatever peace we can find, because we're all in this mess together."

"Rather we weren't," said someone across the cave.

"No," growled the screamer, panting. "NO!" He wrenched himself free.

"YOU shut up!" said another voice. Jax was shoved aside, and he heard fists and feet connecting with the screamer's body.

Jax threw himself at the screamer's attacker. "Let him be! Leave him!"

"I ain't gonna spend another miserable, sleepless night in this hole," sobbed the other man.

"I'm afraid we are all going to spend another goddess-damned night in this miserable hole." Jax held the man. He stood in the darkness, sensing the others around him. The screamer sniveled.

"For goddess's sake, why are we attacking each other?" Jax demanded, releasing the other slave. "Don't we get enough brutality from the trolls? Can't we find a bit of sympathy for each other? Just because the trolls ignore our humanity doesn't mean we have to."

The cave was silent. Slowly, Jax sat down. He wrapped his newly acquired blanket around his shoulders. Rising fear still shivered through his veins, but he heard the others settle into their own blankets and sigh towards sleep.

A blanket fell over his head. Hands and fists covered his mouth and nose. Jax fought back. He was bigger and stronger than the wiry body that clung to him. Fueled by adrenaline, he threw his attacker to the floor. There was a squelching crack. And silence again.

Jax peeled the blanket off his head and threw it over the limp form. Taking his own bit of fabric, he moved slowly through the darkness to the edge of the cave where he sank down, his back to the wall. Eventually his breathing quieted and he laid his head on the folded blanket to sleep.

When the duty troll opened the door the next morning, she frowned. Something was different. Then she noticed the pool of blood and the body. It was that weasel-ish one that the other slaves all seemed to give way to.

In the light of her torch, Jax saw blood stains splattered on his frayed pants. He wondered who should receive the wergild of a slave.

"What happened here?" growled the duty troll.

Softly, Jax quoted from an atonement ceremony his tutors had made him memorize: "*A river has no intent to drown, but it's force and flow will pull one down.*"

"What's that supposed to mean?" The duty troll demanded.

Jax said, "I don't think you want to find out."

The slaves filed out the door and past the breakfast baskets. One of the slaves took two extra buns and tossed them to Jax. "Here you are, Fishman."

"My name is Jax."

"Yes, sir."

A month after Jax's disappearance, the Kordish royal council again gathered around the polished darkwood tabled in the king's privy cabinet. The Duke of Midipex as Lord Chancellor had received a report from his own household. Tallyn listened to his high, thin voice as he read:

"We captured a woman called Felona who was loitering suspiciously around the cliffs of Keffex, apparently waiting for Barians to arrive at a small inlet there. She admitted to having helped Prince Jax steal the treasury documents. As we were binding her to bring her to Kree for trial and punishment, she broke free and leapt off the Rockheart Cliffs into the ragged surf rather than face the protracted horror of a traitor's death."

"Good riddance," Grumbled old Aychex.

"I apologize, your Majesty," said Midipex, shaking his head. "I blame myself for this failure of my household. I have executed the captain and the four guards involved for this unforgivable failure. I am embarrassed and humiliated that this person, Felona, died in a merciful manner, without being fully interrogated or brought here for trial."

Duchess Patrice of Chevvain regarded Midipex coolly. "It's always terrible when our own people let us down."

"Indeed." Midipex turned a careworn face to the king. "We did learn one thing of significance, however. There was certainly Barian involvement."

"What?" shouted the Duke of Aychex. "Speak up, Thorag."

With a flourish Midipex lifted a heavy bag and spilled the contents onto the gleaming table: golden Barian coins. "Felona was found with this Barian money."

Kevlor Brandon, the Duke of Keffex cleared his throat. "That's very troubling."

"It's treason!" shouted Aychex.

"We've already convicted Javix Sharkin of treason," Keffex continued, turning a jaded eye to old Aychex. "But now I wonder if we are leaving ourselves vulnerable by continuing to permit the Barians into our harbors."

The Duke of Midipex gazed thoughtfully at Keffex. "Are you suggesting we take further steps to ensure our safety?"

Keffex nodded. "We closed the Gates of Griffe to the Barians during the dragon interregnum to keep our shores safe. Perhaps we should do so again."

Tallyn knew from Jax about the devastation the Barians suffered when the great fire-breathing beasts descended upon their homeland nearly a thousand years ago. Barred from refuge in Kordon, the Barians had cut the cables of their Floating Islands and drifted for hundreds of years on the Wider Seas. Eventually the dragons left the Knownlands and the Oracle erected its temple on the Barian Island. A Sharkin seaqueen figured out how to direct the Floating Islands and brought the remnants of the Barian people home.

It had taken several hundred years more to convince the xenophobic Kordish to open their ports to Barian shipping. Tallyn remembered Jax's wry suggestion that this opening came about not from any sort of new-found tolerance on the part of the Kordish, but rather from their love of the luxuries Barian merchant shipping could provide.

She knew that closing the Gates of Griffe, denying Barian access to the rich Kordish markets, would be a sharp blow to the island's economy.

"An embargo on Barian shipping will be a hardship for Kordon too." Tallyn entered the conversation for the first time. "We will miss

Farsouthian sugar and have a hard time finding markets for our wines."

Midipex nodded. "Very true, your Highness. My duchy will certainly suffer. We sell a great deal of timber and wine to those shifty Barians."

"I'm willing to drink bitter tea to keep Kordon safe," Earla Stona said, patriotism ringing in her voice. "I vote we banish all Barians and their treacherous trade."

The motion passed amid passionate patriotic declamations.

Hammers clanged in smithies across Keffex and Aychex as links were forged. Frinz of Aychex invented a catapult to heave the length of chain across the water to the Keffex side of the Gates of Griffe. Smiths braved the slippery cliffs to affix the chain to the sea-washed rocks that guarded the narrow entrance to Keffin Harbor so the heavy links swam just below the waves.

The two Barian ships were ordered out of the harbor. The lieutenant in charge of Prince Javix's yacht didn't want to leave without the missing prince, but when old Ambassador Grisham arrived at the wharf with his household and a private message for the new Sealord, she agreed to sail for Baria.

"Keffin Harbor is blocked by chains, your Majesty," Grisham reported, handing Sealord Bryx a sealed case.

Bryx ripped open the case and read. "Sweet goddess," he muttered in Landish as he read of Jax's conviction and sentence. The proclamation spelled out more than condemnation of Jax. It went on to inform the new sealord that he and his people were no longer welcome in Kordon. Any Barians found upon Kordish soil would be taken for enemies of the crown and put to death.

"Dragons fry him!" Bryx threw the paper across the room.

He frowned at the expectant faces surrounding him: the lords and ladies of the Floating Islands, Baria's highest nobles. He considered their dark skin, like his own, and their sea blue eyes, like his brother's, and remembered the softly rolling hills of Kordon, the beautiful horses he kept stabled at Kree, the warm, brown taste of roast boar that no cook in Haven could ever replicate. Still thinking in Landish he spoke it: "Goddess damn that stupid Jax! Where the dragons is he?"

"Your Majesty?"

"Prince Jax isn't there," Bryx spat in Islish, the language of the island nations of Baria, Farsouth, and Jezel. "Evidently, he stole some important documents and ran away. The Kordish have found him guilty of treason and now assume that all Barians are enemies."

"This is ridiculous, your Majesty," Neben, Lord of Rillt frowned. "It's all ridiculous."

"Clearly. But I order all Barians to stay away from Kordon. They'll execute any Barian they find, and I won't be responsible for anyone who disobeys my command."

"What? But the trade!" The assembled captains were all nobles who enjoyed the riches of great merchant fleets.

Bryx held up his hand. The room grew quiet. "Assemble the fleet. I'll take the *Drixa* to Kree and talk to King Kodill myself. Meanwhile, I want Prince Jax found. Get the magicians to scry for him and scour the ports of the Knownlands. He's bound to turn up in one of them."

Ambassador Grisham followed the other nobles out of the palace and across the bridge to the Floating Islands that were permanently moored in the bay. His smile was contemplative and sad. He had seen the shadow of Rax in the new sealord today for the first time: a shadow that left him both relieved and riven with grief for his old friend.

The fleet of huge Barian wing ships swam back and forth through the choppy winter seas outside Keffin Harbor. In Kree, merchants nailed boards over shop windows and the wealthy packed their jewels and fled to country houses or relatives in cities inland.

Again, the Kordish royal council gathered around the broad darkwood table, considering the sealord's request for a meeting.

"He is the sealord now," King Kodill mused. "By rights, young Bryx should get to meet with me."

"But we can't let his ships into the harbor, your Majesty," argued the Duchess of Chevvain. "The town is rightly panicked, and you, Sire, can't go out to him."

"He could land at Griffguard," suggested the Duke of Aychex loudly. "I've a castle there. It's rough, impregnable, and you would still be on Kordish soil."

Thorag Addle's face showed deep lines of worry. "Your Majesty, respectfully, I do not think you need to meet with the half-islish sealord. He's the brother of a convicted traitor. We must assume that the sealord approved of the plot to steal the treasury documents. Your presence would do him too much honor, under the circumstances."

"But then who goes?" asked Rippsmarch. "Princess Tallyn?"

Tallyn leaned back in her chair, wondering how Midipex would take this.

He looked thoughtfully at the princess for a moment. "That's a good idea, Lord Oklan."

Tallyn hid her surprise.

"Bryx knows that Princess Tallyn and Javix were fostermates. He'll probably open up to her more than to someone like me."

"You caused him some trouble in days past," Oklan reminded the duke.

"True. I never well trusted the Barians."

"Wisely, it turns out," noted the Earla of the Tarron March.

Tallyn admired Midipex's manipulation of the council as he began speaking again.

"We must not let the princess meet the Barians alone, of course. Another member of the council should go with her, for safety. As well as Captain Karric and a strong number of troops."

And to corroborate my story, Tallyn realized. Still, she said nothing.

Eventually, the council chose the Duchess of Chevvain to accompany Tallyn at the meeting with Bryx. Within the hour, the two were off, riding over the high moors to Griffguard on the cliffs above the sea.

They arrived by the light of a quarter moon that glowed brightly on the snowy fields around the ancient castle. The next morning, as a cold winter dawn turned the white sails of his fleet a gentle pink, Sealord Bryx rowed to shore.

They met in the icy shadows on the beach below the cliffs. The princess and Chevvain, backed by thirty of Captain Karric's most trusted guards, curtseyed and waited for the sealord to speak.

Like Jax, Bryx had spent years fostering at Kree. Unlike his younger brother, Bryx had proven ambidextrous and had enjoyed the advantages of being a few years older than his cousin Tallyn. His prowess on horseback earned him the respect of his foster class that included Dayne Kora of Rippsmarch and Frinz of Aychex.

Now Bryx watched his cousin bow to him for the first time in their lives. Growing up they had been equals, both of them heirs to powerful thrones. But today Bryx held the Helm of Baria, while Tallyn was still only an heir. He felt a rush of power looking at the two bowed heads before him, a rush of power and anger.

He turned away from the two women and walked back towards the waves. "You speak to them," he growled to Ambassador Grisham. "If the king won't talk to me, I'll talk to no one."

Grisham hurried towards the two Kordish nobles. He bowed deeply to Tallyn.

"Ambassador Grisham." Tallyn, bred to the intricacies of political maneuvering, understood Bryx's actions. She gestured toward her companion. "You remember Patrice, Duchess of Chevvain."

"Of course, your Highness." Grisham bowed again and rose to see a calculating smile on Tallyn's face. He realized that Bryx's refusal to meet with his cousin gave Tallyn the upper hand in the conversation. Grisham knew that Tallyn was aware of her advantage.

"Baria has been a noble ally to Kordon for nearly two generations," she smiled coolly. "But we now have cause to doubt Baria's good intentions."

"Please do not doubt, Princess," Grisham said earnestly. "Baria would wish no harm upon Kordon. Our royal house is allied with yours, and our people value and respect the folk of Kordon."

"Well then, produce Prince Javix."

"We don't have him."

"He's not in Baria?"

"No, Ma'am. No one has seen him."

Chevvain spoke at last. "Then where did he go?"

"We wonder the same thing, your Grace." Grisham understood Landish fluently, but he spoke with a thick Islish accent that often disarmed his listeners. "The sealord orders all our ships to search the ports of the Knownlands for him. We hope he turns up soon."

Tallyn looked at Bryx who stood a few yards away, his back to them, but clearly listening. If Jax was not in Kordon, and he was not in Baria, where could he have gone?

"What will you do once you find Prince Jax?" Chevvain asked.

Suddenly the sealord turned towards them. "I'll give him to you."

"You will?" Tallyn asked softly. "You know, your Majesty, he faces a traitor's death here. Do you believe he's guilty?"

Bryx shrugged. "Knowing what friends you two are, Tallyn, I can't imagine why he would endanger your realm. But I have responsibilities of my own now. Losing our trade with Kordon is a major blow to the Barian economy. I'll give you Jax—once we find him—*if* you reopen the ports."

Tallyn considered her cousin and the ruthlessness of his decision. "You understand, my lord, that the missing documents are of great importance to us."

"I do indeed. I pledge the allegiance of myself and all Baria to you, the king, and the people of Kordon. Prince Jax, when we find him, will be our token to you of our solidarity."

Tallyn looked at the duchess who shrugged and nodded her tentative agreement. "Very well, Sealord," she said to Bryx. "We will relay your offer to the king and his council and await your return when Prince Jax is found."

Bryx smiled. "I hope to see you very soon, cousin." He turned back to his boats, old Ambassador Grisham following in his shadow.

Tallyn and the duchess began the long climb back up the cliffs. The princess had long known that the two Barian princes were often at odds with each other. She had heard Bryx blame Jax for their mother's death. The time spent apart as they alternately fostered at Kree, plus different dispositions and affinities, made affection difficult. But to send his own brother to the horrors of a traitor's death!

She didn't want to believe that the Barians had stolen the treasury documents. That betrayal hit too close to her confidence in her ability to read people, and to her solid friendship with her cousin Jax. But as she trudged up the steep cliff path, she began to wonder if maybe Midipex was right. Were the Barians complicit in some kind of treachery? Knowing both Barian princes, Tallyn recognized how their feelings towards Kordon were different. Bryx had always loved all things Kordish. He'd learned the language from his mother, Valla Brondon Princess of Kordon. Jax had told her that Bryx struggled with the sailing and seamanship that the Barians valued, but he excelled at riding and clearly loved and enjoyed Kordish life.

She had to admit that Jax's feelings towards Kordon were more ambivalent. He had no reservations about pointing out Kordish prejudices and insularity. She knew, too, that while he struggled with Kordish skills, he had mastered the activities that Barians valued with ease. This made the younger Sharkin popular with the Barians in a way that the new sealord could never share.

But now Bryx would have to mend the fences between the two realms in order for him to benefit from the information in the stolen documents. Sacrificing a brother, whose popularity might be a liability, showed a level of intrigue that she hadn't thought Bryx possessed.

Halfway up the cliff path, she paused to catch her breath. Far below on the winter-rough sea she watched Bryx huddle beneath his cloak as his crew rowed the launch back to the ship. Old Grisham sat next to the hunched sealord. The Ambassador's back was straight;

his head high as he faced the sea spray. As she watched, a wave rocked the boat. The sealord nearly fell off his seat. Grisham's head turned only slightly, but Tallyn had the impression that he felt nothing but contempt for his sealord.

As she continued up the steep path, Tallyn considered the dangerous fate that had given Bryx an affinity for the land he did not rule.

Tea was indeed bitter that winter. The Spring Rising came and washed away the last of the snow from the palace courtyard. Brown hills turned green. Daffodils and tulips colored the sunshine. A rider came in from the Tarron March with a torn and dirty Barian Blue cloak. The sigil of the Sharkin cadet embroidered in gold thread gleamed amid the muddy wrinkles.

Tallyn sat in the council chamber after the others had gone. Spring sunshine streamed through the tall windows and flowed like golden cream over the crumpled cloak, where it lay forgotten on the polished table.

She thought about how life had gone on without Jax. Of course, he had often been away from Kree for months at a time. Often enough she had listened with rapt incomprehension to his stories of sea voyages to the far-flung corners of the Knownlands. The Barians were preparing him to be the first captain, or lord admiral or whatever they called it, of the Barian Fleet when his brother became sealord.

She remembered being very small the first time Jax had returned to Baria after his first term of fostering. Tallyn had thrown a fit. A faint smile played across her face as she recalled the druid, Lady Mollish, explaining that he'd be back. They were just six years old, but from then on, Tallyn understood that her Baria cousin was the dearest friend she'd ever have.

Their affinities grew up with them. They liked and disliked the same courtiers (with the notable exception of Carden Yemmel), shared the same sense of humor, a passion for history, and the study of governance.

And now he was truly gone. The ruined cloak spread like an ominous blue stain on the table. The facts of his disappearance felt like a stain on her heart. Only two equally unwelcome options appeared logical. Either he had in fact stolen those Treasury Documents and betrayed her, or Bryx had murdered him in order to consolidate his own power on Baria.

"Here you are!"

Tallyn raised her eyes. No one but Carden Yemmel would address her without a title. He flourished himself into the room followed by Foby Kora.

"It's far too lovely a day to be indoors, your Highness." As usual, Carden's voice hit the title with a sarcastic note. She knew that both Jax and Foby despised the way Carden used his position as her betrothed to push the boundaries of respect.

For the last year or so, however, Tallyn had been willing to overlook Carden's irritating habits as she explored other, more pleasing aspects of the young man. When they were alone together, Carden could be very pleasing, indeed.

"Come ride with us," he coaxed now.

Foby was fingering the blue cloak. She met his thoughtful eyes.

Carden swept the cloak to the floor. "Oh, leave it. Jax is a convicted traitor. Why are you moping over him?"

Tallyn leaned back in her chair and looked up into Carden's fair face.

"That moustache still doesn't suit you," she said.

He smoothed the sparse whiskers with a glint in his eyes. "You'll like it when it's a bit longer."

Foby had retrieved the cloak from the floor and held it out. *"Rooms are now quiet where you used to roam."*

"My heart beats in pain, until you come home." Tallyn finished the line from one of Featherfetch's more obscure sonnets.

Foby looked out the window. "Carden's right," he said. "It is a lovely day for a ride. I think I'll go visit Thikkresh."

"The swamps?" Carden snorted.

"Aye, the swamps."

Tallyn rose. "Yes! Yes! Let's go see what we can find there."

"I'm not going." Carden folded his arms.

Tallyn kissed him, wrinkling her nose in distaste at the prickly moustache. "You and your moustache may stay here, my Lord of Traik."

He grabbed her and held her very close. "I promise you that it will make you scream with pleasure when you return." His voice was serious now and a little rough with passion.

"I'll make arrangements, my lady," Foby said, fleeing with the cloak.

For a week they rode south from Kree over the rolling downs quilted with hedgerows and sprouting green fields. Earla Stona welcomed them at Tar Baravel with wide smiles that did not disguise the questions in her blue eyes.

As the sun bounced dancing light across the gentle waves in the Bay of Swilt, they sat on a balcony sipping sweet Tarron wine.

"Your Highness, I must say I do not understand why you continue to pursue this traitor."

"Shouldn't I?" Tallyn's voice was mild. "If he has truly endangered Kordon, shouldn't we do all we can to track him down?"

The earla made a moue and shrugged. "My lady, all of us develop affection for our foster brothers and sisters. It is surely hard to believe that one of them would betray us."

"It *is* hard to believe, isn't it?" Tallyn sipped her wine. "Especially when the proofs are so circumstantial."

Stona sighed.

"If Prince Jax isn't guilty of stealing these treasury documents, then someone else is," Foby said quietly. "And that person may still lurk among us."

The earla sat up straighter. "I see your point, my lord. I will provide you with the best guides to escort you through the swamps, but I warn you: it will not be pleasant."

This turned out to be an understatement. For the next four days Tallyn and Foby rode through the stinking swamps, assailed by biting flies, great coils of snakes that dropped upon them from overhanging trees, and bloodsucking leeches that came from goddess knew where to attach themselves painfully to their skin. Foby had to use all his considerable skill with the bloodhounds and horses to keep them all moving forward.

They returned to Tar Baravel covered with itchy red welts, but with no greater knowledge of Jax. Their guide had shown them the desolate hillock where the cloak had been discovered, but there was nothing else there other than some cattails and lots and lots of bugs.

Disappointed and uncomfortable, both Tallyn and Foby drank a great deal of Earla Stona's sweet wine that evening. Eventually they found themselves on yet another of the palace's stone balconies. The spring night was warm and the stars clear.

Tallyn stretched on a lounge and laughed again at Foby's wickedly accurate imitation of Carden Yemmel.

"You will scream with pleasure..."

Tallyn howled. Foby came closer, pretending to preen a moustache of his own. "Perhaps already you have an itch my whiskers can scratch."

"I itch all over," she laughed.

He sat on the edge of her lounge. "Ah, your Highness. Let me—" his voice shifted. No longer copying Carden, it became his own. "Tallyn..." Then words stopped.

Tallyn awoke with a crushing headache, the predictable after effect of so much sweet wine. She found Foby, and one of his ubiquitous puppies, tangled in the sheets next to her. She considered him in the new light of morning.

Foby had always been there in the thick of things with her and Jax and Cheshir. When Jax and Cheshir had taken their friendship into more private areas, Tallyn had let Carden entertain her. Foby, she knew, enjoyed such relationships with several other men and women at court.

She was suddenly and uncharacteristically seized with jealousy and rolled toward the young man next to her. Gently she pushed the dark blond hair off his forehead. The puppy awoke and began to lick Foby's face.

His light blue eyes opened and blinked, his smile so sweet, and genuine, and loving. Carden never looked at her like that.

"Good morning, your Highness," he said gently, no sarcasm over her title. "I hope your head doesn't throb like mine."

"I'm afraid it does."

"Perhaps if I kiss it?"

Princess Tallyn rode back to Kree in a daze of happiness that was clearly shared with the young lord at her side.

The fitful summer breeze billowed the full folds of Tallyn's purple cloak of mourning and teased a few more strands of blond hair loose from her elaborate knot of braids. She glanced at the sky, hoping that the rain would hold off. Funerals were dismal enough without rain.

She pulled the cloak around her tightly and looked at the ground. The voice of the priestess rang through the grove as she circled the dark hole that awaited the body, strewing flowers into the soft grass as she went. "All that lives must die. We honor the life of Kevlor Brandon, Duke of Keffex..."

Next to Tallyn, Kevlor's widow moaned softly amid her sobs. King Kodill put an arm around his cousin's widow, his own face wet with tears.

Tallyn felt the familiar tightness in her throat as the duke's body was lowered slowly into the ground. The ceremony was all too familiar: "From her we all proceed, and unto her we all return..."

Resolutely, Tallyn turned her thoughts to something else. She focused on the gray-robed figure of the priestess officiating at the funeral. Tallyn had known Lady Mollish before she was a priestess, when she served the goddess more simply as a particularly gifted druid and healer. Tallyn remembered how intuitive and comforting Mollish had been to Tallyn's dying mother.

That thought wasn't helpful.

She sighed, trying to think of a happier memory involving the druid. She smiled then remembering the joy and excitement on Mollish's face at being chosen to become one of the Oracle's high priestesses. After serving at the Oracle's temple on the remote Head of Baria, Mollish returned to Kordon, wearing the gray robes of one of the Oracle's fully ordained priestesses. She went on to become one of the most talented and sought-after healers in the kingdom.

Tallyn pulled her cloak more snugly around her shoulders and wondered for a moment about the Oracle, the so-called "speaker for the goddess" in the Knownlands. Few people, other than the selected druids who became priests and priestesses, ever visited the Oracle. Occasionally a ruler of one of the kingdoms might consult the Oracle. Even more rarely, the Oracle would summon someone for a specific purpose, but for the most part, the Oracle seemed to influence affairs solely by training a few druids to be priests and priestesses.

Another gust of wind tugged the purple cloak loose. Tallyn sighed again. She'd been wearing far too much purple lately. First for her mother, then Sealord Rax, and today for the Duke of Keffex—dead at age fifty of a monstrous stomach malaise that no druid had been able to either understand or cure.

Keffex was a royal duchy, and since Kevlor and his wife had no children, the lands would revert to the Crown. As the first heavy drops of rain began, Tallyn raised her hood and considered the lines of succession for various Kordish properties and titles, and how those lines had now changed.

"May the peace of the goddess be in our hearts, in this world, between the worlds, in all the worlds. Blessed be."

With little peace in her heart, Tallyn followed her father and the widow through the grove along the path back to Caer Keff. The blue-gray stone of the old castle shone darkly in the summer rain. Looking for Foby in the crowd of courtiers, her gaze snagged on the Duke of Midipex, waiting for the royal family to pass before taking his own place in the procession back to the castle. His face was solemn and weary, an expression he seemed to wear perpetually since Jax had disappeared last winter and the Midipex household had bungled the investigation.

It had been more than six months now since Jax had gone. Bryx had not returned with him.

Tallyn stepped out of the rain into the shelter of Caer Keff. Her lady in waiting took her wet cloak and pushed at the loose tendrils of hair. Foby came up silently to stand next to her. A servant brought steaming mugs of mulled wine.

Tallyn's pale, almost colorless eyes rose with the steam rising from her cup to again snag on Thorag Addle. As he moved across the room to speak earnestly with the widow, Tallyn realized that with the death of Duke Kevlor, and both Bryx and Jax either dead or banished from Kordon, it was Thorag Addle, Duke of Midipex and lord chancellor, who now stood directly behind her in line for the throne of Kordon.

While Tallyn watched the Duke of Midipex mingle with the nobles at Caer Keff, Sealord Bryx sat behind his desk in his privy chamber and watched the light from the setting sun turn the large fluffy cloud bank a glorious rosy pink. With a sailor's understanding of weather, he knew that the storm that had washed the Island of Baria and Haven all day was now moving on and probably sending rain all along the Kordish coast. How he missed those green, rolling downs.

He took a deep breath. Kordon, with its grasslands, its glorious horses, its society rooted to solid ground, was lost to him. Lost to him thanks to his idiot brother, who was the subject of the current conversation.

"I think the Kordish must've done something to him," said Neben de Rillt. "Prince Jax wouldn't just disappear like this."

"We *have* looked everywhere, your Majesty." Koralixa, the Lady of Jeff said. "The fleets of all the Floating Islands have visited every port and harbor and inlet from the Forest Krill to Gilver."

Janil, the Lord of Phlyx, shook his head. "I had both the royal magicians scry for him, and neither Dragon nor Mystic could find him, but they both said it was very strange. Both of them felt that he was alive, but the scry was black. They couldn't see him nor tell where he was. Neither one had ever experienced anything like that. They said if you scried for someone who was dead you'd see a white light then just clear water or flame. This black thing, they couldn't explain."

Bryx surveyed the nobles gathered before him. Neben, Koralixa, Janil, and the two others were the rulers of the Floating Islands. Each one controlled a great fleet of wing ships and merchant vessels as well as their Floating Island. For 600 years now, the Floating Islands had remained moored in Haven, and almost all the Barians continued to live upon them. Unlike his people, Bryx did not enjoy a house that rocked on the waves, so he moved his court from the traditional seat on the Floating Island of Helm, to Valla's Palace that Sealord Rax had built on solid Barian rock for his Kordish wife.

The lords and ladies waited. Bryx knew that these nobles shared a real concern for Jax. Neben especially had been Jax's great friend and rival in the yacht races. The two had been in the same Captaincy class, but Jax had ripped through the trials and tests and attained his Captaincy two years early, demonstrating that at least one of Sealord Rax's sons had inherited the Sharkin gift for sailing. Jax had always been the prince that their father, and the Barians, could be proud of.

But beyond their attachment to the younger prince, the sealord also knew that everyone in the room wanted access to Kordon again. Their great wealth depended on Kordish trade. As for himself, Bryx wanted to go home.

"Sweet goddess," he mumbled to himself, startled by the realization that he thought of Kordon as home rather than the nation he ruled.

Finally Esmee, the oldest noble in the room, spoke. "Your Majesty, you might consult the Oracle on this."

Bryx felt a cold fear in his stomach. The Oracle's temple sat high on a cliff called the Head of Baria. The temple wasn't always visible. Occasionally, the priests and priestesses of the Oracle were seen flying about the temple on the Oracle's winged horses.

As the sealord, Bryx could petition the Oracle. He surveyed his nobles, then rang a bell. When the page entered, he gave instructions: "Send for Mother Ayslic."

The nobles nodded. Mother Ayslic was the Oracle's Priestess to the court at Haven. She arrived almost immediately, as if she had been waiting for the summons, and she probably had.

"We are considering asking the Oracle what has become of Prince Jax," Bryx told her. "Can you go?"

Mother Ayslic was young, but her Barian blue eyes were wise and deep. She nodded. "I will be very pleased to take you to the Oracle, your Majesty."

Bryx shifted in his chair. He did not consider himself a religious person, finding his most spiritual moments on the back of a horse or in the taste of fine Kordish brandy. The idea of going to the Speaker for the Goddess and confronting the greatest magic in the Knownlands scared him. He had no magic himself and didn't much trust it.

"Can't you go and ask our question?"

Mother Ayslic cocked her head. "Sire, only rulers can go. And the great magicians of Mystic and Dragon. You know the Oracle will not speak to the small concerns of individuals."

"But you won't be asking about a small concern. You'll be asking on behalf of all of Baria."

Ayslic glanced around at the other nobles and chose her words carefully. "The Oracle will see only you, your Majesty. Only you can speak on behalf of all Baria."

Bryx had known this all along. He was the sealord. He'd been raised to it, and taught by one of the best, but he just didn't like it.

He frowned at the papers on the table. "Very well," he said finally. "We'll go in the morning. But we're not sailing. We'll ride there." He rang his bell and attendants came running. The nobles of the Floating Islands and Mother Ayslic bowed their way out, keeping their thoughts to themselves.

Hix Sharkin was not lord of any Floating Island, but as the second cousin to Sealord Rax he served the powerful position of Lord Admiral of the Barian Fleets. Charged with teaching the young Barian nobles the ways of ships and seas, Hix had rarely had a kind word for Bryx. So now, Bryx watched with some annoyance as Hix shut the door behind the last noble and turned alone to face him.

"You can't be found by magic either, your Majesty."

This information was so unlooked for, that Bryx just blinked. "How do you know?"

"When we left you at Kree for your first fostering, your father worried about you." Hix paused and cleared his throat. "He asked the royal magicians to scry for you, to see how you fared amid all those self-satisfied Kordish people. But the scrys all went black, just like now when they look for Prince Jax."

"No one ever told me this." Bryx was thinking more about the fact that his father had apparently missed him, implying a deeper affection than Bryx had thought existed.

"Rax and I thought it best not to let people know. We felt it endangered you. At the time, we also learned that Prince Jax was likewise invisible to magic."

"So, you weren't surprised today."

"No, Sire." Hix took a deep breath and sailed straight into his difficult statements. "You were so young when we sent you to Kordon. Do you remember how often your father visited in those days? Or I? We kept a close watch on you."

Bryx distinctly remembered the relief he felt each time the huge Barian wing ships finally sailed away from Kree and out the Gates of Griff, taking his father and the censorious lord admiral far away.

Hix continued: "The sealord swore both the Royal Mystic and Royal Dragon to secrecy. We never even told your grandfather, Lord Fellix. I knew, of course, so that I could help keep an eye on both you and Prince Jax." He straightened his shoulders. "It appears now, that I failed."

Having too often felt the sting of Hix's scorn, Bryx relished the lord admiral's humiliation. Perhaps tomorrow's proposed visit to the Oracle was unnecessary.

"Did you and my father ever figure out why neither Jax nor I can be found by magic?"

"No," Hix paused trying, and failing, to find better words. "Rax felt the two of you were odd enough being half-islish. He didn't want anyone to know there were additional differences."

"Odd enough." Bryx rose. "Thank you for telling me this, Lord Admiral. Maybe the Oracle will have an answer for us, but in any case, we will preserve my father's strategy and not publicize this issue further."

Hix bowed himself quickly out of the room.

Ayslic had ridden the Oracle's flying horses, but like most Barians she'd never mounted a regular horse. She stood the next morning watching one of the sealord's grooms saddle a gentle old mare, recognizing that the prospect of riding a horse all the way to the Head probably made her as nervous as seeing the Oracle made the sealord.

Bryx came into the stable yard with a swirl of rich Barian Blue silk. "Are you ready, Mother?"

"Yes, your Majesty."

Two grooms held the horse who squirmed as Ayslic mounted. Immediately the gentle mare reared and neighed. Ayslic held on mostly by force of will.

The sealord leapt into his own saddle. "None of you Barians can handle a horse." He flicked the reins and headed off at a gallop. Ayslic's horse followed of its own volition. Ayslic just held on.

The ride took three days. The gentle old mare threw Ayslic twice, and the priestess' legs and thighs ached from the hours in the saddle. They spent the nights in the small coastal villages of Bran and Port Jorel. Bryx's grandfather Lord Fellix of Port Jorel was off sailing the south seas, but they stayed in his manor. By the time they reached the Oracle's temple, Ayslic had managed to form a rudimentary understanding of the horse and how to keep her seat. Now, it was the sealord's turn to be uncomfortable.

As they rode up to the Head, they could see nothing but green grass, blowing in the wind.

"Damn," swore the sealord, sliding out of the saddle. "What do we do now?"

Ayslic also dismounted, though with less grace. "We wait, your Majesty."

"Wait?" The sealord was clearly affronted.

"You find the temple by looking into your heart," Ayslic said quietly.

"You mean I could have gotten here without even leaving Valla's Palace?"

Ayslic heard the sneer and frustration in the sealord's voice. "The goddess speaks into our hearts, Sire. And that is generally the best way for us to speak to her."

Bryx rolled his eyes. He found a seat on a large gray rock and took a deep breath. His heart. It was a place of pain. He revisited the aching residue of his mother's death that left him abandoned, small and alone, in this Barian world. He thought of what he loved: a beautiful horse and rolling green downs, the cheering and thrill of a well-mounted joust. There too he found what he hated: his laughing brother embraced by Rax after yet another sailing triumph. He opened his eyes to the rocky coastline of Baria, wave-battered and rugged.

He heard his horse whicker and turned. The white marble temple gleamed in the sunlight. Without magic in his veins, Bryx had never felt anything upon entering a building. He knew that others, even his goddess-damned brother, could sense the power of the Mystic builders, but he never had. Never until now. As he watched, six gray-clad priests and priestesses walked across the grass. He shivered as something seemed to rock in his stomach.

The Oracle's priests took the horses. A priestess bowed to Bryx. "This way, Sealord Bryx. The Oracle will see you now."

They led Bryx through a tall colonnade into a round building. Strange, smokeless lights gleamed from the walls. Curving corridors wound toward the center of the building, which rose to a tower. There, in a round room, with wide windows that opened to the north, east, south, and west, Bryx met the Oracle.

Bryx had come here with dread, but now, facing the small gray figure, he felt his heart lighten, something like joy sang along his veins. He knelt.

The Oracle shuffled towards the sealord and put a wrinkled hand out to touch Bryx's dark hair. "Welcome, Sealord Bryx." The voice was neither male nor female but filled with a gentle warmth that relaxed the sealord in a way he hadn't felt in many, many years. He looked into the strange gray eyes of the Oracle and thought of his long-dead mother.

"Come sit. Sip some tea then tell me why you've come."

Tea sat waiting for him on a low table near a deep chair. Bryx dutifully raised the cup to his lips. The drink was fragrant and steadying. "I've come to ask you what has become of my brother, Prince Javix Sharkin. He disappeared from Kree last winter. We've looked everywhere for him. Our magicians have scried for him, but we can't find him."

"Not even in a scry? They'd know if he was dead."

Bryx took another sip of tea. "So they told me. When they did the scry, all they saw was black water or dark flames, apparently."

The Oracle's eyes continued to stare into Bryx's. A silver bowl suddenly appeared on the low table. "Let's see for ourselves," they said.

Having no magic, Bryx sat back in his chair, wrapping his fingers around the teacup. He felt so comfortable here, so welcomed, more welcome than he could remember feeling anywhere else. He watched the Oracle close their eyes and take a deep breath. Bryx's sense of peace blossomed in his chest. Maybe he should spend more time with Mother Ayslic, if this was what the goddess could do.

The Oracle stared into the water in the silver bowl. Bryx could see a fog of rainbow colors gleam across the surface. The Oracle cocked their head. "Come look, your Majesty."

Bryx rose and looked over the Oracle's thin shoulder into the bowl. Black murk swirled there. A faint scent of sulfur rose from the black water.

The Oracle looked up at Bryx. "This is very strange." They waved a wrinkled hand and the water cleared.

Bryx returned to his chair. "What does that mean?"

The Oracle gazed out the east-facing window. "Your magicians are right. Your brother is not dead. But this gives no direction as to where to find him."

Bryx shrugged. "I can't be found either, apparently."

The Oracle hummed to itself. "We used to know a poem about someone who couldn't be found or can't be seen.... Tell us, Sealord, tell us more about this brother of yours."

"Like me, he's half Barian and half Kordish. He's a notable sailor, but he failed most of the landish tests of merit. It took him an extra year to attain his Knighthood in Kordon because he can't use his right hand with any dexterity."

"You mean he's left-handed?"

Bryx nodded. "In true Sharkin fashion. You know the Sharkin rulers have been left-handed for untold generations."

"Of course," the Oracle mumbled. "Does he have magic?"

"A little Dragon. It's enough to start a fire, and he can play any instrument, including other people, I think."

The Oracle smiled slowly, sadly. "You don't love him."

Bryx shook his head. "He killed our mother. His birth did. And life is just so much easier for him. Everyone just likes him."

The Oracle ran a finger through the clear water in the scry bowl. "Perhaps life is not so easy for him now."

"I need him back," Bryx said firmly. "The Kordish trade is essential to the Barian economy. The Kordish think he's a traitor and have closed the ports to us. If I can give Jax back to them, we can get the trade back."

"Do you think he's a traitor?"

Bryx shook his head. "No. He fostered with our cousin, Tallyn, the Crown Princess of Kordon, and he knows how important the Kordish trade is to Baria."

"So what has happened to him?"

"That's what I hoped you could tell me, your Eminence."

They looked into the clear water in the silver bowl. "You must ask the right question."

"What's that supposed to mean? Where is my brother?"

"Those are not the right questions."

Bryx exploded to his feet. "That's not an answer! My people are suffering. I need to find him!"

The Oracle reached out a wrinkled hand and laid it gently on Bryx's chest. The sealord sighed as a sense of calm and peace washed through him. "We don't have your answers, Sealord Bryx. You have them. You must ask the right question."

"Ask whom?"

"Yourself."

The Oracle turned and walked to the door where a priest had appeared to lead Bryx out. They paused and looked up into Bryx's pale eyes. "He didn't kill your mother, son. You had better learn to see that in a different way. Spend some time with Ayslic." The Oracle folded their hands together and bowed. "Let your heart be forever open."

Again, Bryx was flooded with relief, with peace. He felt tears in his eyes.

The feeling of openness stayed with him for the ride back to Haven. He asked Mother Ayslic to help him maintain an open heart and followed her through a ceremony under the light of the waxing moon. But as the walls of Valla's Palace and the masts of Haven came into view again, he felt the familiar constriction in his chest. He tried to force it away, but it seemed to overwhelm him as he realized that the Oracle had not solved his problem. He still didn't know where Jax was and had no idea what question to ask himself.

Everyone in Haven wanted to know what the Oracle had said.

"Where is the prince, Sire? What did the Oracle say?" People cried out to him as he rode to the palace. Dismounting, he decided he would address the people, his people. He walked down the grassy slope and crossed the arching bridge out to the nearest Floating Island, Jeff. From there he walked through crowded lanes to Helm, to Cabyn Mayne, which had been the home of the Sharkin rulers of Helm. There was a balcony on the second floor that gave onto a plaza. Here, generations of sealords and seaqueens had addressed the people.

Bryx stood there now, looking out on the throng of Barian islish. They were, like him, tall and dark skinned, but whereas he had the round ears and eyes of landish people, most Barians had pointed ears and tilted eyes the color of a calm, deep sea. The nobles of the Floating Islands had gathered in the room behind him.

"People of Baria!" The buildings around the plaza focused Bryx's voice so that it carried out to the farthest fringes of the crowd. "I have visited the Oracle and asked them about Prince Jax."

The people cheered.

Bryx shook his head and raised his hands. "The news is not good. The Oracle says that the prince is still alive, but they can't find him."

Stunned silence.

"We must keep looking. He's out there somewhere. So, listen in the ports of the Knownlands. Listen for reports of a lost prince. Go out and find him!"

Again, the people cheered but not with such enthusiasm.

Bryx turned back to the room filled with the greatest nobles of Baria. None of them spoke. Finally, Neben de Rillt bowed and asked to go.

Bryx nodded and the other nobles followed him. Left alone in Cabyn Mayne, Bryx walked its elegant corridors. The place still seemed to house the spirit of Rax. Bryx could almost see the giant figure of his father in the shadows of the public chamber and again in the small dining cabinet where he took his supper alone.

Later, in the darkness, he walked back through the narrow streets of the Floating Islands across the bridge to the mainland and on up the slope to Valla's Palace. A half-moon rose out of the sea and gilded the white marble.

Bryx paused to look out at the moonlight on the water. Questions paraded through his mind. Why had his mother died? Why shouldn't he blame Jax? How could he make the damn Barians see that he was doing his best for them? And where, by the goddess, was his dragon-blasted brother? The sea undulated darkly and an answer came: Jax must be somewhere deep in the interior of the Knownlands, someplace that Barian ships didn't go.

8

By the time Jax had survived a year in the slave pens, he no longer wondered how Bryx was faring as sealord or what Tallyn might be doing on a given evening. His dreams had followed him to The Hant and were now peopled with trolls and slaves and amorphous terrors that lurked in the shadows of the mine.

He still had to steel himself to go down into the pit every morning, his chest tight and his heart thudding, but he had found a purpose that gave him a reason to keep breathing: Each day he looked for a way to taunt the trolls. He knew that his irreverence angered the trolls but it also earned him their respect. Each day he also found a way to offer a hand or share a burden with a fellow slave, knowing that the others followed his example and helped one another.

The trolls still called him Fishman. The other slaves had started to call him sir, and he accepted the responsibility of the honorific.

The slave wrangler sat in front of Boss Taint on a dark winter day, chewing on a piece of pencil.

"What do you mean we don't need any new slaves?" Taint frowned, causing the purple circles on his jowls to stretch into oblongs. "How is that possible? It's wintertime. We usually lose six or seven a week."

The slave wrangler shook her head. "Ain't none of them died in the last two weeks."

Taint's frown deepened. "What are you doing to them?"

"Nothing different. But I was thinking they might last longer if we feed them a bit more."

"Feed them shmeed them. It's a waste to feed them if they're just going to die right away."

"Well, they ain't dying quite so fast these days. Let me give them a little more."

Taint ruffled the papers on his desk. "If I save two hundred silvers a week by not buying new slaves, then you can have a hundred silvers more to buy food. But if this don't work and we start losing six or seven a week again, the food goes."

"Alright." The slave wrangler pushed herself out of the chair and left the office. Secretly she believed that it was Fishman who was making the difference, but she was not ready to tell Taint that. There was always a slave who seemed to rule the others somehow. It was her experience that all creatures from dogs to slaves, and even trolls, liked to be told what to do and liked to have someone in charge of them. She had noted over the years that the slaves were usually ruled by the most ruthless and hardhearted of them all. She'd never seen one like the Fishman. Rather than brutalize his fellows into submission, his leadership came from some strange sense of responsibility. Sustained by him, the slaves were still miserable and still died, but they seemed to have a better heart because they knew that someone was looking out for them.

"Look, sir!" A slave named Ollie shoved his bowl at Jax. "I got a whole chicken wing! You want it?"

Jax had gotten used to being offered food. The gesture always reminded him of how people used to try to placate the screamer. "No, thanks, Ollie."

"Maybe you're more of a leg and breast man?" a woman named Ahno said slyly. Jax laughed. "Maybe."

"Aren't we all," Ollie offered.

That night Ahno rolled next to Jax in the dark. "Care to try a bite?" she whispered.

Indeed, he did. Unlike taking food from a fellow slave, sex was an act of mutual pleasure, and he had no qualms sharing this warm refuge from the dark misery of the slave pens.

In the baths the next morning, Jax helped the new woman in Cave Three dunk her head the obligatory two times, holding her so she would not panic, as most landish people did when submerged.

"Oh, it's awful!" she cried as she came up spitting sulfuric water.

"But it might keep you healthy," Jax reassured her. "You're done now. Climb out and get some clothes."

"Right, sir."

"It's Jax. Just Jax."

As she got out, Jax pushed himself deeper into the warm black water.

"Get OUT, Fishman!" shouted the duty toll. "For goddess's sake, why do I always have to yell at you to get out?"

"I thought you liked yelling. You do it so well. And so often."

"Shut up," growled the troll, but Jax saw the hidden grins on the other slaves' faces.

The long Hantish winter wore along with periods of brilliant but frigid days punctuated by howling blizzards. To him the days underground were black and identical.

Then one night deep in the darkness of Cave Three, he felt Ahno's arms reaching for him, as they often had. He rolled toward her and came fully awake. She was burning with fever. He sat up and pulled her into his arms.

"I'm hot," she shivered, "but freezing."

"Hush." He slowly rocked her back and forth.

"You shouldn't touch me. You'll get it too." She began to sob. "I'm done."

He held her tighter. "You'll be free, Ahno," he whispered to her hair. "You'll be out of this pit."

"I'm scared."

"It can't be worse than this place."

She didn't answer, but she clung to him. He rocked her slowly back and forth in the dark.

When the duty troll arrived that morning, Ahno was no longer conscious; her breathing was thick and labored.

The other slaves stayed away. They all knew the fever was terribly contagious.

"What's this?" the duty troll grumbled at the sight of the Fishman holding one of the other slaves.

"She has the fever."

The troll noted the fatigue around the Fishman's weird, slanted eyes and realized he must have spent the night trying to comfort her.

"Alright, off to the baths. Hurry up." The troll sighed, knowing she'd be chastised for the group being late to the work sites.

Jax stood up, carrying Ahno's inert body.

"Put it down, Fishman," the troll ordered. "I'll get a troll to come get it."

Jax shook his head. "I'll take her."

The duty troll was speechless. Usually, the slaves stayed far away from a sick one.

Jax moved past the troll and down the dim passage. He knew of the death cave where the sick were taken, never to emerge again, but he had never been in it.

He followed a long tunnel to its end and pushed a door open. Inside, a troll with a torch knelt among several still forms.

"What? Are ye bringing me another?"

"Yes."

Jax set Ahno down gently on the dirt floor, wishing he'd brought her blanket. The troll peered at her and felt her head.

"It don't have long."

"No." Jax looked at Ahno's thin face. The flush of the fever made her look more healthy than she had been in months. She wasn't the first of his people in Cave Three to die of fever, but she had reached out to him more than any of the others. He wished there was something more he could do.

As he crouched near Ahno, Jax watched the troll drag the body of a dead slave to the back of the cave. There, a broad, deep canal of steaming water ran through the room and disappeared under a wall. A deep rumble echoed from somewhere beyond the cave. The troll tossed the body into the water. It sank as the current carried it from the cave.

"Where does that go?" Jax asked.

The troll twisted his head. "No one knows. There's a deep cavern down there beyond the falls. No one's ever been down to it."

"Goddess damn you," Jax muttered.

"You probably damned yourself," said the troll, "bringing in your friend. I'll probably see you back here in a couple of days."

Jax knew this was true. Still, he bent to give Ahno one last kiss. As he squeezed her hand, her eyes fluttered, but did not open. "Fly free, Ahno. Goddess bless you."

Without another word he went to the bath. The others had already left. An hour later, the duty troll came back to fetch him out of the hot dark water, after the engineer had yelled at her and sent her off to find the Fishman.

Two mornings later Jax could not get up.

"What's wrong, Fishman?" sneered the duty troll. Jax only rolled away from the light of her torch, which burned his dry eyes. Undeterred, the guard grabbed Jax's collar and tugged at him.

Woozily he sat up and leaned against the wall of the cave, shivering uncontrollably. The guard recognized the signs.

"Ah well, Fishman," the troll sneered. "This is what you get for holding that sick one the other night. You've gone and killed yourself."

She left Jax sprawled, sweating and shaking, on his blanket and herded the rest of the sorrowing slaves to the bath.

Jax couldn't make sense of the troll's words. He could not seem to do much of anything. Rolling over and pulling the blanket up around his shoulders seemed to take forever.

Alternately freezing and burning, he suddenly found himself in a different cave. Hearing the rumble of the waterfall, he knew where he was.

He heard someone sing an Islish lullaby, and he tried to ask for a drink. For a long time there was nothing but hot and cold and the thunder of falling water.

"It's still alive, Wrangler, and it's been two days."

The slave wrangler turned from the infirmary troll and gazed speculatively at the unconscious Fishman. The fire of the fever still flushed its disgusting, whisker-shadowed cheeks. Yellow dirt caked the sweaty skin.

"Let's put it up on a cot. Clean off that mud and give it some water." She turned away. "I'll send a druid down with some broth."

"This one will be the first slave to ever survive the fever."

"I know." The slave wrangler left the death cave wondering. Maybe its islish blood enabled it to withstand the fever; after all, trolls did not get it. The Fishman had already proven to be a good buy, surviving more than a year in the mines. That was almost unheard of too.

Jax's eyes didn't want to open. They were sticky, gummy around the rims. Foggily at first, then more distinctly, he saw the grotesquely painted faces and orange eyes that belonged to the voices he'd been hearing.

"It's awake."

"Welcome back," said the infirmary troll, cheerily.

"Dragons," Jax croaked.

"You've turned out to be a good buy, Fishman." Boss Taint's face creased in a way that might have been a smile.

The slave wrangler thumped Jax's leg with her huge hand. "We thought of breeding you, since you're so hardy."

Jax did not feel hardy; he felt as if a troll was sitting on his chest and his head hammered with every beat of his heart.

"Unfortunately, the goddess forbids that kind of thing," said a fourth troll, whose green-trimmed robe and pentagram pendant identified him as a druid. "It could be construed as rape."

"Rape, shmape," grunted Boss Taint as he lumbered out of the cave.

The slave wrangler grabbed Jax's head by the hair and poured some water down his throat, oblivious to his choking gasps.

"You'll be just fine in a week or so," she said gently. "Ready to go back to the mines."

"Splendid."

A week later a duty troll harried Jax down the tunnel back to Cave Three. He unlocked the door and held his torch high. "Look who's back."

"Sir!"

"Sweet Goddess."

Several of the slaves stood up and went to touch Jax. "We heard you had survived." Two of them hugged him.

The troll slammed the door, plunging the cave into darkness.

Jax swayed, but someone caught and steadied him.

"Here, sit down, sir."

Jax sat. Someone put a blanket into his hands.

"How did you do it? How did you beat the fever?"

"I don't know." He coughed. "I just didn't die."

Jax awoke the next morning only when the duty troll prodded him with her boot. "Up now, Fishman. You gotta earn your keep."

Mechanically, Jax followed his fellow slaves to the bread baskets, across the courtyard, and down into the mine. Slaves from other caves thumped him on the back and hugged him, welcoming him back. He stumbled along feeling weak and dazed.

At the end of the tunnel the others began to hammer at the rock. The banging pounded painfully in Jax's head.

"Get to work, Fishman," the engineer growled.

Jax swung at the rock, but the impact shuddered through his weakened body. He dropped the pickax and reeled away to the opposite wall and slid to the ground as the horror of his survival became graphically evident.

The fever hadn't released him. His recovery condemned him to more endless days, weeks, months, maybe years of sweating in this dark, stinking hole.

He buried his head in his hands. The other slaves crouched down next to him. "You'll be all right, sir. When you get your strength up."

"All right for what?" Jax whispered.

"All right for us. We need you, sir."

"It's Jax. Just Jax."

"What's going on here?" The engineer raised his lantern and glared at the inactive slaves.

"He ain't strong enough to dig yet," one of the slaves answered.

The engineer deployed his crop, and the other slaves jumped to resume their work. "The druid says the Fishman is fit," he said.

Jax rose to his feet. "Your druid is a hypocrite."

The engineer grinned. "That's what Boss Taint says, too. Now get to work!"

Jax leaned against the tunnel wall and stared at the troll. He'd be damned if he'd let them order him around anymore.

The engineer frowned, he could beat the damn slave into submission, but Taint wouldn't like that. He snapped his crop back onto his belt. "At least make sure these others keep working," the troll said stomping off up the tunnel.

Jax lifted his ax again. He steeled himself and swung at the rock.

"What's a *hypo-crate*?" one of the other slaves asked.

Bang. Jax's ax slammed into the tunnel. "A druid who condones slavery." Bang. "A slave owner who pretends to value life." Bang. "A noble who abandons their people."

Bang. Bang. Bang.

"Hey, Fishman, here's a new one for ye." The guard's smoky torch reddened the bundles of slaves lying on the floor around Cave Three. A few of them sat up.

The guard raised his light, looking around the cave. He held a trembling young woman by a leash clipped into a new collar. With a frown the guard walked into the cave, finally finding the Fishman, already sound asleep. The troll kicked him.

Jax rolled away and sat up, rubbing his eyes. "What?"

"I'm bringing ye a new one."

"Great." Jax was puzzled. Usually, the trolls just opened the door long enough to shove a new slave into the darkness. Why was this one getting such an introduction? Jax looked at the woman the troll was shoving toward him. His eyes widened in amazement: she was beautiful.

"Take care of it. It was pricey."

She flinched as the troll unclipped the leash from her collar.

"Right," Jax said, staring at the young woman, noting her lovely curves and the tracks of tears glimmering on her cheeks. "Someone give her a blanket," he said as the troll left and darkness returned.

"Take mine," offered a male voice from across the room.

"She can share with me," offered another man.

"We don't have any extras?" Jax asked.

"I have two," sighed a woman. "Here."

Jax groped in the dark, found the blanket then found the new lass and put the blanket into her hand. What were the trolls up to now, sending this beautiful person down into Cave Three with a personal introduction? Jax could tell from the rustling of other blankets in the cave that he was not the only one intrigued.

By her breathing, he knew she was crying. He had heard plenty of tears over his year in the slave pens. She sniffled loudly.

The voice of Nyle, a young man from Ohe, spoke from the other side of her. "Hey now, lassie. May I hold you?" Jax heard Nyle put his arms around the girl. "Hush now."

Jax frowned. Wasn't it his role to take care of people? Still, he lay down again and resettled his blanket to keep his head off the dirt. Eventually, he slept.

"Let's go!" The duty troll slammed open the door of Cave Three. She dumped the large basket that held the slaves' breakfast bread on the floor and leaned against the wall, munching her own bun as she watched the slaves roll wearily out of their blankets.

"Hey, you!" She strode into the room and kicked at Nyle, who was lying with his arms around the new girl. "Let go. It ain't for you!"

Nyle got up slowly. "What do you mean by that?"

The duty troll smacked him with her crop. "You just let that one be."

Jax stepped between the duty troll and Nyle. "You trolls never cared about this kind of thing before."

"Well, I care now. Ain't you the lord around here, Fishman? Ain't you the one who's supposed to sort out the new slaves?"

Jax shrugged and looked at the new girl. Her brown eyes were swollen from last night's tears, and she was rubbing her face with her sleeve.

"Sure I am," Jax answered. "What's she supposed to do?"

The duty troll grinned slyly. "Well, today, Fishman, it's supposed to learn to carry."

Jax stared in amazement at the troll. "And tomorrow? The next day?"

Again, the troll just grinned. "Whatever. Let's go now."

Jax looked around at the other slaves; all of them seemed puzzled by this. The new lass kept her gaze on the floor. Jax bent down to find her gaze. "What's your name?"

Her brown eyes met his and something flickered there. "I'm Jolira. And you're the Fishman."

"I'm Jax. Here, have a bun. Take an extra for lunch."

"Lunch?" Jolira whispered.

"It's his fancy word for tiffin," Nyle grumbled.

"It's the proper word," Jax noted. "I'll show you the carry-house, Jolira."

The duty troll grunted. "That's more like it."

In courtyard, Jax noted the way the sun found auburn highlights in Jolira's brown hair. "You'll start over here at the smelters," Jax said to her, reaching for her hand to pull her out of the line of slaves headed for the mine mouth. She flinched, and he dropped it. At the smelter he found the duty troll in charge. "This is Jolira. She's supposed to carry."

The troll smiled widely at Jax. "She's pretty, eh, Fishman?"

"She is. But I thought trolls found all of us as unattractive as we find you."

The troll frowned, working his way slowly to the insult in Jax's reply. Finally, he swatted at Jax with his crop. "Git on with you, then."

Over the next few weeks, Jax watched the other slaves jostle to sit near Jolira in the mess and look for ways to give her something or impress her. He kept himself aloof from all this as best he could.

Jolira seemed to have come to terms with her fate. He'd seen her smile and even heard a rare laugh. Jolira was far more lovely and shapely than the usual slaves who ended up here. Everyone knew that the iron mines were the last stop for a slave. None left this place alive. They worked until they died. The mine tended to look for bargains, buying cheaper, older slaves, or those, like Jax, who might be a risky purchase.

He did not want to believe that the trolls would really buy a slave just to seduce him. He did not want to be the reason that she had ended up in the slave pens rather than in an easier place with a rich trollish family.

Jolira had continued to sleep near Nyle in Cave Three, but everyone was perfectly aware that Nyle wasn't touching her. They did, however, often sit together quietly in the mess hall. Jax made a point of sitting somewhere else. Maybe, he thought, if their plan didn't work, the trolls would sell Jolira away from this horrible place.

Instead, they sold Nyle.

One day he was gone. When Jax asked the duty troll where he was, she glowered. "We beat it and sold it for bait."

"Bait?"

"You don't know much, do you, Fishman?"

"I wasn't raised among trolls. I don't know all your vicious ways. Tell me what you mean by bait."

"Well." The duty troll spoke slowly as if talking to a child. "We hunt for monsters in the Forest Krill. And we use slaves as bait. Monsters, you see, like to eat live meat. So, we take an old slave or a particularly bad one and beat it until it ain't but barely living. Then we tie it up to some trees. The monsters smell the blood and come in for the kill. When they're in the thick of it, crazed with the blood lust, we kill them. Usually with swords, but some trolls prefer pikes. Myself, I like..."

"Enough," Jax snapped, sickened. "Enough."

"Naw. It's a great sport." The troll leered at Jax. "And I'll tell you what, Fishman. That lassie will be bait too, if it don't please you."

Jax turned from the troll in horror.

"Come on now, Fishman. You git down to your dig."

Jax shook his head and strode off across the courtyard. He found the slave wrangler in her office, throwing papers around.

"What are you doing here, Fishman?"

"Did you buy Jolira to make her..." he choked on the words. "So that she would..."

"Breed with you?" The slave wrangler's teeth were coated with her orange lipstick. "Yeah."

"But the druid said you can't do that. You can't breed people!"

"Hey, you folks breed horses and dogs and nobles. Why can't we breed slaves?"

"Because it's wrong. And because it won't work. You know the goddess never gives a baby to anyone here."

The slave wrangler shrugged. For all the ardent worship of the goddess' rituals of love and pleasure in the Knownlands, children rarely resulted from these activities. All babies in the Knownlands were considered gifts from the goddess and a sign of her blessings upon the parents. Still, pregnancies were rare enough even for married couples, and those who had not gone through a handfasting ceremony and committed themselves to each other in the eyes of the goddess and their community almost never found themselves gifted with a child.

The slave wrangler knew that the slaves sought solace in each other's arms in the dark of their caves, and she'd always encouraged it. She figured that whatever relief they could find might keep them alive a little longer. But in all her years in the slave pens, the slave wrangler had never once seen a slave get pregnant. The Fishman was right: the goddess didn't give babies into a place like this.

Boss Taint strode into the slave wrangler's office growling. "What are you doing here, Fishman?"

Jax strove for his temper. "Boss, you might as well sell that girl out of here. I'm not going to play your damn game."

Boss Taint made a face. "If you don't like it, we'll sell it as bait and get you another one."

"NO!"

Taint's smile was evil. "Yes."

"Go on, Fishman," said the slave wrangler. "Enjoy it."

That night Jax took his allotment of gristly stew and sat down next to Jolira. Two other slaves were already there. "Please leave us," Jax ordered. "I need to speak to Jolira alone."

Jolira's smile was nowhere as she watched him with wary dark eyes. Jax lost his appetite. "Jolira. Do you know what happened to Nyle?

She shook her head, her eyes fearful.

"They sold him for bait."

She gasped and put her hand to her mouth. Tears filled her eyes.

"I'm so sorry," he whispered finally. "When I recovered from the fever the trolls said they wanted to... to get more slaves like me who are resistant to the fever."

Jolira nodded. "I know, sir."

"I'm just Jax," he said, filled with shame. "You're here because of me. They sold Nyle because they thought he was between you and me."

"I should have thought of that," Jolira said in anguish. "The trolls told me about you, sir. They said if I could get a child from you for them that they would set me free."

Jax took a deep breath. "The goddess doesn't give babies here."

Jolira shrugged. "I wouldn't mind sharing blankets with you sir, but I couldn't buy my freedom with my own baby."

"No. But, Jolira, they'll sell you to be bait unless I...unless we—. Dragons." He swore for lack of a better finish to the statement.

"Bait?" she trembled and went white. "I don't want to be bait. Don't let them do that to me, sir! Please, don't let them do that."

He thought for a moment. "Listen, here's what we'll do. We'll pretend to carry on, alright? We won't have sex, but we can sleep beside each other. If you seem to be doing what they ask, they'll keep you here. And that will buy us time."

"Time for what?"

"An easier death for either one of us."

"Oh." She took a deep breath. "Alright then. Just don't let them take me for bait, sir."

"Jax," he said, drawing her into a hug. "My name is Jax."

That night they wrapped themselves together in their blankets and slept, both of them comforted by the other.

"I won the lottery," Jolira explained, leaning into Jax as they sat side by side on the bench in the mess.

"I knew a village that had something like that," the Crone said slurping the last of her soup. "T'was in the poor scrubland north of the Y-Gren. Them people had a hard time growing anything but rocks."

"I'm from Ohe," Jolira said, "and we can't seem to grow more than rocks either."

"So, your village takes up a lottery and sells one of its people to the trolls?" Jax was horrified.

"Yep. They split the money among everyone, but the family who wins gets a bit more. Folks who have little ones under the age of sixteen don't have to participate. My husband will have gotten enough to buy a cow...." Jolira gave her self-deprecating smile. "It's not a terrible trade for him, once he gets done missing me. With a cow, he'll be able to get a new wife."

"You had a husband?" Yory, a tall Norledgian leaned across the table.

"Handfasted for a year." She nodded.

Jax moved to pull away a bit, but she put a hand on his leg. "He could have won the lottery too. I know that this way, he won't starve to death, and neither will I."

Jax considered the meager food. "What about your nobles?" he asked. "Isn't there someone who can alleviate the suffering before you have to sell yourselves as slaves?"

"What's *alleviate*? Nobles ain't got much either," Jolira shrugged, "but they don't have to put their names in for the lottery because the trolls don't pay much for 'em."

"Why not?"

She laughed and winked at him. "Everyone knows nobles is lousy as slaves, *sir*."

"That's the truth," Jax muttered. He hadn't specifically told Jolira of the titles he'd been born to, only saying that some of his family sold him to the trolls, but like everyone else in the slave pens, she'd recognized the aristocrat in him.

As weeks rolled into months, Jax marveled at Jolira's good natured acceptance of her hideous fate. She admitted to missing her husband and occasionally talked about him or her family with sad fondness. But she took up the heavy mine work and ate the dismal food with the nonchalance of someone bred to labor and meager rations.

"T'was a lovely day," she'd say as they sat in the mess hall, or she'd compliment someone on a new twist to her hair, or tease one of the men about his growing muscles.

On the one hand Jax thought that her lack of misery suggested a certain simplicity, but she was truly a joy to be around.

Sleeping next to Jolira's lush curves became increasingly difficult. Abstinence wasn't something people practiced in the Knownlands, where all acts of love and pleasure were considered the goddess' rituals.

Finally, one night, Jax's hand brushed across her full breasts and stayed. She exhaled softly, so he continued to fondle the soft flesh.

"Jax," she whispered a half-hearted caution.

He was peeling away the top of her dress, his mouth going where his hands had just been. "There are other paths to pleasure," he offered.

"Your accent drives me crazy."

He didn't answer with words, but she felt his whiskered cheeks between the soft skin of her thighs. A few minutes later she shuddered with relief and release and then moved to return the favor.

10

"You, Fishman! The mine boss wants you." A duty troll collared Jax as he crossed the courtyard on his way to the pit. Jax shrugged off the troll's large fist, but he followed her to the mine boss's office, fear growing in his stomach. He was afraid Taint was going to question him about Jolira. If she didn't get pregnant, he feared the goddess-damned trolls might sell her and find another young slave to try to breed him with. But the trolls had something very different in mind.

Inside, the office was as cluttered as when Jax had first arrived. The slave wrangler stood against the wall watching Boss Taint talk to a third, beefy troll who lounged in the chair that faced Taint's desk.

"You're smart, Oblek," said Taint flipping through a set of neatly written pages. Jax could see columns of figures and colored graphs. "You've always had an eye for a new opportunity," Taint admitted. "But this...." He put the papers down.

Oblek grinned. "My numbers are conservative, so even if it only works half as well as I've estimated, you still save significant time and money."

Boss Taint put a thick forefinger on the papers. "Yeah, but according to your proposal, a significant percentage of my savings goes right into your pocket."

Oblek stood up. "Well, I'm the one doing the work, taking the risk, and it's my idea."

"Alright," Boss Taint shrugged. "Let's give it a try. Here's the Fishman for you."

Oblek, his orange eyes underlined by heavy smudges of black kohl, turned to consider Jax. Once again Jax found himself amazed by the violence of trollish cosmetics.

Oblek noted Jax's scrutiny, and he frowned. "You're Barian?"

"Yes."

Oblek smacked Jax across the mouth.

"Don't you teach your slaves humility?" Oblek demanded of Boss Taint.

"Not this one."

Oblek's eyes narrowed as he turned back to Jax. "Can you sail a boat?"

"Yes."

Oblek, hands on his hips, frowned down his nose. "Bring him." He gestured to the slave wrangler and stalked out of the mine boss's office. Jax caught a grimace on the fe-troll's round face; clearly, she did not appreciate being treated like a slave herself.

She and Jax followed Oblek across the courtyard. As they passed the group of slaves bundling the iron for shipment, Oblek thoughtfully pulled a leather crop from his belt and deployed it randomly, wordlessly among the slaves. Jax finally remembered where he had seen the meaty troll before: Oblek oversaw the mine shipments. Occasionally, he came to view the extraction process, but he spent most of his time at the mine's sales offices in The Hant, or along the road between the iron mines and the little outpost at Southant, where caravans from the south came to pick up ore, allowing the iron merchants to stay as far away from The Hant as possible.

Now, Oblek shoved open the thick wooden gate and led Jax and the slave wrangler out of the mine compound. Jax walked through the gate with a trembling sense of awe. He had not been outside the walls since his arrival more than a year and a half ago. The air out here seemed noticeably cleaner and fresher.

Oblek strode ahead of the other two, leading them around the walls of the mine buildings and down to the shore. Hanter Lake gleamed blue and green in the morning sunlight. Jax felt an incredible longing to dive into that beautiful water.

Seeing the wistful expression on Jax's face, Oblek quickly snapped a leather leash onto Jax's slave collar.

"Look at this," the troll gestured to an oddly shaped sailboat that lay on its side a few yards from the shore.

Jax considered the craft. Only the sprites would build a boat with such confusing lines and misplaced timbers. It had a mast and some rigging for a mainsail and a jib, but it also had oarlocks placed so that they would certainly foul the sheets. Gaping holes where the wood had buckled rendered the craft useless as it stood.

Jax pushed his hair back from his face. "The sprites don't know how to make boats."

"Can you make it seaworthy?" Oblek asked.

"Maybe. Whose is it?"

"Mine."

"Ours, actually," the slave wrangler inserted. "It belongs to the mines."

Jax looked from one troll to the other, astonished. The trolls, like all landish creatures, disliked water. The sprites occasionally built boats and ventured to sea, but usually found tragedy there—as anyone might, who went out in a rickety tub like this one. "Why did the mines buy a spritish boat?"

"Because the stupid Barians wouldn't sell us one," Oblek growled.

Jax laughed and Oblek responded with his fists, sending Jax to his knees.

"Shut up, or I'll kick you. Now, tell me. Can you make it seaworthy?"

"Probably." Jax stood slowly, eyeing Oblek with contempt.

"Good!" The slave wrangler clapped her hands.

"This is my ticket to fame and fortune," Oblek said. "The ferry will carry bricks of pig iron across the lake." He pointed south. "It's a three-day journey from here around to Southant on the Vrillbridge road. I want you to fix this boat so we can ship the ore across the lake and save the three days. It'll be cheaper too: no mules to feed."

"Who'll sail it for you?" Jax wondered if the trolls were foolish enough to go to sea with sprites.

Oblek stared with dislike at Jax. The slave wrangler answered for him: "You will, Fishman. Oblek or another overtroll will go with you."

"Really?" Jax gazed thoughtfully at Oblek. The idea of being out of the mine thrilled him. Oblek was surly and cruel, but Jax would be in the open air, on the water even! He'd finally be out of those terrifying tunnels.

He walked around the boat again, mentally listing things he would need, then looked at the shallow shore of the lake. "We'll have to build a loading dock. You'll probably need one at Southant too."

Oblek nodded. "You'll build it and repair the boat. Wrangler will assign slaves to help."

Back inside the compound, the slave wrangler sent Jax to her office to draw up a list of necessary materials.

Boss Taint joined the wrangler and Oblek in the courtyard. "You think it'll work?"

"Sure it will," the beefy troll answered with confidence.

"We'll see," Taint lumbered off.

The slave wrangler put a hand on Oblek's arm. "The Fishman doesn't eat as much as a mule, but it's not docile," she warned.

"I'll tame it."

Jax could hardly contain his relief at being freed from the mine tunnels, but Jolira was horrified.

"You'll be on water," she wailed. "You'll surely drown."

Jax shook his head. "I don't think I'll drown. But maybe I can escape. And If I'm gone, they'll have no reason to keep you."

They were lying together in the darkness of Cave Three, her arms warm around him. "I'll miss you. We'll all miss you, if you go."

Jax enjoyed taking her mind off these concerns.

Jolira and the other slaves, who all shared her fear of open water, finally accepted that Jax really was happier on the lake. Those who were assigned to help build the loading dock watched how he easily moved in and out of the water. Used by now to the Fishman's crisp accent, neither the slaves nor the duty trolls questioned Jax's easy assumption of command, but Oblek did.

"Dragons, Oblek," Jax gasped, wiping blood from his split lip. "Can you stop hitting me? Your beatings don't motivate me to work harder, and they don't prove you're superior."

"I don't have to prove anything to you, Fishman. You slaves are puny rodents, hairy and furtive. But here in the Hantland, we value individuals for their innate qualities. Clearly, I am smarter, larger, stronger, and superior to you in every way!"

"Not to mention your deft hand with cosmetics," Jax said blandly.

Oblek came at him again, and Jax scrambled back. "You don't prove you're superior by beating up people who are smaller than you!"

"Maybe that's not what I'm trying to prove." Oblek caught him in the stomach with a thick fist.

"What then?" Jax grunted.

"I'm proving that I am in charge. You need to cringe before me like a mouse before a cat."

"Why didn't you just say so?" Jax snapped.

"I'm a troll of action, not words."

Jax laughed, then bowed low in an elegant abasement he'd learned long ago when having to beg forgiveness from Kordish authorities.

"You are so damned stupid." Oblek turned away, and Jax made a rude gesture to the troll's back. The other slaves sniggered.

Oblek spun around. Jax shrugged innocently. "What, master?"

"Dragons fry you, Fishman. You've wasted enough time here. I'll beat you as it pleases me. Get to work."

Jax took the ferry for its first voyage on a beautiful late summer day when sunlight spangled the ripples on the lake and a balmy offshore breeze filled the sail. Jax glowed, ignoring the constant stinging of Oblek's crop.

The troll had never been on a boat, and its rocking unsettled his belly. Another young troll, hoping for rapid promotion by volunteering for the risky position of ferry mate, came along for the maiden voyage. Both trolls clung to the sides of the boat in fear.

After a few hours, Jax pulled the boat up to the little loading dock. The mate sprang off the boat and ran for shore. Jax never saw him again. Oblek had trouble keeping mates for his ferry project. Most of those who were willing to undertake such a hazardous occupation were either young trolls out to prove themselves, or trolls who had failed at other jobs and wanted to reestablish themselves as overmasters. No ferry mate lasted more than a month. They could not stand the fear, or the seasickness, or the terror of a sudden squall. Jax, who still cringed at the thought of the dark mine tunnels, could understand how they felt.

Oblek didn't like being on the boat either. He had hoped to delegate the job of sailing across the lake to a ferry mate, but none stayed long enough.

Now, after the first voyage, Oblek stood on the shore and watched the other troll's retreating back as the sun slanted to the western horizon.

"I'll need more pitch," Jax called as he shoved the boat up onto the coarse sand of the beach. "She's pretty tight, but water is still coming in here, and here. Over here too." He knelt, peering closely at the hull. Oblek looked too, but he saw nothing.

"I'll have to move this jib-line as well." Jax stood and thoughtfully pulled a loose thread from his shirt.

"How long?" Oblek demanded. He wanted to get the ferry running regularly as soon as possible. Even though the iron caravans that took the metal south only traveled in the summer, Oblek planned to run the ferry year-round, storing the iron at Southant instead of in the mine compound as they did now.

Jax walked around the boat, already loosening the jib line. "Two days. The pitch has to cure."

"Make it one." Oblek clipped the leash onto Jax's slave collar.

Jax shrugged. There was one more thing he needed. He stowed the bailers and stood once more to face the troll. "I'm going to need another hand to sail this ferry and to help load it."

"You want a slave of your own, do you?" Oblek snarled.

"I've never needed to enslave someone to get help," Jax noted.

Oblek turned and strode away, dragging Jax behind him.

Satisfied, Jax stumbled after the troll up to the mine compound. He knew Oblek would get someone to crew with him. Over the last few weeks, Jax had come to understand that Oblek's anger stemmed from the conflict between his sense of superiority and the reality of his reliance on a "slave." That essential paradox pointed a knife at Oblek's ferry scheme and his entire worldview. Jax couldn't stop the abuse, but he knew how to twist the knife.

Jax stared up at the dark clouds blowing through the afternoon sky. He recognized the rush of nausea and panic flowing into him as Rising Fear.

"Stop lollygagging and get the boat loaded!" Oblek shouted.

"We shouldn't launch now." Jax turned to face the troll. "The Rising is just about here."

"I told you to load up." Oblek punctuated his order with a vicious flick of his crop.

"No one sails in a Rising." Jax dodged the blows.

"You will." Oblek finally landed a stinging blow then another.

With no choice, Jax helped the other slave, Moiry, load the ore onto the ferry. He clenched his teeth against the Rising Fear and cast off. The steady wind wasn't quite a gale. Jax directed Moiry to help with the sails, while Oblek and the ferry mate clung to the sides of the heeling boat.

"Damn you, Fishman! Make the boat flat!" Oblek growled.

"If you want to get to dry land before the Rising starts, we have to go as fast possible," Jax answered curtly.

The sun set into a purple bank of clouds as they tied up to the little wharf at Southant and unloaded the ore. Moiry sat exhausted on the dock, while the trolls chatted on the shore. Jax paced. Moiry wondered where he was finding the energy. Oblek had pushed the slaves to their physical limits for days as the summer waned, insisting on at least three, and often four, trips each day as he strove to supply the last caravans of the season.

Finally, Jax marched up to the trolls. "We should leave the boat here and find another way back to the mines."

"It's a three-day walk around the lake," said the troll who lived at Southant.

"I'm not walking." Oblek snapped a leash onto Jax's collar and hauled him down to the wharf. Oblek fastened the leash to a wide leather strap around his bulging waist. The ferry mate attached a similar system to Moiry. This was Oblek's insurance that the Fishman wouldn't just jump overboard one day and swim away or toss the trolls off the boat and sail off into the open sea.

Overhead, a thick cloak of clouds hid the stars, but the wind had died. Jax shuddered. "The Rising will come tonight."

"Fine." Oblek shoved him onto the boat. "Row."

Jax settled his tired muscles into the rowing frame as Moiry cast off. The night was close and windless. Jax smelled the ozone of Rising storms.

About an hour out onto the lake, it began to rain heavily but stopped after all four on the ferry were thoroughly soaked. The night was completely black.

"Do you know where you're going, Fishman?" The mate looked around at the dark water and black sky.

"I'm trying to get us off the water before the Rising," Jax answered between strokes of his oars. There was no wind to fill the sail. He could sense the northern shore of the lake, still a few miles off, but he could see no lights.

Oblek said nothing. The Fishman had rowed them home at night before, but it had never been quite so black.

"How do you know it ain't just rowing us in circles?" the mate screeched.

"I'm not."

"I'll beat you to a pulp if we're not home in an hour."

Moiry dredged deep into his own reserves to keep stroke with Jax. He was used to the nervousness of a new ferry mate, but Jax's uneasiness frightened him. What made him row so hard? Where was he finding the energy?

They arrived at the mine dock shortly before midnight. Jax insisted that he and Moiry haul the little craft out of the water and well up onto the beach.

"You'll just have to put it back in again tomorrow," Oblek taunted, as the two slaves strained their tired muscles.

The Rising hit with a scream and a bang a few hours later. Jax awoke with a start in the blackness of the cave. He sensed, more than heard, the roar of the storm. Shuddering, he rolled toward Jolira and fell into uneasy dreams.

Glaring at the driving sleet and wind of the storm the next morning, even Oblek realized they could not venture onto the lake in this weather. Moiry and Jax relished the rest provided by two weeks of stormy seas. They repaired sails and ropes, carved a new tiller, and even accompanied Oblek on some errands into The Hant, where he enjoyed bragging about the success of his vision in getting ore delivered to Southant in hours rather than days.

Shivering in the raw weather, Jax always looked for Barians on these trips, but he knew there was slim chance of finding any of them here during a Rising. Barians despised trollish slavery, and having no use for trollish goods or trade, they seldom came here. Jax noticed a few free people, but none that he could identify as someone who might help him.

Oblek required fewer trips across the lake during the cold winter months. While the steaming water kept them warm as they made their trips back and forth, Oblek hated getting caught in the blinding Hantish blizzards that would blow across the lake with little or no warning.

Moiry died one day when he fell off the dock at Southant as they were unloading the cargo. Jax moved to dive into the warm water to fetch him out, but Oblek held him back.

"Let me get him!"

"No. I'm tired of it."

Furious, Jax stood and watched Moiry drown. None of the trolls made any move to help. They didn't even bother to fish his body out of the water, but let it lie in the lapping waves for weeks, rotting slowly.

"Let's go!" The grumpy voice of the duty troll with her ruddy torchlight broke into the silence of Cave Three. Jolira sighed softly and disentangled herself from Jax. He sat up and flexed his shoulders.

Oblek's head appeared behind the duty troll. "Come on, Fishman."

Jax squeezed Jolira's hand, pulled on his shirt and followed the troll. Oblek looked over his shoulder at Jax, scrambling to keep up. "You must not be very potent if you haven't fetched a baby on that girl yet."

Jax said nothing.

Oblek sniggered. "Maybe you're like a mule: sterile. Crossbreeds sometimes are."

"Goddess damn you, Oblek."

"She surely damned you."

Jax couldn't argue with that.

Oblek led him into a small office where several slaves stood waiting, their eyes wide with nervousness and fear. "Go stand against the wall there, Fishman. You others stand next to him."

Jax frowned. "Where's Alemm?" He looked around for the other ferry slave.

"Dead." Oblek spat. "Fever. Now shut up and stand still."

Jax shoved his hair back from his face and waited. He knew that Oblek liked to have a matching pair of slaves. Of course, none of the other slaves had Jax's sea-blue islish eyes or pointed ears, but Oblek could choose tall, light-haired Norledgians or Ohites to match Jax's fair Kordish coloring.

Now Oblek scowled at the other slaves. "Who brought these?" he looked around for a duty troll. "None of these matches the Fishman."

"These are what the slave wrangler sent," explained the duty troll.

Oblek growled. "I'll take the woman. Bring her, Fishman."

"No!" the woman wailed.

Jax offered his hand to the woman. He recognized her from Cave Four. "It's not that bad, Chora," he said gently. "At least you don't have to go down into the pit."

The lake undulated black and steamy under the low clouds of late winter. A fitful breeze stirred choppy waves. Both Chora and the ferry mate were sick, leaving Jax to handle the boat alone. The trip took longer than usual due to the inconsistent wind. Even Oblek looked queasy, his orange eyes almost yellow by the time Jax tied the craft up to the dock that evening.

Jax helped Chora back to the slave pens, got her a left-over breakfast bun and sent her to her cave. Finally, he went to the mess hall where the mine slaves hunched over their dinners. He knew the moment he walked in that something was wrong. No one would meet his gaze. He didn't see Jolira.

Nausea rose in him. "Where's Jolira?" he asked the room in general.

"Cave-in, sir,"

Pain ripped through him. "No. NO!" He kicked over a bench. "Dragons fry you! Dragons fry us all!"

He turned from the room and bounded up the stairs to the courtyard. Two duty trolls followed him.

The day's fitful breeze had developed a purpose and Jax shivered at its force as it drove out of the north. Ignoring the snow, Jax stood against the high, rough wall and clawed at the stone.

The slave wrangler, summoned by a duty troll, found him hunched at the base of the wall, face and hair running with melting snow.

"Come on now, Fishman. Let's get you a bath and heat you up again. You know Oblek will want you in the morning." She hauled Jax, shivering silently, to his feet.

Later, after the slave wrangler locked the door of Cave Three behind her, Jax began to shiver again. He hadn't realized how much he loved Jolira and her happy heart. He grieved for never having told her.

Finally, someone put a gentle hand on his shoulder. "Sir, she's free now. Let her go."

"Free?" he choked, "Dead is not my idea of freedom."

But as he stared open-eyed into the darkness of his pain, he remembered that he and Jolira had hoped for this, for a kinder death, kinder than being bait, anyway.

But was it? Smothered, trapped in the muddy dark? He rolled into a ball of horror and heart break.

"Where's the girl, Fishman?" Oblek jerked Jax awake, back into his grief.

"Dragons fry you," Jax swore, following Oblek out of Cave Three while the others still slept.

Three weeks later, Jax stood on the dock with Oblek and Chora, watching the first storms of the Spring Rising whip and churn the black water of Hanter Lake.

Oblek's mouth twisted into an ugly frown as he viewed the Fishman. The slave had grown gaunt since his little friend died. Worse, he had become even more insolent.

Stupid, lovelorn slave thought Oblek sourly. The Fishman had, however, rowed like a fiend since the girl's death. Often, he was already awake in the morning when Oblek came to fetch him, sitting against the wall of the cave, shirt on and ready to go.

Unaware of Oblek's scrutiny, Jax pushed back his wind-tangled hair. "That's the Rising." He turned back toward shore.

Oblek watched his two slaves walk away. "Where are you going?" he snapped, frustrated by the Rising that left him nothing to do for the next few weeks, and not much for his slaves to do either.

Jax turned and shrugged. "Where do you want us to go?"

Oblek's mouth twisted evilly. He wanted to hurt someone. He would hurt that damned, insolent Fishman.

"To the pens." Once there he bound Jax to the whipping post and beat him unconscious.

"Had enough, Oblek?" The slave wrangler stood by, hands on her wide hips watching the beefy troll. She understood the need for the whipping post but discouraged the overtrolls from using it too much. "They all die soon enough without whipping 'em."

Oblek's orange eyes glared at the fe-troll, who was now directing the druid to take the Fishman to the infirmary.

"Bind the other one!" Oblek shouted. A guard brought Chora forward. "The Fishman didn't scream. I want to hear screams."

Chora obliged him.

By the time the Rising ended, the cuts on Jax's back had healed into a spider web of pale scars. Once again, he walked with Oblek down to the dock and set about training a new ferry slave. In the mess hall he sat with the rest of the slaves from Cave Three, but remained silent with his grief that, like the beating, left him hollow and numb with occasional twinges of incredible pain.

11

"Now, Fishman!" Oblek clipped the leash to Jax's collar and folded his waxed canvas cloak about his bulk.

Jax resigned himself to another day of chattering teeth as he followed the troll about his errands in The Hant, unprotected from the Rising weather. Another Fall Rising. Six months now, since Jolira had died. Memories of her still hurt, even through Oblek's abuse and now the Rising's pounding sleet. But when they walked out of the compound gate, Oblek headed for the dock instead of into town.

Jax knew without looking that black Rising clouds roiled overhead. The rain had stopped this morning, but the black waters of the lake rose in ominous, uneven waves under a whipping wind, evidence that the turmoil of the changing currents was far from over. Jax, of course, didn't need external evidence. The Rising Fear jangled through his veins.

Down at the shore, Nevan, the other ferry slave, was untying the knots that lashed the ferry to the rocks high above the waterline, while the ferry mate stood by watching.

"What are you doing?" Jax asked.

"That's a stupid question," Oblek snapped. "Get to work."

"Stop, Nevan," Jax ordered, turning face the large troll. "The Rising isn't finished," he said evenly. "The boat can't sail today."

"It can. We can't just stop shipping for three weeks."

"Use wagons, then." Jax shrugged.

Oblek slapped him hard across the face. Jax stumbled to his knees, and Oblek kicked him to the ground.

He looked up at the troll, Rising Fear searing through his blood like lightening. "I won't do it."

"Yes, you will, Fishman."

Jax sat on the wet sand. "If we put the boat out it will capsize in these waves."

"You goddess-damned lazy half-isle!" Oblek kicked, but Jax rolled away.

"Hold him!" Oblek snapped at his mate. The troll hauled Jax to his feet.

Thunder rolled overhead and sharp lines of lightning crackled down from the sky to stab at the black waves. The wind suddenly rose to a roar, and the rain came down, heavy with hail.

"Dragons!" cried the mate, pulling up his hood.

"Don't you wish we were in the middle of the lake right now?" Jax asked.

Oblek's orange eyes glowed with rage. He turned abruptly back to the mine buildings. Everyone followed. Once inside the gate, he continued to drag Jax across the courtyard and then into a small building behind the smelter. Worn steps led down into ancient tunnels, the usual reek of sulfur here was overlaid with a musty staleness of disuse. Jax guessed this must be the remains of one of the oldest parts of the iron mine. Down and down they went, until the stairs disappeared into a small hole covered by an iron trapdoor. Hinges squealed as Oblek pulled up the door.

"In!" He shoved Jax into the hole. The trapdoor slammed down, and a bolt slid home.

"The Rising isn't my fault!" Jax shouted, as Oblek's footsteps receded up the stairs.

He pushed against the trapdoor, even knowing it was futile. Finally, he sat down, his wet clothes sticking to him. The space was too small for him to stretch out his legs. He could stand upright, but his arms met the crumbling dirt walls in all directions. There was nothing here but dirt and metal, nothing he could burn with his bit of Dragon magic other than his own clothes, and that didn't seem like a good idea. In a corner, his feet kicked something metal, and a faint reek told him this would be his slop bucket.

He sat with a sigh; his knees drawn up to his chest. Goddess but he hated these damn tunnels. Hours slowly passed. He dozed, awoke cramped, wiggled, and slept again. Hunger woke him finally. He stood up.

"Hey! Hey!"

Nothing.

Eventually he sat down and slept again.

His hunger faded as thirst consumed him. He couldn't even sleep now for want of water. Even awake, he didn't at first recognize the sound of footsteps coming down the stairs. As the trapdoor opened, he rose to meet whoever was there, but had to look away as the light burned his eyes.

Jax recognized the voice of the ferry mate. "Better make this last," he said, dropping a bucket of water and loaf of bread into the hole.

"Wait!" Jax put up his hand, but the trapdoor clanged shut again. "Let me out!"

The footsteps climbed away. "Come back!" He shouted, ashamed of himself even as he said it. "Let me out!"

More black hours crept past. The bread was long gone and then the water too. No one came. His mind began to cannibalize itself. He felt the dirt walls closing in on him, squeezing the breath from his lungs. Something grumbled, something in the dark hole with him.

Panic flushed through him. He stood and banged on the trapdoor. "Let me out!" he shouted. "Let me out of here!"

He heard the grumble again. This time he recognized it as his own stomach. He sank again to his haunches and put his head in his hands. "Dragon blasted trolls," he said. "I'm in a fix this time." He felt foolish talking to himself, but the sound of his own voice was a relief in that dark, empty place.

A thought occurred to him. Softly he began to hum the First Tune. Music had been an integral part of his life as a prince, and the bit of Dragon force in his blood gave him a facility with instruments and harmony. He hummed his way through the First Tune, a haunting song that any Dragon could sing and play.

He'd found no time or heart for music since he'd been taken from Kree. But now, it came to him: Barian songs, with lyrics in a language he hadn't thought or dreamed in years, and the Kordish ballads that Tallyn had loved. Singing to oneself wasn't crazy the way talking to oneself could be, and the sound was comforting.

He sang until his dry throat cracked and his voice failed him. Then he slept again.

"Hey, Oblek!" The slave wrangler stood at the door to the barracks, staring into the rain. Oblek was beating a slave, but it wasn't the Fishman. When the slave was unconscious and bloody, the troll turned to the slave wrangler.

She detailed a couple of duty trolls to take the slave to the infirmary or the graveyard as necessary then frowned at Oblek. "Where's the Fishman?"

Oblek smiled and shrugged. "Damned lazy half-isle is probably in a hole somewhere enjoying its Rising holiday."

The slave wrangler frowned as Oblek sauntered away under the heavy rain.

That evening the slaves in Cave Three looked up with dull interest as the door opened and the slave wrangler herself appeared. She raised her torch and looked around at each of the slaves on the floor.

"Where's the Fishman?"

"We don't know," a woman said defensively.

"How long has he been gone?"

"Most of the Rising, I guess," a man said.

The slave wrangler frowned. Could the half-isle have escaped? No. She thought of Oblek's insouciant attitude. He'd be enraged if the Fishman escaped. The troll must have his slave stashed somewhere.

She left Cave Three, shutting the slaves in the dark again.

"I don't think he escaped," a voice said, continuing the discussion that had been going on in Cave Three for the last ten days. "The trolls would be executing us all if anyone ever got free."

"The big troll flogged the other ferry slave to death today."

"Dragons! That means someone else will get taken for ferry duty."

"They won't kill Sir Jax. They don't have anyone else to sail their ferry for them."

"Where is he then?"

A long pause.

"Goddess help him."

Clean autumn sunlight splashed across the Hantland and sparkled on the smooth water of the lake as the last of the Rising storm clouds floated gently away to the west. The slave wrangler bustled amid trolls and slaves, searching for Oblek. A string of three slaves trailed behind her.

She found Oblek at last, standing in the bright morning sun beside the warehouse. A dirty creature sat at his feet.

"I've brought three for you to choose from, Oblek," she said, gesturing to the slaves cringing in her wake. "But I'm not giving you another slave until you tell me where the Fishman is."

"It's right here," Oblek kicked the creature, which looked up from blue islish eyes.

The slave wrangler squatted down and peered at the crumpled figure. It was the Fishman, alright, but it was hollow-cheeked, pale, and covered with dirt and those rough whiskers.

"What've you done to it?" She stood slowly.

"Taught it some respect. Get up, Fishman. It's time to go."

Using the wall of the warehouse for support, Jax pushed himself to his feet. With the eyes of experience, the slave wrangler identified the marks of starvation and deprivation.

Oblek was looking at the new slaves. "I'll take the Norledgian."

"Dragons!" Yory gulped. "Not me."

Oblek just swatted him.

The slave wrangler watched the Fishman shuffle behind the troll as they headed for the dock. She turned to take the other two slaves back to their regular duties, thinking of the spark she'd seen in the Fishman's queer blue eyes. Oblek might have taught it something over the past two weeks, but she didn't think it was respect.

Jax's arms shook with weakness as he leaned into the tiller to hold it steady against the force of the autumn wind. Yory, naturally, was busy being sick over the side of the boat. Beyond the miserable figure of the Norledgian, Jax could see the dark shoreline. It wasn't close enough.

"Pull the mainsheet tighter, Oblek." After two weeks of starvation and darkness, he didn't have the strength to set the sails, hold all the lines and guide the tiller. Not in this wind.

The troll grabbed the wrong line.

"No, not that one," Jax snapped. "The mainsheet! The thick one!"

Oblek found the right line and pulled.

"That's enough."

Oblek looked without comprehension at the sail above him, then turned his orange eyes to the Fishman. He may not have any understanding for the damned boat and its stupid ropes and pulleys, but he knew slaves. His satisfaction with the Fishman's clear physical weakness was soured. He picked up a bailing bucket, filled it with grimy water from the bottom of the boat, and flung it at the half-isle.

The boat slewed around and came into the wind as Jax lost his hold on the tiller.

Yory almost fell into the black water, and the mate, a troll called Tillish, slipped onto the planks.

"Dragons, Oblek!" Tillish shouted. "Can't you just let the Fishman sail the damned boat? Beat it on land, if you must."

The water had made mud of the dirt covering Jax. Yory happened to be looking back and saw the flash of a feral grin beneath the grime as the half-isle pulled himself back to the tiller and set his course again for the land.

Both slaves had to be physically dragged back to the mine compound. Two duty trolls took them to the baths and then dumped them in the mess hall.

"Sweet goddess, sir, where you been?" The other slaves gathered around Jax.

"Oblek locked me in a hole," he answered, swallowing his food with desperation.

The others noticed. "Here, sir, you can have the rest of mine."

"Mine too,"

Jax considered refusing, as he usually did, but his body was still starving.

He didn't see the slave wrangler come up behind him. She put a full bowl of food in front of him. He looked up at her for a moment. Her fleshy hand landed on his shoulder. "You can have double this week. There ain't no ferry without you."

He was already wolfing the food. "You should remind Oblek of that."

Later, as the duty troll locked the door to Cave Three, Jax choked at the darkness and slumped to the floor, fumbling with his blanket.

"Are you alright, sir?"

"I've had enough of the dark."

He heard a shuffle then friendly arms enclosed him. His heart thumped a minute as he missed Jolira, but he had been alone too long. He drew the warm body close and shuddered.

"There, now," she crooned. "We've got you back, now, sir."

Her sympathy unlocked his self-control and he shuddered again, choking on his sobs. "I didn't think he'd let me out. I couldn't breathe...."

"Hush. It's alright now. Here...yes, there. Isn't that better, sir?"

"Better," he mumbled and, tangled with her, his breathing finally deepened. She felt his heartbeat grow steady and knew he slept.

After a few moments of silence someone spoke from across the cave. "He's naught but gristle."

"And grit," Yory said, admiration in his voice. "You should see him handle that boat. He stands at the tiller-thing despite the rocking waves, holds the ropes in his teeth, and tosses insults at the trolls all the while."

"I pity you, Yory, on that boat."

"Yeah. The water's so black...." Yory admitted. "But that Overtroll Oblek is the real terror."

Jax mumbled something unintelligible.

"Quiet," said the woman holding him. "Let the poor man sleep."

12

Despite the burning sore on his neck and the unambiguous weight of the iron collar, Corvyd Cale could not accept the idea that he had become a slave. This kind of thing did not happen to the son of a baroness, not even the admittedly irresponsible and possibly stupid younger child. He'd known the dangers of hunting alone on the northern boundaries of his mother's woodland, but he was sure he could get a prime buck in those forsaken stretches of forest.

Of course, he'd also known that trolls theoretically hunted for slaves under the same dark pines, but he hadn't really believed that. Plus, it was the dead of winter.

"You'll be in Cave Three," the duty troll stopped before a heavy wooden door. Corvyd's fine, aristocratic nose wrinkled in distaste at the smell of sweat mixed with the wet sulfuric vapors that pervaded all these tunnels. Sweet goddess, the infamous Hanter Iron Mines. Would his mother ever think to look for him here?

"In ye go." The troll shoved Corvyd into the dark. The door slammed shut behind him.

Corvyd turned to pound on the door. "Let me out! Let me out, I say! I am not a slave!"

"Afraid ye are now." A woman's voice spoke gently. "There's no use shouting. The troll won't come back."

"You don't understand. I am not a *peasant*." He practically spat the word. "I am not fodder for trollish slavery."

"Well, whatever ye are, sit down and be quiet." A man's voice came from the back of the cave. "We need our sleep."

Corvyd's blinked into the darkness. Finally, he sat down near the door.

"It ain't easy for anyone," the woman said softly.

Corvyd assumed it would be far more challenging for someone like him, a noble, an aristocrat, to adapt to the hardship and servitude of a slave's existence than for a poor peasant or merchant who would be accustomed to light food and dark work.

"I don't have a blanket," he fumed, aggrieved.

Sighs. A new voice spoke, quite near him by the door. "Axster, don't you have two?"

"Aye, sir, but one belonged to my sweet Yesta."

"So, keep Yesta's for yourself and share the other one with our new friend."

Corvyd couldn't place the crisp accent, but he recognized the tone of authority. Axster evidently did too. "Here ye go," the slave mumbled.

"My lord," Corvyd added sourly. "You address me as my lord, or sir."

He heard the fellow by the door make a soft, ironic noise, but he ignored this as he smelled the blanket. "UG! This thing is foul!"

The crisp voice was firm. "If you don't want it, *sir*, Axster will have it back."

"I don't want this foul rag. I don't want some slave teaching me manners!"

"Then show us some, friend."

"I am not your friend! I am a nobleman. I can't be here. I can't be a slave! My mother is Baroness of Norgren." Corvyd felt his voice crack with his heart. He folded the dirty blanket to his face to muffle his sobs. He heard more sighs around the room, but no one said anything. At last, exhausted by his grief, he slept.

The acrid smell of torch smoke woke him. He rubbed his itchy eyes. "Now, Fishman." An especially large troll had grabbed a slave by the collar and hauled him to his feet. In the ruddy light, Corvyd saw the white scars on the slave's bare back as he wrenched himself free of the troll and bent to grab his shirt from the floor. A second slave rose as well and followed the one called Fishman.

Then the door slammed shut and the cave was dark again. No one said anything, but Corvyd was sure that the scarred slave, this Fishman, was the insolent one with the snooty accent.

He'd gone back to sleep when the duty troll slammed open the door again. More torches brightened the corridor now. "Let's go, Cave Three!" the troll growled.

Corvyd stood along with the others. The duty troll lifted her torch. "Is the Fishman gone already?"

"Aye," a few slaves answered.

"Damn. Well, then, which of you is a digger?"

Five of the other slaves raised their hands. "You, then. You take the new one here with ye. It's to be a digger too."

"Me?" Corvyd asked.

"You."

The day was a horror. Breakfast was a stale bit of bread. Then he had to slog across the courtyard where the frigid winter wind cut through the scraps of clothing the trolls had given him. His feet chafed in the cold wooden clogs. Trolls seemed pleased to beat him no matter what he did, their crops raising stinging welts on his skin.

The tunnel was comfortably warm, but he soon found it too warm as the work of hammering away at the rock wall caused sweat to pour off his face.

The slave who was showing him the work paused to wipe his own brow. "I'm Mik. What's your name?"

"Lord Corvyd, to you."

Mik shrugged and offered Corvyd a canteen. "Have a bit of water."

"Sir. You have to say, *have a bit of water, sir!*"

Mik took the canteen back and shook his head. "Down here, Corvyd, you ain't nobody more than me."

Corvyd's arms and back shook with fatigue, and his head pounded from the echo of pike and hammer long before the slaves were allowed to ride the lift up to the courtyard. Here the wind was even colder than before. The sweat froze on his face. Suddenly Mik in front of him stopped to watch two slaves stumble in through the gate. Icicles hung from their hair and Corvyd could hear their frozen clothes crack as they moved, their feet bleeding as the frozen ground cut through their wet socks.

The slave wrangler came out of her office, screeching. "Sweet goddess, Oblek! What've ye done to them?"

"Don't yell at me. It's the Fishman's fault. The Norledgian fell in and the Fishman went in after it."

"He pulled me out of them black sucking waves," the Norledgian mumbled through blue lips. "The damned trolls were casting my chains after me into the sea as fast as they could." He choked and shivered.

"Get to the bath, both of ye," the slave wrangler ordered. "It'll warm ye up."

Corvyd watched them go, the Fishman wiping a bit of blood from his chin.

"You're going to kill the Fishman one day," the slave wrangler said accusingly to Oblek.

"Yeah. I'm looking forward to it."

Corvyd shuddered with the cold and the even colder look in the big troll's orange eye, but he had little time to think of someone else's woes as the mess hall proved to be a further assault on his well-bred sensibilities. The slaves huddled together on wobbly benches at filthy tables. Trolls prodded the slaves from one table at a time to approach the food servers. Each slave received a steaming bowl, a hot mug, and a bun. Corvyd's stomach clenched and his head spun with exhaustion, hunger, and growing hysteria.

Before his table had been given food, the Fishman and his fellow ferry slave entered and joined them. Their hair was still wet, but the bath had warmed them up. Several other slaves patted the Norledgian as he sat opposite Corvyd. All of them made way for the Fishman.

Corvyd had seen Barians when he visited his cousins in Brakkle, and he recognized islish ears and sea-blue eyes. But Corvyd had never seen a fair-haired Barian, and he thought they spoke a different language.

"Cave Three," the duty troll growled. The slaves rose and got their food. Corvyd resumed his seat, his nose wrinkling at the rotten stink of the soup. It was the color of chalky mud. He looked around doubtfully, as the others slurped noisily. Only the Fishman seemed familiar with the proper use of a spoon.

Corvyd picked up his own spoon and took a sip. Even famished as he was, his throat refused to swallow the vile stuff. He spat it back out. "That's disgusting!"

A tanned, sinewy arm reached across to take his bowl away. "You don't have to eat it, sir," the Fishman's blue eyes regarded him and Corvyd recognized the crisp accent from the night before. "But don't ruin it for someone else."

He passed the bowl to a boy whose bones were terribly visible beneath the taught skin of his face. "Take it Ablemar. Get your strength back."

"Thank you, sir!"

"Now look here, you, you Fishman—."

The other slaves grew suddenly silent. The Fishman smiled slowly. "You'll eat when you're hungry enough." He tossed Corvyd half of his own piece of bread. "And don't call me Fishman. Sir."

Corvyd ate the bread. The slaves started talking again, horribly enthralled by the Norledgian's story of nearly drowning. The woman next to the Fishman touched his lip. "Did Oblek beat you for saving Yory, sir?"

He finished the last of his soup. "Oblek beats us because he's trying to prove something."

"Prove what?" she asked.

The Fishman shrugged, and Corvid thought he smiled like a wolf.

Yory answered "Maybe he'd lay off you, sir, if you didn't tease him so mercilessly."

The Fishman shook his head. "It's how I know I'm winning."

"Winning?" Corvid asked. "How are you winning when the troll beats you?"

Again, that wolfish grin flashed. "I'm proving who's in charge."

Corvyd shook his head frowning at the paradoxical idea that the person getting beaten was actually the one with the upper hand. He noted that the woman's fingers had slipped beneath the Fishman's shirt.

"You've got a fat lip, sir," she said.

"Kiss it better?"

Corvyd watched the kiss develop heat and intent. In a minute, the woman lifted her head and stood from the table. Without a word the Fishman followed her. Corvyd watched them leave the room, noting that the trolls didn't seem to care. With new interest Corvyd considered the women and men around the table. They were a scraggly, worn-down lot, drab and drudge-like. But then again, some of them did have a nice swell of breast beneath their dresses, and the man called Ablemar had a very fetching mouth.

"Does your Fishman always get the choicest partners?"

"Depends on who's choosing," answered one of the women.

"He don't make it easy," Mik conceded. "He's got a lord's pretty face and a lord's pretty words."

"Remember Jolira?" Yory mused. "Beautiful Jolira."

"Who's Jolira?" Corvid turned to look around the room.

"She's dead," Mik answered. "But the trolls didn't want no one else messing with her. When some other feller tried to spoon up to her, the trolls sold him for bait."

"The trolls gave the Fishman a girl?" Corvyd was astonished. This demonstrated a depth of blasphemy he wouldn't have thought possible.

The old woman called the Crone leaned towards the conversation. "They wanted more islish slaves, 'cause he's so hearty," she explained.

"But that would be rape!" Corvyd snorted.

"It might have been," the Crone nodded. "But it weren't."

Mik filled in some details. "The trolls would've sold her for bait if Jax hadn't taken to her. And he was mighty tore up when she died."

"Who is he?" Corvyd asked. "This Fishman?"

"Don't call him that," Yory cautioned. "He's half-islish obviously. Been here years, they say. The trolls can't seem to kill him. He even survived the fever."

"Is that why you all call him sir?"

"No."

"Time's up!" A duty troll came by, obviously ready to be off shift. He prodded the tired slaves. "To the caves with you."

When they got to Cave Three, Corvyd noticed that the Fishman and the woman were rolled together in a couple of the blankets by the door. He was sound asleep, but the woman winked at one of her friends.

Jax tied off the freezing lines, his insides as cold with fear as his fingers. Oblek stood at the shore end of the dock waiting for him. He'd taken a chance today, and it hadn't worked. For the first time all his months sailing on Hanter Lake today he'd finally seen a Barian ship come into the harbor. It had anchored off The Hant and its boat had put out and rowed to the town.

Jax had tried to be surreptitious in aiming the little ferry towards the Barian ship, but Oblek had figured it out.

"Take us home, Fishman," he growled.

"You know I can't sail in a straight line when the wind is off the sea," Jax answered calmly, hoping that this ruse would allow him to get close enough to hail the ship.

Oblek wasn't buying it. He threw Jax to the boards and let the sails loose so that they flapped loudly. "You!" he roared at Yory. "Row!"

"Dragons, Oblek! Let me sail!" Jax shouted.

"I'm not stupid, Fishman." Oblek wrapped the chain leash around Jax's arms and secured it with a spare lock he carried in a deep pocket. Hunched in the bow, Jax could only stare at the distant

Barian ship, which finally disappeared when a dark squall blew in from the ocean.

Now back at the dock he knew from the set of Oblek's shoulders that he'd pay for taking that chance.

Oblek marched him across the courtyard to the door behind the old smelter. Dragons, Jax swore to himself. Not the pit again.

"Hey, Oblek...."

"You aren't going to talk your way out of this."

"Don't put me down there," Jax hated himself for begging, but the thought of that pit pushed against him. And maybe those Barians would still be anchored in the harbor tomorrow.

"Ask nicely," Oblek turned to him, smiling.

Jax steeled himself for humiliation. "Please, don't put me in the pit again, Oblek."

The troll slapped him across the mouth. "Overmaster. You call me Overmaster."

"Don't put me in the pit...Overmaster."

"Hah!" Oblek crowed. He noticed the way the other slave, the Norledgian, cringed at the Fishman's capitulation. "Hah!" He grabbed the Fishman by the collar and pulled him towards the stairs.

"No." Jax choked. "Please, no."

"Overmaster!" snarled Oblek, pausing on the stairs.

Looking down those dark stairs, Jax gave up the last of his dignity. "Please don't, Overmaster."

Oblek laughed. "I love it! The Fishman is beaten at last!"

He plummeted down the stairs dragging Jax with him. The trapdoor opened and swallowed Jax. "You're beaten, Fishman. Beaten!"

The door banged shut over his head. Jax sank to his haunches, his hands over his face as the blackness closed in on him. He choked back a sob. As always, he felt the earth push against him, suffocating him. He had to force himself to breathe and will himself to stay calm in the face of his instinctive fears. This was the third time this winter that Oblek had shut him in here. He knew that the troll would come back in a few days, but by then the Barians would surely be gone. He choked again. Indeed, he was beaten.

After a while he slept, but later as he stood to let his cramped muscles get some blood, he started to think about the coming Rising. Oblek would confine him down here for the entire three weeks. Stomping from one foot to the other, Jax determined to take back his destiny. He would not let Oblek drown him in the earth. If he was going to drown, it would be on his own terms and in his own element.

The slave wrangler chewed on the end of her pencil and frowned at the inarguable proof of mathematics. The slaves were dying again. True, it was winter, and one of the coldest she could ever remember, but still she had thought the Fishman was helping....

She stood up and waddled to the mess hall to survey the herd of slaves. Inured by years at her job, she didn't notice the reek of their tired, sweaty bodies, but she did sense their dejection. Shoulders hunched in despair as they ate listlessly.

Her orange eyes swept the tables. There was the group from Cave Three, but where was the Fishman? Did Oblek still have the ferry out? No, the other ferry slave, that Norledgian called Yorbit or Dorby, sat among the others.

She walked to the table. "Where's the Fishman?"

Yory glanced up at her. "Oblek put him in the pit again."

"Again?" She'd already spoken to Oblek about this.

"Third time this winter," a woman muttered.

"*Third* time?" The slave wrangler scowled and stomped from the mess hall. Overtrolls generally enjoyed unlimited powers over the slaves assigned to them, but the Fishman was different. She needed that one alive, alive and among the others.

"Taint!" She marched into the mine boss's office. "Oblek's gonna kill the Fishman."

Taint looked up from the thick steak he was eating. "Can't say as I blame him."

"Without the Fishman there'll be no one to sail the ferry."

"You're right. I'll remind Oblek of our investment in his project."

Jax recognized the footsteps coming down the stairs and he rose to his feet. As soon as Oblek pulled up the trapdoor, Jax scrambled out of the hole. He sat at the troll's feet gasping at the fresher air.

The troll sneered at him and dropped a bucket of water. Jax picked it up and drained it.

"Let's go, now." Oblek started back up the steps. "I'm going to have you train that Norledgian to sail the ferry."

Jax wiped his mouth and stood to follow the troll up the stairs. He knew that his ability to sail the ferry was the one insurance on his life. If someone else could sail, Oblek would immure him in that pit and leave him there. But he had yet to meet any landish creature who could develop any facility for sailing.

The winter sun, bouncing off the snow in the courtyard, blinded him. Oblek was already half-way to the gate, but Jax turned toward the mess hall.

"Fishman!"

"If I'm going to row, I need food."

The other slaves in the courtyard slowed their steps to listen, but Oblek didn't respond with words. Jax jumped away from the crop, just barely keeping out of reach. He knew the other slaves counted on him to face down the trolls. He also knew that they were losing heart this winter. More were getting the fever, and more seemed to just die of despair. He couldn't be there for them while Oblek had him locked in the damned pit.

Those long days and nights without food, without light, were taking their toll on him too. He didn't have the strength or stamina to row multiple trips across the lake. Even his wits seemed dulled.

Right now, he needed to flaunt his disrespect as much as he needed food. So, he winked at the surprised duty troll next to the breadbasket as he snitched three buns. He knew the other slaves were silently cheering for him as he turned back to an empurpled Oblek.

"Alright." He chewed. "I'm ready now."

Oblek had noticed Boss Taint looking out the window of his office, so he contented himself with whipping the Fishman viciously with his crop.

As Jax anticipated, Yory had no ability to understand the set of sail or how to compensate for the push of the current. Oblek realized that he wasn't learning how to sail and vented his frustrations on the Norledgian's hapless back. Jax tried to shield Yory by giving him only the simplest of tasks, but he couldn't hide the fact that Yory had no idea how to run the ferry on his own.

"I'm from Norledge, you know," Yory was saying to no one in particular in the mess hall one night, as he gazed morosely at the weeping sores on his raw and chafed hands. "I'm no stranger to cold, but I'll be glad when this winter is over."

Corvyd glanced at the half-isle slumped next him on the bench, his elbows on the table, his own chapped hands in the tangles of his hair.

"The Rising will be here in a few weeks," he said quietly.

"Aye, sir. Then we'll get a bit of rest, won't we?"

"I hope so." Jax muttered, but Yory heard a false note in his voice.

"You should go lie down, sir," one of the women said.

"I should learn to keep my mouth shut."

Yory considered him. There was something different about Jax these last weeks. Something frightfully resigned. And if Jax was resigned, goddess help the rest of them. "No, sir. You don't want to let Oblek win."

Jax considered Yory for a moment, but he couldn't find a smile or a word of encouragement. He rose stiffly and left the mess hall.

"I still don't know why everyone calls him sir," Corvyd griped. "He's just a slave like all the rest of us."

"No, he ain't." Yory sighed. "No one else stands up to them damned trolls. The rest of us keep our mouths shut. The rest of us just try to survive each day."

"He's still just a slave," Corvyd pouted. "I *am* a lord, but no one calls me sir."

Mik leaned against the wall. "I told you before, you ain't a lord here."

"And he is?"

"Pretty much." Yory answered.

Two days later, Corvyd winced with sympathy as the half-isle pulled off his shirt and moved into the bath with the others.

"Why do you provoke the trolls, Jax?" Corvyd asked as they sank into the warm water.

The half-isle lay back to let his hair float in the water. "It does everyone good to see someone stand up to the trolls."

"But you pay for it."

"The price of being milord."

"Lord of the slaves?" Corvyd's voice was scornful.

Jax splashed over in the water. "They need us more than free people."

"Us?"

"Weren't you raised to care for your people, Lord Corvyd?"

"Yes, but these aren't my people. I don't think they're yours either."

"They are mine. And I am theirs. Someday, maybe they'll be yours."

Corvyd got out of the water. The duty troll started yelling at Jax, as usual, because he had swum off into the dark depths of the pool. Corvyd pulled on the itchy clothes, understanding at last why they called him sir.

13

"Steady... Steady, sir.... Good. A bit more, now." Yory called instructions to Jax who stood at the boom which lowered the cargo of iron onto the ferry. Jax leaned his weight into the crank wheel to ease the heavy load into the hold of the boat.

"Almost!" Yory shouted. The Norledgian reached up to grasp the descending load. Gently he guided it into the cargo frame.

"That's it, sir!" The small boat shuddered and bobbed in the water, creaking under the burden of pig iron.

Jax shoved himself back from the crank and stood for a moment looking at the sky. The towering black clouds had been bundling by all morning, pushed by a wintery wind. Now, they gathered together in a dark, rolling mass. Jax pushed strings of hair out of his face with a shudder of Rising Fear. The Spring Rising had finally arrived.

He glanced back up at the gray wall of the mine compound. He thought of tombstones and the long dark year since Jolira had died.

"What's the matter, sir?" Yory asked as Jax jumped into the hold to help tie down the cargo.

"It's the Rising."

"How can you tell?"

"Rising Fear. All Barians get it." Jax saw the two trolls coming down from the mine buildings, clipping their leashes to the leather belts at their waists.

"You need to get sick, Yory. Right now."

"What?"

"Go take three or four big gulps of water."

"Yuck."

"Do it now. It will make you sick. You'll stay here, when Oblek and I shove off."

"Why?" Yory swayed as a gust of wind pushed at him.

Jax looked him in the eye. "I'm going to take this boat out into the Rising. It isn't coming back."

Yory stared at him, comprehension coming slowly.

Jax glanced away at the approaching trolls. "Hurry!"

Yory leapt to the lake and swallowed three gulps of the warm, sulfuric water. He gagged and fell to his knees.

"What's wrong with it?" Oblek demanded.

Jax shrugged. "He's felt sick all morning." In the gravel by the lapping waves, Yory began to vomit.

"Goddess damn it," Oblek snarled.

"Stop that." Tillish kicked Yory. This just caused more vomit to spew from him.

Oblek clipped his leash onto the loop in Jax's collar, his orange eyes sharp. "I'll deal with it when I get back," he snarled to Tillish. "Take it back to the mine."

With that, Oblek shoved Jax into the ferry. "You'll have to sail alone today, Fishman."

Jax felt like vomiting too, the Rising Fear was so strong in him, but he cast off and pulled the little sail up. The boat jerked to a gust of wind and tore a white wake across the black waters of the lake.

"Dragons, Fishman! Make the boat flat," Oblek ordered.

Every instinct and nerve in Jax's body was screaming against taking the boat to sea in the face of the Rising. Currents pushed the tiller first one way then another. Waves rose unpredictably on all sides, steaming into the cold air. Clouds coalesced, and first snow then an icy sleet poured down upon them.

Oblek shifted nervously on his bench and the sleet pounded loudly on his waterproof cloak. Jax enjoyed no such protection and was quickly soaked.

Bigger, blacker waves tilted the boat up then plunged her down.

"How long before we get to Southant?" Oblek asked. His growl trembled with his fear.

"Couple hours," Jax kept his voice calm. He wanted to be well into the middle of the lake before he let the waves take him. Even with the sail reefed, the boat careened through the water. Maybe the wind would rip the sail or even carry away the whole mast. If the Rising didn't capsize or break the boat, Jax would turn her sideways to a wave and let her broach. Bound as he was by the leash to Oblek, Jax hoped the two of them would quickly sink and drown.

These sharp needles of sleet against his cheek would likely be the last sensations before the water took him. He felt the wind in his wet hair with abnormal clarity, and the jitters of Rising Fear seemed to recede, leaving him calm and resolved.

Briefly, he smelled the open ocean, clean and fresh and free of the stinking reek of sulfur. The wind veered around again, slammed into the sail, and upended the ferry. Oblek screamed. Wood snapped. A heavy piece of beam knocked Jax on the head and he fell unconscious into the warm embrace of the waves.

Oblek was tangled in the ropes around the mast, but this saved him. The mast, broken free from the rest of the boat, floated on the waves and kept the troll's head above water. Something was pulling him down, though, something connected to his belt. The troll freed one hand and hauled on the chain leash. Soon enough, the Fishman's bloody head came out of the water.

Oblek used one arm and a leg to kick and shove the slave onto the mast and then bound him there with more of the loose ropes. Somewhere in this process, Jax opened his eyes. He coughed, realized what Oblek was doing, and fought to get free, but it was too late. The troll had him tightly tied to the mast.

"If you sink, you'll drown me too," Oblek shouted over the wind and rain. "And I ain't going down with you, Fishman."

Night swallowed the grim wet day. Jax and Oblek, blind in the dark, bobbed up and down on the thrashing waves. Rain mixed with wind and spray, blurring the line between air and water. As his arms and legs grew numb, Jax hoped the troll would get chilled and let go of the mast. Not even Oblek could float forever.

The sun of a new day eventually penetrated the dark clouds, but the rain, wind, and waves were as thick as ever.

Something solid pushed against Jax's legs. He kicked at it.

"Ha!" Oblek grunted. Triumphantly he untangled himself from the ropes and rose out of the waves to tower above Jax. He untied the half-isle and pulled the leash free of the mast.Jax sat in the water, devastated.

"Where are we?" Oblek asked.

"South shore of the lake."

"Get up." Oblek ordered conversationally. Jax ignored him. "Damn you, Fishman. I said, get up!" He pulled the leash so hard that Jax gagged against the metal of his collar, but he stood up finally. Neither of them noticed the wagon drawn up beneath some trees or the elegant group of people who watched them from under the protection of a delicately wrought stone shelter.

Oblek shivered as the cold wind pushed through his wet clothes. He picked up a piece of driftwood to use to allay his frustrations on the half-isle and caught sight of the people in the shelter. They stood around a small, bright fire, enjoying steaming mugs of something.

"What's this?" Oblek walked up the beach, toward the group, dragging a stumbling Jax along by his leash.

Nine people of diverse backgrounds stared back at the bedraggled troll, black streaks of his eye makeup running down his cheeks. Through the throbbing in his head, Jax recognized Ilyian, Norledgian, Vitran features among the group, even the characteristic black skin and green eyes of the Farsouthian islish on one young woman.

Oblek moved nearer the fire. Suddenly, seven gray-faced, grayhaired creatures jumped out of the wooden cabin on the back of the wagon. Jax realized that they were Sagehamites—servants to the magicians at Castle Caledra, the font of all Mystic power. They moved protectively around the people.

Oblek held up his hands in a disarming gesture. "Would you share your fire with a poor, shipwrecked troll?"

The oldest man in the group, a short Norledgian with gray streaks in his blond hair, frowned as he stepped forward. "We'll share what we have with both you and your slave."

Oblek stepped under the shelter and crouched near the fire, holding his cold hands almost in the flames.

Jax moved to join the troll, but something held him back. Something more than Rising Fear now pushed against his nerves.

"Not the Dragon!" One of the gray creatures placed himself between Jax and the fire.

"Dragons fry me," Jax mumbled and sat in the sand where he was, rain running down his hair and nose. The cold of it felt good on the bloody gash in his scalp.

"Dragon?" Oblek looked around at Jax. "You have magic?"

"Yes." Jax shrugged at the obvious.

No one said anything more. A gray creature handed Oblek a steaming mug. The troll slurped the hot liquid.

Jax hunched his shoulders against the cold rain that pelted his head and ran in icy fingers down his back and into the despair around his heart. His plan had failed. He would die now in whichever slow and horrible way Oblek chose. He dropped his head to his shivering arms, as cold inside as out.

His Dragon force continued to jangle his nerves and turn his stomach. Cross-magic, he realized after a while. These people were brimming over with Mystic, and his little bit of Dragon repelled and revolted against it. He knew they would also feel his magic like a small festering splinter in the fabric of their own power.

Neither Jax nor Oblek was aware of the silent, telepathic conversation going on in the ancient language used by those with great Mystic power.

"This doesn't seem right," the Farsouthian sent.

"He's a Dragon, Klaris. He's not our problem."

"He's wounded and cold. Our tea would do him good."

"I agree with Klaris. We can't just let him sit there in the rain with nothing."

"If we help the slave, we'll anger the troll."

"The troll seems angry enough already."

"Yes, but in the Hantland we can't risk having trollish anger directed at us."

"Oh, come on. He's one overtroll. What about common decency?"

"Slaves don't get common decency."

"Not from trolls, but we're not trolls."

"He's a Dragon. He hurts us!"

"And we hurt him. See how he's moved as far from us as that leash will allow."

"He doesn't mean to hurt us."

"Fine. Fine." The Norledgian spoke aloud in Landish. He turned to the troll. "Could we offer you and your slave a bit of bread?"

"Yeah. I'll take some. The slave doesn't need any. Don't waste your food."

"It's no waste. And he's cold." The Farsouthian spoke Landish with a thick Islish accent.

Jax, folded in upon his misery, wasn't listening.

Oblek shoved the bread into his mouth, considering the small, Black woman who had spoken. He'd never seen hair curl like that. Then he looked at Jax who still sat in the rain, his back to them all. "It'll be warm enough when we start walking home."

"But—."

"Klaris," the Norledgian interrupted. "I'm sure our guest knows how to take care of his slave."

Oblek's orange eyes glinted in the firelight as an unpleasant grin split his fleshy face.

Klaris tucked her curls under a deep green hood, rose from her camp chair, and climbed into the cabin on the back of the wagon. One of the gray Sagehamites went with her. The others began packing up gear and stowing it.

Oblek reluctantly stood back from the fire and watched in awe as the pot vanished and the gear leapt to storage holds on the wagon. Four horses walked up to the empty harnesses at the front of the wagon and waited patiently as the Sagehamite servants buckled them into place.

"You're Mystics." Oblek said.

"Yes." The Norledgian man settled his cloak about his shoulders. "We study at Castle Caledra. We've been testing our skills near here for a week. I'm Emmil Rohan."

"Magic." Oblek grumbled. He was still soaking wet, but his waterproof slicker and heavy boots kept more rain from getting to his skin. His ferry was lost, and now he found himself alone with just his useless slave and a bunch of Mystics.

The trolls tolerated the comings and goings of the most powerful Mystics in the Knownlands, who gathered to study at Castle Caledra, which sat atop Sageham Isle off the Hantish Coast. For their part, the Mystics themselves hurried through the trollish homeland, trying to be as unobtrusive as possible. Even with their great magic, they had no desire to anger the large, contemptuous trolls who ruled the Hantland.

Now, Oblek watched as three of these magical people gathered hands, forming a small circle around the fire. They stared into the flames. Slowly, the fire compressed itself, rose in a red ball that glowed in the gray rain, and sailed into the back of the wagon. Its warm glow oozed merrily from the small round windows in the wagon's cabin.

Three more magicians raised their hands to the lacy carved stone of the shelter. Slowly the rock seemed to melt back into the earth. When they were done the ground was covered with early grass, as if no structure had ever stood there.

Jax hunched over the nausea in his belly caused by all this Mystic power. Oblek did not notice.

The Farsouthian woman came back out of the wagon and looked from Jax to the troll. "Where are you going?"

"Back to the iron mines."

"We can give you a ride," she offered. The others gasped.

"Klaris!" Emmil Rohan spoke sharply.

"I'd like a ride." Oblek stated.

"Then please join us." Klaris smiled.

Oblek hauled on Jax's leash. "Get up, Fishman. We're leaving."

Jax followed the troll towards the wagon.

"No Dragon! No!" Three gray Sagehamites moved in between Jax and the wagon.

He lifted his empty hands. "I can't hurt you."

"But you do."

"I'll hurt you," Oblek promised Jax ominously. "I'll not have you messing this up."

"Overtroll!" Despite her throaty accent, Klaris's voice cut through the evil mood and the rain. "Overtroll, we take you and your slave to the mines, but you stop beating him."

"I'm not beating it."

"Klaris!" Again, Emmil Rohan tried to stop her.

She raised a hand in a gesture that Jax recognized but could not quite place. "We're helping this poor troll. And perhaps we can weave a Protect spell around the Dragon. That will keep us all comfortable."

"Can you do a Protect?" asked one of the men. "I can't."

"I can try," Emmil said slowly.

"I can help." Klaris offered.

Jax had been watching the small Farsouthian woman, trying to gather his thoughts. "What's a Protect?"

"It's a ...shield." She shrugged as she groped for the word in Landish, her green eyes sparkling with the audacity of the attempt. "You will feel not our magic."

"If you can do it," whispered the Ilyian woman.

"Let's try." Klaris looked to Emmil.

The Norledgian bent his head in concentration.

Jax grunted as he felt the man's magic like a fist in his stomach. Then there was something else there, something soothing and green. Suddenly he felt nothing. The tingle and pressure of cross-magic was gone. He felt almost light. He sighed in relief, then shivered as he realized how cold he was.

"Sweet goddess," one of the men smiled in admiration.

"Nice," the Vitran woman squeezed Emmil's shoulder.

He answered with a scowl and retreated to the wagon. Klaris hadn't 'helped' him weave the Protect. She had done it herself, but she had done it so subtly, using his own magic, that the others had not realized that he had not been able to do it himself. Dragons fry her.

The gray Sagehamites disappeared into the cabin on the back of the wagon, followed by the other magicians. Oblek and Jax climbed onto the back, still exposed to the wind and rain.

"Here." The Farsouthian woman handed Jax a horse blanket.

"Thank you, my lady. You're Farsouthian?"

She smiled, aglow with the triumph of her magic. "I am. What are you?"

Oblek almost pushed the woman back into the wagon but stopped himself just short of physically connecting with her. "It's my slave. Let it alone."

The horses started walking and the wagon jolted down the rough Vrillbridge Road. Jax huddled under the blanket and soon settled deep into a shivering despair. He had lost. Worse, he had abandoned his people in the iron mines for nothing. Sure, the ferry was sunk, but Oblek would live, while he would suffer some dark and bloody horror of Oblek's devising. And he'd have to face it with stoicism. It was the only weapon he had left.

But he didn't feel stoic now. Despite the freezing numbness of his fingers and toes, he felt a sheer, stomach-cramping terror.

Eventually the wagon stopped in a clearing as night closed on them.

Shoved by the troll, Jax stumbled stiffly off the wagon and stood back with Oblek to watch as the Mystics and their gray servants called on their magic. A sturdy stone cabin rose from the ground.

When it was done, the magicians quietly congratulated themselves. Jax didn't blame them. This was a beautiful structure, far nicer than the simple shelters Felona had built during their journey up from Kordon. But then, these people wielded far more power.

The Farsouthian, her head tilted to one side, raised her arm. A separate, smaller structure rose next to the cabin, its chimney already smoking warmly.

She turned and smiled at Jax. "This is for you and the troll."

"I don't sleep with slaves," Oblek growled ungratefully.

"I don't sleep with trolls," Jax answered.

The woman laughed.

Oblek's lips twisted unpleasantly as he stomped into the main cabin. Inside, the gray servants roasted some meat over the fire and handed around mugs of steaming grog. Shoved into a corner, Jax gently scratched the scab on his head and watched them eat.

The young Farsouthian tried to hand him a shank of meat, but Oblek took it from him. "It doesn't need food, Lady."

"Surely you feed him."

Oblek shrugged and kicked at Jax's legs.

Something within Klaris bristled at the indifferent way the slave took the abuse. "The deal," she said firmly, "was that you would not beat him."

"I'm not beating it."

Klaris frowned down at the bedraggled half-isle. He looked back at her, his startlingly blue eyes full of a devastation she could not fathom.

Unsettled, she returned to the fireplace and sat with her own thoughts amid the soft conversations of the others. Soon they all climbed into beds laid inside the warm cabin.

Oblek pushed Jax outside into the dark sleet. There he wrapped the chain leash tightly around a tree trunk and fastened it with the lock he kept in his pocket.

"This is a good idea," Jax said. "Maybe I'll freeze to death."

"You can hope." Oblek kicked the back of Jax's leg and a ligament snapped. He fell to the muddy ground. The troll disappeared into the smaller shelter Klaris had built.

Famished and freezing, Jax lay exposed to the wind, the rain, and his own grief and fear. He had not slept at all the previous night, lashed to the floating wreckage of the ferry. Exhaustion soon brought merciful oblivion.

Later, as the moon peeped through a brief break in the storm clouds, Klaris opened the cabin door. A gray Sagehamite head appeared next to her. Light from the warm room behind streamed out and just touched the miserable figure of the slave bound in the mud beneath the tree.

The Sagehamite watched silently as Klaris made the customary tilt of her head and began to weave the magic. Nothing appeared. Finally, Klaris snapped her fingers. Only then, did the Sagehamite see a thick woolen blanket drape itself over the sleeping slave.

"I haven't seen an invisible structure in many years," the Sagehamite whispered, using the ancient language.

Klaris was far more fluent in Ancient than Landish. She glanced up at the moon. "I read about it."

"How did you learn to do it?"

Klaris looked at him, perplexed. "The Mystic tells me, of course."

The Sagehamite raised his eyebrows. "You know the magic doesn't tell everyone."

"I think maybe they don't know how to listen."

The gray creature turned his eyes back to the slave, who had stretched and relaxed a bit warmed by the blanket and now protected from the wind and dripping water from the tree. "Why do you care so much about him, about a Dragon?"

The moon disappeared behind fast-sailing clouds. Klaris could see a faint green glow that spoke of her magic, but not the sleeping slave. "I don't know, Laddie. There's something about him that calls out to me."

"You're compassionate."

"Maybe, but it's something else. "It's not just pity that I feel. My magic seems to want him."

"Want him? He's a Dragon."

"Yes, but there's something more. Don't you feel the odd eddy of Mystic around him?"

The Lad considered the slave out in the dark for a few minutes. "I think it's just his bit of Dragon force."

The Farsouthian shook her head and frowned. "It's not just that. I feel like I've noticed this type of disturbance before, but I can't remember where." For a few moments they stayed there quietly. Then Klaris ducked back into the cabin and the Lad found his own bed again.

14

Oblek woke warm and delighted. Today he would begin at last to kill the damned, insolent Fishman, and he was going to thoroughly enjoy it. He'd waited for this day long enough. Focused on this gratifying thought, Oblek could forget the loss of his ferry. He marched to the larger cabin and shoved his way to the fireplace. A Sagehamite handed the troll a mug of tea. He wrapped his thick fingers around the hot mug and turned to look at the Mystics around him. None of them spoke. After downing the tea, Oblek went out into the rain to wake his slave, who still slept, curled against the tree.

Where had that blanket come from? And why wasn't it wet? Oblek kicked viciously at the Fishman's sleeping form. His boot hit something hard, and green sparks flew about mixing with the rain. The invisible shelter shattered. Jax awoke when the wind and rain and then Oblek's boot found him.

Oblek kicked him again. Jax tried to roll away, but the tree and the chains held him. Another kick.

"Enough, Oblek. I'm awake."

"Overtroll!" Klaris's thick Landish cut through the cold rain. "Please, stop that."

"I'm just waking it up."

Oblek opened the lock and Jax disentangled himself from the chains and the tree and stood slowly, rain soaking into his shirt. How had it been dry?

Back inside the main shelter, Oblek shoved Jax down to sit in the same corner in the back of the room. Jax rubbed his swollen knee.

He felt surprisingly rested but the delicious scent of the Mystics' breakfast gnawed at his empty stomach. Goddess, he'd been hungry too much this winter. The others gathered around the fireplace eating steaming piles of scrambled eggs, potatoes, and cheese.

Never much of an eater herself, a few mouthfuls satisfied Klaris. She considered the slave in the corner, noting again his air of defeat as he leaned his head back against the wall.

He had to be famished, but there was more misery to him than that. She watched him gaze at the disappearing pile of food on Emmil's plate. He ran a hand over his mouth and rubbed at his whiskers. They were golden. She didn't think she'd ever seen a person so crushingly brutalized, and yet there was something so compelling about him. Despite the rags and misery and pain, he wasn't subservient. And those sea-blue islish eyes and sun-streaked hair were rather beautiful, or might be if he were clean.

Klaris looked down at the cooling food on her plate. She spared a glance and half an ear for her colleagues. They were speaking the ancient language as usual, discussing a detail of the rock beneath the shelter that had complicated their weave. The troll had stepped outside.

She seized her chance, rose from her chair, and handed her tin plate to the slave. "Quick," she said, but she need not have bothered.

Jax shoveled forkfuls of food into his mouth so fast he almost choked. The plate was almost clean before Oblek stomped back in.

"Hey!" The troll kicked the plate out of Jax's hands. "I told you it doesn't need food." Klaris stared up into the orange eyes of the troll who towered over her. "You're wrong."

"He often is." Jax jumped up and took the troll's anger. Oblek slammed him up against the wall.

Klaris placed a hand on the troll's arm. "That's enough."

The troll glowered at her, but he let Jax go.

Klaris gave a curt nod of acknowledgement then went out into the rain, pulling her cloak over her hair.

Jax watched the others follow her. This woman was by far the youngest magician in the group, about his own age, maybe, and so petite that she seemed younger. The Norledgian man was clearly the leader of this group, but the others all treated the Farsouthian with a deference that had nothing to do with her youth.

While the magicians worked together to reduce the stone of the cabin back to untouched earth, Jax and Oblek resumed their seats on the back of the wagon.

When the cabin was gone, the magicians and their Sagehamite servants climbed back into the wagon. Jax watched the Farsouthian fire an insolent glance at the troll and realized that her willingness to defy Oblek probably came, like his own, from the arrogance of a noble birth.

Hunkered under the horse blanket, Jax's thoughts briefly swirled around the girl. He remembered visits to tropical Farsouth like something out of a confused dream. Sealord Rax had always liked the beautiful Farsouthian Queen. In fact, Rax had betrothed Jax to Queen Jeress's daughter. Such betrothals were a well-known way that aristocratic parents flirted with each other, projecting their own feelings onto their toddlers. Jax didn't remember ever meeting his betrothed princess, and now could not recall her name. But he remembered the feline beauty and green eyes of the elegant Queen Jeress as she laughed at something Rax had whispered into her ear.

The wagon bounced him up against Oblek. The troll grunted and swore. Jax's memories faded as he contemplated the horrors that surely awaited him back at the iron mines. Oblek would immure him in that pit and never let him out. As they rode along, he took slow steady breaths of the sleety wind, thinking it would be last fresh air he would ever know. He tried to take strength from it, strength to hide his fear and anguish from the troll.

Late that afternoon, Oblek shoved Jax off the back of the wagon. The gray walls of the iron mines were black with wet.

Klaris jumped out of the cabin. "Wait! Wait! Who are you?"

"Dead, Lady. It's dead!" Oblek took a menacing step toward Klaris. He held Jax tightly by the leash. "It'll be bait before the Rising ends."

Jax's stomach dropped. Not the pit. Bait.

"I buy him," Klaris offered, her Landish breaking as she strove to speak quickly. "Let me buy him from you. Right now. I'll pay whatever you ask."

Jax was stunned.

Oblek smiled blackly. "No. You're a bossy little thing, and I won't sell it to you. It has been a nasty, insolent slave and it sank my ferry. I want to kill it. That's what I want. I want it to die slowly, thinking of me—or maybe," the smile became even blacker, "thinking of you."

Oblek turned and began to drag Jax into the mine compound.

Jax fought free of the troll. Suddenly, he remembered his betrothed princess, whom he never met because she was always away studying her magic at Sageham. "You're Klaris," he said, speaking Islish for the first time in three years. "Princess Klaris de Farsouth."

"Yes." She answered in the same tongue.

He pulled aside his shirt to show the mutilated tattoo beneath his collar bone. "I'm Javix Sharkin, your Highness."

"Javix Sharkin?" She stared at the scar. "*Prince* Javix Sharkin?"

"Yes."

"But how are you here? Like this?"

Trolls had come out of the mine gate, and the other Mystics were spilling out of the wagon. None of them understood a word of Islish.

"Bring me the Fishman!" Oblek ordered the gathered trolls.

Jax took a step towards Klaris. "Help me."

One troll grabbed Jax's collar. Another pinioned his arms. They began to haul him back through the gate, where Oblek had found a stout pole and was swinging it through the rain.

"Stop!" Klaris yelled, but she was still speaking Islish. "Stop! Stop! Stop!"

Emmil Rohan pulled her away. Other trolls came running out of the mine buildings, waving clubs, crops, and menace.

"No!" she cried.

Emmil thrust her into the wagon.

"Klaris, be quiet! He's not our problem."

"Don't you understand?" she snapped back into the ancient tongue. "That's Javix Sharkin, Prince of Baria. He's been missing these three years. He asked for our help!"

A gray Sagehamite shut the door of the cabin, and the wagon started off down the road.

Six trolls closed around Jax. He heard Klaris's shouts, but he could not see what happened to her as they pulled him into the mine compound. The gate clanged shut and Oblek came at him with a club. There was no help and no place to hide.

Blood splashed into the puddles. The mine slaves climbing out of the pit stopped to watch.

Oblek paused for breath, sweat mixing with sleet on his face.

Jax lay panting in the mud.

Yory, amid the crowd of watching slaves, took a step forward. Corvyd put a cautionary hand on his shoulder.

"We have to help him," Yory explained simply.

Corvyd looked at the crumpled figure, thought about that wolfish smile, and remembered courage. He nodded, and together with Yory, moved toward Jax.

"What do you think you're doing?" Oblek snarled.

"We'll take him to the infirmary," Corvyd said calmly.

Jax shook his head and held up a warning hand.

Oblek lifted the club for one last blow. It crashed into Jax's face, obliterating his final view of the slave pens.

"It ain't going to the infirmary!" The troll kicked the inert form savagely. "I'm going to hunt monsters tomorrow, and I've got some fine bait."

"Dragons," Yory whispered. Several of the slaves moaned in grief.

Boss Taint stomped into the courtyard. The sleet eroded rivulets through his magenta rouge. He frowned down at the Fishman, who was choking, unconscious, as rain and blood filled its mouth. Taint booted the slave so its battered face was turned away from the rain then looked to Oblek.

"You're free to go hunting tomorrow, Oblek. And every day after that, but you can't use mine property as bait."

"That's all the Fishman's good for," Oblek spat.

Taint's frown was focused on Oblek now. "You lost the ferry and its load of ore."

"That was the Fishman's fault!"

"You're the overtroll. It was your responsibility."

Oblek's voice dropped to a low growl. "You firing me, Taint?"

"Yea."

Oblek's nostrils flared. He raised the club once again and would have dealt Jax a killing blow, but the slave wrangler grabbed his arm and pulled him away.

"Goddess-damned Fishman!" Oblek raged.

"Goodbye, Oblek," Taint said.

Oblek threw his club. It crashed through the window of Taint's office. Without a word he turned and shoved through the crowd of trolls and out of the iron mines.

Taint's face twisted as he lumbered back toward his office. "Sell the Fishman for bait," he said to the slave wrangler.

"But—."

"No. Sell it," Taint insisted. "It's been a damned nuisance. I want to be rid of it."

Seated on cushions in the warm cabin, Klaris glared desperately at the faces around her. They stared back, confused. None of them came, as she did, from an islish country; none of them came, as she did, from a royal house.

"Sweet goddess," she slumped, her head in her hands. She had never felt so isolated among Mystics, who had been a family to her for years.

"Klaris, you know we can't interfere with the trolls," Emmil said.

She shook her head. "Don't you understand? We've just found the answer to the greatest political mystery of our time! Javix Sharkin has been here, as slave. Sweet goddess, it's inconceivable."

"It is indeed," the Ilyian woman agreed. "Nobles don't survive as slaves."

"Everyone's been looking for him," Klaris continued. "His disappearance caused Kordon to banish all Barians from Kordish soil. And once, we were betrothed."

Several of the others laughed. "Betrothed?"

"Klaris, you have too much magic to marry a prince." The Ilyian woman smiled gently at her. "Even a prince who's a slave."

"The betrothal was a joke, of course," Klaris snapped. "But I can't believe we've found him. I *knew* there was something about him. My Mystic knew."

"The Mystic doesn't belong to you, Klaris." Emmil's voice was hard and cold. "You will not endanger us and the Mystic weave's relationship with the Hantland by raving about islish politics, showing off your power, and mooning over some slave."

"Mooning!" Klaris felt as if she'd been slapped. "Showing off?"

She frowned around at the others. These were all the most promising Mystics, people of incredible discipline and understanding. Surely, they did not think she was as flighty as Emmil implied.

The faces looking back at her were mostly cautious. Klaris took a deep breath. Her power was, and had always been, exceptional. These others were good, but they all knew that she was better. They all knew that Emmil Rohan was leader of this little expedition to The Hant only because of his age, not his magical ability. But no one spoke of it.

A daughter of a ruling family, Klaris understood politics. She knew the Mystic flowed more deeply through her than Emmil, but she also knew that leadership carries responsibilities. She had been content to let others run things so she could concentrate on her studies, until now.

She had found Javix Sharkin. She knew Sealord Bryx had been searching the Knownlands for him for the last three years. Their betrothal was not the issue, but her magic was drawn to him, entangled almost, and suddenly she remembered that the Mystic made that same slight snag around Bryx also, although she certainly wasn't drawn to him in any way.

The wagon jerked through the gate in the old stone wall around The Hant. She looked at Emmil, who was staring out a small window and spoke quietly. "I must get him out of there."

"No!" Emmil snapped. "You will not anger the trolls or put us in any danger."

The Ilyian woman, who had grown up with trollish raids and knew all about the cruelties of slavery and the realities of bait, put a hand to Klaris. "It's probably already too late."

A few minutes later, the wagon rocked to a stop in front of the townhouse that the Mystic magicians maintained on a quiet back street. A thin fe-troll darted out of the door, holding an umbrella.

"Come in! Come in! I've some beetroot tea ready for you, and the radiator is hot. You must be freezing."

The Mystics climbed out of the cabin and sought refuge in the house. As promised, a tea tray steamed in the cozy sitting room. Most of the travelers gathered around it, but Klaris headed up the stairs to the bedroom where her small valise had been neatly stored before the expedition left for Southant.

She dove into the back pockets of the case, searching for her seldom-used royal seal. Then she sat at a small desk beneath the window and began to write.

By the time Emmil knocked on her door, she was sealing two letters with Farsouthian Green wax.

"What are you doing?" Emmil leaned against the door jam.

Klaris wanted to say that it was none of his business. She let the dripping wax pool on the parchment then firmly pressed her seal into the warm mass.

"I'm sending some letters," she answered, finally.

"To whom?"

"To my mother. And the sealord."

Before he could stop her, Klaris threw open the window and tossed the letters out. Emmil grasped for his magic, but Klaris was too quick and her hold on the weave too sure. The letters vanished into the sleet.

"Fine." Emmil dropped his powerless hands. "You can send word, obviously, but not even you have enough magic to bring people here through the Rising."

"I have to do something."

"Why, Klaris? You'll just cause trouble."

"Why do you assume I'll cause trouble?"

Emmil frowned. He didn't like Klaris. He hated the way the magic always came to her so easily, so effortlessly. "You know it is our policy to leave the trolls alone."

Klaris tossed her head. "I don't expect to bother anyone. But Javix Sharkin is a prince of Baria and Kordon. I intend to get him away from those trolls."

"You won't! I forbid you!"

"I'm going to scry for him. Do you want to watch?" She waved her hand; again Emmil moved too slowly, and before he could intervene a silver bowl appeared on the desk.

"You'll do no such thing!"

"Emmil, I don't know why you're so insistent upon this. It's not Mystic business. You don't have any authority over me on this kind of issue."

Emmil's face turned red. She was right. He was the leader of this little expedition, but he had no jurisdiction over the magicians' personal lives.

"Look, Klaris, someday you may be the Weaver and then I'll follow you. But until then, Feilor is Weaver and he designated me as the leader of this group, and that includes you!"

The princess cocked her head, aware of the fact that Emmil's reply did not address the issue of her personal life.

"I don't need you to follow me, Emmil. I just need you to let me tend to my own business."

Emmil slammed the door behind him. She heard him stomp down the stairs and the rise and fall of his voice in the sitting room below. Klaris ignored all this and centered herself for the scry. The clear water swirled and became a murky black. Puzzled, she pulled back and started afresh. Again, the black water. This was odd. She attempted to scry for someone she knew was dead, her beloved granny, Queen Essa. When she did this, the water in the scry bowl flashed a brilliant white then remained crystal clear. So, she reasoned, Javix must still be alive, but under what grim conditions, she did not want to imagine.

Below her in the sitting room, Emmil was intently modifying Klaris's condition. He couldn't stop her magic, but he could confine her. He ordered the other magicians to help him move the stones and rebuild the house so that Klaris's room became a windowless tower. Alone in the room, Klaris felt them weave the spell that imprisoned her. She studied the way each of them pulled on the power and constructed the walls. She knew the places where the magic was weak, where the weave was loose, or a spell untidy.

Strong as her own power was, she couldn't counteract the working of all these magicians, but she could, and did, cut through their weave to give herself one small window onto the black Rising night.

This was small consolation, and she never knew how it maddened Emmil to know that she could rip a window into what he had intended to be a solid wall. Imprisoned with only the sound of the Rising rain pounding on the slate roof to keep her company, Klaris faced the devastation of this betrayal. She was astounded that these people would refuse to listen to her. These were the people she'd shared so much with, studied alongside, experimented with. A few tears of frustration tracked down her cheeks.

She was trapped. And Javix Sharkin was lost again.

Again, she reviewed the way the magic seemed to tangle itself around him. Again, she considered what she knew of the politics of his disappearance and thought about what it meant to find him in the slave pens after all these years. Who, by the goddess, had done that to him?

When Lad Yob brought up her food, he found her sitting next to the radiator, her gaze distant.

"I could bring you some books, if you like, my lady," he said, apology in his gray eyes.

"I can't find him," she said.

Lad Yob had served the Mystic and its magicians longer than anyone knew. He easily followed Klaris's train of thought. "Perhaps he's dead?"

Klaris shook her head. "No. The scry goes black, not white."

The fat gray tabby that had followed the Lad up the stairs jumped into Klaris's lap and looked into her face. "He can't be found," she said to the cat.

Lad Yob felt the magic lurch within him. Both Klaris and the cat turned green eyes to him.

He stood, staring at them, his gray face ashen. "Is it time?" he muttered.

"Time for what?"

The cat purred loudly.

"Sweet goddess," Lad Yob whispered. He turned and fled down the stairs.

"What was that all about?" Klaris asked the cat. She reached around him to pick up the bowl of soup and a spoon.

"Meow."

"You can have some when I'm finished," Klaris said, but as the cat continued to stare at her, she had the impression that the cat had meant to express something other than an interest in the food.

For two more long weeks, during which the Rising pelted the tower with rain and sleet and even snow, Klaris endured her imprisonment with just the company of the cat and the daily, subdued and silent visits of Lad Yob. He brought her food and books, but he said little. She noticed his distraction, but distracted herself, she didn't say anything.

All the magicians in the house could feel Klaris's magic flare and swell from time to time as she pulled on the power that came so fluidly to her call, but they did not know what she was doing up there in that tower. After the window went in, Emmil had made the Lads and Lassies bolster the spells that created the tower so there was no way Klaris or any magician other than the Weaver himself could modify the prison.

When the Rising finally ended and the magicians were ready to return to Sageham Isle, Emmil and the Lads climbed to the tower to escort a silent Klaris down to the carriage that would take them all to the dock and the boat to Caledra. The gray cat sat and watched the procession file down the stairs. Slowly, his tail straight up behind him, the cat followed them down, slipped out the door, then padded softly down the street.

Lad Yob watched Klaris sit silently among the other magicians. He was puzzled by the look of bewilderment on her face.

"I'm sorry, Klaris," the Ilyian woman whispered to her.

Klaris turned her confused gaze to the woman but didn't answer.

Lad Yob looked at those eyes. They were the color of sage, not the leaf-green of the Farsouthian royal house. He leapt away from the carriage in time to see the striped cat slip around the corner of the street.

"Wait!" he ordered tersely, sprinting down the street after the cat.

Fat as it was, the cat moved more quickly than the Sagehamite. But Lad Yob was more familiar with the neighborhood. He took a shortcut and pounced on the cat from the shadows of a side alley.

"Where are you going, my lady?"

Leaf green eyes looked up at him. *You know where I'm going,* Klaris's voice spoke in his head.

"The trolls will harm you."

I'm just a cat.

"Then a dog will get you."

I'm not exactly defenseless.

"And if you find this Barian slave prince, how is a cat going to save him from the trolls? Will you pay for him with dead mice?"

I have to find him first. A cat can slink into many places.

Lad Yob heard the tension in Klaris's voice and realized with awe that not only was she maintaining this spell, but also the sham image back in the carriage, all while carrying on a telepathic conversation. No one had exhibited such a command of the magic in many, many generations.

"Lad Yob! What are you doing?" Emmil Rohan came around the corner, followed by two other magicians and a Lassie.

"Playing with a cat?" sneered the Vitran magician.

"That's no cat," gasped the Lass.

Emmil's magic flared and snagged. "Klaris!"

"Dragons," swore the cat. It shimmered, and suddenly Lad Yob stood in the sunny street holding Princess Klaris in his thin gray arms.

"You can shape shift?" the Vitran demanded, rather foolishly.

"No, of course not." Klaris blinked benignly.

Emmil's grip on Klaris's arm was not gentle as he strode back to the carriage. There they found the other magicians fighting to hold a yowling cat.

"Klaris just morphed into this fiend!" shouted the Ilyian woman, long red scratches bleeding on her cheek. "We're containing her."

"The cat is a tom," Klaris noted quietly.

"Let the cat go," Emmil snapped. "Get in, Klaris. We'll let the Weaver deal with you."

The carriage jolted into motion. Inside, the magicians and Sagehamites rode in silence, but Klaris could see the speculation and amazement on their faces. Every magician at this level knew that no one had been able to shape shift for at least eight hundred years. But what, by the sweet goddess, did these people think she would do with her time, locked away in a tower for two weeks?

When they reached Sageham that evening, Emmil brought Klaris to face the Weaver and the five tutors. These were the most powerful Mystics in the Knownlands. Klaris had studied under all of them and surpassed most of them. She watched their faces as Emmil told of finding the troll and the slave on the Vrillbridge Road, of how Klaris had defied him there and again at The Hant, and the measures he'd taken to keep her from "imperiling our careful relationship with the trolls."

"Thank you, Emmil," Weaver Feilor croaked, his face gray with the disease that was slowly killing him. "I understand you acted in the way you thought best."

"I did, Weaver, but Klaris's insubordination must be punished. The other junior magicians need to respect what their tutors and trainers demand, for their own safety and the safety of us all."

"I may be young," Klaris said. "But you can hardly consider me a junior magician."

"You are what, twenty-five years old?" Emmil snapped. "You know how few magicians even get to Caledra before they've seen thirty summers. You are a junior magician despite your power, and your rashness is proof of it!"

"Enough," Feilor's weakened voice rang with the force of his magic. "Leave us, Emmil. Leave us to deal with this."

"I'm twenty two," Klaris said succinctly, as he walked past her.

Silence filled the room. Klaris felt Feilor's magic soothe her. She did not realize that all the Mystic tutors felt a similar joy in the presence of her magic.

"Do it, Klaris," Feilor said finally. "I want to see it."

"Yes, Weaver."

She closed her eyes to center herself for the strenuous magic she was about to do, so she did not see the ecstasy on Feilor's face as she pulled together the weave and constructed the spell.

Her slight figure shimmered and shifted and suddenly Emmil Rohan faced them.

"Ah," Feilor smiled.

Professor Lellyn, Tower Tutor, pursed her lips. "Does poor Emmil have *your* shape now?"

"No. I didn't shape swap this time." Klaris answered out of Emmil's mouth with Edmmil's voice.

"The eyes aren't right," complained Professor Essen.

"Really? I had to practice without a mirror," Emmil/Klaris said. "I didn't want Lad Yob to suspect what I was trying to do."

The magic swelled, and Emmil's eyes were now a bright Norledgian blue.

"Uh. That is better," choked Hiddicot, the tutor for the Dock and Portal acolytes.

"Eight hundred years," Feilor breathed. "No one has seen this done since Weaver Anelwyth died over eight hundred years ago."

Emmil bowed, shimmered, and rose as Klaris.

"I did not intend to be insubordinate," Klaris said. "Javix Sharkin is a prince of both Baria and Kordon. Surely anyone would have an obligation to help him and to alert his family as to his whereabouts. I, especially, have such an obligation."

Feilor relaxed back in his chair and pulled the heavy fur blanket further up his chest. "But there's more, isn't there?"

Klaris nodded. "As Emmil told you, we found him and a beastly overtroll shipwrecked on the shore of Hanter Lake. We didn't know who he was, and he didn't tell us, but from the moment I saw him I sensed an oddity about him. Of course, his Dragon force irritated me—all of us. But there is something more. The weave wants him—don't you feel it?"

"I've never heard of a Mystic being drawn to someone with the dragons' magic." Feilor wheezed.

"It's not about me." Klaris knelt at the Weaver's knee and took one of his cold hands. "He needs help. The Mystic wants him."

Feilor looked at her young hand on his vein-riven old claw. "What more do you need to do?"

"I want to find him."

Feilor felt Klaris's magic as a soft, warm blanket. Her power had always been so extraordinary. But he also knew that, just as her magic was unique, so were her challenges. Few Mystics faced the kind of conflicting responsibilities that would confront a Princess-Weaver. In fact, everyone knew that the goddess disliked concentrating so much power in just two hands. Because of this, Feilor was not sure Klaris would ever be the Weaver, despite her obvious magical qualifications.

"You could consult the Oracle," Feilor said softly.

"I could?"

He nodded.

"But the Oracle..." Hiddicot protested. "Weaver, do you think this puzzle warrants going all the way to the Oracle?"

"Well, it is a puzzle that involves a very high level of the magic and royal families as well."

Klaris stood, with a queer sense of dread rising in her belly. She had seen the Oracle's white temple blazing in the sun as she sailed past the Head of Baria on her way to Sageham from her home on Farsouth. Everyone knew that the Oracle spoke for the goddess, but they wouldn't see her. She was a tower-tested Mystic, true, one of the dozen or so most powerful Mystics now living. But she wasn't the Weaver. Feilor was too ill to travel, and Klaris would not willingly go anywhere with Emmil Rohan again.

Weaver Feilor's voice continued. "I went once to the Oracle with Weaver Bizzelworth. Something strange had happened to the fabric of the magic, you see, and none of us could quite figure it out."

"What was it?" asked the Foundation Tutor, who had been listening in fascinated silence.

"It was as if someone had taken the fabric of the magic and shaken it—like one would shake a blanket." Feilor answered.

"Really?"

The Weaver's old eyes bore into Klaris's. "No one had ever felt such a thing before. We could not find any account of a similar situation in any record anywhere. The whole fabric of the Mystic had shifted, you see. Old wrinkles vanished and new ones arose. We expect this kind of change when a new Weaver is made or when an old Weaver dies. But out of the blue, this was...uncanny."

"Did the Oracle tell you what it was?" she asked.

Feilor nodded.

Everyone waited, everyone except Professor Lellyn, who had been at Castle Caledra in those days and already knew.

"It was you, Klaris." Feilor's voice took strength from the admission.

"What do you mean, me?"

"It was you. The moment of your birth shook the weave and changed it forever."

"Why?"

Feilor stared at her. A funny gulping noise rose in his throat. Soon he was choking on laughter. Klaris watched in confusion.

"Why?" he coughed, wiping tears from his eyes. "Why? You know, we didn't think to ask that."

Klaris went to the window. "I want to know what has happened to Javix Sharkin. I want to find him," she repeated.

Feilor suddenly felt the magic of the weave billowing through his veins and recognized its words speaking through his voice. "He'll find you."

"He will?" Klaris had also felt the magic move. She knew that it was the Mystic speaking to her.

"Patience, my child. Patience."

"Patience," Klaris echoed.

"That will be your punishment." Professor Lellyn smiled slyly as she rose. As Tower Tutor, Lellyn was teacher, mentor, and guide to the most powerful of all Mystics. "The weave itself seems to have decreed that you must leave Prince Javix Sharkin to his own devices. One day, he will find you."

The old woman took Klaris by the arm and led her from the room. Klaris allowed herself to be drawn away, but she was remembering his desperate plea for help and knew he had precious few devices against whatever the trolls had in store for him.

As spring melted the ice from Sageham's rocks, Klaris barricaded herself behind mountains of ancient texts. Everyone, including Feilor himself, knew that he would not last much longer. Soon there would be no hands to guide the Mystic weave. It was a void Klaris was determined to fill. But she was not the only one.

Emmil sat in a chamber high in the tower of the castle, surveying the wreckage of yet another spell. Professor Lellyn looked in and saw the ruin and the dejection in Emmil's shoulders. She knew from personal experience how frustrating it was to be so close to one's own chance at taking the weave, to feel such power, and yet to know that someone else had more.

"I think Klaris is sabotaging me," he grumbled. "I used to be able to make these spells work, and now I can't."

Lellyn's voice was gentle: "She used to interfere with your work. She would watch you and quietly help you. I told her she shouldn't, but she thought she was being kind."

Anger surged through him. He remembered the steady sensation of support he used to get when working these difficult weaves. He had always assumed it was the Mystic helping him. Now he realized that he had not felt that support since the Spring Rising and the unpleasant trip to The Hant.

"Dragons fry her!" He swept the detritus of his spell onto the floor and pushed past Lellyn to head loudly down the stairs.

The professor looked at the talismans and broken glass on the floor. A gray Sagehamite came in with a broom.

"Thank you, Laddie," Lellyn said softly, as she too headed down the stairs.

15

Consciousness returned with such agony that he tried very hard to push it away. For an indefinite time, he could think of nothing beyond the painful draw of each broken breath, the throb of cracked bones, and the burn of open wounds. A horrible, sickly smell finally began to drive thoughts through the blanket around his mind. The overwhelming odor, vile and inescapable, forced him to open one eye. The left one remained swollen shut.

He found himself sprawled on rancid straw in a small, dim cell. The stench emanated from the dead body on the floor next to him.

Gagging, and gasping with the effort, Jax pushed himself away from the corpse. By the murky light of distant, smoky lanterns, the body's sunken cheeks and moldering orifices gleamed ghoulishly. It had been dead for some time.

Jax sat up slowly. Where was he? Where was Oblek?

"Hey!" he called hoarsely through the bars of the cell.

Several cadaverous people eyed him from similar cells down the long, sooty hallway, but no one spoke.

It took him several minutes to muster his breath and his voice against the pain. ".... This guy's dead in here."

A woman in the cell across from him shrugged. "Been dead a couple days, he has."

"Well... He stinks."

"Don't we all?"

Too weak to be frustrated, Jax leaned back against the stone wall and watched in horror as a large, greasy beetle crawled from the slack mouth of the dead man. Uncontrollably, Jax vomited. He retched until every bone and muscle in his body convulsed in pain and merciful darkness closed in upon him.

Smells woke him again. This time it was a chipped bowl that was leaking stewed cabbage onto the rancid straw.

"Hey," he whispered to the troll, who ignored him to shove similar fare into the cell on the other side of the corridor.

"Hey!"

A second troll loomed over him outside the bars. "Whaddye want?"

"This one's dead, here."

The guard frowned and glared back into the shadows of the cell to where the corpse lay. "Ye may be right." Sharp orange eyes glared down at the half-isle, who was now using the bars of the cell to pull himself up.

Without another word, the troll strode from the hall. Jax swallowed some of the cabbage. Chewing hurt; everything hurt. He tried to find a position that didn't crunch a broken bone, twist a torn ligament, or reopen black scabs, but he had little success.

A screech of rusty metal startled him as the cell door swung open. Two trolls stomped in and nudged the body with their boots, aggravating the stench.

"Stop that," ordered a third troll. The white makeup caking his face indicated that he was an overtroll. "Just remove it."

Jax rolled as far from this operation as the cell permitted. He didn't notice the speculative expression on the overtroll's painted face.

"Druid!" The overtroll called down the corridor.

"I'm here," grumbled an ancient fe-troll. "Surely ye don't need me to tell ye that one's dead."

"No," the overtroll snapped. "It's this one I want you to look at."

"Me?" Jax squinted up through one eye.

"Stand up," the overtroll ordered.

This took considerable effort. Eventually he attained his feet and stood swaying.

The druid frowned, drew a long thin blade from a sheath at her belt and advanced toward him.

Clumsily, Jax stumbled back, but the bars of the cell stopped him. The knife slashed his mud and blood-stained shirt, parting it down the middle. It came off with a jerk of the druid's deft fingers.

"Dragons," Jax swore bleakly.

"Dragons, indeed," grumbled the old fe-troll, surveying the massive bruising above the broken ribs, the cuts and welts and other swellings on his emaciated body.

"Well?" The overtroll demanded impatiently.

"Well," the druid mimicked. With unexpected gentleness she turned Jax around to look at the old scars on his back. "Ain't none of this fatal," she said, turning Jax around to face them again.

The overtroll pursed his whitened lips. "I didn't think so. We can sell it for more than bait."

"Probably," agreed the druid. "It's got good muscles and plenty of scars."

"Take it upstairs." The overtroll left the cell.

"Come on then." The druid put her shoulder under Jax's right arm, away from the broken ribs on his left side.

Slowly he limped down the corridor then, gasping with the effort, up a flight of stairs. The druid said nothing, just supported his halting progress.

"Here ye are." She unlocked another cell.

"So...." Jax paused for breath. "So.... I'm not going to be bait?"

She shrugged. "Not if ye can walk by auction time."

"When's that?"

"Couple o' weeks. Get on in there now."

Pushed, he stumbled into the cell and came up hard against the stone wall.

A man and a woman already sat there, watching the shirtless half-isle subside slowly to the straw.

"Sweet goddess," the man said as he saw the extent of Jax's wounds. "What happened to you?"

"I think... I've just been rescued."

"Rescued, lad? You don't know where you are."

"You don't know... where I've been."

Over the next weeks his fellow cell mates pumped him for information on how to survive in the iron mines, which just increased their fear of ending up there. They counted his many scars and watched in awe as he wolfed the bad food. By the end of the two weeks, they had grown tired of his tedious exercises. Several times each day, Jax would haul himself to his feet and limp around the little cell. At first, he could only make one gasping circuit.

Jax had found something new in Klaris de Farsouth's confident gaze that gave him the will to push past his pain and force his aching body to regain its strength. He'd caught a glimpse of hope for the first time in three years.

The Princess of Farsouth would let the rest of the Knownlands know that Javix Sharkin still lived and could be found in The Hant. The Barians, or someone, would finally extract him from this nightmare, if he could make it to the open auction.

By the time the trolls came to clean the slaves up for the auction, Jax could make more laps than his cell mates could count. Un-bandaged, his cuts gradually crusted over and the bruises turned green and purple. Eventually he was able to open his left eye, but his knee and his right hand were still swollen, and breathing was still torture.

On auction day the trolls herded the slaves into scalding showers, scrubbing the dirty bodies with coarse brushes and shaving the men with rough indifference. Dressed once more in baggy cast-off trousers and a scratchy and unraveling sweater, Jax stood in line with the other slaves while the trolls roped them all together.

Prodding and cursing, the trolls hauled the string of slaves out of the dark corridors and into a narrow, cobbled street.

Jax blinked at the overcast sunlight. The air was pleasant, with a gentle breeze and the fresh scent of spring rain. The Rising was well finished. Jax calculated that he must have been in the auction pens for three weeks. That should give a fast Barian ship time to sail here, if word had gotten to Haven immediately following the Rising. His heart beat with excitement.

Limping along in line, he smiled. Oblek had failed. He had made it to the auctions; Klaris or the Barians would find him now.

A guard shoved each slave, one by one, into small upright cages. The thing was almost too narrow for Jax's shoulders, and his head brushed against the bars on top. Locked inside, Jax watched the prospective buyers stroll along the street, perusing the merchandise.

He thought about what he'd do as a free man. Eat, for one thing, eat real food until his belly couldn't take any more. And then he'd have a few words with his damn brother. The cool morning wore on, and his thoughts began to fray under the physical strain of standing in the cramped cage. Knee, ribs, head, hand everything ached. Finally, he slumped down, sticking his sore knee through the bars and out into the street.

"Stand up, damn you!" One of the merchants kicked at Jax's leg. "If you don't look like a good buy, you *will* end up as bait."

Slowly, Jax climbed back to his feet and wedged himself upright into a corner, trying to think of something other than his pain. He noticed the shadows on the street had shifted from leaning east to leaning west. Eventually a harassed runner, followed a more harassed guard, stopped in front of Jax's cage.

"Wake up, you!" The runner shook the bars. The little cage rocked violently, snapping Jax out of his daze, as he tried to keep his balance. The troll looked at the number on the cage, then peered at his clipboard.

"Yeah. Number seventeen: half-isle." He turned to the guard. "It's next." The runner took off down the street, squinting at the clipboard to find the next lot for the auction.

The guard fumbled through a ring of keys, finally finding the one for Jax's cage.

"Don't move, or I'll club ye." He clipped a leash into the ring on Jax's collar and jerked the lead. "Come on."

When they got to the base of the auctioneer's platform, the guard pulled off Jax's sweater and cuffed his hands behind his back.

"Dragons fry you," Jax whispered, dizzy with pain.

"They'll want to see yer scars and know ye can take a beating."

Up on the platform, another guard held a trembling girl while the auctioneer bellowed at the audience.

"This beauty from Northern Ohe came to us from its own family, just last week." The big bones of the girl stood out under her milky skin. She sobbed disconsolately. Jax thought of Jolira, but his heart was racing with anticipation. He flexed his shoulders against the bonds that pulled at his broken ribs.

"Don't try any funny stuff," the guard growled into Jax's ear.

"There's nothing funny here."

"Git on up now." The guard shoved Jax onto the auction block.

"Lot seventeen," the auctioneer called, "is our half-isle. Look at these muscles, the good color of its face. It has been in the Hanter Iron Mines, so you know it's strong and ready for all kinds of work. Do I hear twenty-five silvers? Twenty-five silvers for this marvelous—twenty-five silvers, thank you. Thirty?"

Jax looked around the marketplace. The platform stood at one end of the town square. From this raised perspective, he could see over the faces watching the aution to the various booths that lined the other sides of the square. The crowd consisted mostly of trolls, but there were also humans among them. He looked for Klaris. Surely, she would be here. Surely, she would have gotten word to Bryx.

A rough hand grabbed his hair and jerked back his head. "Stop favoring that leg and look meek."

A scab on his scalp came off and blood oozed into his hair. Jax pulled himself away from the troll. "I'm not meek."

"Fifty silvers!" cried a voice from the back of the crowd. A low murmur of surprise echoed through the assembly.

"Fifty silvers going once! Twice! Sold! To the gentleman in the back for fifty silvers!"

At the title stand, set up next to the auctioneer, the guard stuffed Jax back into his sweater and cuffed his hands together again. Wary and a little confused, Jax watched a Hantish man sign the deed papers. This fellow wasn't the rescuer Jax had anticipated.

He spoke with the same broad Hantish accent that the trolls used, but he was human, maybe forty years old, dressed in warm layers of woolen clothes. His unremarkable light brown hair blew about in the wind, while sharp blue eyes gleamed through the thick lenses of wire-rimmed spectacles. An iron goddess charm hung on a long leather thong about his neck, and a black satchel sat on the ground where he had set it carefully.

"Fifty silvers." The man counted out coins for the cashier.

"Here's his key, sir. Thank you."

The man turned to look Jax up and down, noting the scars and bruises. "You're a sight lad. Bleeding, even."

Jax just stared at the man.

The man made a face. "You looked better from a distance."

Jax found his voice: "Did Klaris send you?"

"Who?"

"Klaris de Farsouth or the Barians?"

"No. No one sent me. And I don't know any islish folks. Turn around now, lad."

Jax did as ordered, panic rising in his stomach. He heard the key click in the handcuffs, and his arms were released.

The new owner placed the handcuffs on the cashier's table. "I don't use these."

"Fool," mumbled the cashier.

Hope again bloomed with the physical release, but it withered when the man handed Jax his black bag. "You can carry this for me. It weighs a ton." He started off into the crowd, still speaking: "I'll bandage your head when get to my cart. We'll be going home now to Hilsen Vale..." The man stopped and turned sharply, realizing that his new purchase was not with him. Struggling with the heavy black bag, Jax limped along grimly.

"Sorry about that." The man took back the bag. "I guess you have more than a bump on the head, eh?"

Jax stared at him, baffled. Where, by the goddess, was Klaris? She was a princess and a powerful Mystic. Surely, she had the resources to find and rescue him.

The fact that this Hantish man had evidently bought him to be a slave astounded Jax, both because he did not know that people would engage in the practice of slavery, and because he had expected Klaris, or someone, to buy him his freedom today.

"Here's my cart." With a grunt the man shoved the bag behind the seat of a covered two-person buggy. He opened the bag, rummaged around for a moment and came up with some white cloth. "Sit down, lad."

Jax sat on the buggy's seat. With gentle fingers the man probed Jax's hair. "This isn't a new wound," he said, wrapping the bandage.

Before Jax could find a useful answer to this comment, the man had tucked in the end of the bandage and seated himself. He flicked the reins, and the cart jerked into motion through the wet and cluttered streets of The Hant.

"Wait," gasped Jax.

The man glanced at him but didn't stop the cart. "I'm sorry, lad." His eyes behind his spectacles were gentle and kind. "You were hoping someone else would buy you?"

"I hoped...." He could not go on.

The cart rattled over the cobblestones. "I expect most slaves hope that their family will show up at the auction and buy them back. But you were in the mines, weren't you? Your family's probably given up on you."

Jax shivered, stunned. He remembered Klaris's sparkling green eyes and the warmth of hope that had spurred him for days to get up and push his aching body around and around that cell. Pointlessly.

Soon they were out of town, trotting along the Vrillbridge Road. The man continued to comment on the road and the fine spring weather and finally about Jax.

"You don't look Hantish."

Jax didn't answer.

"Do you understand Landish?"

"Generally."

The man stiffened at the aristocratic tone. "Well, you haven't said two words to me."

Jax stared at him. "I have nothing to say."

The simple answer conveyed such a sense of disgust that the Hantish man pulled the horse to a stop and turned to look at the lad he'd just purchased. Probably the slave was more deeply wounded than was apparent. Surely there was great pain in those strange, sea-blue eyes.

"Well, why don't you tell me your name?"

"My name?" Jax ran a hand over his face. Fishman? Sir? He choked. How could he claim to be Javix Sharkin here, now? He was nothing again. Nothing but forsaken.

Jax grabbed the side of the buggy and slipped out. His knee buckled, but he caught himself, and turned, limping grimly back toward The Hant.

"Whoa! What are you doing?" The man jumped out of the buggy and easily caught up with the slave. He wished he hadn't been so quick to give up the fetters and ran an inventory through his mind of things he might use to confine the lad.

Jax stumbled again, and this time he went down hard. He closed his eyes, shaking with pain and desperation.

The man crouched down beside him. "You're not really in any shape to escape, are you?"

"Dragons fry you," Jax panted.

"Now, that's no way to talk." The man helped Jax stand. "I can get you up and running in no time."

Jax gasped past his broken ribs for breath and looked away from the man's kind face.

"Here, I'll introduce myself," the man began walking Jax back to the buggy. "I'm Mrac Appandel. Everyone calls me Doc, of course, because I'm the village druid. Up you go, now. Pull some of this fur over you. Now stay put; I don't want to have to bind you."

Jax leaned back, defeated. Doc got himself in and settled. He flicked the reins and the cart jerked over the rough ruts in the road.

Doc drove in silence. Jax knew the man was waiting and recognized that Doc's kindness deserved an answer. Finally, he mumbled "Jax," through clenched teeth. "You can call me Jax."

The druid flashed him a smile. "Jax. What kind of a name is that?"

"Barian."

"Barian! Well, that explains those eyes of yours and the pointed ears. I've never met a Barian before. Not many come to the Hantland."

"Because we don't condone slavery." Jax bit.

"*Condone?* I guess you do speak Landish, then. Well, I don't really condone it either. But it's these trolls, you know. They're the ones in charge, and around here you don't want to mess with them."

The druid spoke about the trolls, The Hant, the road, the steaming Vrillian River. But Jax could not pay attention. He did not want to talk; he did not want to think. He felt as fractured as his bones and closed his eyes in utter despair.

Eventually, Doc glanced at the sleeping slave and fell silent. He saw the spring breeze finger through the sun-bleached hair, revealing white scars and fading bruises. The goddess had spoken to him as he watched the lad stand up there half-naked before the crowd of trolls, spoken with an imperative he'd never felt before. After a long while, he muttered to himself: "Fifty silvers! Sweet goddess, Mam is going to skin me."

Jax awoke in the chilly twilight. The buggy stood amid a few trees; the horse had been staked in some grass. Doc was busy doing something with a large piece of canvas. Jax looked around for the shelter but saw only the rocky steppes of the Hantland stretching away from the lakeshore.

"Give me a hand with this, will you?" Doc was trying to prop a pole underneath the fabric.

Stiff and sore, Jax climbed slowly from the buggy. He limped to Doc who handed him a corner of canvas.

"I got in the habit of making this spring trip to The Hant with my husband. He has the Mystic. It's been years since I had to use the tent here, and it's not as easy as I remember."

"Tent?" Jax repeated, confused.

Doc's response was lost to the shrouding fabric as he stuck the pole in the ground and raised the canvas. It nearly blew away, but Jax grabbed the flapping corner nearest him.

"Good!" Doc came out. "Hold on there, while I hammer in the stakes."

Doc moved around the tent with his mallet. "There! Home for tonight!" Doc headed back to the buggy and began to lug out rugs and blankets. "Grab that fur," he said to Jax. "I didn't bring bedding for two, and it's going to be cold tonight. We'll have to make do."

Jax looked at the flimsy walls of the tent bowing in the wind.

"Go ahead and lay out the blankets," Doc said. "I'll get dinner going."

Jax spread the rugs and quilts inside the tent. Panting with the effort, he finally lay down and pulled the fur up over himself. By the time Doc turned to offer him some hot tea with whiskey, he was again sound asleep.

Doc drank his own toddy and then Jax's. He warmed a meat pasty he'd bought in the square before the auction had caught his attention. Steam rose as he cut the pasty in half and turned to give Jax his share, but the lad still slept soundly. As he ate, Doc considered the partially healed wounds and remembered the anger in the weird islish eyes, wondering if the lad might be dangerous.

He took several precautions before tucking himself into the blankets, a dagger uncomfortably snuggled against his chest.

Jax woke hungry and bound the next morning. These undeniable signs of enslavement pushed him up with a roar that choked to a whimper of pain. Doc glanced up from his pots over the small fire.

"Morning, lad. You want some tea?"

"I want to be untied."

"Alright." Doc fiddled with the ropes and pulled them free. "I just didn't want you running away or strangling me in the night."

Jax rose unsteadily. He was a good head taller than the druid. "I'm only accidentally murderous." The crisp accent was hard, but the voice was attenuated.

Doc considered this paradox. He bent over the pot on the fire and poured some tea into a mug, adding a dollop of honey. Jax lowered himself slowly to a log near the fire. He sipped the sweetened tea. It was delicious.

Next, Doc handed Jax a small bowl of porridge. "Let's avoid accidents, then. And please don't run away."

Jax took two quick bites. It was heavenly. "Feed me like this, and I'll stay."

"At least until you can actually walk again, eh?" Doc laughed.

Jax's bowl was empty. Doc refilled it. "Why did the trolls beat you?"

"They didn't need a reason." Jax gulped the porridge and finished his tea. "My overmaster wanted to use me for bait."

"Wonder why he didn't."

Jax had no answer. He too had wondered how he ended up in the auction pen rather than in some Rising-soaked forest waiting for monsters and could only conclude that maybe the slave wrangler had diverted Oblek's bloody plans. This thought led him back to the painful reality that faced him today: He might be alive and healing, but he was not free.

Doc was collecting his breakfast things and rinsing them with water from a canteen. "Still, the trolls appear to have made a mess of you. Tell me where it hurts, and I'll see if I can't fix you up a bit."

"Ribs. Knee. These fingers."

"How long were you in the iron mines?"

"Three years."

"Sweet goddess." Doc shook his head. "No one survives three years in the iron mines. How did you do it?"

"Bad luck."

Doc frowned at the bitterness in this response and rummaged in his bag. "What did you do for them?"

"I dug in the mines, and I sailed the ferry."

"The one that sank a few weeks ago?"

"Was there another?"

Doc grumbled at the saucy answer as he manipulated the broken fingers on Jax's right hand. "These need to be re-broken to set right."

"Re-broken?"

The sauciness was gone. Doc heard the pain beneath the fancy accent. He rose and went to the small fire. "It will hurt, lad, but I'll make you some poppy tea to dull the pain."

Jax said nothing, but Doc sensed his trepidation. While the poppy brewed, the druid pulled up Jax's shirt to look at his bruised ribs. "By the goddess," he whispered in horror, as he saw the old scars colored by new cuts and bruises.

"Look, Jax, I've never had a, uh, slave, but I can see that it's been hard on you."

"Just a little."

Doc placed Jax's left arm in a sling to take weight off the broken ribs. "Like I said, as a druid, I don't really approve of slavery, but I do need an assistant. My husband went to Castle Caledra a year ago to study his magic. That leaves my mother and me with all the druidical and doctoring responsibilities for the Vale, where we live, you know. We realized that it's too much work for just the two of us. On top of that, Mam has these crazy travel plans."

He turned his attention to Jax's knee. "Anyway, when I saw you standing up there looking so disdainful, but forlorn, I thought, why not? You could be our assistant as easily as you could work for some trolls. Fifty silvers, though, by the goddess!" He looked up into Jax's face, his blue eyes huge through the lenses of his glasses. "Mam is going to have a fit. She's pretty thrifty."

Doc patted Jax's knee gently. "You know there are strings in there that connect bone to muscle."

"Ligaments, you mean?"

"Well, yes," Doc was surprised. He had never had a patient who would have known the correct anatomical word. "The ligaments can heal, given time. How's it feel now?"

"Fine."

Doc knew the lad was lying. Whatever he had done, the trolls had very nearly beaten the life out him. "Fine, eh? Let me look at that eye." With gentle fingers he probed the tender bones around Jax's left eye. He held one hand in front of his good right eye and tested the half-isle's vision. "This is a nasty business."

"Slavery is."

"Sure, it is." Doc grunted as he stepped away, while Jax shrugged his ragged clothes back into place over the bandages. The druid handed him the poppy brew. "Drink this now. When it takes effect, I'll fix your fingers."

The tea was bitter and left a taste on his tongue of something greasy and burnt. Soon, his eyes were drooping. He felt warm and more comfortable than he could remember. The aches in his ribs and knee were still there, but he didn't mind them as much.

Doc removed the bandage from around the lad's head. "This is healing nicely now," he said, moving the pale hair away from the scab. "You don't need the bandage here if you can keep the scab intact."

Healing. But for what? Jax swallowed, trying to get the taste of the poppy out of his mouth.

Doc set about striking camp while he waited for the tea to sedate the lad. He watched surreptitiously as Jax leaned back against the log. How old could he be? He had youthful muscles despite the obvious signs of starvation. Sinews, veins and bone stood stark beneath taught skin. Doc thought of the scars under the newer abrasions and began to understand the hardness in those strange islish eyes and the coldness of that wolfish grin.

The eyes were not hard now. Dilated with the poppy, they were wary and resigned.

"Alright, son." Doc knelt next to Jax and took his slack hand. Crack!

Jax took a sharp breath. Deftly Doc set the finger then took its neighbor. Crack!

"Dragons," Jax swore thickly.

The third finger was the most difficult. Doc had to re-break it in two places to get it aligned correctly. Jax had turned his head away and covered his face with his good hand, trembling.

"All done." Doc said rising. "I know that hurt, but you'll want the use of your right hand."

Woozily, Jax stood up then sat back down. "I'm left-handed," he mumbled.

"What?"

"I'm left-handed."

"Oh." Doc wouldn't have been so quick to save the off-side hand, knowing how much pain it would cause. He placed the last of his things in the buggy and helped Jax settle himself around the stiffness of the bandages. As they started off again, Doc spoke. "Left-handed, eh? I... I didn't know that."

To cover his discomfort, Doc chatted non-stop, going on about the geologic oddity of the steaming river, the route they would take across the Hantish steppes, and the massive granite peaks of the Ledden Rises that surrounded his home in Hilsen Vale. Jax listened silently, his hand throbbing. As they crossed the Vrillbridge and took the track to Steppash, the poppy had worn off enough for Jax to realize that Doc was taking him away from the sea. In Baria, Kordon, and even in the mines, Jax had always lived near the ocean. Now, as the buggy rattled across the rolling steppes, he could no longer smell the salt and water of the sea.

He listened to the druid and tried to ignore the increasing discomfort in his soul.

By midafternoon Doc had exhausted his store of small talk. Frustrated by the lad's lack of response, he decided to try more direct tactics.

"Where are you from?" he asked directly.

"Baria. Kordon."

"So that's your accent then, Kordish?"

Jax didn't reply.

"Do you speak Islish too?

"Yes."

"So, how did you end up in the Hanter Iron Mines?"

Jax looked at the man, not sure how to take all this civility. Doc glanced at him and squirmed. Finally, Jax answered. "Some of my relatives decided they would be happier without me."

"And this was three years ago?"

"Yes."

Doc thought about this silently for a little while. "How old are you, Jax?"

"Twenty-two."

"Naught but a boy," Doc murmured, almost to himself.

"I'm not a boy."

Doc glanced at him. "It's a matter of perspective, lad."

"Exactly."

16

For two more days Doc tried to wriggle information from Jax, but he slipped around questions and innuendos like some slithery water creature. As they made their way across the Hantish steppes, Doc continued to check the bandages and to wonder, not always silently, about this strange person he had bought.

Each night Doc roped Jax's feet and wrists together with lumpy knots. Jax watched with a sailor's practiced eye. Each morning Doc found the rope coiled neatly, his slave sleeping unbound. He found this increasingly exasperating and each night he devised ever more complicated knots.

"It's not the size that matters," Jax told him, as the druid admired a particularly tangled mass of rope. "It's about tension and counter-tension."

"Surely complication has something to do with it."

Jax shook his head, lay down and closed his eyes. Doc tried to stay awake to see if the lad could extract himself from his masterpiece, but the long day took its toll and he was quickly asleep. In the morning, the rope was again coiled neatly.

On the second day of the journey it started to rain. Doc struggled to light a fire, so Jax used his Dragon force for the first time since the day Broog had been killed when the tunnels caved in. The bundle of sticks Doc had collected for the fire burst easily into flame.

"Oh-ho! So, you have a little Dragon in you."

"Better if I had some Mystic," Jax mumbled, shivering in the damp tent. Still, he watched the druid to see how this display of magic would be received, but Doc seemed unconcerned. In fact, as they continued their trip, Doc encouraged Jax to use his gift. After all, Dragon force was by far the easiest way to light and maintain a campfire.

Doc finally asked for help with the knots and was surprised when Jax showed him how a simple slip knot would keep him tethered quite effectively. That night Doc used his new technique to tie him up, trying to ignore the lad's wolfish grin.

In the morning the rope was again coiled neatly, but it had been burned through.

"I should have kept the fetters you came with," Doc growled.

He was further exasperated by the animosity that developed between Jax and Doc's horse. Pol, usually a docile, unimaginative old nag, often nipped or kicked at the half-isle without any provocation.

"Horses don't like Barians," Jax explained after one of Pol's more violent outbreaks.

"Do Barians like horses?"

Jax shrugged. "Most Barians don't ever have anything to do with them. There's no place for a horse on the Floating Islands."

"Hum." Doc sat by the fire chewing on the end of an unlit pipe. He thought for a minute about the knowing way Jax had handled Pol, even in her disobedient moods. Barians may not know horses, but Jax evidently did.

"So, where did *you* learn to care for a horse?"

"Kordon."

"And what were you doing in Kordon?"

"Fostering."

"Fostering? Were you an orphan then?"

Jax shook his head. "It's the Kordish custom." He paused, juggling his bowl and spoon with his left hand. "They send their children to other people to learn etiquette, history, horsemanship... politics."

"Really? Don't they miss their children?"

Jax shrugged. After a few minutes he spoke softly. "I missed my dad."

"Not your mother?"

"I never knew her."

"Ah. I'm sorry, lad."

Both Doc and Jax had had enough of the continual rain by the time they reached the yellow stone walls of Steppash. Fuming geysers north of the town sent steam up the rain to join the clouds.

"I'll be glad to sleep under a roof tonight," Doc said, as he guided the buggy through the wet, narrow streets to a small inn just inside the town gate. "Hi, lad! You've grown a foot since I saw you last week." Doc leapt down from the buggy and handed the reins to the lanky stable boy.

"Yer slave can't go inside, Doc," the boy warned, his adolescent voice cracking.

"I know trolls don't let their slaves inside, but this is different." Doc ducked into the inn. "Come on, Jax!"

"Hello, Doc." The innkeeper, a Hantish human with the same light brown hair and blue eyes as Doc, looked up from his ledger and smiled then frowned. "Hey! Who let the slave in?" He came around from the desk and began to shove Jax back into the rain. "Out with you! Out!"

"Wait, Kajjon!" Doc protested. "He's with me."

Kajjon stopped pushing Jax and blinked at the druid. "It's *your* slave?"

"Well, yes. Mam and I need help up in the Vale, you see."

"Stand by the door," Kajjon ordered Jax. He returned to his ledgers. "I do see the craziest things," he muttered, mostly to himself.

"So, there will be two of us tonight," Doc went on. "We'll want baths of course, and I've been looking forward to your antelope pasty."

"Sure, Doc. You can have your usual room and we got a fresh antelope in yesterday, so the pasty's been cooking all day."

"You'll love it, Jax." Doc turned to smile at Jax, who leaned against the wall by the door.

Kajjon continued as if Doc hadn't spoken. "I got a spot in the pen for your slave. Only one other in there tonight. We'll get it groomed and fed for five irons. Or three irons for just grooming or just feeding."

"No, Kajjon. He can stay with me."

The innkeeper scratched the bald place on his head. "Doc, I can't have a slave in the inn. You know the trolls won't put up with that."

"But—."

"My pen's clean. It'll be out of the wet, and I feed them only the best table scraps."

Horrified, Doc turned to face Jax, but before he could speak the stable boy stuck his head in the door. "Come on, slave. You ain't allowed in here."

Jax saw the embarrassment and discomfort on Doc's face and wondered what the druid had expected. The stable boy was tugging on the slave collar, so Jax followed him out into the rain.

The boy didn't let go until he'd gotten Jax securely locked into the same kind of shaving chair the trolls had used in the mines. "You must be a lot of trouble for a druid like Doc to beat you so." The boy lathered Jax's whiskers, noting the bandages and scabs.

"Trolls did it," Jax explained carefully so as not to jar the razor.

"Ah," the boy smiled, relieved. "That makes more sense. I wouldn't've thought a druid would own a slave, much less beat it." He unlocked Jax. "Wash there."

Harboring similar thoughts, Jax splashed himself and dunked his head.

"Come along, now." The boy spoke to Jax in the same tone he used with the horse. He led Jax to a stall at the back of the stable. The straw on the floor was reasonably fresh and a stack of blankets was neatly folded in a corner. Thick chains hung at regular intervals along the wooden walls. A plump man with salt and pepper hair, looked up at them, as the boy hefted one of the chains and padlocked it to Jax's collar.

"There you go, now." The boy swung the stall door shut behind him.

The man considered Jax as he sat gingerly. "Hello. I'm Birn."

"Jax."

He smiled. "What'd you do to get so beat up?"

"I sank the Hanter Iron Mines' ferry."

Birn frowned, confused. "You've a queer way of speaking, Jax. I didn't know there were fairies in the mines."

"A ferry is a boat that goes back and forth across a river or a lake. This one carried the iron ore."

"A boat! Goddess preserve us."

"I guess she did," he grumbled and changed the subject. "Why are you here?"

"I've been a house slave these twenty years to the same trolls. Raised their two trollings. Now I travel with the mistress a bit. She gets mournful sitting around that empty house, missing her young that are all grown and off on their own."

"Here's yer food." The stable boy banged back into the stall. He carried a bucket of table scraps, another of water, and a tin cup of brown ale. "Doc paid extra for this," he handed the ale to Jax.

Birn was already digging through the bucket of scraps. "Seriously?" He held up a bone, nearly picked clean and wiggled it at the boy.

Jax took it from him. "I'm not choosy," he said.

"There's plenty in there," the boy said defensively, slamming the stall door again.

Birn fastidiously chose a few morsels and pushed the bucket to Jax.

Jax wolfed the food. There were a few more bones, pasty crusts, the heels of some bread, and a bunch of cooked carrots. This was by far the best food he'd had in years. Doc's trail rations were plentiful, but plain.

He sipped the warm brown ale and shared it with Birn.

"The mistress gives me drink only on the sabbats." He smiled.

"There wasn't any in the mines." Jax took another big swallow, enjoying the almost-forgotten glow in his head. "I think my new master feels guilty that I couldn't stay in the inn with him."

"What kind of crazy troll is that?"

"He's not a troll. He's human. And a druid."

"Sweet goddess!" Birn shook his head. "You're either lucky or damned with a human master. The good ones will treat you like a servant, but the evil ones are worse than the cruelest trolls."

"Doc's not cruel." Jax finished the ale. "Not intentionally."

"That's often the way of it," Birn said. My mistress and the trollings love me. If I were to die, they'd cry at my funeral. But if they don't have grandbabies for me to care for, I'm not sure what they'll finally do with me."

The beak reality of a slave's future caught Jax like a blow to his belly. He'd seen plenty of slaves like Brin in the Iron Mines, sold by the families they'd served for years. "Why wouldn't they set you free?"

Brin laughed. "That's frowned upon. If slaves could be freed it makes keeping them a choice. That's why folks usually sell off old slaves. If I'm lucky they'll put me down when my mistress dies."

"You want them to kill you?" Jax asked.

Birn nodded. "They see it as a way to honor our years of service. But of course, they don't get any money for us if they put us down, and I'm not sure they'll be able to afford that."

Despair engulfed Jax and a sob, loosened by the ale, wracked his broken ribs.

Chains clanked as Birn moved to wrap his arm around Jax. "It's a kind of freedom," he said gently.

Jax couldn't speak. He closed his eyes and tried not to breathe.

Brin rocked him gently.

This silent kindness soothed Jax. He sat up and wiped his face. "It's not my idea of freedom."

The stable boy came for Jax in the early dawn and tried to lash him to the horse's traces, but Ol' Pol put up such a fuss that he finally settled for tying Jax's hands behind his back and leaving him to stand and wait.

Doc took a second fried egg sandwich with him out to the yard. The rain had stopped in the night, but he found his buggy, horse, and Jax standing in a thick, geyser-infused fog. Jax handed him the stable boy's ropes, now in several pieces.

"You've made your point." Doc grumbled. He turned to the stable boy. "How much for those?" He pointed to a pair of iron fetters rusting on a peg.

"You don't want them, Doc," the boy answered. "The key's lost."

Doc flipped the stable boy a coin for a tip and climbed into the buggy. He waited while Jax, moving more slowly, did the same. "Did they feed you this morning?"

"A piece of bread." Jax nodded.

Doc handed Jax the egg sandwich and clicked the reins. "I.... I'm sorry, Jax. I didn't realize that you'd be treated like a beast."

"You tie me up each night," Jax said, his mouth full. "How is that different?"

"I tether you because I don't know if I can trust you. I can't afford to let you run away, and I'm not sure you won't kill me while I sleep."

"I haven't killed you yet." He swallowed the last of the sandwich and grinned.

Doc found that smile exasperating but not dangerous. A grin of his own bloomed on his face. "I can't wait for my mother to get ahold of you."

Spring sunshine bounced brightly off melting snowbanks as the little buggy rocked over the Roaring Pass and headed down into

Hilsen Vale. Although the Spring Rising was more than three weeks past, winter's white grip held the Vale. A large alpine lake lay grayly frozen in a bowl created by massive granite peaks. Jax looked at the vast scenery in awe. He had never been to such an altitude before. The dry mountain air seared his sinuses, and the intense sunlight bit into his eyes.

As the buggy rolled down the muddy ruts of the track, the streets of Hilsen Vale appeared below them, curling along the shore of the lake.

"That's home!" Doc crowed, gesturing to the town below them. "Isn't it beautiful?"

Jax looked up at the surrounding peaks and felt familiar tremors of claustrophobia.

Doc went on, oblivious to the discontent in Jax's sea-blue eyes. "Takes your breath away doesn't it? This scenery attracts quite a tourist trade, by the way. That's why you'll find so many different races living here in the Vale.

"Of course, we're technically still in the Hantland, so trolls run the place, but they're a reasonable group for the most part. Especially since they're definitely a minority, just the magistrate and the blacksmith really. And a couple of tour operators, too, but they're seasonal."

"I didn't know that people could live with trolls."

"Oh, sure. Once you get out of The Hant you realize that most of the Hantland is populated by humans and nyads."

"And monsters?"

"Well, yes, there are the monsters. But they keep down to the Forest Krill, away from the geysers and out of the high country."

Jax winced as the buggy lurched over a particularly deep rut and jarred his broken bones. "Do the trolls take the villagers here as slaves?" he asked when he could breathe again.

"No! No. Certainly not." Doc shook his head. "You'll notice that most of the slaves are from the border regions of other countries: Norledge, Ily, Ohe."

"Is that why you Hantish humans support the slave trade, then—because you're exempt?"

Doc stiffened. "I told you, Jax, I know that there are moral problems with the practice of slavery, but what are we Hantish humans supposed to do about it? Only trolls get to vote. We don't make the laws here."

"I guess it's not your problem then."

"Look, no one in the Vale has a slave," Doc said as the buggy bounced on the rutted road. "Not even the magistrate. Things won't be so discriminatory here."

The muddy lane wound down the slope and between narrows created by two large boulders. Doc paused here and made a brief prayer of thanks for a safe journey before continuing. As they drove on through the trees, Jax noticed that there were doors and windows in the hillocks and mountainsides. Not one built structure stood anywhere he could see.

Finally, Doc pulled the horse to a halt outside a burrow with a bright green door.

"You live underground?" Jax said with consternation.

"Of course. There's too much snow here in the winter for regular buildings." He jumped out of the buggy, calling to the burrow, "Mam! I'm home!"

Jax climbed down, and the druid handed him a few light parcels. "Welcome home, Jax."

"By the sweet goddess..." A small woman with gray hair and crinkled lines around bright blue eyes stood on the stone stoop, hands on her hips.

"Hi, Mam." Doc dropped his bags to hug her.

She looked over her son's shoulder at the person, who limped slowly up the path.

"Sweet goddess," she repeated. "Is this a slave?"

"Well, yes. There's his slave collar and all. I figure he can be our assistant."

"You mean he's *our* slave?"

"Yes."

The woman's eyes swept up and down Jax, noting the islish point to his ears and cast of his eyes. With the long practice of an old druid, she recognized broken bones beneath the stiffness of his movements. She turned to frown at her son. "I am ashamed of you. How can you, a druid dedicated to the value of all life, do something so antithetical as purchase a slave?"

"Don't lecture me," Doc said wearily. "You know how over-worked we've been since Adgar left. We need an assistant, and that'll be Jax here."

"Jax." She looked back to where he waited, halfway up the path. "What do you know about healing? Or the call of the goddess? Can you read?"

"I can read Landish, Islish, and Ancient." Jax's tone conveyed a level of affront that was at odds with his beat-up body and ragged clothes. "And I know what healing feels like."

"Ancient?" The woman pursed her lips. "That's unusual, as unusual as your mixed blood. I'm Mother Marith."

"Look, Mam," Doc spoke earnestly. "I figure Jax can work for us for a couple years. When he's worked off what I paid for him, then he can be free."

"Really?"

"Really?" Jax cocked an eyebrow.

"Yes," Doc said with growing exasperation. "Jax may still be a slave, but life with us will certainly be better than what the trolls would have done with him."

After a moment of silence Jax asked: "So, how long will it take me to work off fifty silvers?"

"Fifty silvers!" Marith shrieked. "You paid fifty silvers?" For a long moment she stared into those cold, islish eyes. "He's broken," she muttered, shaking her head. She came down the steps and passed by Jax. "Broken," she said again, walking away through the trees.

Jax watched her go and began to laugh, which hurt.

"She's not really funny," Doc sighed and bent to pick up his bags. "Come on, let's get this gear inside."

Jax stepped reluctantly through the doorway and into the hillside. He expected to smell dirt and sulfur, like in the mine tunnels, but instead the burrow smelled of the herbs that hung in bunches from the ceiling. Jax's bit of Dragon force prickled in response to layers of Mystic that stabilized the walls and held up the roof.

As they carried in the boxes of herbs and medicines that Doc had bought at The Hant, Jax inspected the layout of the burrow. The walls were plastered and painted creamy yellow. A huge hearth stood to the left of the door aiming its warmth into a cozy room. Beyond the fireplace a kitchen sink and shelves of pots and plates were lit by a thick glass window.

Three wing-backed chairs stood in front of the fire. Candlesticks, pentagrams, books and other druidic implements covered the mantle and the floor between the chairs.

Behind the kitchen a large alcove could be curtained off from the rest of the room. Obviously, this was the area that the druids used for their surgery. There was a small cot littered with candle holders, pentagrams, and embroidered cloth. A long wooden table stood under another thick window, holding vials, jars, and glass tubes.

When the buggy was unloaded, Doc directed Jax to the stable around the side of the burrow and vanished up a small flight of stairs. Jax found that the stable was also built into the hill. Inside, a fat, marmalade-colored cat eyed four hens. Jax opened a door in the back of the stable and found it connected to the burrow.

Huffing in the thin air, he brushed Ol' Pol, who squirmed and kicked at him. He wondered how long it took to earn fifty silvers. Jax generally knew how much things cost, that was the Barian merchant in him, but he had no idea how wages were awarded. Not only had he never worked for pay, he had never been subservient to anyone other than trollish overmasters.

He took the inside door back to the main room of the burrow, followed by the cat. Opening other doors, he found a toilet, a root cellar, and at the very back of the house, a door that opened to impenetrable darkness. A very small oil lamp glowed dimly in the tunnel above the druids' lintel. He closed that door quickly. Returning to the main room he stood a moment staring out the window at the spring sunshine.

"Jax?"

"Yes?" Jax walked to the stairway and looked up.

"Here's some stuff you can use for bedding." Doc tossed down a cloth-filled mattress, some blankets, a down comforter and pillows. "There's a niche under the stairs you can use for a bed. It'll be warm, and I think it's big enough for you."

Jax pressed his face into the soft bedding. It was fluffy and smelled gently of some sweet herb. The scent stirred old memories so deep that specifics did not surface, just a feeling of security and peace.

He opened the cupboard under the stairs. It took him two tries to figure out how to manage the various items of bedding, because he'd never made a bed before, never sheathed a pillow in a case nor used a fitted sheet. Once the quilts and blankets were arranged the tabby settled herself atop them staring at him smugly.

Marith swung back into the house and came to see Jax's progress.

"I see you've met Jelly."

"The cat?"

Marith nodded.

Doc stomped down the stairs, and Marith turned to glare at him. He ignored her and went to arrange his new herbs in the surgery.

"Look at this lovely valerian root I found, Mam," he said in a conciliatory voice.

"Don't try to wriggle out of this, son."

"I'm not wriggling," Doc insisted, still messing with his herbs. "We needed an assistant, and if you really do take this crazy trip of yours this summer, someone has to go with you. Besides, when I saw Jax up on that auction block with that wicked grin of his, something moved me. I didn't think he should get bought by some beastly troll."

"So he got bought by a beastly druid instead."

"Mam." Doc set down the root. He glanced at Jax then turned his blue eyes to his mother. "Mam, I think the goddess wanted me to buy him."

Marith's face registered nothing but skepticism.

"Really," Doc explained quickly. "When I saw him standing up there, I felt something compelling me. I knew I had to get him. I felt he needed us, and we needed him."

The skepticism had faded from Marith's face, but it was plenty evident on the lad's features. She turned to him now. "Why would the goddess want you here, Jax?"

"I don't think the goddess gives a damn about me."

Marith considered him for a moment. "Perhaps living with druids will change your mind about that." The wrinkles deepened around her blue eyes. "And Doc is right. We do need help. I hope being here will be better than serving trolls."

"It is."

Doc strove to change the subject. "I'm starved," he said. "Why don't we go 'round to the pub for supper?"

Marith gave her son a sly smile. "You want to get this all out in the open right away, eh?"

"Will they let me in?" Jax asked. "Or should I expect to wait at the hitching post?"

Marith stared, again taken aback by the aristocratic tone so at odds with the slave's bedraggled figure.

"Kajjon wouldn't let Jax in the inn at Steppash," Doc explained a little grimly. "But Aric is different."

"Why don't you just set me free?" Jax suggested. "I'll stay and work until the fifty silvers are paid off, but then you won't have to worry about the stigma of owning a slave, and I won't have to be one."

"Did you say *stigma?*" Doc marveled at the slave's elevated vocabulary.

Marith simply answered. "It's against the law to set a slave free until you've owned it for a full year."

"Slaves are people. Not things."

"Him, her, them." Marith frowned.

"Look, Jax." Doc spoke gently. "This is going to be at least as awkward for me as it is for you. Let's get cleaned up and go on down to the pub so everyone can get a look at you and so I can explain."

Getting cleaned up involved shaving. "We keep clean-shaven to mollify the trolls," Doc explained. "Here, you can use this razor and there's the lather."

Jax looked at the implements. He'd never done this himself. Valets had taken care of his grooming as a prince, and the trolls' rough ministrations sufficed while he was a slave.

"I don't much care about mollifying the trolls," he noted.

"I suppose you don't," Doc said, lifting his chin and scraping away the lather. "But we do it anyway."

Jax watched him. "I don't know how."

"That's why you have so many scars," Doc quipped.

Jax gave him half a grin. "I don't know how to shave either."

Doc wiped the last of the lather off his face. "Ah. I'm sorry, lad. You were awfully young when you were taken, weren't you?"

His face now covered with the foam, Jax didn't clarify. He carefully followed Doc's directions, peering at himself in the small mirror, thinking that the man who stared back at him was a sorry mess.

"We're ready, Mam!" Doc called up the stairs, handing Jax one of his own cloaks.

Marith came down the stairs, looked up at the slave, and was struck by the straight lines of his face. "Well," she said, and headed out the door.

Jax put on the cloak, which was too short for him, and followed the two druids out into the twilit streets of the Vale. He was beginning to wonder if life with Doc and Marith really would be easier. At least with the trolls his position, his loyalties, and his hatreds had been clear.

17

Jax limped behind Doc and Marith down a stone-paved path through the deepening twilight. He noticed doors and windows in most of the small hills and hummocks. Other people greeted Doc and Marith easily and stared at the stranger with them. Jax had never spent much time in country villages. Although he had ridden through them in Kordon, his destination had always been manors or castles. Even then, his visits to the country had been brief, for his life had revolved around the capital cities of the Knownlands.

Aric's Pub was delved into a large hill that also housed a bakery. Inside, two huge fireplaces roared at opposite ends of a long room. Benches and tables stood around the floor, and a long darkwood bar curved along the back wall.

Several of the customers hailed the druids as they walked into the pub. Everyone stared openly at Jax.

Doc and Marith took a table by one of the fires.

"Ah," Doc sighed comfortably. "Sit down, Jax. This is our table, and we'll make sure it'll be your table now, too."

Jax sat, looking around the room. A few trolls stood drinking from heavy steins at the bar, but most of the clientele was human.

"Doc! You're back." A thin man emerged from the kitchen behind the bar, carrying steaming plates of food.

"Hi, Aric!" Doc leaned over the table towards Jax. "Aric makes the best ale for miles around, and Mam Aric is absolutely the best cook."

"I see." Aware that almost everyone in the pub was staring at him, Jax squared his shoulders and lifted his head from old habit. He'd often been stared at as a prince.

Aric returned to the table bearing three mugs of black ale. He folded his lanky body into a chair. "Hello Mother Marith. Who's your new friend?"

"Let Doc tell you."

Doc drank deeply from his mug. "This is Jax."

"Jax." Aric smiled at him, noting the bandages. "Looks like you need a good druid."

"Indeed."

"Kordish, are you? I recognize the accent. Where's your master? Or did they leave you to heal with the druids?"

"Doc is my master."

"What?" Aric sat up and glared at Doc in disbelief. "Why'd you beat him? Is he dangerous?"

Marith watched Jax grin.

Doc squirmed in his chair. "I didn't beat him, Aric. He came that way."

"You bought him like that?"

"He's actually healed up quite a bit. But yes, I sort of bought him while I was up at The Hant."

By this time a young woman had come out of the kitchen bearing four platters of roasted apples and potatoes, sprinkled with goat cheese and thyme. She set them on the table and stood back to consider the stranger.

"How do you *sort of* buy a slave?" She had a dimple when she smiled. "Maybe I'd like to buy one."

Jax looked up at her, intrigued by her deep blue, almost violet eyes.

"All right, all right," Doc grumbled. "I happened to be passing through the square while the auction was in progress. I saw Jax up there and figured we could use the help. So, I bought him."

"How much did you pay?" Aric asked, tucking into his dinner.

"Fifty silvers."

Aric swallowed and looked at Jax with new interest. "That's a lot of mugs of ale."

The serving girl flounced back to the kitchen. "Too pricey for me."

Aric sat back in his chair. "You know I'm not supposed to serve slaves," he told Doc. "It says so right on my license." He motioned towards a stained parchment pinned to the wall near the kitchen door.

Disliking the direction of this conversation, Jax ate voraciously.

"Stop a minute, Jax." Marith took the plate and pint of ale away from him. He sat back and swallowed. She stood up, walked around the table and put the food down again in front of him. "Now *you* haven't served him, Aric; *I* have."

Jax fell upon the food before it could be taken away again.

With varying degrees of discomfort, the other three recognized the years of hardship behind Jax's desperate eating. Aric gave a resigned shrug. "I'll let you take it up with the magistrate, Mother."

"Vloggan hasn't won an argument against Mam yet." Doc took a long pull of his ale.

"And he won't this time either," Marith said firmly. She considered Jax again and his now empty plate. "Try the ale." She smiled.

Jax could have eaten more but was afraid to push his luck. He took a sip of the thick, dark ale.

"It's bitter."

"Aye, and lovely too," Doc said with a beatific smile.

Unconvinced, Jax took another sip.

"It packs a wallop," Marith warned.

Aric was still watching Jax. "I see a lot of folk here, Jax. You speak like the Kordish tourists, but you ain't as pale as them."

Jax set down his mug. "I'm half Barian."

"Never seen an isle before." Aric's eyes roved up and down Jax with frank curiosity. "You do have pointy ears, don't you?"

"And I like boats," Jax said pointedly.

"Yikes! That is frightening. Maybe you should tie him up, Doc." Aric laughed.

"Tried that, but it didn't work." Doc grumbled.

The conversation turned to local business that had gone on while Doc had been away. Marith joined a group of women at another table. Jax finished the ale, watching the two druids interact with other Vale locals. Clearly, the people here respected and cared for their druids. Just about everyone in the pub talked to one or the other of them.

The serving girl brought two more steins of ale and set them both in front of Doc and watched as the druid pushed one of them to Jax. "I'm Dylith. Who are you?"

"Jax."

"Jax What?"

"Just Jax."

"Well, welcome to Hilsen Vale, Just Jax." Her smile grew wider.

Aric stood up sharply. "All right now, Dyl. Get on to work."

Dylith winked a violet eye at Jax and swirled away.

"I'd better get to work too," Aric sighed. "With all my girls flirting, somebody's got to run the business."

"It's the goddess' way," Doc shrugged.

"That's what I get for complaining to a druid." Aric marched off to the kitchen.

Doc raised his full mug of ale to Jax. "Cheers, lad. Welcome to Hilsen Vale."

Jax raised his glass in response.

"Hi, Doc!" A pair of nyads came into the pub and ambled over to Doc's table.

"Florin. Borrel. How've you been?" Doc smiled warmly at the two.

Jax had not seen many nyads since they were primarily forest dwellers and did not frequent the coast. For once Jax found himself staring as much as stared at. The two tall, brown-skinned, brown-eyed, brown-haired creatures sat down at the table. The woman wore sturdy leather leggings and a tunic. Her long hair hung in a thick braid down her back. The other, a man, was dressed more simply in cloth pants and woolen sweater, much like Doc.

"You bought a slave, Doc?" The male nyad stared at Jax.

"I'm fine, Borrel, thanks. And you?"

The woman grinned as Aric ran by, setting two more mugs of black ale on the table. "I'm Florin Starrish. This is my brother Borrel."

"You've got some Dragon force!" Borrel announced enthusiastically.

"I wondered if you would notice." Doc smiled. "Allow me to introduce my new assistant, Jax."

Florin turned back to Doc: "Your new *assistant*? That slave collar is for real, isn't it?"

"Oh, yes. It's for real," Doc answered.

Jax sat back to listen to Doc tell their story once again. He watched the two nyads curiously as they listened to the druid. Dylith walked by and smirked at him.

Borrel gulped some of his ale and leaned eagerly across the table towards Jax. "Tell me about your magic."

"I can light a fire and play a tune, but that's about it."

"Really? That's it?"

"The rare presentiment that I'd usually rather not know about."

"Maybe I could teach you more?"

Jax shook his head. Borrel looked disappointed, but Jax remained silent. When he was five, Jax's magical talent burst forth during a squabble with his brother. In a fit of inarticulate rage, young Jax had set Bryx's small sailboat on fire. Servants doused the flames and hauled their bawling prince off to see the Barian Royal Dragon. The old Dragon soon determined that Jax's magic lent him the occasional presentiment, the predictable Dragon talent for music, and the ability to start fires. It had taken longer to keep him from lighting them at inappropriate times.

"Borrel's been studying Dragon force for years," Florin explained. "Last summer his tutor died, leaving him to study on his own."

Jax had been carefully considering the two nyads. "Are you twins?" Jax asked, looking from one nyad to the other.

Florin smiled. "Yep."

Jax answered her grin with one of his own. "I've never met a nyad before. I thought you all lived off in the forest."

"Well, we've never met an isle before," Borrel noted.

"Most nyads do live in the forest," Florin said. "But we live here in town."

"Why?"

"Because," Borrel answered, "Florin was in love with a human, and I needed a tutor for my magic."

"Now I take tourists trekking into the mountains," Florin continued, "and Borrel helps me, when he's not studying."

Jax noted that no human seemed to be involved with Florin now.

"Trekking? Lots of people like to do this?"

"I take about twenty groups every summer."

Dylith sauntered by. "How do you like our Vale Ale, Just Jax?"

Unused to these easy interactions, Jax looked down into his half-empty mug realizing it had been a long time since he'd been among free people. "I suppose I'll get used to it."

"You will," Dylith assured him with a warm smile. "The more you drink it, the better you like it."

Borrel speculatively followed Jax's gaze, which followed the barmaid as she went to serve other customers. The nyad's white teeth flashed against his dark skin. "I hope you like it here in the Vale, Jax."

Realizing he was caught, Jax's wolf grin slid into place. "It's better than the mines."

"The mines?" Borrel frowned. "The *iron* mines?"

Jax nodded.

"Whew," Florin said. "I didn't think people got out of there in one piece."

"They don't," Jax answered in a voice so factual that no one else spoke for a long time.

Jax couldn't sleep in the niche under the stairs. It wasn't long enough for him, and the cramped space reminded him too much of Oblek's pit.

In the dark he pulled the bedding out and tossed it beneath a window near the bottom of the stairs. He took some deep breaths, staring up at a crescent moon, listing for himself the many differences between the druid's burrow and the dark, dank hole of Cave Three. Eventually he slept.

Marith came quietly down the stairs as the dawn first began to lighten the sky. She stumbled over something on the floor. "Sweet goddess," she said. "What are you doing there?"

"I was sleeping." Jax sat up and shivered as the down comforter fell from his bare shoulders. He made the fire bloom.

"But why on the floor?"

"The niche is too close." He pulled the quilt around his shoulders.

"Too close?"

"Like the mines. I was immured, Marith."

Marith considered Jax for a few moments. In the brighter firelight she'd seen the scars before he'd pulled up the blanket. *Immured.*

She took a key from her pocket, unlocked the inner door to the stable, and went out. Jax tossed a couple logs on the fire and lay back on his blankets. Jelly meowed petulantly as Jax's movements disturbed her nest on his legs. A moment later Marith returned, holding two eggs aloft triumphantly.

"The hens have been at work today." She placed her treasure gently on the kitchen table.

"You and Doc can have these for breakfast." She bustled briskly around the room, gathering up certain odds and ends. "I'm off to do the sun salutations." This time she unlocked the front door and went out into the gray dawn.

Sun salutations. Jax had not thought about the goddess' high holidays for the past three years, much less the more quotidian practices. But life with druids would revolve around these rituals.

Relishing the softness of the quilts, he had decided to go back to sleep, much to Jelly's satisfaction, when Doc clopped down the stairs.

"Whoa!" Doc stopped just short of stepping on the bundle in the blankets. "Why are you sleeping there?"

"I am not sleeping anymore." Jax rolled onto his back and looked up at the druid.

"I bet you gave Mam a start, didn't you?" The druid bundled himself into a fur-lined cloak against the cold spring morning. "I'll run down to the bakery and get some of Ma Vlarn's sweet rolls. You can fry the eggs and make some tea."

The lock clicked behind him as Doc left the house. Jax realized they weren't taking any chances with him.

He rose, splashed himself with cold water and pulled on his worn trollish cast-off clothes. Returning to the pump, he filled the kettle and set it over the fire. Raised as a prince, Jax had never cooked anything in his life. He did not know how to fry an egg or brew tea.

After thoughtfully regarding the black strands of tea with a cocked eyebrow, he scooped one small spoonful into the teapot. The kettle had begun to steam, but not boil. Impatient to have his tea, Jax poured the tepid water over the leaves and left them to steep while he worked on the eggs.

He found a saucepan on the shelf and cracked the eggs into it. Two yellow yokes peered back up at him. He stirred them with a spoon, wondering if he should fish out the bits of shell.

Unable to get the small pieces of shells out of the eggy slime, he gave up and set the pan over the fire. Five minutes later, he burned his hand on the pot handle as he removed the eggs from the flames. They were brown around the edges and stuck fast to the bottom of the pan. He was trying to scrape them out onto plates when Doc unlocked the door and came in with a blast of chilly air.

"Eggs ready?" He set a steaming package of fresh rolls on the little kitchen table.

"I think so."

Doc poked at the black and brown eggs on the plate and peered at the weak and lukewarm tea. "Is this how you eat in Baria?" Doc forsook the eggs and concentrated on the rolls.

"Not at all."

Doc was puzzled by the disparity between this answer and the way Jax ate every scrap of burnt egg.

"You like burnt eggs?"

Jax looked up from his empty plate. He saw the confusion on the druid's face. "I like being fed."

"Here." Doc pushed his own plate of eggs towards Jax. "You're welcome to mine." Jax polished them off.

"Maybe I'll do the cooking tomorrow and let you fetch the bread." Doc offered Jax a roll.

The honeyed bun filled his mouth with such sweetness that tears came to Jax's eyes. "I'll be happy to fetch these buns every day."

"Self-defense." Doc muttered.

Jax's own defenses no longer seemed effective. Here, among these decent people, Jax could not retreat to the insulating aloofness and open disrespect he had used with the trolls. Nor were these "his" people in the desperate way of the other slaves in the mines.

Acting as an assistant to the druids either in their rituals or in their healing was never physically demanding, but these duties required things from him that were harder to give than mindless labor. Often, Jax had to sit with families while Doc or Marith worked with a patient. In these situations, he offered what caring words he could think of and consoled them as best he could, but always he knew that no matter how upset they were, or how terrible their loss, worse places and harsher deaths existed in the Hantland. This left him feeling dishonest.

After a few weeks, he realized that by forcing himself to pretend sympathy, he had actually come to feel it. He knew that their pain was no less real for being felt here in the Vale instead of in the iron mines. This thought brought him no comfort, because it seemed to belittle the horrendous experience of the slave pens.

By the time the last of the snow melted from the streets of Hilsen Vale, Jax could walk without a limp, use his right hand, and breathe without an ache in his chest. He learned that the whole village was connected by tunnels, like the one at the back of the druids' burrow so that they could meet and visit when winter snows buried the paths and blocked the doors. The tunnels were only rarely used in the warmer months because people relished the ability to get outside. Jax understood that sentiment.

As tulips and daffodils glowed above the mud, Jax wove his way into the fabric of Vale life. He had received plenty of stares at first, both because most people had never seen either an islish, or even half islish person, and because they wanted to know more about this fellow who had somehow convinced their druid to buy a slave.

Many of the children wanted to touch Jax's pointy ears, not believing they could be real. With the unconscious arrogance of his aristocratic upbringing, Jax resorted back to the manners he had been so thoroughly taught as a young prince. He boldly met the confused stares and took refuge from awkward situations in politeness or sarcasm.

Jax stood with Borrel exchanging jokes one evening in the pub, when Jax was suddenly drenched by a tankard of ale.

"You!" the village notary sputtered, his now-empty tankard dangling from his fingers. "You, slave, you spilled my ale!"

"I didn't spill it," Jax laughed, looking down at his wet shirt and trousers. "But I did catch it."

Others in the crowd laughed.

"Slave!" the notary snarled. "I demand that you replace my ale!"

Jax spread his arms. "You're welcome to lick it off me."

"You're impertinent, slave!"

"I'm Impertinent Jax."

"I might lick it off your impertinence," Dylith offered, as she pushed through the laughing crowd.

The notary, noting that the folk of the village were unsympathetic to him and his lost drink, threw his mug at the barmaid. The last of the ale splashed across her blouse.

"I'll return the favor," Jax offered her. The crowd laughed and offered several graphic suggestions to both Jax and Dylith.

After that no one cared to refer to him as anything other than Jax. Soon the townsfolk were used to seeing him out on various errands for the druids, with them in the pub, or acting as their assistant in various medical or druidical procedures.

He did his best to avoid the few trolls in the Vale. Marith had a conversation with the town magistrate. She told Doc and Jax about it at dinner one night. "He said we couldn't let our slave wear free-folk clothes."

Jax looked down at the shirt and trousers that Marith had made for him. They were cut from unbleached homespun, but at least they fit him.

"Am I supposed to walk around naked?" he asked.

"No," she said rising from her chair. "Viscal had these in a box in the back of his store." She went to the surgery and brought out a bundle of fabric tied with brown string. "He said he keeps some slavecloth on hand in case a traveling troll with a slave needed something."

She untied the string and shook out a pair of cast-off trollish trousers, two shirts, one of them in a flamboyant flower print, and a sweater. "Try them on, Jax. If they're too big, I'll take them in for you."

"I'd rather go naked."

Marith had gone back to the surgery and came out again, this time with a box. "I figured you'd feel that way, so I got you these too." She opened the box. Inside were a pair of new soft leather boots.

Jax ran his fingers over the soft leather. "What will you tell the magistrate about these?"

"I'll tell him you need to have proper footwear to fulfill your duties as our assistant. You can't trek all over the Knownlands in those wooden clogs."

Jax pushed the boots away. "I'll go barefoot."

"Why?"

"Because I am your slave."

Doc pushed the boots back towards Jax. "Don't be silly, son. You'll want these."

Jax put the clothes and boots in the cupboard under the stairs. The next morning, he dressed in the garish shirt and tied the brown string around his waist to hold the trousers on. It wasn't until they were a half mile on the path around the lake that Marith noticed his bare feet.

"Why aren't you wearing those boots?"

"They don't match the shirt."

Marith considered him for a moment then turned to walk on. "Standing on principle only hurts yourself."

"Yes, Master."

Marith chose to ignore him.

Two nights after a full moon Doc, Marith, and Jax all headed to the pub for some well-earned mugs of Aric's Vale Ale. A nasty spring 'flu had swept through the population and only abated last week, but then it was time for Beltane, which was followed a few nights later by the full moon ceremonies, keeping Doc and Marith up late even more nights.

Inside, the pub bubbled with the voices of tourists and locals. Several groups had pulled chairs outside to enjoy the fine spring evening. The druids and Jax joined Borrel and Florin at the bar.

Jax leaned across the polished darkwood and waved to Dylith. She smiled saucily when she saw him and sauntered over, carrying mugs of ale for him and the two druids.

"I haven't seen you since Beltane." She smiled.

Jax lifted her hand and kissed the long fingers that had so wonderfully found him staring into the big bonfire on May Eve and taken him to several places of holy joy. He smiled into her beautiful eyes.

Dylith leaned her elbows on the bar and gazed up at him. This action gave him a lovely view down the front of her wide-necked white blouse. Jax leaned his own elbows on the bar. Their faces were very close. Her fingers drifted from his lips down to touch the steel collar around his neck.

"Does this bother you?"

He shrugged.

"Is it heavy?"

"Figuratively." Slowly he rubbed the smooth skin of her arm.

Dylith still fingered the slave collar. "What does that mean?"

"It means I don't like being enslaved."

"Dylith!" Aric stood at the tap with his hands full of tankards. "Come help me, like you're supposed to!"

Dylith winked. He squeezed her hand as she pulled away.

"Are you through flirting?" Florin grinned.

"Never."

"You ought to stop flirting and get down to business, by the goddess," Marith suggested.

"Ah, springtime," Doc said gloomily. "It makes me miss Adgar."

"He'll be back before we leave for Dishroc, won't he?" Florin asked.

"Dishroc?" Jax asked. "You're going to Dishroc? In the Nomad Range?"

"Yes, Dishroc. We're all going," Marith said, her eyes sparkling with excitement. "Doc told you, didn't he?"

Jax looked from mother to son in disbelief. "No. No one said anything to me about Dishroc."

"I told you that Mam had crazy travel plans." Doc took a long drink from his glass.

"Yes, but I didn't know she was thinking of going to Dishroc." Jax leaned back against the bar amazed. "And I didn't realize that I was expected to go along as well."

"It's why I bought you those boots that you refuse to wear." Marith noted. "We'll leave after Lughnasad. Florin and Borrel are coming too. Doc and Adgar will stay here, so the Vale won't be left without any druids."

"None of us has Mystic. Are we going to sleep in a tent?"

"Yes. I have a nice big one."

Jax blinked at her. "Seriously? How long do you expect to be gone?"

Marith shrugged, an adventurous light gleaming from her blue eyes. "I expect we'll be back about a year from now."

"Dragons," he swore grimly.

Marith raised her mug. "A toast to our journeys together!"

Pointedly, Jax sat his mug on the bar and did not drink. Marith watched him with some exasperation, but Borrel soon changed the subject and had everyone talking about the sprite who had moved to town that spring. Jax's thoughts continued to roll over and around one another. He was angry that the druids should make such sweeping plans without consulting him, but then he was just a slave: there was no reason they should discuss plans with him. Slaves went wherever their masters ordered.

Marith went home after one beer, and Doc followed her after three. Jax stood around brooding until Aric hollered out last call, then he waited outside the kitchen door in the light of a waning moon, frowning at the way the peaks blocked off so much of the sky. At least he would be leaving at the end of the summer. But Dishroc! Dishroc was in the desert, even farther from the sea than the Vale.

Dylith slipped her arms around his waist. She followed his gaze up to the stars. "Mmm. Lovely."

"Better now that you're here."

Dylith took his hand and led him into the soft summer night.

18

Lord Foby, sweating into his silk shirt, stepped through the open doors onto the dark balcony, took a deep breath of the summer night, and blessed the silence after the loud music and laughter of the ball in the room behind him.

Except that it wasn't silent out here either. Soft voices mumbled from the balcony on the floor below.

"That half-isle couldn't have been him, your Grace," a voice with a thick northern accent grumbled through the night. "That half-isle was a slave."

"It is unthinkable that our prince would end up as a slave." The Duke of Midipex's alto voice rose softly on the night breeze. Foby stopped breathing.

"Anyway, that slave was beat near to death and sold for bait."

"Bait?"

"Aye, my lord. The trolls love to hunt for monsters on the Hantish steppes. They use old or dying slaves for bait. The monsters kill the bait then the trolls kill the monsters."

"I see."

"You want me to keep my eyes out for your Lost Prince, then, my lord?"

"No." Foby heard the jingle of coins as a purse changed hands. "No. I think three years of looking is enough. Thank you."

"Thank you, my lord. It's been my honor."

Foby pushed through the rainbow crowd of drunken, dancing nobles. He found Tallyn hiccupping with laughter over some story Carden Yemmel was telling.

"Come with me, your Highness." He pulled her arm.

"What?" Tallyn frowned. The look on Foby's face hit her like a bucket of cold water.

"What?" Carden mimicked sourly to no one, as he watched Tallyn and that damned Lord Foby slip through a side door.

Foby wouldn't speak until they reached Tallyn's sitting room. There he told her all he had heard.

"You're sure it was Midipex?"

"He has a distinctive voice."

"Yes, he does." Tallyn stood by the open window, fanning herself. "So apparently our lord chancellor has been paying people to watch for Jax in The Hant." She paused thoughtfully. "I wonder if he has spies elsewhere in the Knownlands."

"I wonder if that half-isle was Jax after all," Foby said quietly.

Tallyn turned to look at him. "How could it be? A prince as a slave?"

"It would explain why no one can seem to find him. Who'd think to look among the trolls' slaves?"

For several moments Tallyn considered this. "Let's get a magician and scry again."

Tallyn and Foby had time to share a cool glass of wine while the servants extracted the royal Mystic from the lord's chamber where he had happily anticipated ending the evening.

His robes somewhat askew, Carte Serge presented himself to his crown princess and her current favorite, Lord Foby of Rippfell.

"We want you to scry for Prince Jax again." The princess explained.

Serge sighed. When Prince Jax had first disappeared three years ago, the princess had insisted on scrys from both him and the Royal Dragon almost daily. All of them were frustrated and baffled by the black water that greeted each search. But as time passed and no magician, priest, or priestess could explain this phenomenon, the princess had asked less and less often. Serge had felt her scorn for his ability grow with each failure.

Now he set up his silver bowl, poured the water, centered himself and drew on his magic. The clear water in the bowl swirled and darkened, as if someone had added ink.

Tallyn and Foby watched the familiar result.

"So, we think he still lives?"

Serge swept his hand across the bowl and the water cleared. "I believe so, my lady. But I can't be sure."

"Of course not." Tallyn's voice was barely civil.

Serge gathered his implements and left the room grumpily. He hoped that Lord Phynn would still be in an accommodating mood.

Tallyn shook her head as the door closed behind the magician. "I think we have to agree with Midipex's man. That half-islish slave must be dead by now, so he can't have been Jax."

Foby had used bait to hunt for bear and boar among the wildlands of the Rippsmarch. With newfound horror at this practice, he gathered Tallyn into his arms. "Sweet goddess, I hope not."

"And finally, Admiral, we've had a curious report from one of Rillt's schooners that the sorry excuse for a ferry boat that the trolls were running up on Hanter Lake sank in the last Rising."

Hix Sharkin, Lord Admiral of the Barian Fleet, pushed himself out of his chair, turned to look out the stern lights of his cabin and stretched. "That's no surprise," he said, his spine cracking audibly. "Damned spritish-built boat."

"Yes, sir. The thing is that the trolls are apparently blaming the wreck on the slave who sailed the boat for them."

Hix turned, waiting.

"It was a half-islish slave."

"Steward!" Hix's voice boomed from one end of the great ship to the other.

"My lord?"

"My cloak. And the launch. Signal the sealord that I request an audience. Immediately."

Sealord Bryx grimaced as he watched the gray head of his lord admiral push through the crowds on the Floating Island of Jeff and make its way across the green lawn. What the dragons did the damned old Isle want with him now? He had already agreed to go to their stupid Gather again.

A few minutes later the door crashed open and Hix, red-faced and breathing hard, blew into the room like a hurricane.

Bryx leaned back in his chair and watched the wild swings of Hix's bow. "Yes, my Lord Admiral?"

"Your Majesty listen to this! We've received a report that a half-isle was sailing a boat for the trolls up on Hanter Lake."

Bryx sat up. "Really?"

"Yes, Sire."

"Interesting. I too have received a report of a half-isle slave near The Hant."

Hix put his hands on the sealord's desk and leaned forward. "By your leave, I'll go at once to investigate."

Bryx smiled. "No. After the Gather, Hix."

"But the Gather's in the South Seas this year," Hix sputtered.

"Right. And we have planned the trip to visit the Dranstyllians and Jezellians afterwards."

"But—."

"But, no. You and I and the lords and ladies of the Floating Islands need to make those trade visits."

Hix had regained his breath, but his face became even more empurpled.

Bryx raised a hand. "I know. I know you want my brother back. I know you miss having him as your vice admiral, but I think he's dead, and our economy will be dead too if we don't find some new markets and find them quickly."

As lord admiral, Hix had a close view of the effects of Barian poverty, visible in broken spars and frayed ropes, and the results in shipwreck and tragedy. Indeed, he had been one of the leading proponents of this summer's embassies to the countries around the Southern Seas.

"We will go to The Hant," Bryx said finally, his round, Kordish eyes holding the slanted sea blue gaze of the lord admiral. "We will go after the Gather and after our trade mission."

Hix shook his head. "It will have to be after the Fall Rising then."

"Yes, I suppose so."

Hix pushed away from the desk and glanced out the wide windows at the view of the Floating Islands and the ships moored in the sun-spangled harbor.

"But meanwhile, the poor lad..."

"My *poor* brother is the cause of our troubles," Bryx noted succinctly. "He's been away for six Risings. We can surely do without him for one more."

"Yes, Sire. But then, let's go find the rascal." Hix again executed his windy salute and left, the door slamming behind him.

Rascal or rogue? Bryx wondered. From a drawer he pulled a lavender envelope. It glittered subtly as he opened it and read again.

"*...believe I've found your brother, Prince Javix Sharkin....*" He traced the graceful script, having already memorized the words. Unlikely as it seemed, Klaris de Farsouth was clearly convinced that his brother was, in some incomprehensible fashion, enslaved by the trolls.

Bryx walked to a window and looked down upon an inner courtyard, one that was sheltered from the constant sea breezes. Woodland scenes danced in bas-relief along the walls. Bryx smiled as he remembered Klaris standing there, shyly wondering if he liked her work. In fact, he liked everything about her.

He ran the sparkling letter over his lips, the letter she had sent to him during the last Rising. Yes, they'd go to The Hant and hopefully confirm that Jax was dead. Dead, so Bryx wouldn't have to deliver him to the Kordish. And after that, he'd sail to Sageham and visit the delicate little Farsouthian princess.

19

As the snowfields shrank slowly into the shadows of the highest peaks, the Vale began to fill up with tourists. Florin was often gone, guiding groups of visitors along the high paths to beautiful views and stunning waterfalls. The additional population of tourists kept the druids busy too, by constantly spraining ankles or catching colds from underestimating the hard frosts of Vale nights. The druids also spent the warmer months visiting tiny outlying settlements and farmsteads that had been isolated by the deep winter snows.

These treks often took all the long spring day. Usually Jax, carrying the pack full of medical supplies, followed Marith, who bounded along the steep paths like a mountain goat, talking the whole time. The rocky paths were hard on his bare feet, but he still refused to wear the boots. Between his tender feet and the high altitude, he struggled at first to keep up with her, but as his soles toughened and lungs adjusted to the thin, high-altitude air, he began to join the conversation. Marith's stories about her patients and friends in and around the Vale gently invited Jax to respond with anecdotes from his own life. Without realizing it, he reopened thought patterns that had long been closed.

After Marith had discussed a young farm boy's broken ankle, Jax told her about the time he had broken his arm in a fall from a horse. Mam Aric made a comment on his accent that led to a conversation about how he had first learned Landish when he arrived in Kree as a boy of six. A story about Doc as a youngster reminded Jax of various escapades he and his cousin Tallyn had engineered.

One afternoon while Marith was assisting a woman giving birth, she heard the music of a dragonpipe coming from the room where Jax was keeping the woman's older child entertained. Later, after the birth of the baby, Marith emerged to find that it was Jax playing the instrument. She stopped, staring.

Jax finished the piece and handed the pipe back to the boy. "There you go. That's the kind of music we make in Baria."

"Play some more!" The child handed the instrument back to Jax. He looked at Marith who nodded and began to pack her things back into her pack.

Several songs later, Jax and Marith finally stepped from the cottage into the cool blue evening and began the long walk down the mountain and back to the Vale.

"You play well," Marith said.

Jax shrugged under his pack. "It's the Dragon in me." He did not mention that as a young prince his inherent talent had been rigorously exercised.

When Jax awoke the next morning, he found a dusty lute on the kitchen table. Its strings were warped, and some were broken. He picked it up and rubbed off some of the dust. Doc clomped down the stairs.

"Where did you find that old thing?"

"Sitting here on the table." Jax continued to fiddle with the instrument.

"I think a patient gave that to Mam years ago." Doc filled the teakettle and set it on the cold fireplace.

Jax glanced up for a second and the fire roared into life. He strummed the lute and winced at the sour sound. Again, he fiddled with the knobs and plucked at the strings. Finally, he strummed again.

"Wow," said Doc, slicing some bread. "I've never heard that thing sound so good."

Jax continued to strum and pick. This lute was not as fine as the instruments he had enjoyed as a prince, but he loved to feel the music coming from his fingers.

An hour later when Marith returned from the sun salutations, she found Jax and Doc sitting in the morning sun on the front step. Doc quietly smoked his pipe while Jax played. Without a word, Marith poured herself a cup of tea and joined them, listening to the music Jax could make.

The music soothed Jax, just as it had helped him weather the dark of Oblek's pit. He felt it mend some of the rawness the mines had left within him. The fingers on his right hand ached, but he didn't want to stop.

The sun climbed higher and burned with its high-altitude intensity. Jax finally set the lute down. The music had taken his thoughts back to iron mines. He wondered how his people in Cave Three were faring on this lovely summer morning. Had that Corvyd fellow stepped up to care for the others? He flexed his newly healed fingers and caught Marith's blue eyes watching him. "Thank you, Marith," he said softly.

She smiled and stood up. "No, Jax. Thank you. It's a joy to have music in the morning. But now we must be off. We're going out to the Merffystead today. It's not far, but the path is steep."

As she climbed the steep, narrow path up the rocky mountainside, Marith listened to Jax's steps behind her. She knew, even if Jax did not, that he was finding himself again as he remembered his past.

Remembering his past, however, made Jax more aware of the anomalies of his present. Once again, he knew that he had been a prince, but was now a slave. So while he began to relax into his duties with the druids and even enjoy his interactions with the people in the Vale, the imprisoning landscape still clotted his dreams, and the inevitable trip to Dishroc still rubbed raw against his desire for self-determination.

"Mother Marith! Doc!" Someone was banging on the door that led to the tunnels. "Open up! You're needed!"

Jax sat up and conjured a light on the small bear grease lamp. He rose from his blankets on the floor and went to the tunnel door.

Viscal Crane, raised his lantern to look up at him. "Ah. Jax."

Jax's nose wrinkled at the thick smell of dirt. "You want the druids, Mr. Crane?"

"Oh. Yes. Listen, Lagga's Canyon Lodge collapsed. You and the druids have to come. People are wounded, maybe dead."

"We're coming, Viscal," Marith called from above.

Jax's stomach turned at the idea that one of the borrows had collapsed, but he pulled on his own clothes and went to the surgery to gather supplies into their satchels.

"Let's go!" Doc trotted down the stairs.

Jax handed him one satchel and shouldered another. All together they headed into the tunnel. Jax had only taken the tunnels once, when they'd gone to the pub in the midst of a late spring blizzard. Other folk, most carrying lanterns like Viscal, now joined them all flowing like water through a straw to the site of Lagga's Lodge.

"Tell us what happened." Marith took Viscal's arm.

"Old Grag, who can't sleep you know, since his husband died, he said he saw water running under the lodge's front door. Hot water, because it steamed into the night."

"Lagga always lets the hotspring water flow freely." Doc noted.

"Well, I think someone fell asleep without turning it off. So the water overflowed and eroded the supports for the whole lodge." Viscal shook his head in despair at the thoughtlessness of tourists in general. "The whole place just crumbled."

"I felt the impact at home," Viscal continued. "When I ran outside and heard the screams, well..." He paused for a moment, shaken. "Gragg was out there yelling that a flood had caused it. I figured you and Doc would be needed."

As they got closer to the site of the disaster, the tunnel became more humid. Jax wasn't sure if this was the result of the increasing crowd or the hot water that caused the disaster. Either way, he was relieved when the crowd eventually left the tunnels and came out into the Hilsen Mercantile. From there they plunged into the cold night air and surveyed the crumpled hill that had been Lagga's Canyon Lodge. Muddy water still streamed from the rocks and ran steaming towards the lake.

Three people with Mystic desperately wove their magic together to raise the muddy earth. Jax and Borrel and others like them with Dragon force, stood aside creating light. Villagers and tourists without magic took shovels and picks and dug into the rubble, throwing it aside to find survivors, or bodies.

Marith, Doc, and Jax were soon surrounded by the cries, moans, and deathly silences of the wounded. They bandaged, applied splints, removed huge splinters of wood, and even, in two cases amputated crushed legs. Jax had never seen such carnage, nor assisted in such bloody surgeries.

The sun rose upon a blood-spattered Jax and Doc kneeling in the path, laboring to save the last person pulled alive from the destroyed burrow: Lagga herself.

"Come on, Lagga, breathe!" Doc pleaded with the unconscious woman while Jax blew air into her lungs. Doc bound the bloody gash on the woman's forehead, but he feared her internal injuries would prove too grave.

"She's not having any," Jax gasped between breaths. He felt her warmth ebbing away into the cold dawn air.

Doc pressed a hand against her hardened stomach and grimaced. "Damn." He checked her pulse. Nothing. He sat heavily down on the ground and rubbed his face with both hands.

"You can stop, Jax."

Jax also sat back into the grass, pushing a long strand of hair out of his eyes.

Morning light filtered through the blue mist off the lake. Jax surveyed what was left of Lagga's Canyon Lodge: a huge pile of mud and a rough hole in the ground. Already Magistrate Vloggan had the Mystics shut off the water source and was detailing crews to dispose of the twelve bodies. Marith had gone with the wounded to see them properly bestowed in beds around the village.

Jax pushed himself off the ground then gave Doc a hand up. Together they walked in silence back to the burrow. The horror of what he had seen crept up from Jax's stomach with a hot stream of bile. He vomited into a neighbor's bushes.

"Sweet goddess." He wiped his mouth.

Doc waited patiently for him.

"It was an ugly mess," Doc agreed.

Jax shook his head, trying to clear it of the crushed and bloody bodies, glowing red in the sooty light of the torches. But the memories of the night seemed to coalesce with memories from his dark hours in the pit. He had never seen bodies of slaves killed in mine cave-ins, but now he knew how a body looked when the life has been crushed out of it. He could picture Jolira in horrible ways.

"Come on, son." Doc put his arms around Jax's shoulders and led him home.

His nausea subsided a little once the blood and dust were washed away, but as he wrapped himself in his blankets, he began to fear his dreams. The nightmares woke him to the green afternoon. Choking on the bile that rose again, Jax stood up from the floor and dunked his head into a basin of cold water.

Marith came in from the barn, the lines around her eyes deep with fatigue.

"Hey, Jax. Do you think you could give Pol's stable a good cleaning sometime today? Doc won't have time to do it, with all the injured to see to."

"Sure." Jax hated attending to the horse. Doc usually took that chore, knowing how Pol misbehaved around Jax. But occasionally, when the druid was too busy, the job fell to Jax.

Marith collected some bandages and ointments, preparing to visit more patients. At the window she paused for a moment, then turned to Jax who sat slouched at the little kitchen table.

"That was a nasty business, son." She put a hand on his shoulder. "You were a big help."

Jax closed his eyes, but in his mind, he saw again his nightmare: Jolira's crushed and bloody face.

Marith squeezed his shoulder and quietly left the cottage.

He tried to eat some bread and cheese but could not get it down. Finally, deciding that even dealing with that diabolical horse would be better than brooding here, he went out to the barn.

Pol was even more ornery than usual. She reared and kicked and bit, and the more Jax coaxed her, the worse she acted. Eventually he got her into the little corral out back, but not before she ripped the shoulder of his shirt with her big yellow teeth.

"Dragons fry me!" In his fatigue and frustration, all his miseries seemed to rise up and swamp him. He took a deep breath and looked up to the sky, but those damned mountains rose like vast, solidified waves. His breath caught in his chest. There was a scent, something on the breeze, something like the sea. A bird cried overhead.

The mountains seemed to tilt and Jax felt himself rushing down the slope of a great wave, rushing to get away from the encroaching peaks and escape his nightmares. Before he knew it, he had crested Roaring Pass and was descending towards the lower ridges of the steppes. But wait, he did not want to go that way. Not back to the monster-infested steppes; not back to the trolls at The Hant.

He left the track and cut towards the west, across the slope of the great mountains. He supposed he would eventually hit the road towards Brakkle and the sea: the sea, which had come to him on that strange gust of wind. By the time the long evening had played its symphony of color on the clouds and granite peaks, he was well down the mountain and into warmer, lusher forests.

Then he began to get hungry and realized that he had run away. He ignored that line of thought and continued to shove his way through the scrubby brush. When it got too dark for him to see his way around thickets and rocks, he sat down near a big boulder that still held the warmth of the sun.

"What have I done?"

Drawing his knees up to his chest and hugging them to his grumbling stomach he thought of Mother Marith's goat cheese suppers and her compassionate eyes. Then it was Jolira again in his mind's eye, and the horror of her death swept him away into the tragedy of her short life.

He bowed his head to his knees, grieving for Jolira, then for others: Moiry, Chora, Ahno, his mother, and finally his father, Rax.

What had he ever done to deserve so many losses? Everyone he cared for, everything he cared about ripped away from him. Even his name.

He raised his eyes to the stars, which blinked coldly back at him. And now he'd finally lost himself, betrayed himself irrevocably.

In the moonless dark he faced this last and greatest loss.

He had forsaken the trust of the druids. They had offered him healing and compassion and he had run out on them. Jax Sharkin did not betray people. Jax Sharkin did not shirk his responsibilities. Jax Sharkin did not steal. But he had done all of this.

As the sun rose to push long fingers of shadow away to the west, he admitted that he had become someone he did not want to be.

He began to walk, still vaguely heading for the long road to Brakkle. At a stream he drank and splashed his face. His stomach grumbled, and he shivered in the crisp air. He took another drink and pushed back his damp hair.

Where was he going? He did not have any idea how far it was to Brakkle, and he had no food, no money, no shoes, not even a cloak.

Once he got to Brakkle he could probably get onto a ship. Any merchant would give Jax free passage back to Haven once they knew who he was.

But that was the problem. He didn't know who he was anymore, and he didn't like the man he'd become. Returning to Baria would mean that he would have to grieve formally for his father. He would have to see his brother Bryx sitting on Rax's throne, taking Rax's place. He would have to explain where he had been all these years. Without realizing it, Jax's steps slowed, but he did not stop.

He could not picture awkward, land-loving Bryx as sealord. How could he explain his experiences as a slave to his old friends like Neben de Rillt, or his cousin Tallyn, or Foby and Cheshir? The Kordish had taken his name and sent him to The Hant, but all of them had left him there: left him to the shame of Oblek's pit and now the final betrayal of himself.

They must all think he was dead, anyway. And they were right. Prince Javix Sharkin, Viscount Norbay, etc., no longer existed. A man who couldn't even help some country druids with their horse was in no way fit to fulfill the responsibilities and play the shifty political games that he would face in Kordon and on Baria. If he didn't exist, then he didn't have a home either.

He came out of a thick stand of pungent pine trees into a meadow full of spiky blue lupine and bright yellow balsam flower. Through the field a road ran down to the west. Jax stood there gazing down the slope for a long time. The sun beat upon his rumpled hair.

Lost. Completely, utterly lost to himself, his past, his future.

There was no home for him, but there was no way he wanted to go back to the Vale either. He shuddered at the thought of those entombing peaks and the confining kindness of the two druids.

Suddenly six trolls strode around the bend, coming up the road towards him. Surprised out of his self-absorbed confusion, Jax dashed for the trees.

"Hey!" shouted one of the trolls. "It's a runaway slave!"

"Get it!"

Jax did not stand a chance against the larger trolls. Three of them tackled him, rolling in a giant ball of arms and legs in the matted pine needles. Jax felt his knee, only just recovered from Oblek's beating, twist and pop as the trolls rolled him. His head hit a rock, and everything went dim.

When he could see again, he found himself sat upon by two trolls while four more pinioned his limbs rather redundantly.

"What are ye doin' out here without a master?" the troll on his chest demanded.

"Sightseeing."

"Why'd ye run from us?" another troll asked.

Jax shrugged his shoulders in the dirt. "You're ugly."

All the trolls growled, and the one on his chest slugged him in the face.

Again, his world went dim. He heard the trolls telling him that he was a runaway and that they would take him back to the Vale. Roughly they hauled him to his feet, causing his head to spin.

"Yer little vacation is over now," the first troll said. He fished a leash out of a pack and clipped it to Jax's collar. Another troll bound his hands. Then they decided that the half-isle might as well be useful, so they loaded their heaver items into a pack and strapped it onto his back. With a jerk on the leash, they started off up the road once again.

Jax stumbled after them; his knee throbbed. When he could not keep up, they pulled switches down from budding willows to swat him.

Jax took the abuse in silence. He recognized that he might deserve a beating this time.

Would the druids decide to sell him back to the trolls? He knew they could not afford to let fifty silvers up and walk away. Angry with himself and his own stupidity, he followed the trolls up over the pass, down through the Hilsen Gate and into the Vale. They took him straight to the town hall. Magistrate Vloggan came down the steps and replaced the leather leash with chains. Pretending not to notice the crowd of locals and tourists that was gathering, Vloggan aimed a few sharp kicks at the half-isle.

"Humans obviously don't know how to discipline a slave," he said loudly. "This one is owned by our two druids. I see it out by itself all the time."

"Mam Marith won't be too pleased if you damage him," said a voice from the crowd.

"A runaway must be whipped!" Vloggan kicked again. The slave grunted as the boot took him in the belly.

"Come along, slave. I wonder if Doc and Marith will want you back after this. Maybe I can buy you cheap."

The crowd silently watched the troll drag Jax away through the darkening streets.

A tall, fair-haired tourist with pale blue eyes behind round spectacles turned to one of the local lads next to her in the crowd.

"Who was that slave?" she asked in the clipped Landish accent of the south.

"That's Jax. He's our druids' slave."

"Jax? His name is Jax?"

"Aye."

"How long has he been here?"

The boy shrugged. "Doc bought him off the trolls at The Hant this spring."

"He doesn't look Hantish."

"Naw, he's islish! Or half, anyway. Didn't you see the fey tilt of his eyes?"

The blond tourist took a silver coin from her purse and handed it to the boy. "Thank you," she said with a smile.

The boy took this treasure and dashed off to the Hilsen Mercantile to diversify his windfall through an investment in candy and trinkets.

The tourist herself walked slowly back into the cliff-face that held the Hilsen Lake Hotel. She found her groom and maid discussing the spectacle of the beaten slave with other tourists.

"Come along," she ordered. "We're leaving at first light."

"Leaving on an expedition or leaving Hilsen Vale?" The groom frowned. The plan had been to stay here another week.

"We're leaving for Kordon." The answer was clipped.

Light gleamed from the windows of the druids' burrow. Marith was still making rounds of the survivors of Lagga's Lodge, but Doc was home, washing medical instruments in a basin of soapy water.

"Here you are, Doc," Vloggan said chummily, shoving Jax down onto the floor with a clang of chains.

"Thanks." Doc looked at Jax. The half-isle was a dirty mess. His hair hung in straggles as he wiped a bloody nose on a torn knee.

"I can whip it for you, if you want," Vloggan went on, carefully smoothing the thick blue paint on his eyebrows.

"Thank you, sir, but I don't think we need to do that just now."

"Well, you have to make sure the other slaves roundabout know that we don't tolerate runaways."

"What other slaves?" Doc muttered absently, watching Jax, who sat where he had been dumped, staring dejectedly at the floor.

"Well, it's the law," Vloggan noted pompously. "Here's the key. You can return the tackle to my stable. And if you don't whip it, I will be obliged to do it for you."

"Thank you, sir." Doc took the key then saw the magistrate to the door. "I think we'll take care of Jax's punishment."

Vloggan looked down his nose at the druid. He might have said more, but Doc spoke again.

"Thank you for bringing him home, sir." Gently, Doc closed the door. He waited a few minutes, listening to the troll's receding footsteps before turning to Jax. "Are you all right?" He bent to unlock the chains that bound the half-isle's hands behind his back.

"Sure."

"Did they feed you?"

"No."

Doc ignored the insolence in Jax's tone and moved to the kitchen for some food. Jax remained on the floor, covering his face with his hands.

Marith came in with a bang, and Jax stiffened at the sound of her voice.

"I heard they'd brought you back. How could you run away from us, Jax, after we took you in?"

"You didn't take me in. You *bought* me."

"That's a technicality."

"It wasn't a technicality to the trolls who hauled me back here."

"Do you want us to chain you?" Marith matched his insolent tone. "Should we keep you fettered like a beast? We *trusted* you!"

Jax slowly got to his feet, his knee popping audibly. "You shouldn't have. Do what you have to. Sell me back to the trolls if you want. I don't care." He hobbled to the window and looked out at the thick green evening. Behind him, he could hear Doc and Marith whispering. He tried not to listen.

"Come sit down." Doc said gently.

Marith poured tea for all of them as they took chairs around the little kitchen table. Automatically, Jax lit a candle with his magic.

"Just tell us why you ran away, son." Marith asked finally.

Jax knew they deserved a true response, but his indignation answered. "I am not your son. I'm not your servant. I *am* your slave. It would be easier for all of us if you would remember that."

"Don't you get high and mighty with me, Jax." Marith's voice was stern.

He rose. "High and mighty? For goddess's sake, Marith, I'm a slave. I have *nothing*: no choices, no dignity, no self. Pretending otherwise merely... makes it worse." His voice cracked and he stopped.

Marith jumped up from her chair and walked slowly around the room until she came abreast of Jax. "I still don't understand. You're better off with us than with the trolls."

Jax looked away from the kindness in her eyes. "In some ways it was much, much easier when I didn't like the people who were enslaving me."

"Dragons, Jax," Doc muttered.

Jax eased himself back into his chair. The candle burned lower. Marith stared out the window as the world darkened, and Doc watched them both.

Jax finally lifted his blue gaze past Doc to Marith. "I thought I wanted to go home." The voice with its crisp Kordish accent was hard. "But I was wrong. I don't have a home."

Marith turned away.

"This is your home, Jax," Doc said softly. "Go to bed. We'll deal with all this later."

Jax did as he was told, unrolling his blankets on the hearth rug. His body ached from the trolls' chains and beatings, and the soft quilts received him warmly. The cat settled onto his legs. He fell into a deep and dreamless sleep.

Doc and Marith, however, sat out on the front stoop watching a waning moon climb across the sky.

"What are we going to do, Mam?"

"If he can't see all that he has, and all that we've already given him..." Marith grumbled.

Doc packed tobacco into his pipe. "Some of the things he says just about break your heart."

"Like that snide remark about liking the people who enslave him?"

"Think what three years in the iron mines would do to a person."

"That ought to make him grateful to us!"

Doc struck his flint. "He doesn't seem ungrateful, to me. I keep thinking we should fear him, but he's never violent."

She sighed. "I don't fear him. His heart is generous, more generous with others than with himself. He doesn't seem able to accept what we give him."

Doc puffed on his pipe for a moment. "Maybe because what we're giving isn't what he wants, or what he needs."

"Decent food, reasonable work?"

"I was thinking about when I fixed his broken hand the day after I bought him. I did what I assumed he needed. Most people would want the use of their right hand. But it turns out that Jax isn't like most people."

"No, he isn't." Marith thought of the scraps of conflicting information Jax had revealed about himself, the surprising things he knew and the obvious things he didn't: like technical words and historical facts, but how he couldn't cook, and goddess he was awful with the laundry.

"What does he need now?" Doc asked.

Marith smiled slowly up at the moon. "A choice."

20

The next morning Marith plodded down the stairs as the first pink rays of dawn streaked across the summer sky. She stepped carefully around the lump of quilts at the bottom of the stairs. He'd been sleeping there on the floor for months. Only now did that seem problematic. She wondered why she hadn't cleared off the cot in the surgery for him. She went out to greet the sun, her heart unsure of itself.

Doc came down a little later, stoked the fire and set about making breakfast. He shook Jax awake and gave him a mug of tea.

"Here, son."

Jax sat up and winced. "Please, don't call me that."

"What then?"

"Jax. Just Jax."

Finding his own patience tried, Doc turned away from the coldness in the sea blue eyes. "You'll have to wash those pillows, Just Jax. You've bled all over them."

When Marith returned from the sun salutations, she joined Jax and Doc at the table, poured herself a cup of tea, and looked with determination into the cold islish eyes.

"Doc and I decided to ask you if you want to stay. If you do, you'll have to continue assisting us, like you have been, and I'll expect you to go to Dishroc and back with me as well."

Jax sipped his tea and waited.

Doc continued to outline Jax's options. "We understand that you may not want to stay here in the Vale. Since we can't afford to let you just go free—which is illegal in any case—we'll try to find a place where you'd be happier. We wouldn't just sell you indiscriminately back to the trolls."

"Although Magistrate Vloggan offered me twenty silvers for you on my way home this morning," Marith said slyly.

"Twenty silvers!" Doc hooted. "That troll knows nothing about humans."

"Too big a loss?" Jax struggled to keep his voice polite.

"Damn right," Marith muttered.

"Look, Jax." Doc returned to the topic at hand. "Even though you are still a slave, we want you to make the choice here. You don't have to answer immediately. Think about it."

"Alright, I will."

"Fine." Marith drained the last of her tea. "Now then, I'm off to see that Ohite boy whose leg we amputated. He's not too happy about it."

"Marith," Jax called as she was just about out the door. "Thank you."

"You are welcome."

Doc poured more tea into their cups. "She was madder than a wet dragon when we found out you were gone, and we had all the wounded from Lagga's Lodge to care for."

Jax watched ghosts of steam dance up from the tea and felt ashamed again. "Doc, I don't know how to do this. How to be...this."

The druid was startled into silence by the remorse and loss in the sea-blue eyes.

After a moment Jax spoke again. "How long do you expect me to work off those fifty silvers?"

"Well... I was thinking somewhere about two and a half or three years. My husband expects to be done with his studies at Sageham in about three years, so we won't need as much help around here."

"Two and a half or three years, if I decide to stay with you?" It seemed like forever.

Doc shrugged. "I suppose we could renegotiate, once you get back from Dishroc."

Jax stood up faster than his bruised body could handle, and he swayed heavily against the table. "I'll let you know," he said shortly, limping to the door.

"Hold on," Doc called him back. "Let me patch you up again." He helped the lad into the surgery where he examined Jax's bruises and bandaged his cuts.

"I did say I could get you up and running, didn't I?" Doc mused as he wrapped Jax's knee in the familiar, tight bandage. "I guess I didn't really think you would." He daubed stinging ointment on several cuts, and finally put three stitches above Jax's pointy eyebrow to stop the bleeding. "Mam and I both feel betrayed."

Jax held a compress over the stitches, the pain minor compared to his guilt and remorse. "I'm sorry, Doc," he whispered.

"Good. Now, best do your laundry before the stains set."

Jax scrubbed the pillowcases in the wash basin, watching his blood slowly dissolve into the water. When they were clean, he hung them dripping on the clothesline, grabbed the lute and headed down to the shore of Daylor Lake where he found a large, sunny boulder to rest upon. He gazed wistfully out over the clear water, his fingers absently picking out notes and chords.

Doc and Marith were doing all they could to accommodate him. He could hardly imagine finding more gentle masters—especially ones who would pay fifty silvers for him. But could he stand to be here in the Vale for two or three years more? Of course, much of that time he would be on the road for Doc's supply trips and Marith's wild journey all the way to desert Dishroc.

He sat there, playing simple tunes, letting the piercing, high-altitude sun warm his bones. Staring at the glassy water, Jax suddenly realized that the mountains stared back at him, reflected in the placid lake.

With a groan of horror, he stopped playing mid-song. The reflection in the water seemed another betrayal, as if his native element was subservient to the mountains in this place. Oh, how he wished he could go home.

But he had no home.

He dropped his lute into the grass, lay back and closed his eyes against the mountains.

"Well, if it isn't our runaway slave." Dylith's voice, full of angry sarcasm cut through his unhappy meditations.

He sat up slowly. She stood, arms akimbo, with sunlight washing over her, violet eyes snapping and cold.

"I'm waiting," she said.

"For what?"

She took two tense steps towards him. "For an explanation! You ran out on Doc and Mother Marith who treat you like family. You ran out on me. I trusted you, too. Can't you at least tell me why?"

"Dragons," he swore, feeling cornered. "I left because I don't want to be here."

"I thought I made you happy."

"Happy? I'm a slave, Dylith. I don't get to be happy."

Dylith gazed down at him. The sun glowed through the thin fabric of her dress revealing the shape beneath.

"Why do you even care?" he asked, his voice a little ragged. "Marith is taking me away in a couple of months, and goddess knows when we'll be back."

"I don't know why I care. Maybe I don't." She looked away from him. "But I couldn't believe that you had actually run away. You didn't seem capable of such a betrayal."

He gave her a slow, saucy grin. "I'm evidently capable of all sorts of nasty things."

"By the dark goddess," Dylith whispered. She turned away.

But he had seen the hurt on her face. "Wait," he said, almost against his will. "Wait. I am sorry, Dylith. Look, I..." What could he say?

Dylith came to stand very close to his seat on the warm boulder. She looked deep into his sea-blue eyes.

"I'm not who you think I am," he said, feeling foolish as the words came out of his mouth. "But then, I don't even know who I am anymore."

Dylith ran her hand thoughtfully down his face. "It doesn't really matter who you are, Just Jax. What matters is what you do."

"Do this with me," he asked softly, pulling her down to kiss. The kiss deepened into something more. He pulled up her skirt. Her hands released his trousers.

Later, Dylith straightened her clothes and pushed her short dark hair behind her ears. "Sometimes I wonder where your heart is."

"It's in a lot of little pieces."

She kissed him deeply, her violet eyes looking into his. Then she left him there in the long, lakeshore grass.

Alone, he sat up and pulled on his shirt. Born a prince and raised a lord, Jax had always assumed that who he was dictated what he did, but now he considered Dylith's reverse opinion: that what he did defined who he was. Warmed by the sun and by Dylith's sensual attentions, this new view didn't negate the other. Both seemed possible.

All around the mountains soared towards a deep blue, cloudless sky. Dishroc. Well, at least he would get away from these looming peaks, even if he could not get to the sea.

He stood up and walked slowly back to the druids' burrow. Marith sat on the front step, sipping tea with Jelly in her lap.

"You have grass in your hair," she told Jax as he limped up.

He brushed at it with his fingers as he sat down next to the druid. His gaze roved down the path toward the other homes as he imagined these simple places forming the limits of his existence. He thought about the people he'd met here in the Vale. These were the kind of people who had been his subjects in Kordon and Baria. They were good-hearted, but, like the unfortunate folk in the slave pens, all too willing to follow whatever scoundrel, or troll, dared to take charge. Now, Jax was himself a subject to the subjects.

At last he spoke: "For so long I wanted to get out of the slave pens. I wanted to go home, back to my life."

Marith nodded but said nothing.

Eventually he continued. "The fact is, I don't have a home to go back to, but I still don't want to be a slave."

"We honestly forget that you're a slave, Jax," Marith said quietly. "You're not exactly subservient."

"I wasn't raised to be subservient."

"What *were* you raised to be?"

"A knight. An admiral."

"So, you're a nobleman."

"No, Marith. I am a slave. *Your* slave. I do what you tell me to do, go where you tell me to go, eat what you deign to give me, and sleep on your floor."

"Sleeping on the floor is your choice. And I've *deigned* to give you another choice. Do you want to stay, or do you want to go?"

"Either way, I'm still a slave."

"Few of us get to choose what we are, son."

Jax groaned and flopped onto his back. Jelly jumped from Marith to Jax, turned once on his belly and settled down, purring.

Jax covered his eyes with his arm. Marith watched him breathe, grief overtaking her. "We've all gotten used to you. Even the cat."

He heard something in her tone and sat up. Tears ran down her face. "What's the matter?"

Marith stood and took a deep a breath. "It might be a relief to be done with your sharp tongue, but I don't want to watch what the trolls will do to you."

"You're selling me back to the trolls?"

"Isn't that your choice?"

"No. No." He watched the tears glitter on her cheeks. "Marith, I'm choosing to stay with you. I'll go with you to Dishroc. I'll help you here, as best I can."

"You chose to stay?"

"Yes."

"Well, you might have said so up front." She wiped her face with her sleeve.

"I'm sorry, Marith. Sorry for a lot of things."

"I can't imagine what you've been through, Jax, and I know you have scars that can't be seen."

He looked away. Trust a druid to get to the heart of things.

Looking at his clean profile, Marith recognized generations of fine breeding beneath the cuts and bruises on his face. He must have lived in manors, maybe even castles. She spoke gently. "The way home lies within you."

"I don't have a home."

"You'll find it when you learn to live with those scars on your heart." She stepped past him, her hand on his shoulder. "I'm going to fix supper. Will you play the lute for me while I cook?"

"Of course."

As he lay on the floor that night watching the fire die, Jax considered another option that Marith and Doc knew nothing about. He could have asked them to sell him to the Barians.

Anger flushed through him, and he rolled restlessly in his blankets. He wanted revenge. Bryx, Tallyn, Midipex, even that Klaris de Farsouth. He wanted them all to pay for abandoning him, for putting him through this pain and humiliation. He imagined himself exploding back into the courts of Baria and Kordon. Blood would flow.

And what would be the point of that?

He groaned. Marith was right. He had to learn to live with his scars, or he would kill them all.

"And what's this one?" Marith pointed to a plant growing alongside the trail.

"Silvery Lupine," Jax answered.

"Uses?"

"The leaves, brewed in tea, will induce labor," Jax recited, stomping along, sweating under the pack.

"And?"

"And the petals are hallucinogenic, but you have to mix them with peppermint and mullein because they are also a purgative."

"Very good." Marith trotted on up the trail. "And what's this?"

"Sickle-leaf—whoa." He stopped, suddenly. A strange wave of nausea stole his breath and spun his head. "Ow." He sat down with a thud.

"What's wrong?"

"I don't know." The nausea subsided as smoothly as it had come. His head cleared, and he felt fine once again.

"That was strange." He stood up.

Marith watched him, puzzled. "What happened? Are you all right?"

"Yes, I am now."

They walked on a bit in silence, Marith forgetting to test Jax's growing herbal knowledge. Finally, he spoke. "It felt like magic. Big magic."

"Hum," Marith frowned. Then a rare, but extremely useful plant caught her eye. "Oh, looky-here, Jax! These are Arielle's Lilies. See them?"

That evening Aric's pub buzzed with the news: the old Weaver had died that afternoon. The death shook the whole fabric of magic in the Knownlands, and everyone who had any magic felt the loss.

"All of us Dragons felt that wave of nausea, Jax," Borrel explained. "It's a mild kind of cross-magic. Anyone with Mystic in the blood would have first felt a wave of joy, then a deep, almost inconsolable grief."

"Grief because the old Weaver is dead?"

Borrel nodded. "How old are you, Jax? Don't you remember when the last Dragon Highlord died? It was about 20 years ago."

Jax shrugged. "I don't remember it clearly."

"You are magically hopeless," Borrel sighed.

Jax took a big swallow of ale. "It's to be expected."

Borrel was going to question Jax about this cryptic response, but Dylith brought another round and he got distracted.

"I wonder what it was like for Adgar today." Doc stared into the white foam atop his ale.

"I'm sure Sageham is a sorrowful place tonight," Borrel said. "Every Mystic feels the hole that the Weaver's death leaves in the fabric of magic."

Jax resolutely shoved the image of sharp green eyes out of his thoughts. He turned to Borrel. "When will there be a new Weaver?"

"It depends." Borrel paused to take a long drink of ale. "It takes years to work one's way through all the necessary levels of study, and then more years preparing for the big mastery spells. I don't know all the details, but you don't want to attempt to master the Mystic or harness the Dragon force before you and the magic are absolutely ready."

"Could Adgar be the next Weaver?" Jax asked Doc.

"I don't think so, and I certainly hope not. I'd never get to see him if he were the Weaver. He'd have to spend so much time on Sageham."

"And you'd have to keep Jax as your assistant forever," Borrel noted.

"Goddess save me," muttered Jax.

"I think she already has," Doc said dryly.

21

The funeral left Klaris drained. She sat in the Great Hall that afternoon, her eyes on the fire, but her vision focused on the altered magic. Around her the castle itself had morphed and moved. Doorways led to new passages and staircases ended abruptly in blank walls.

Professor Lellyn, noting the absence in Klaris's eyes, took a deep chair next to the princess and let her own grief be soothed by the calm elegance of the girl's magic. Emmil Rohan found them there and took a third chair.

The other magicians noticed the three and felt the air shimmer with some shared magic, but they did not hear the telepathic conversation.

"I will organize the Corridor Cadets and have the stairways fixed," Emmil said with an assumption of authority.

"Couldn't you wait a bit?" Klaris asked. *"I sense a curious pattern in the remake of the castle."*

"No. I don't think we should wait, young Klaris," Emmil snapped. *"The stairs are damned dangerous now."*

"Yes, but why?" Klaris asked.

"It doesn't matter why. It just needs to be fixed."

Lellyn sat forward and entered the silent conversation. *"No, Emmil. The fix will come when the next Weaver takes up the threads."*

"In the meantime, we're all in danger."

Lellyn answered. *"I'll look after the novices and acolytes. The Foundation and Corridor level people will be fine."*

"*You!*" Emmil snorted silently. "*Forgive me, Professor, but you should save your strength and energy to continue to tutor those of us who are Tower Tested, so one of us can master the Mystic.*"

Lellyn's dark eyes snapped. "*Emmil. Did you not know that when we are without a Weaver, it is the Tower Tutor who directs the Mystic weave—and its magicians?*"

Emmil shook his head. "*I assumed it should be the senior Tower.*"

"No." Lellyn looked down at the ubiquitous pile of yarn in her lap and began sorting strands. "*You can review the policy in the* Weaver's Rede."

Klaris watched Emmil pull himself together. He rose and spoke aloud. "The *Weaver's Rede.* Very well, Professor."

As he walked away, Klaris frowned. "He doesn't realize that his Secret lies amid all those jumbled staircases. Why can't he see that?"

Lellyn's fingers grew still amid the yarn. "I don't know. The greater question, perhaps, is why can you?"

Tallyn ripped off the purple mourning cloak and flung it from her. "Bury that thing!" she snapped to her lady-in-waiting. "I'm right sick of mourning."

The lady gathered the crumpled silk and slipped from the room. Tallyn walked to a side table and poured herself a glass of pink wine. Sweet goddess. Enough of death and dying and mysterious disappearances.

Her head came up at a gentle knock on the door. "Your Highness?" The priestess Lady Mollish stepped into the room.

"You may come in, Priestess, but leave off your purple."

Mollish pulled the purple surplice over her head and laid it over the back of a small chair. She walked to a casement window that overlooked the royal gardens abloom with summer's bounty. The smell of flowers and fresh air filled the room as she pushed open the window.

Tallyn stood next to her, looking down on the glorious colors. "Here we are amid so much color and life, honoring yet another death."

Mollish glanced at the princess. "Your Highness didn't feel the Weaver's death, did you?"

"No. You know I have no magic. I'm just tired of mourning, of loss, of missing someone."

Lady Mollish had noticed Lord Foby among Earl Kora's party that had ridden out of Kree for the Rippsmarch two weeks ago and suspected that the princess's current mood had little to do with the death of the old Weaver.

"Separations often teach us to cherish the times we have to hold one another, my lady."

"Thank you, Priestess." Tallyn said, without any gratitude apparent in her voice. She drained her glass and went to pour more. "Would you care for some? It's a new rosé my lord Frinz has been developing."

"Thank you, yes." Mollish smiled. "Lord Frinz has been working on a claret too, I believe."

Tallyn sat on a velvet chair and motioned for Mollish to do the same. "Yes, ever since he became Duke of Aychex he has been obsessed with improving his vintages."

The banging on her door this time was not gentle, but urgent.

Tallyn felt her mood sour again. "Come in Carden, before you break the door down."

The Lord of Traik entered wearing yet another outfit of expensive, and these days hard to get, Dranstyllian silk in purple and scarlet.

"Sweet goddess, such colors, my lord." Tallyn squinted.

"I'm pleased you noticed me, your Highness."

Tallyn noticed but did not comment on the familiar sneer. "What brings you here, my lord? Lady Mollish and I were having a private conversation."

Carden didn't even bother to look at the priestess. "Your Highness, may I present Wishalore Allowan."

A tall blond woman, her pale eyes gleaming from behind round spectacles, sank into a rather awkward curtsey.

"Wishalore Allowan?" Tallyn repeated the unlikely name.

"Your Highness, I am a scholar of botany. I have traveled across the Knownlands searching for varieties of primrose, which as I'm sure you know, have many medicinal and magical properties, as well as being a beautiful and extremely hardy—."

"Yes, yes," interrupted Carden. "Just tell the Princess about the, eh, primrose you found in Hilsen Vale."

Wishalore's blue eyes looked with confusion at Lord Carden. "The violet multi-foliate-."

"No, no, no!" Carden laughed. "The slave, good woman. We're interested in the slave, of course."

"Of course, my lord." Wishalore frowned at the gaudily dressed lord who was, she knew, betrothed to the crown princess.

Wishalore cleared her throat and addressed the princess. "Your Highness, I may have found the traitor Prince Javix."

Tallyn spilled her wine. "Tell me."

"I was in a village called Hilsen Vale. It's very high in the Ledden Rises of the Hantland."

"Get a map, please," Tallyn ordered one of her ladies.

"I saw the trolls there bring in a runaway slave, and I thought I recognized him. I'm just a scholar, my lady, and you wouldn't know people like me, but we all watch you and your court. I remember your cousins, the half-islish princes. I always thought it so curious how different they are from one another.

"You have the elder one, the sealord now, with his dark Barian coloring but normal landish features—eyes and ears like ours. But the younger one, the Prince Javix, fair hair and skin like their Kordish mother, but with islish eyes and ears. I find it fascinating the way traits pass from one generation to the next—."

"Excuse me, Wishalore," Tallyn gripped hard on her patience. "Are you saying that the runaway slave you saw in...in the Hantland was Javix Sharkin?"

"I believe so, my lady." Wishalore's eyes gleamed with sympathy. "They called him Jax, which I believe is how his friends here called him."

"Truly a slave?" Priestess Mollish frowned.

"Most horribly, so. I saw a large troll beat him, but the people there told me he is owned by the village druids."

Mollish shook her head in disbelief. "Druids wouldn't own a slave."

"I was surprised, too." Wishalore nodded. "I was told the druids had bought him from the trolls at The Hant."

Tallyn stood abruptly. "Carden, I want you to ride to Rippsgate and fetch Lord Foby."

"Oh, that's rich, my lady," he complained.

Tallyn stared at him until he flourished an insolent bow and left. Then the real work began. Tallyn sent her ladies running with messages through the palace and the town, and a second, more reliable rider was dispatched to Rippsgate.

On her way out of the palace, Wishalore Allowan enjoyed the feel of the heavy purse bouncing against her leg and thought of the expedition to the primrose fields of Ohc that it would pay for.

"Good day, Madam Scholar," a fluty voice stopped her in her tracks. "I understand you may have found our traitor prince after all these years."

"I believe so, your Grace." Wishalore's powerful observational skills identified the Duke of Midipex.

"And he was a slave, you say?"

Wishalore marveled that the duke seemed to know all about her conversation with the princess. "Aye, my lord. I recognized the half-islish prince."

"You are sure? I mean, how could a prince of Baria and Kordon end up as a slave?"

"Indeed, your Grace, I was shocked to see him there, but I am a scholar and I observe."

"Well thank you, Professor Allowan, for reporting this to us."

"I felt it my duty, your Grace."

"Yes. Just so. It is our duty to bring the traitor to justice."

Wishalore left the palace and walked through the streets of Kree to her home. Remembering the sight of the bleeding slave and the thunk of the troll's boot hitting his body, she mused about the nature of justice.

The summer had stretched past Lughnasad before Tallyn could gather up Foby and organize a suitable retinue for the ride to Hilsen Vale. Carden Yemmel had not returned from his leisurely ride to Rippsgate. Midipex insisted on sending a number of his personal household along as guards in recompense for losing the prince's accomplice three years before.

From the balcony of her apartment, Wishalore watched the colorful cloaks of the nobles and their attendants billow as they rode out through the streets of Kree. She turned back to her papers, wondering what would be left for Princess Tallyn to find.

Jax followed Marith down the narrow path, his nose wrinkling at the overwhelming smell of pine coming from the boughs in his pack and in his arms. For three days he'd helped the old druid collect just the right branches from trees on the mountainsides and carry them back to the village grove. There, Doc had nearly finished constructing the figure of the Corn King.

When they arrived at the sacred grove, the headless Corn King stood alone in the sun.

Marith, her hands on her hips, looked around in exasperation. "Where has he gone?"

Jax dumped his load and tried to rub the sticky pitch off his hands. "Maybe someone needed him."

"He needs to finish the Corn King if we want to burn him tomorrow night." Marith muttered. She turned and stomped off toward her burrow, Jax trailing behind her.

Just inside the door, Marith stumbled over a large valise. "Sweet goddess!" she snapped, then began laughing. "Hello, you two!" she called up the stairs. "Hello! We're home."

Jax knew Doc had been waiting anxiously for his husband to return from his studies at Sageham. He heard murmurs from above, and a new voice called: "We're coming, Mam. Give us a minute."

Marith set about organizing things for dinner. Jax took a little butter to get the pine sap off his skin. He was wiping off the last of the sticky grease when a stout man, his dark hair salted with gray, swept down the stairs into Marith's warm embrace. Mystic force slugged into Jax, closing iron bands around his chest.

"Welcome home, Adgar!" Marith smiled.

"It's good to be home."

"It's good to have you home." Doc's eyes glowed in a way Jax had never seen.

"And you are Jax?" Adgar smiled at him, his deep blue eyes sharp. "Jax with some Dragon in you."

"Jax with all kinds of things in him," Marith said dryly, returning to her preparations for dinner.

Increasingly uncomfortable with both cross-magic and the intimacy of the druids' family, Jax moved to the door. "I'll sit outside."

"Play some music for us!" Marith called.

With palpable relief, Jax sat on the front stoop and ran his fingers through his hair. After collecting himself for a few moments, he picked up the lute and began to play. He could hear the druids' voices inside.

"But that's an extraordinary coincidence," Adgar said. "I'm sure your Jax was the slave that Klaris de Farsouth was so upset about. He told you he was shipwrecked with his overtroll, right?"

Doc laid utensils on the table. "Yes. In fact, now that you mention it, when I bought him he asked if someone named Klaris had sent me."

"How terrible for him." Adgar scraped chopped shallots into the frying pan and set it over the fire. "He probably expected her to buy him out of slavery."

Doc glanced out the open door to where Jax sat in the sun, apparently lost in the interweaving harmonies of the lute. "I think he did."

Marith added a large bunch of greens to the pan of simmering shallots. "Who is this Klaris and why didn't she buy him?"

"I don't know all the details, since I am just an acolyte, far below Klaris's level. But the rumor was that the Senior Tower magician, Emmil Rohan, wouldn't let her help the slave, and he was in charge of course. But Klaris is the most gifted Mystic in many, many years. She's also the Princess of Farsouth."

"So why did she care so much about a slave? A slave with Dragon force, no less?" Doc asked.

The music stopped. "She didn't care, apparently," Jax said from the doorway.

"No, Jax. She was distraught." Adgar stepped further into the room, to keep distance between himself and Jax. "I don't know what she knew about you or why she wanted to save you, but Emmil wouldn't permit it."

"Jax," Marith rose from stirring the greens. "Do you know why Klaris wanted to save you?"

He set the lute down and stood up. "Marith, I would hope that any goddess-loving creature would wish to help someone who was beaten, starved, and sold for bait." He paused, watching the hurt and remorse cross their friendly faces.

"Doc did." Jax said finally. "Her Highness Klaris de Farsouth didn't save me. But Doc did."

He turned and strode away from the house, away from the cross-magic and their continued inability to see the horrors of slavery.

Dylith gave him dinner in the pub kitchen, several pints of black Vale Ale, and a friendly bed for the night.

The embers of the Corn King were still sending gray wraiths into the clear summer sky as Marith embraced her son and son-in-law one last time. "Take care of each other."

Doc walked with them out to the boulders that marked the Hilsen Gate. Florin led the way, followed by Marith, then Borrel and Jax leading Ol' Pol who nipped at him.

"Watch out for her, will you, Jax?" Doc said softly.

"I have to watch your damned horse every second."

"Not the horse, son. Jax." Doc corrected himself dryly. "Mam's sharp and spry, but you know she's old enough to be your grandmother."

"I know."

"And she is my mother."

"Yes?"

"Bring her back safely."

Jax looked into Doc's blue eyes and saw the loss he was facing. "Doc.... Alright."

The druid smiled. "Here." He held out a small wooden dragon-pipe. "I'm glad to see you wearing the boots finally."

Jax took the simple whistle. "It's a long walk to Dishroc."

He looked at the small instrument and thought of all the other gifts he'd been given during his long years as a slave. Finally, he met Doc's eyes: "Thank you, Doc."

"We'll see you next year."

For four days Jax followed Marith, Florin, and Borrel through the narrow paths that lead down from the mountains towards the stockade city of Fort Rim in Ily. Overgrown with the late summer grasses, the paths snaked faintly among the trees, sometimes fading altogether. Several times Jax watched Florin lean her head against a tree then straighten and pat the bark affectionately, convincing him finally that the rumors were true: nyads really could talk to trees.

This time she stood away from the tree with a frown. As she led them down the invisible path, she muttered something softly to her brother, who just laughed and shook his head.

"Fine. Laugh. You won't think it's so funny if they show up and bewitch you."

Unrepentant, Borrel chuckled. Trudging along under his pack, Jax wondered what the trees could have told Florin that so amused Borrel.

"See?" Florin pointed to a fairy ring in a clearing.

Jax cocked an eyebrow at the nyad's worried expression. As far as the islish knew, there were no fairies on Baria, and the Kordish scorned fairy-lore, so he had little knowledge of the supposedly mythical creatures other than old tales from the nursery.

Jax fell in step beside Marith. "Fairies?"

"They're mostly just mischievous. They'll upset a camp or release pack animals. But once they tried to kidnap the male members of Florin's trekking party."

"Really?"

"Really. They feed their victims fairy gems, shrink them down to fairy size, and take them off to the fairy queen. Florin had a terrible time getting her party back from them. I've never heard the whole story, just enough to know that the men were none too happy to leave the fairy queen, and that Borrel thinks the whole affair is absolutely hilarious."

They walked along for a few moments. "The fairy queen is supposed to be one of the most beautiful creatures in the world," Borrel noted.

"And one of the most dangerous," Florin added darkly. "She'll seduce you, and you think you're only spending an evening with her, but when she finally releases you, you find out that fifty or sixty years have passed, and you have aged, wasted your life for an evening of dallying."

They slept in the open, not needing to trouble with a tent in the warm summer nights. Borrel set wards with amber bands of his force around their camp each night. Ostensibly this was to keep the fairies out, but the nyad knew that his magic could not match the fairy queen's. They also took turns watching the dark forest for any sign of the small creatures.

"I don't like the look of this place." Florin glared around the twilit clearing. "We've seen *three* fairy rings near here."

Jax gazed up at the small patch of pink-tinted sky and flexed his sore knee.

"We can't walk any farther." Marith dropped her pack with a thud. "We're all too tired after last night." Distant fairy lights had made them all jumpy last night, and no one had slept well.

"I'd rather walk all night than camp near the fairy queen's lair." Florin frowned at her exhausted companions.

"Marith's right, Florin," Borrel said reasonably. "Besides, so far my wards have kept them away from us."

"Alright. Fine." Florin gave in with ill grace and flung her pack down into the grass. "But don't blame me when one of you gets kidnapped by the little bugs."

Too tired to eat much, the group rolled into their sleeping quilts after munching a few handfuls of dried fruits and nuts.

Borrel took the first watch. The hours passed quietly, punctuated only by the occasional hoot of a night bird and the silent movement of the stars across the sky. Jax took his turn next, sitting with his back to the fire, gazing out into the dark forest beyond the faint amber glimmer of Borrel's wards. Once he heard a trilling giggle, but it was so brief, and followed by such a pure silence, that he began to think he had imagined it.

Suddenly a rainbow-colored batch of glowing fairies popped out from behind various trees and bushes and flew in dizzy circles around the clearing. Most of them were about twelve inches long, with elongated features and pointed ears, but one was much larger, almost human sized. It lumbered and crashed through the leaves.

"Marith!" Jax shouted. "Florin! Wake up!"

The others jumped out of their quilts.

"They're beautiful," Jax whispered.

The fairies sparkled pink, violet, green and blue, and their laughter filled Jax's heart with a strange, wild joy.

Unmoved by the spectacle, Florin spoke to the fairies in a firm voice: "You have the half-troll with you tonight, I see."

"He's our brother!" The smaller fairies danced around the large one, who executed a wobbly pirouette.

Florin was unappeased. "Be off with you!"

"Why? Your magic won't let us touch you." A purple fairy with glittering yellow hair and wings spoke in a tinkling voice.

"Good," mumbled Borrel.

Marith tried to take the situation in hand. "In the name of the goddess, I bid you to leave us in peace."

The purple fairy fluttered up to eye level with the druid, her arms crossed in front of her and a petulant frown on her fairy face.

Suddenly all the companions found themselves gently floating up off the ground. Borrel laughed hysterically, and Jax giggled at the funny feeling of the fairies' magic working on him.

"Put us down!" Florin ordered.

Borrel, laughing so hard that tears streamed from his eyes, finally managed to mutter a word of force to counteract the fairies' spell, and the whole group crashed down into the soft grass.

"No fun!" cried several of the fairies.

"Plenty of fun," Borrel gasped, wiping tears from his eyes. "Goddess, but your magic tickles."

"Tickles!" The purple fairy became a ball of lavender indignation.

A glimmering gold and rose fairy, larger than the others but not as big as the half-troll, shimmered into existence against the dark backdrop of the woods. Trailing a sparkle of lights, she slipped right through Borrel's amber ward. "The nyad gulped his giggles as her magic tickled his.

The fairy floated over to Jax. "You are a pleasant sight, now that I can see you." Her voice was a lush contralto. Her eyes swept him, and he felt her magic touch his skin. It didn't tickle. "Javix Sharkin, isn't it?"

"How do you know me?"

"Magic," she shrugged, scattering sparkles and looking closely at Jax's companions. "Where's the Weaver?"

"I believe the Weaver is dead, your Majesty."

The fairy waved her hand, sending more sparks in a glowing arc. "Not the old man. I'm looking for the girl. Klaris de Farsouth."

Jax's blood cooled a bit. "I can't help you there."

"Javix," she lingered over his name, her tongue playing with it in a way that sent his heart thudding again. Without a doubt, she was the most incredibly beautiful creature Jax had ever seen—all twenty-four inches of her. "Javix, Klaris needs you."

"I don't think so."

"You don't care about Klaris and her needs?" The fairy queen twisted her body voluptuously in midair.

Jax felt a warm rush low in his belly. "No, Ma'am."

She frowned. "The two of you have work to do, together."

"We do?"

"Of course, you do. Don't you know the prophecy?"

"No."

"Mortals!" snapped the fairy in exasperation. "Those stupid Axterran Oracles ruined everything."

Jax and the others stared at her without comprehension. Axterre was an ancient empire that had fallen over 1,500 years ago and lay in ruins somewhere far to the east, almost beyond the bounds of the Knownlands.

The fairy queen shook herself, scattering sparks. "Listen, Javix Sharkin. You are a paradox, are you not?"

"You could say that."

"And she'll be the Weaver."

"Klaris?"

"Of course! Klaris. Look. You had better go find that sorry excuse of an Oracle and get them to tell you what to do. I'm not going to have my people devastated again. Our populations haven't recovered from the last time. I'm sure you've noted that there are no fairies on Baria."

"I don't know what you are talking about." Jax said, a weird and wary feeling spreading through his chest.

The fairy queen squared her shoulders. "No, of course you don't."

"And I can't go see the Oracle."

"You could."

"I am not a ruler."

The Queen's bell-like laughter rang out through the clearing. "Aren't you?"

"And I am not free."

"Who is?" she snorted. "You're the Paradox, Javix, although our half-troll might do in a pinch." She glanced at the big fairy who was busy adorning himself with tiny night-blooming flowers. "Only a very, very tight pinch," she muttered turning her violet eyes and inviting smile back to Jax. "*You* must fulfill the prophecy. You and Klaris both."

"That's not a paradox; that's just more slavery." Jax argued.

Tinkling bells began to jangle discordantly all around them. "Dawn is coming! Dawn is coming!" sang the smaller fairies, who glimmered outside Borrel's amber rings of magic.

The fairy queen looked up to the sky. "Your mortal days are so short." Her rich voice held concern and pity and a little scorn. Purple or green or turquoise eyes bore into Jax's and finally she ran her cool fingers down the side of his face. "Klaris has been looking for you. *I've* been looking for you, but of course you can't be seen."

"I'm not invisible."

"You are to magic."

"Dawn! Majesty! Dawn!" The jangling, jabbering fairies were screaming now.

"Go! Go!" The queen waved a negligent arm. The little fairies popped out of sight.

"Go to the Oracle, Javix." She looked at him now, her mockery gone. "Goddess bless you." With a snap she was gone.

Jax sat down and pushed both hands through his hair. Borrel turned to stir his magical fire. Florin walked the perimeter of the clearing, glaring into the shadows.

"Javix," Borrel mimicked the fairy queen's lascivious tone.

"It's just Jax," Jax grumbled.

Marith still stood, her hands on her hips frowning down at Jax. "You are never just one thing, Jax. You're a paradox or an enigma."

"Dragons, Marith. What do you want of me?"

"The truth. How did the fairy queen know you?"

"You heard her: Magic."

"Don't get smart with me."

"I am anything but smart."

She considered his straight profile against the light of Borrel's fire and sighed. "You certainly walk strange paths."

"I'm just following you."

They decided to close their eyes for a few hours before full light. Jax's thoughts traveled in a tedious circle: invisible to magic; he could not be seen. That would explain why no one had managed to find him during his years in the iron mines. But how could such a thing be? Surely the most powerful royal magicians in both Kordon and Baria would have scried for him. Finally, exhausted by unanswered questions, Jax fell asleep and dreamed of the fairy queen. He sensed her need and felt his own, but as he reached out for her warm promise, the image shifted, and he found himself looking into the green eyes of Klaris de Farsouth.

22

Morning frost crusted the grass and defined the shadows as a large party riding beautiful horses streamed through the Hilsen Gate and into the village green. They circled in front of the Hilsen Lake Hotel and dismounted. Grooms and village children came running to take horses and ogle the foreigners in their brilliant cloaks.

The leader was clearly the young blond woman with the aquiline features and the pale, almost colorless eyes. All of them spoke in the clipped accents of Kordon. In fact, they sounded a lot like the druids' slave. And sure enough, here they were asking about him.

"Thank you," the young lady said to the owner of the hotel, who had explained the available accommodations. "But what we really want is to see your druids and their slave, immediately."

The hotel owner motioned to a boy who ran down the path calling for Doc. "Do come in, my lady. The druids will come."

"No. I'll go to them." She set off to follow the running boy, her whole entourage walking with her, until she stopped and turned to them. "Lord Foby and I will go find the druids, and we hope, Prince Jax. The rest of you stay here and see to our rooms and our gear."

"Your Highness, respectfully," the captain of Midipex's household guard stepped forward. "The prince is a traitor and likely dangerous. Please allow me and my men to accompany you and Lord Foby."

Tallyn saw the running boy disappear into the trees and snapped. "Fine, Almac. You and Captain Karric may come. The rest of you stay here."

She surveyed the crowd of children around her and chose one of the largest girls. "You, lass, lead us to your druids."

"Yes, m'lady!" The girl glowed with pride. "Is it their Jax you've come to see?"

"It is. How did you know?"

"You talk just like him."

"Ah." Tallyn smiled at Foby. It was him!

"But Jax is gone," the girl continued.

"What?"

"Yes, m'lady. He went away with Mam Marith just after the Corn King."

"Dragons, no," moaned Foby.

"But Doc's still here and Adgar. And here's their burrow."

Doc, summoned by the boy, came to the front steps, his mouth gaping at the colorful nobles at his gate. Adgar stood behind him in the doorway, watching as the Kordish lord and lady came up the path. Two tall guards with long swords followed behind. As they reached the house, one of the guards drew his sword.

"Put it up, Almac." Tallyn ordered.

"But my lady—."

"He isn't here, apparently. And you are scaring people."

She turned away to the sound of the sword sliding home.

Doc arranged himself in his best idea of a bow. Adgar, having seen more of the world at Castle Caledra, managed his obeisance with more credibility.

"I am Tallyn of Kordon. This is Lord Foby of Rippfell. We understand that you have a slave named Jax?"

"Your Highness, we do. Or we did." Doc stuttered.

"Will you come inside, your Highness?" Adgar stood back from the door.

Tallyn and Lord Foby seemed to fill the room with the jewel tones of their rich clothing. Tallyn took the offered chair by the fire. Foby remained standing at her elbow, but he picked up the fat orange cat, who began to purr loudly. The two guards positioned themselves by the door.

"Did you say Dishroc?" Tallyn couldn't keep the incredulous disappointment out of her voice. "Where is that?"

"It's the capitol of the Nomad Range, Ma'am," Foby offered.

"The Nomad Range?" Tallyn frowned up at him. "But that would take months, years even, to go there and back."

"Yes, a year, we expect." Doc nodded.

"A year. And he went willingly?" Tallyn asked.

"Well." Doc cleared his throat. "More or less. We didn't keep him bound. Not anymore, anyway."

Tallyn considered the druid with cool ice-blue eyes. "Right. He is your slave."

Doc realized he had seen a similar imperiousness on Jax's face. "Honestly, Ma'am we thought of him as our assistant. We came to realize that he wasn't 'just Jax,' but we never would have thought him a prince of two countries." He shook his head. "Nobles just don't end up as slaves. Or if they do, they don't last...." Doc reddened with shame.

"So how did Prince Jax become a slave?" Foby asked.

Almac's dagger whispered from its sheath, and he stepped further into the room.

Doc had just begun to answer when Almac's knife flashed through the room and sliced into the druid's throat.

"Almac!" Tallyn leapt to her feet, but Karric already had the other guard down and held.

"Help me," Adgar snapped at Foby. "Take his feet. And you, my lady. I need those bandages there."

Without pausing for thought, Adgar settled Doc on the cot in the surgery and withdrew the knife. Deftly he wrapped the bandages around the wound.

"It's alright, Doc," he crooned, glancing at the shock in his eyes. "I know it hurts, but the knife missed the big veins."

Doc made gurgling noises.

"Hush." Adgar settled a pillow under Doc's head. "Just breathe. That's right. Deep belly breaths."

Tallyn turned to Almac who still lay prone, immobilized by Karric's grip. "Explain yourself."

"He aided the traitor, my lady. They all did, it seems. Beware of them."

"They didn't know who Jax is," Foby snapped. "They didn't know he'd been convicted of treason."

Tallyn looked at Foby. "Jax doesn't know that either," she said softly.

"Don't trust them," Almac grunted as Karric's knee bore into his back.

"I don't trust you," Tallyn stated.

With practiced skill, Karric got Almac to his feet and together with Foby marched him back to the hotel where they bound him tightly and placed him under guard in a storeroom.

Tallyn stayed with Adgar until Doc's pulse stabilized and his bleeding stopped. The druid opened his eyes and smiled wanly at Adgar. When he spoke, his voice was as pale and bloodless as his skin.

"Jax told me some of his relatives decided they'd be better off without him." He paused, looking into the princess's nearly color- less blue eyes. "That's how he ended up with the trolls. His family sold him."

"His family?"

Doc spoke again with some effort. "Aren't you his cousin?"

Tallyn nodded. "That I am." She turned to Adgar. "I apologize for my guard's attack on Doc. We will have food sent to you and I'd like to come back when he is stronger."

"Thank you, my lady." Adgar rose, wiping bloody hands on a damp cloth. "You might like to know that Klaris de Farsouth dis- covered that Prince Jax was enslaved by the trolls last spring. She couldn't free him, but I believe she sent word to the Barians."

"How is a princess of Farsouth involved in all this?"

"She studies at Sageham, my lady," Adgar explained. "Her magic is very strong. She saw Jax somewhere along the Vrillbridge Road."

"And she knew him?"

Adgar nodded. "She wanted to get him away from the trolls but couldn't."

"Why not?"

Adgar hesitated. "She is young, my lady. About your age, maybe. That's unusually young to be studying at Castle Caledra, you understand."

Tallyn took a deep breath and looked at Doc, who lay on the cot, his eyes closed, his breathing painful.

"I understand very little when it comes to my cousin Jax and his adventures," Tallyn said finally. "I'm going to send Captain Karric back to guard you as well, Father Adgar."

As she walked through the late summer sunshine towards the hotel, Tallyn catalogued Jax's relatives, most of whom were her relatives as well.

"Your Highness!" Tallyn woke up to the urgency in the tone, and Foby's dog barking. "Oh, your Highness!"

"Yes? What?" She sat up, pushing her long white-blond hair behind her ears. Foby sat up next to her.

One of her ladies-in-waiting opened the door to the guard. "Almac is gone, your Highness. All of the guards from Midipex have gone."

"What?" Foby sat up straighter and hushed the dog.

"Orriston was guarding Almac in the night. He was knocked on the head and doesn't remember anything," the guard said, keeping his voice firm and impassive. "It must have been Midipex's people because they're all gone this morning, including Almac."

Tallyn and Foby exchanged a glance. "All of Midipex's people are gone?"

"Aye, my lady."

"Where is Captain Karric?"

"With the druid family, my lady."

"Fetch her."

"Yes, my lady."

Karric paced back and forth across the hotel sitting room, ignoring the food and tea. "I don't understand why Midipex's people would take Almac and leave."

"The good duke will have a lot to explain," Tallyn said grimly.

"He begged you to bring his people with us," Foby said, staring thoughtfully out the window at the stunningly blue lake.

"He did."

"But Midipex isn't one of your relatives, is he?"

Tallyn shrugged. "He's a second cousin once removed."

Foby thought about royal genealogy for a few moments.

"What does that have to do with anything?" Karric asked, pausing in her pacing.

"Jax told Doc he was sold to the trolls by his relatives."

"You think Midipex would have done such a thing?" Karric breathed. "That would be treason."

Tallyn shook her head but didn't answer. She thought of Bryx's apparent lack of concern for his brother, and realized she knew nothing of Jax's other Barian relatives.

They took lunch on a sunny table on a terrace overlooking the lake. Foby decided he liked the black ale with the creamy foam on top. Tallyn longed for some decent Kordish wine.

A large troll, wearing something scarlet and official-looking, strode up to their table and looked down his powdered nose at them. "I hear you are looking for a slave."

Tallyn nodded. "Yes."

"I am Grobber Vloggan, the Magistrate of Hilsen Vale. I can tell you that the druids' slave was no good. No good at all."

"How so?"

"Insolent, cocky, damned smart mouth."

Tallyn smiled. "That's the fellow."

"I know it isn't here, but even if it were you can't take it."

"It?"

"It's contraband. It tried to run away, which means that it can't be released."

Tallyn looked at Foby, who answered slowly. "Thank you for alerting us to the situation, Magistrate. We'll make sure we purchase *him*, if we decide we want *him*."

The troll made a sour face. "You may be able to purchase it, but I'm going to make sure it gets the beating it deserves when the bill of sale changes hands."

"Can you do that?" Foby asked.

"I have to do that," the troll growled. "It's the law that any slave that runs be beaten. The druids never did it, and now the slave is gone. I have to sign any bills of sale and I won't approve the sale until it's been beaten to within an inch of its life."

"Thank you," Tallyn said, turning away. "We appreciate your dedication to your duty."

"Dragons," Foby grimaced as the troll left them. "Do you realize what Jax must have gone through these last four years?"

Tallyn sipped the bad wine and shook her head.

The barmaid set platters of sausages, pickles, and cheese in front of them and paused.

Foby looked up into the girl's beautiful violet eyes.

"You are friends of Jax, my lord?" she asked.

"Friends and family," Tallyn answered crisply.

"But they say you are the Princess of Kordon," the girl stammered.

"They are correct."

"But Jax—."

"Yes. He is a prince of Kordon. And Baria too."

The girl's shoulders slumped, and she turned quickly back to the building.

"You just broke her heart, Tallyn."

The princess's clear blue eyes gazed at the lake. "All our hearts are breaking."

Two days later Doc was well enough to sit up. A violent thunderstorm banged among the peaks. Tallyn and Foby huddled before the fire in the druids' cottage while rain came down in buckets.

Foby had pulled a bag of coins from his pocket. "How much does a slave cost?" He put a few golden coins on the table. "I think we would like to buy Jax, so that when you see him again you can send him home to us."

"I thought you said he was a traitor." Doc's voice was weak, but anger sparkled in his eyes.

"He's been convicted of treason, but we don't think he's a traitor," Foby answered. "We grew up with him, you see."

"What I don't see is why we should trust you, my lady." Adgar said fiercely. "You claim to be Jax's friends, but your man nearly killed Doc, and it was Doc who saved your Jax from the trolls."

Tallyn made a small bow. "Indeed, Father Adgar. I believe that this incident is forcing us to see some things we weren't meant to notice. And we beg your forgiveness for Doc's injury."

"We are truly sorry," Foby added.

Adgar had no wit to match the princess's pretty words and fine manners, but he sensed the sincerity in Lord Foby's pale eyes.

Doc heard Jax's accent in Tallyn's words and wondered how he hadn't realized that the lad was noble. "I'm not sure I'll release him to you," he said finally. "He's not safe with the Kordish, apparently, and neither are his... friends." He pulled at the bandage around his neck.

"I understand," Tallyn smiled tightly. "Again, I apologize for our man's mistake." She turned and glanced at the bag of gold on the table. "You can keep the gold. Let Prince Javix decide what he wants to be, and where."

Long after the Kordish nobles left the Vale and the winter snows blocked the passes, Doc wore a thick scarf around his neck to support the severed tendons. Dylith lost a lot of weight. Adgar tried without success to send a magical letter to Castle Caledra. Finally, he resigned himself to waiting to tell Klaris in person about Jax when he returned to his studies next summer.

"You executed him?" Tallyn frowned at the Duke of Midipex who sat across the polished council table from her.

"Of course, I did, my lady. When I heard the other guards' report of how he had endangered your investigations. I had his home searched. We found a large stash of Barian coins. Clearly the Barians were paying him to help them find the traitor prince."

"Clearly," Tallyn's voice proved that there was nothing clear about any of this.

Midipex shook his head and opened his hands. "I beg your pardon, my lady, and yours, your Majesty," he turned to the King, who was looking out the window at the autumn storm building in from the west.

"Once again, my household guards have proven inadequate and even traitorous." Midipex looked down in shame. "Perhaps you should banish me."

"What?" Earla Stona rose. "Don't be stupid, Thorag. You've been the staunchest opponent of the Barians. No one would suspect any of your people to be spies. That's why your household is the perfect place for them to hide."

"I fear you are right, my lady." The duke rose. "By your leave, Sire. I am going to interrogate my entire household from the seneschal to the garden boy and make sure no more perversity lurks in my house."

"Perhaps we should all do the same," the Earla said thoughtfully.

"Fine. Fine, Midipex." The King rose as well, and his council stood with him. "I'm going to ride before it rains. Tallyn, come with me."

Tallyn followed her father from the chamber, her wide smile masking how exactly she noted the depth of each noble's bow.

 23

The rest of the trip to Fort Rim passed without further fairy interference. They spent one night in the stockade city. Marith was up hours before the sun, performing her usual salutations, hoping to calm her exuberance. Fort Rim had formed the limit of her travels until today. She roused her grumbling companions and had them on the ferry across the River Frode as the sun rose over the bluffs of Ohe.

Hawks circled overhead in the vast cloudless sky as they climbed up the bluff and faced the wide Plains of Ohe. Jax scuffed through the dust of the road, relieved by the freedom of far horizons. Neither mountain nor forest imposed themselves between him and the sky. North, east, and south, the land stretched away from the high bluffs above the River Frode, covered with thorny dryherb bushes and precious little else.

Occasionally a winding stream, often dry, cut across the dryherb flats, making a deep wrinkle in the land. Cottonwood trees grew tall along these washes, sheltering herds of shaggy deer and flocks of black-winged ravens.

Out on the plain Florin and Borrel both felt exposed. Marith pointed out that the only creatures paying them any attention were the distant, circling hawks. Florin hunched closer to one of Borrel's wind-whipped fires, as they made camp that evening. "It just seems so big."

"It *is* big," Marith answered. "What do you expect?"

"It makes me feel small, vulnerable," Borrel grumbled.

"You ought to see the ocean, if you want to feel insignificant," Jax noted.

"I don't particularly," Florin said dryly. "But thanks all the same."

Day after day they walked south, further into the Ohite hinterlands, on the track to the village of Rangohe. Along the way, occasional clusters of dilapidated buildings rose unsteadily from the dust and dryherb. With empty windows and collapsed roofs, none of these places showed any sign of recent human habitation.

Three days after crossing the River Frode, the group shuffled into the dusty village of Rangohe that sweltered in the late summer sun. The town, like the other buildings they had seen so far, stood in near ruin. A barkeeper sat on his front stoop swatting flies, his tavern filled only with shadows. The inns were closed; the houses boarded shut against the empty street. Marith had hoped to buy supplies here, but the one store had only a handful of dried cactus fruit and a few leathery strings of antelope jerky.

"Where is everyone?" Marith asked the shopkeeper.

"Gone."

"Why?" Jax watched a small brown cockroach rummage futilely in an empty cracker barrel.

"Drought."

"But those farms looked like they'd been abandoned for years," Borrel offered.

"Well, they have." The shopkeeper put his elbows on his counter. "It was the cattle that caused the drought, you see. Too many cattle, not enough grass. Then the winds came, and all the exposed dirt blew up into the air and away to Norledge, or Ily, or I don't know where. So now, even though the cattle are long gone, the grass don't come back, and folks hereabout can't make a living. So, they leave."

Marith clucked her tongue. "Don't bite the goddess or she'll bite back."

"Yeah, well. She done bit us."

Rather than stay in the dying village, the travelers continued on the track towards Langohe. All along the way, the story seemed to be the same: abandoned ranches and farms crumbling slowly back into the earth. They passed through no other towns.

"I can't believe anyone would think to try cattle ranching out here." Jax squinted across the mirages at a herd of prong-horn antelope.

"Maybe they thought cattle would eat dryherb." Borrel kicked at a scraggly bush.

"Well, my map designates this part of Ohe as full of cattle ranches," Marith noted.

"Where did you get that map, anyway?" Florin wiped dusty sweat off her face.

"A patient gave it to me." The druid's excitement rang in her voice. "Years and years ago, it was. The fellow was a tourist from Kordon, of all places Jax, and he had fallen ill in the Vale. He ran out of coin and couldn't pay me or his bill at the inn, but he offered me this map instead. He said it had been made by a committee of druids and magicians, all of them wise and well-traveled."

Jax, who had caught only a brief glimpse of the rolled parchment map, silently raised a skeptical eyebrow. He knew what scholarly maps looked like—the Barians naturally had a passion for them— and the thing Marith had was nothing but a lot of vague lines designating spurious landmarks like "the twisted tree," and offering strange promises like "water here," or "gold dust rocks."

Still, Jax knew that good maps were rare in the Knownlands. The Barians, out of necessity, had detailed descriptions of the coastlines, but the landish people seemed content to know only vaguely that such and such a road supposedly led to such and such a city.

They made yet another windy camp in among the giant dryherb bushes, hobbling Ol' Pol loosely so she could forage for the meager grass. Borrel stared about him at the dryherb tossing in the wind above spiny clusters of cacti.

"Sweet goddess, Ohe is ugly."

"I like it," Jax said. "You can see the sky."

"But nothing else."

"That's the beauty of it," he answered, pulling out the little wooden dragonpipe. He tried a few notes, then ran through the First Tune. When he was done, he paused, smiling at the mellow notes the pipe made. He put it back to his lips and played a tune as wild and free as the dry Ohite wind.

Finally, nearly two weeks after leaving Fort Rim, the group crossed the wide stone bridge over the Shadd River and entered the bustling town of Langohe. After days of isolation on the high prairie, the teeming town seemed infested with people. The throbbing crowds made even the nyads nervous.

They spent the night at an inexpensive inn, all of them glad to get a bath and a hearty meal. Early the next morning Marith had them up and moving out of town, on the road once again. Despite the early hour and the disappointment of being roused out of the first real bed they had enjoyed in weeks, all of them were relieved to leave the city.

Langohe sat on a tongue of land between two fat rivers that flowed down from the distant Barthrobar Mountains. A second stone bridge, as wide and well-constructed as the one over the Shadd, arched over the River Blin, south of town. As they crossed this bridge, Ol' Pol's hooves clopping hollowly, Jax wondered if the cities of his youth had been as crowded as Langohe. Both Haven and Kree stood as capitals to their countries and were full of all the people and services necessary for royal courts and national governments. Still, Jax did not remember them as over-crowded. Even the Floating Islands never seemed so densely populated. Sure, space was always efficiently used, but there was always room for trees or gardens, squares and statues, or calm canals that widened into ponds and bays. Langohe showed none of these amenities. People hung from every window and filled each alley and gutter.

Walking farther from the city, watching the brown rolls of the Levenloes push up into the sky, Jax decided that all the people from the abandoned buildings up on the prairie must have flooded into Langohe. And yet, the move could not have been recent. He remembered how many of his fellow slaves in the iron mines had come from Ohe, including Jolira, and he began to think about the relationship between poverty and desperation.

That evening, Jax sat warming his toes at Borrel's magical fire, trying to remember what the rulers of Baria did to ease the plight of their poorest subjects. He knew that Rax had occasionally visited the bilge slums in the holds beneath the Floating Islands, but beyond that, he remembered nothing.

"You're looking mighty thoughtful, Jax," Marith teased.

"I was thinking about poor people." He poured more hot water into his tea mug.

"What about them?"

"Nothing."

"Oh, don't give me that," Marith snapped.

"All right, all right," Jax's said with exasperation. "I was thinking about the poor people on Baria, and what sort of programs existed to help them out."

"What brought that on?" Borrel frowned.

"Langohe. All those people. And the fact that so many of the slaves in the iron mines came from Ohe. It's obviously a poor country."

For a few minutes none of the others spoke. They just looked at him, his face ruddy in the firelight.

"You weren't raised poor, were you, Jax?" Borrel asked quietly.

"Not exactly."

"So why do you care about these poverty-stricken Ohites?" Florin often felt like she did not understand Jax at all.

He shrugged. "Don't you care? Doesn't it bother you to see these people so destitute that they sell their children, their brothers, their wives into slavery?"

Jax watched in amazement as the others frowned or shrugged sheepishly.

"There's not much we can do about it," Borrel said, finally.

"As a druid, I can heal their bodies and offer them the goddess's consolations," Marith mused. "But I can't help them beyond that."

Jax sipped his tea. "Well, there you have it then."

No one spoke much more, and they all went to bed feeling vaguely guilty.

In two days, they had traversed the winding trails through the Levenloes and the last hill rolled them down onto the vast savanna of Thequis, which swept off to the south, east, and west. Late summer grass, long and golden, bowed and swayed under the wind. Far in the distance, a vast herd of bison darkened the prairie.

"Wow." Borrel glumly shaded his eyes against the sun. "It's like Ohe all over again. Only here there's grass instead of dryherb."

Jax squinted against the glare and inhaled deeply. "It's like a vast golden sea."

"How do we cross it?" Marith stared at the untracked plain.

"We follow the sun," Florin answered confidently. "And navigate by the stars."

But the next day the Fall Rising began.

Jax, wading through the grass behind Florin, suddenly felt his stomach lurch. "Oh no..."

"Oh no?" Florin turned to look over her shoulder. "What?"

Jax gazed up at the far blue sky, sniffed the wind and frowned. "It's the Rising."

"Well, we won't drown out here." Florin resumed her stride toward the east.

Within an hour the sky clouded over, and a driving rain pelted the travelers. The plain offered no trees and few sheltered lees. Huddled in cloaks against the rain, the group continued to trudge eastward—at least they hoped they were still headed east.

At night they sheltered in their large tent, but even its waxed canvas could not keep out the downpour. By morning, wet and chilled and barely rested, they all huddled around Marith's map arguing about the best way to get to Stede, which was the only permanent town on the prairie.

"According to this, Stede is due east from the pass we came over." Borrel pointed to the map with a long brown finger.

"But we can't be sure this map is that precise," Jax noted.

"We could head south to this river," Marith offered. "Then follow it east to the city."

Florin peered at the map. It looks like the river ends in some kind of swamp. We don't want to mess with that. What's this river called? The lettering is too messy to read."

"It's *Rysk*." Jax said without looking. He remembered the name from his geography studies in Kree.

Florin continued. "The city lies on the river's northern bank. Surely it won't be that hard to find."

A particularly vicious blast of wind shook the tent; a corner ripped shortly, loudly.

"We should have brought a Mystic to build us shelters," Borrel said.

Florin laced up her pack. "But then you and Jax would be miserable with cross magic the whole trip."

Jax stood up and hefted his pack. "We'd better make a decision before this goddess-damned hurricane blows us all away."

"You know, Jax." Marith rose to her feet and gathered her gear. "As a theological point, the goddess doesn't *damn* anything. Not trolls, not hurricanes, not even half-isles."

"She damned me."

"You damn yourself. Let's do it Florin's way," she decided with an abrupt change of subject. "So far the map has been close enough to accurate."

They folded the tent as best they could in the screaming wind and set out on to the east. At least they hoped it was east. Jax held Marith's arm to steady her, as they all lurched across the windy plain, under a sky so low and so uniformly dark that there was no way to be sure exactly which direction they were headed.

Before long, the thick clouds and constantly shifting wind forced the group to stop traveling during the middle of the day when the gray light and unmarked landscape provided no hint of direction. Only at dawn and dusk, when they could be certain of their course, would Florin lead them through the wet and blowing grass. During the middle of the day and at night, they huddled together under a dripping tarp or tent and tried to warm themselves over smudgy fires of damp grass.

As they sat the next afternoon, seeking the meager shelter offered by the crumbly sandstone along the bank of a shallow wash, they saw their first tornado. Lightening crackled in blue-white forks down to the dancing grass. Thunder followed, rolling across the plain in loud, un-breaking waves of sound. Hail, the size of river stones, pounded down on them, spooking the horse.

Amid all this, they managed to rig a tarp for shelter and even, much to Jax's discomfort, pull Ol' Pol under it for protection. Across the wash, away in the distance, they watched amazed, as the heavy clouds lowered a black finger to touch the earth.

"What is that?" Florin asked in awe.

"I think it's called a tornado," Jax answered.

"A tornado?" Marith repeated the unfamiliar word slowly.

Jax thoughtfully recalled his political geography lessons back in Kree. "I think they're caused by the Risings. They sweep all along the prairie, destroying everything, sucking up stone shelters or tents or people or livestock, and uprooting trees."

"What trees?" Borrel wondered.

"How do we avoid them?" Marith watched the swirling cloud roar westward.

"Out here, I don't know." Jax pushed strands of windblown hair out of his eyes. "The Herders all shelter in Stede during the Risings. I guess the city can withstand the wind."

"How do you know all this?" Florin frowned.

"I had insistent tutors."

"Yes, well now that you've decided to enlighten us about our danger, perhaps you'd care to remember something more useful," Marith said dryly. "Like how to get to Stede."

"I don't know."

Marith noted his impudent grin and laughed. Outside the tarp, large hailstones hammered into the mud.

As miserable as they were, slogging through the wet grass, beaten by the hail, deafened by the thunder, and threatened by the tornados, Jax was still glad to be out of Hilsen Vale. While his three companions nostalgically reminisced about Aric's warm pub and black ale, he relished the freedom of the distant horizon, waving with undulating grass.

They saw more than six tornados in the seven days it took them to reach Stede. One roared by in the night, ripping the tent up around them and dragging it several hundred yards. Inside they and their belongings tumbled about like beads in a rattle. The experience shook them all, and even Jax was relieved to get out of the open and into the city.

The city of Stede rose from the flowing savanna like an island amid a great running river. Vast, roughly hewn blocks of stone, stacked without mortar, formed the walls, towers, and even the roofs of the single permanent town in Thequis. As they approached it from the north, the sun was setting over the cloud-filled west, casting long, blue shadows to meet the darkness in the east. Ceaseless Rising winds blew across the grass and howled around the city's sun-reddened stones.

"Giants must have built this place," Florin whispered in awe as they approached the towering walls.

"That's what the legend says," Jax told her.

"What legend?" Marith asked skeptically.

"*Giants strode across the plains,*" Jax quoted. "*And though they're gone, there still remains/ The vast and towering town of Stede/ Where Herders show their finest breeds.*"

Borrel began to wonder if going to Stede was such a good idea after all. "I've never seen such a building that didn't have at least a residue of the Mystic that built it. But there's none here. What happened to the giants?"

"It's thought that they retreated underground." Jax answered. "The prairie is prone to earthquakes, possibly caused by the giants down there. Herders found Stede as it is, standing abandoned, but they don't have any other built cities because they can't withstand the earthquakes and the tornados."

"So, the giants are gone?" Borrel wanted to be sure.

"You're asking the wrong person, Borrel. My Kordish tutors didn't think fairies existed either."

"Great," Borrel muttered, but he followed the others down the muddy track to the city.

Tall, long-haired Herders appraised the four travelers through small windows in the sturdy wooden gate. Around and above them, the heavy walls stood unperturbed in the wind.

"We're seeking shelter," Marith explained with some asperity to the wary eyes of the guards. What, by the goddess, did they think she and her three windblown friends wanted?

Grudgingly the guards let the travelers into the city. Staring with wide eyes, the group walked into Stede. Everything within the walls was made of the same massive stone blocks. The buildings sloped up to conical roofs, constructed of carefully balanced stones. The Herders themselves stared at the four travelers suspiciously, but surreptitiously. Kordish, Ohite, and Nomad merchants often visited Thequis to buy horses, which were the finest in the Knownlands, but horse traders usually had enough sense to leave the tornado-swept savanna long before the Risings descended.

The Herders merely tolerated foreigners or ignored them altogether. In this unfriendly atmosphere, Marith had to use all her charm and plenty of her coins to arrange lodging. Stede, full of Herders sheltering from the storms, had few extra rooms for the strangers. Most Herders occupied vast dormitories that housed their extended family groups, while their herds of fabulous horses, cattle, and sheep stamped in covered barns. Filled with almost the entire population of Thequis, Stede exuded a holiday atmosphere that Jax found familiar.

After a bath and a hot dinner, he and the two nyads relaxed over mugs of Herders' mead—a milky drink made from things he did not want to think about. At one end of the tavern, four Herders rolled among the tables in a private brawl. Elsewhere around the room couples sat in the shadows, embracing purposefully.

Jax grinned at all of this. "This place is just like Haven during the Risings."

The twins glanced around at the unruly Herders.

"Everyone in the country is washed up together for the duration of the storms. We Barians go through the same thing each Rising. Haven is a wild place those weeks."

"But why?" Borrel asked. "I should think that these three weeks would be the perfect time to read books, or contemplate life, or the goddess, or whatever."

Jax shook his head. "The Risings make us too tense. First there's the Fear, and then the storms rock the Floating Islands in crazy ways. Besides, even at the best of times, Barians don't like to sit still. The seas keep us moving."

"I suppose these Herders feel the same way," Borrel conceded.

Before long, unimpressed by the supposed merits of Herders' mead, they found the room Marith had rented and went to sleep, glad to be sheltered from the pelting hail and the black, tornadic winds.

24

Much to everyone's surprise, especially considering their obsession with horses, it was Jax who befriended and was befriended by the Herders. Sensing some fundamental affinity with Jax's islish heritage, a number of them sought him out and eventually took him home. None of them seemed to understand that the iron ring around his neck was anything other than a rather heavy-handed taste in jewelry.

By their third day in Stede, Jax, and by extension Marith and the two nyads, were invited to stay for the remainder of the Rising in the "hotel" belonging to the Westfork Herd. These hotels were vast stone buildings with several floors of bedrooms and large common rooms for dining and socializing. Since the Westfork Herd was one of the more affluent Herds, their hotel gleamed with light from blown-glass sconces from Vitrus. Bright, richly woven Nomad carpets hung from the stone walls and covered the floors.

Florin frowned, Borrel laughed, and Marith shrugged as their hard-eyed half-isle drank, gambled, and generally ran amok with two cousins, Tolomund and Frola.

"But you can't even lead Ol' Pol down a trail without getting into a fight with her," Florin pointed out to Jax. "You don't have anything in common with these Herders."

"Yes, I do." Jax took another swig of Herder mead, which, he had discovered, went down easier after the first four or five mugs. "In some ways these Herders are more like Barians than any other people I've met."

So, when betrayal came, it hit Jax doubly hard.

For the better part of a week, the travelers shared the shelter of Westfork Herd's hotel. Jax amassed a pile of Herder coins by consistently winning at cards. Borrel spent hours chatting with the Westfork Herd's two Dragons, while Florin, for lack of anything better to do, spent her time "studying horseflesh" with a couple of very handsome Herders. Marith exchanged medicinal lore with the Westfork's druid, but she found a better resource in an old trader who claimed to have been to places as far flung as the city of Seare in Vitrus and Lake Cronkie deep in the Verwood.

Day after stormy day, Marith left Westfork's hotel and scurried through the blustery streets to sit for hours with Pop Gulligan. With an inconsistent pen, he scrawled blotchy amendments on her map, and filled her head with confusing tales of lost cities and vanished giants.

Marith listened and questioned and nodded, knowing that glimmers of truth probably lay deep within even the most improbable tale. Of course, she could not always know which bit of Gulligan's fable was truth, but she figured that when the time came, she would know.

"Come on up!" Tolomund called down to Jax and Frola, who stood far below on the walkway.

"Watch how I do it." Frola winked at him then climbed nimbly up the massive stone blocks to stand on the parapet next to her cousin.

Indeed, Jax watched how she used small pits and crevices in the stone for finger and toeholds. Still, it looked like a tricky climb, especially in this wind.

With a Rising-reckless grin, Jax followed the Herders up to the parapet.

There, the view of the vast flowing savanna curved away to the distant horizons. Black clouds grumbled overhead.

"Great, isn't it?" Frola shouted over the howl of the wind.

"It is impressive."

"Whoa! Look at that horsetail!" Tolomund used the traditional Herder term as he pointed to a thick tornado that plummeted to the ground not far from the city walls.

Thunder pounded through the clouds.

"This may not be the best place to stand at the moment." Frola squinted at the sky.

"How do we get down?" Jax looked at the walk far below.

A crack of lightning struck another parapet not a mile from where they stood.

"Quickly!" Tolomund deftly lowered himself towards the protection of the walkway below.

Thick rain poured suddenly from the sky.

"Damn," Frola swore. "This will make the stone slippery. Go carefully, Jax."

With rainwater splashing into his eyes and nose, Jax clambered down as quickly as he could. Above him, Frola flattened herself against the parapet.

"Sweet goddess!" she shouted, as hail began to thicken the rain. "Tolomund, look! That horsetail is coming right towards the city!"

Both Jax and Tolomund looked to where she pointed and watched in horror as the black cloud smote the city wall and whirled into the streets. People, horses, crates, chickens flew up into the air.

Frola more slid than climbed down to the walkway, and all three of them started back to Westfork's hotel at a run. Undamaged, the hotel nevertheless shook with the uproar as Westfork Herd tried to account for every member and each animal. Marith came in shortly after Jax, her hair flying away in a wild tangle, her face nearly as gray and distracted as her hair.

Concerned by her appearance, Borrel and Jax got her some tea and sat her by the fire.

"Where's Florin?" Marith looked around the room with a dazed air.

"With the horses, helping to calm them."

"Thank the goddess." Marith took a deep sip of tea.

"Did you see that tornado?" Borrel asked.

"See it! I was right there when the black beast touched down. People, carts, all sorts of stuff just went flying everywhere. Even Pop Gulligan would have blown away if I hadn't grabbed hold of his belt. I was wrapped around one of those hitching posts they have all over the place. Sweet goddess! That wind blew so hard it practically sucked the breath out of our lungs."

Tolomund joined them by the fire looking grave.

"Are your people all right?" Jax asked.

"I don't know yet, but nine horses damaged themselves in their terror and will have to be put down." His lips closed in firm, unfriendly line.

"I'm sorry." Jax knew by now that the Herders valued their steeds almost as much as their human family members.

Marith drained the last of her tea. "Tolomund, how often do tornados hit Stede?"

The Herder shook his head. "They don't. That's why we all stay here. There is no story or record that the Westfork Herd knows that tells of a horsetail ever touching Stede."

Florin reappeared from the stables, straw sticking out of her brown hair, manure on her boots. She glanced at Tolomund then frowned at Marith's haggard appearance.

"Mother, are you all right?"

"I'm fine. Considering the tornado literally swept me right off my feet."

Again, Florin glanced at Tolomund. "Well," she hesitated before continuing. "Some people in the stables mentioned that you had been seen at the site of the horsetail, and they were blaming you for it, saying you drew it down, called it into the city."

"That's ridiculous. I'm just a druid."

"No, but the other nyad there has magic," Tolomund supplied darkly.

"I've never heard of any magician with enough power to influence the weather." Borrel would have laughed at the egregiousness of the suggestion, but the expression on Tolomund's face scared the humor out of him.

"But it's a little too slick for coincidence that the first horsetail to hit Stede in memory comes while you foreigners are here."

"But, Tolomund," Jax stood to face his erstwhile friend. "You know us. You know we wouldn't wish you any harm."

"We thought we knew you," Frola came to stand next to her cousin. "But maybe you fooled us."

"I'm the fool." Jax turned away and pushed angrily at his hair.

"Look, Tolomund, Frola," Marith interposed, "We did not cause this tornado to hit Stede, and we certainly wish you no harm. But we'll go ahead and leave your hotel for now, so you can settle your affairs. We'll go back to the inn where we were staying before."

"That would be for the best." Frola spoke coldly.

Angrily, Jax followed Florin to the rooms they had shared in the hotel.

"This is ludicrous," he growled.

"Obviously." Florin stuffed their belongings indiscriminately into the packs. "But it isn't just Tolomund and Frola who are talking like that. Out in the stables people were already convinced that Mother Marith called down the wrath of the goddess on the city."

"But why?"

"I don't know, Jax. But in the confusion, I loaded Ol' Pol." She handed him two of the packs and shouldered the other two. "I'll take these down to the horse. You and Borrel get some food, if you can. I'll meet you in the alley behind the hotel."

"You mean we're leaving Stede altogether?" Jax grasped the implications of Florin's plans.

"I think we'd better run for our lives before these crazy Herders arrest Mam Marith."

Jax lugged the two bulky packs back down the stairs, tromping down the sick feeling of betrayal with cold anger. Back in the salon where Marith still sat near the fire, he could sense the evil mood of the Herders who milled, muttering, around the room. Panicky and confused, they were all too ready to strike out at the first target of blame.

Jax handed one of the packs to Borrel and helped Marith to her feet. As they shuffled out the door he casually waved back at the Herders. "Goodbye, Tolomund," he called, only barely muffling his sarcasm.

"Goddess, Jax, don't provoke them," Borrel whispered.

Despite the clear accusation in their eyes, the Herders let them go. Out in the street, the travelers felt the sting of malevolent glares. A few Herders even spat into the road as they saw the strangers pass. Indignantly, Jax stared down the most threatening people.

They tried to buy bread and dried fruit from some stalls in a square, but the merchants refused to sell their wares, even when offered most of Jax's winnings.

"Hey, Marith!" Pop Gulligan shoved his way through the crowd to join Marith, Jax, and Borrel. "I think you'd better leave Stede."

"We've reached the same conclusion."

"Yes, well..." Gulligan's glanced around at his frowning compatriots. "Meet me behind my house in about fifteen minutes. I'll show you a less public way out of the walls."

"We'll be there."

Pushing though increasingly ugly crowds, the three soon reunited with Florin and Ol' Pol and set off to find Pop Gulligan's house. Fortunately, rain began to fall again, washing the crowds from the street. As evening slowly shrouded the city, they met Gulligan in a narrow passage between rain-damp stone buildings. Silently, he led them to a ragged wooden gate that closed over a solid block of stone.

"Only it's not solid," Gulligan chuckled. He wiped rain out of his eyes and considered the wall for a moment. Coming to some decision, he began to push and shove on different faces of the stone.

With an earsplitting shriek one of the giant blocks slid aside to reveal a long dark tunnel.

"See!" The old Herder nearly danced with delight. "I bet you thought all me old stories was just tall tales. But they're true! True!"

Marith regarded the old fellow with new admiration. "You're a wonder."

"I am that. Here." He handed Florin the large sack he had been carrying. "Food."

"Thank you." The nyad roped the satchel onto the horse.

"Now, don't take the road," Gulligan said seriously to Marith.

"What road?" Jax asked, having seen no roads whatsoever since coming to Thequis.

"The road to the south, on the other side of the river," Gulligan explained. "This Rising is nearly spent, and when they count up the dead from the horsetail today, plenty of folk will mount up and ride out after you. You all may walk pretty fast, but you won't outrace Herder horses."

"So where do we go if we can't stay on the road?" Florin frowned.

"Take to the canyons." Gulligan smiled slyly. "Horses can't go far in that rocky maze."

"But how will we find our way?" Borrel remembered the area designated as 'the Maze' on Marith's map.

"There's a trail. Once you get outside the walls here, go east along the river until you come to a ford. Cross the Rysk there, and on the far shore you'll see a wash that leads towards the south. Follow it all the way into the canyons. Well, I don't really remember every twist and turn, but you'll see the footprints of people who were there before you. Footprints stay in the desert for years."

"So, we follow a trail into the Maze, and then where are we?"

"No, no, no," Gulligan shook his head. "Not into the Maze. You don't want to go there. No one gets out of the Maze. Besides, the Eldar ghosts are in there."

"But you just told us to go into the canyons," Jax said, exasperated.

"Right, right. You go up this wash and follow this trail. It skirts the Redrock Maze, but you won't actually get into it. The canyon leads beside the flat-topped mesas and finally you come out into the brown desert. Just keep heading south. Soon you'll find the Owh River. Follow it west and south. Cross the Owe Canyon at Ropebridge and take the caravansary from there to Dishroc.

Jax, who had been watching up the street while Pop Gulligan rambled on, saw ruddy torchlight reflected on a distant wall. "I think we'd better get going."

"Yeah, yeah. The mob's a-coming," Gulligan chuckled.

"Thanks for your help." Marith gave the old Herder a juicy kiss and ducked into the tunnel.

"Yippee!" Gulligan hooted. "Yippee!"

The stone gate slammed shut behind the four travelers, leaving them surrounded in thick darkness.

Jax choked. "I hate tunnels."

No one moved; no one could see a thing. Behind them they could feel the tramp of feet passing along the street they had just left.

"Why don't you make us a light, Borrel?" Marith asked impatiently.

"Oh. Sorry." Borrel's magical amber light filled the tunnel.

"Yep, I hate tunnels," Jax said again, as a collection of dried bones—human and animal— and numerous spiders came into view under Borrel's light.

"Let's move," Florin ordered. They were all glad to obey.

Within five minutes they came to the outer edge of the passage. Gusts of fresh wind blew through chinks in the stone.

"Our hero forgot to tell us about this part," Florin muttered.

"Just push around, like he did," Jax suggested. "The mechanism is probably here somewhere."

With the practiced eye of one who was raised in castles riddled with secret passageways and hidden doors, Jax began to press here and there on the cold stone. It was Borrel, however, who leaned up against the wall and triggered the switch. The screech echoed loudly through the tunnel, but the stone slid open and the blowing savanna grasses waved at them in the lighter dark of night.

Without a word the four travelers left the shelter of Stede and walked onto the dark, windswept plain. Behind them the stone door squealed shut. They found the River Rysk, mostly by sound, and proceeded along the bank, heading east.

After an hour Florin called a halt. "I think we should stop for the night. In this darkness we won't know if we come to that ford or not."

In no time they had pitched their tattered and patched tent and lain down, exhausted by the day's ordeal.

"I really thought I was going to fly away," Marith said softly into the darkened tent.

"We're glad you didn't," Borrel answered.

Florin poked her nose out of her blankets. "I still can't believe they would blame us for that tornado. After all, Jax had practically become one of them."

Jax stared up at the blowing fabric of the tent, wondering if he would ever become accustomed to betrayal. It seemed to happen to him far too often. What did he do to make everyone, from his mother, to Tallyn, Bryx, Klaris, and now Frola and Tolomund always abandon him?

He tried briefly to reason with himself, to take the Herders' side and see how strangers could be threatening in an already incomprehensible situation. But reason could not answer to his feelings. Betrayed he felt, so betrayed he was. Despite his fatigue, it took him hours to find sleep.

The winds continued to blow fiercely for the next two days. The group crossed the River Rysk at the ford Gulligan had described, found the wash that meandered southward, and followed it into the canyons.

Had there been any water in the wash, they would have been walking upstream, but the wash was dry. Their only potable water came from the occasional pool left here and there from passing Rising storms.

The canyon walls rose higher and steeper as they went on. Twice they had to backtrack when the canyon ran them into cliffs too steep to climb. But as Gulligan had promised, Florin always managed to find signs of human passage. It was not much, but Marith and Florin remained confident that this wash led to the trail to Dishroc.

By their third day out of Stede, the sand-filled wind finally let up, but the clouds hung lower and lower and finally came down in a light rain. Exhausted, Marith threw down her pack in the shelter of a swaying cottonwood tree, even though it was only mid-afternoon.

"At this point I don't much care if the Herders catch us," she told a frowning Florin. "But I am not going to walk on in the rain."

"It's not much of a rain." Borrel slung his own pack onto the sand.

"No." Marith put out a hand to catch the tiny drops. "But it will make a gentle lullaby for us on the roof of the tent. Besides, I think we all deserve an early night." None of them had slept easily since their precipitous flight from Stede.

With the ease of long practice, they had soon pitched the tent in the sand under the tree, staked out Ol' Pol, eaten a little food and rolled into their quilts. As Marith had predicted, the soft sigh of falling rain lulled them all into a deep sleep.

In the dead of night Jax awoke with a start. He sat up, listening, but the rain had stopped, and the desert was silent. Jax's heart pounded; sweat beaded on his brow. He did not know what was wrong, only that a rare magic-given premonition was screaming inarticulately. Suddenly he understood.

"Get up!" He jumped out of his blankets. "Marith! Florin! Get up! Move! NOW!"

"What?"

"Jax, what's the matter?"

"MOVE!" He dashed out of the tent, his arms laden with packs and loose gear. He threw the bundle of stuff up onto the bank, well out of the wash, and ducked back into the tent one more time.

The others were up, looking at him in confusion. Borrel had made a dim light.

"Get out now!"

This time they obeyed, grabbing what they could carry and following Jax back up the bank. Marith was still in the wash when a giant wall of water careened around the bend. Jax grabbed her arm and dragged her up onto the bank.

With a roar the water plunged past them, sweeping away the tent.

"Pol!" Marith wailed.

"Sweet goddess." Borrel watched the bubbling flood in awe. In the cloud-shrouded moonlight the four travelers stood shaking on the bank and watched as tree trunks and even, it seemed, boulders washed by in the rumbling torrent.

Eventually Marith collapsed onto her pack. "Poor Ol' Pol. She's been with us nearly thirteen years."

Pol had been tethered to the tree on the other side of the tent. No sign of her remained anywhere. Like the tent, she was probably far down the canyon, swirling towards the River Rysk, miles in the distance.

Borrel shook his head and turned to Jax. "How did you know that was coming?"

"Once in a great while my magic is actually useful."

"Your magic told you that flood was coming?" Florin asked skeptically. "Why didn't Borrel's magic warn him?"

"Ask Borrel."

"It's the way with the gift." Borrel sat down next to his sister. "Sometimes the best benefits come to those with the least power."

"I still don't understand how Jax knew," Marith muttered.

"Presentiment," he explained. "I get them from time to time. I never really know what's going to happen, just that it won't be good."

Marith considered his dark form in the moonlight. "So, you do have feelings."

"Mostly bad ones."

Sunrise found them still sorting through their belongings. They had managed to salvage all four of their packs, most of their food, and their sleeping quilts. Jax had a straw hat that he had picked up in Langohe to shield his nose from the intense southern sun, and Marith had remembered to grab her money. But the map, their spare blankets, Borrel's books and the coins Jax had won gambling were gone.

For three days they camped on that bank, trapped by the flood-waters. The desert nights proved comfortably warm, so they did not miss their tent. With the extra time, they climbed the canyon wall to try to see where they were and where they were going, but even after they got to the top, which proved to be much higher than they expected, all they could see were crinkle lines of the maze of canyons stretching away in every direction. Giant, flat-topped mesas rose in ruddy monoliths to the east. Florin estimated that these strange mountains were no more than ten or twelve miles away as the raven flew but following the looping convolutions of the canyon would quadruple the distance.

"Too bad we're not ravens." Jax followed Florin down the canyon walls through different layers of red, blue, and green rock.

"Oh, I don't know," she said. "I'm pretty happy to keep my feet on the ground."

"We'll see if you still feel that way after we've walked eighty miles and only gone twenty."

25

By the time the flood subsided, they had resigned themselves to their losses, although Marith kept thinking that she saw Ol' Pol out of the corner of her eye. Despite the flood in the wash, very little rain had fallen on the surrounding desert, so Florin still hoped to find signs of Gulligan's trail. Nevertheless, within two days they were hopelessly lost.

Some critical turn in the trail had been washed away, and they had gone too far into the Maze before they realized their mistake. Although they studied the sandy floor of each side canyon, they could find no sign of human passage. Plodding heavily though the sand, laboring under their packs, they gradually realized the desperation of their situation.

At first, they tried to backtrack, following their own footprints, but they lost the track when they crossed the rocky waves of petrified sand dunes. In grim silence they climbed once again to the canyon rim to try to get their bearings. Vast blocks of sandstone the color of dried blood towered above the canyon maze.

Jax took off his hat and wiped his brow with a rolled-up sleeve. Borrel stared up at the hot autumn sun shimmering above them in a blue-white sky. "I can't imagine where that flood came from."

Marith sat on an outcrop of redrock and drank from her water skin. The surrounding landscape grabbed at her heart. She found it eerily beautiful in a pure sort of way: bare rock, bare sky, sun. But it was so vast, and so arduous to cross. She knew they were running out of food.

"That way is south." Florin shaded her eyes and squinted at the multiple layers of canyon walls and strange spires that laddered away until a distant blue mountain rose towards the implacable sky.

They all followed her gaze, knowing that was the way they had to go.

"Maybe we should leave the canyon floors and strike across country," Borrel suggested.

Jax frowned. "That'll mean lots of up and down."

"But these canyons meander around so much, we're never sure they will end up where we want them to."

Borrel was right, Jax realized, but going overland would be much more strenuous, and many of these canyon walls were too vertical to climb.

Three days later when their food ran out, they had only reached the jagged spires that Florin had noted from the distance. Here, narrow pillars of rock rose up from the sandy canyon floors like giant fingers. Amazed, the travelers wandered among these formations.

"Let's keep moving." Florin snapped them out of their daze.

Tramping along, Jax found himself, like Marith, alternately entranced then horrified by the canyon maze. Each time they climbed out onto a rim he felt the freedom of the sky and the sun and the sere desert wind. But each time they descended into another canyon, the walls closed overhead, shutting out the sun and the view and bringing back his old claustrophobia. It did not help that Marith and the two nyads always preferred to make camp somewhere down inside the canyon walls, though they never again dared sleep in a "dry" wash. They had learned that lesson.

Even so, their precautions were in vain. No more rain fell upon them. As they continued from one canyon into the next, they found less and less water. They learned to stop at each small pool, no matter how bug-infested, drink deeply and fill their water skins.

Marith began to wish for a straw hat, like the one Jax had. Florin eventually wove ragged, but effective, hats for herself, Borrel, and Marith from some brushy plant she found near a drying canyon pool.

Slipping and sliding along their way, bearing their packs and their growing fears, they went on towards the blue mountain far to the south. It did not seem to come any closer, but the ravens and the vultures that circled overhead did.

At first Lexyl thought they might be monsters. Their strange heads, over-sized and rather wispy, looked more like the weird illustrations on the ancient scrolls than any contemporary people. Of course, Lexyl had never seen any of the other races of the Knownlands, other than the Caveharts who lived on the mountain, one nyad, and the occasional dead Nomad. She had, however, read about them.

She cracked another nut on the warm rock where she sat and watched as the four odd-shaped creatures descended awkwardly into Blath Canyon. Several hours later they reappeared, this time on the south rim of the canyon. Before long they again dropped from sight into Whisper Gulch.

Lexyl folded her book closed and frowned. This time she realized that the four were people; their voices had carried to her across the two canyons that still separated them from her watcher's perch. Her sharp amber eyes, bred to the desert, recognized that it was hats and packs that distorted their forms. When they climbed out of Whisper Gulch it was noon. She watched as they rested for a while in the shade of a tree. They did not eat. Neither did Lexyl, until they once again disappeared below the lip of a canyon.

As she sucked a chewy pink lump of dried cactus fruit, Lexyl faced her dilemma. For generations, watchers from Arandy had sat in this perch, under this same tree, surveying the rolling griprock wilderness that stretched away to the north and west. Nowadays watchers usually just accepted messages sent from one of the other Eldar Collectives in the Maze or kept an eye on a lost Nomad, near enough to death to ignore. The desert took care of the careless.

Once watchers had played more active rolls. When this perch was established centuries ago, the watcher knew that he or she held

Arandy's safety. Outsiders were to be led astray, deeper into the Maze, or dealt with even more definitively: canyon walls were steep; canyon floors lay hundreds of feet below the rims.

But over the centuries the desert grew slowly larger, extending further and further to the lands north and west, so fewer outlanders reached the watcher's post. Eventually even the inhabitants of Arandy forgot the watcher's original purpose. Lexyl knew only because she had illegally read the ancient scrolls.

As the four strangers again emerged from a canyon, Lexyl realized that they were still a couple of days from death. Precedents for what she should do were so ancient that most Eldars would not know of them. Conveniently, this left Lexyl the opportunity to make up her own rules.

The strangers finally came onto the mesa where she sat. Their shuffling footsteps and slumped shoulders demonstrated the extent of their fatigue. Canyon Nkai seemed to defeat them. Five hundred feet of empty air separated them from the small stream that gurgled among autumn-colored trees and a herd of desert deer. But unlike the other canyons they had climbed through today, these walls appeared impossibly sheer.

Lexyl listened to their voices, mildly surprised that she could understand their Landish, despite their funny accents. One of the men threw down his pack and took off his hat to run his fingers through sun-streaked hair. Two of them looked liked the nyads she'd seen up on the mountain. The smallest stranger, a woman by her voice, sat down with a heavy sigh, while the nyads continued to stare down into Canyon Nkai. With a shiver of shock, Lexyl realized that one of them was a Dragon. She had never met a person with the dragons' force.

Although they were now no more than thirty yards from her perch, they still had not seen her. But then her thick-soled sandals, linen pants, and loose shirt were all the same ruddy color as the rock around her. Only her blue scarf of rank, which she wore irreverently tied around the brim of her wide straw hat, did not blend with the rocky landscape. Since her back was to the sun, she did not worry about glare reflected from her blue-tinted sunglasses.

Briskly, she cast her entrapment spell, making sure she sewed the Dragon in tightly. She sensed depth to his magic but had no way to gauge his power or his means of using it. As her net fell upon them, she realized that the other man had a little Dragon too, but not enough to bother her.

Three blue bands of Mystic snapped around the strangers. Their cries of alarm bounced off the canyon walls. Lexyl waited without moving, watching their reactions. The Dragon sent out a finger of his magic, but the bright resistance of her rings had him penned. At last Lexyl stood from her spot under the tree, drawing their gaze for the first time. Brushing bits of nutshell from her pants, she grabbed one of her water skins and strolled over to her captives, who stood, silently watching.

At close range, the signs of exhaustion, dehydration, and sunburn were clear on their faces.

Silent and wary, they stared back at her.

Following proper Eldar etiquette, she removed her sunglasses so her captives could see her amber eyes as she tossed the water skin through her blue rings. "May the sun always grant you his shade." She offered them the traditional Eldar greeting.

The nyad woman stooped to grab the water skin, opened it and threw back her head to drink.

"Wait!" cried the older woman. "It may be poison."

Lexyl grinned, but her eyes narrowed. "Why should I do what the desert would do for me?"

The nyad gave Lexyl a hard look then took a long deep drink. "It's water, Mother." She handed her the water skin.

"I'm Florin Starrish." The nyad turned back to Lexyl. "Thank you."
"You needed it."

"We did." The other nyad wiped his mouth and handed the skin on. "I'm Florin's brother Borrel. This is Mother Marith, and Jax."
"I'm Lexyl St. Clare."

"Are you a Nomad?" Marith wondered.

"Of course not. I am of the Eldar People." Lexyl's voice was mild, but her eyes snapped. "But I am beside the point. Were you looking for Canyon Nkai, or are you lost?"

"Are you a ghost?" Florin narrowed her eyes at the Eldar woman.

Lexyl laughed. "Not yet."

"We're lost," Jax confirmed.

"We were trying to get to Dishroc, Lexyl." Borrel liked the feel of her foreign name on his tongue.

"Dishroc!" Lexyl found herself responding to Borrel's rather attractive smile. "You certainly are lost."

"There was a flood in the middle of the night," Florin explained. "It washed away most of our gear and the track we were following."

"I see."

"This is very good." Borrel gestured to the rings. "Why aren't Jax and I suffering cross-magic?"

"Hard to say," Lexyl prevaricated, although she was puzzled herself. According to all she had read, the use of her Mystic ought to have severe effect upon the two Dragons. She had read that powerful magicians of either Mystic or Dragon could erect barriers of protection to prevent cross-magic, but Lexyl had never studied such precautions. "I've never met a Dragon before, much less used my magic on them."

"Well then, Jax and I are pleased to be emissaries of Dragon force to your Eldar People." Borrel bowed gallantly.

Jax laughed, but Lexyl's eyes narrowed behind her blue lenses. "Come sit by this tree." As she gestured, the three rings began to drift toward the shade. Herded by her magic, the four moved as directed. Once they had seated themselves on the rock, the rings faded so that they were only visible by an occasional blue shimmer.

"Great control," Borrel admired softly.

Lexyl tossed the group a pouch of nuts then settled herself on a higher rock with her back to a stone ledge. Here she could keep an eye on her territory and her captives. Silence returned to the canyon.

Only the occasional cough of a raven, or puff of breeze echoed among the rock walls.

The strangers ate the nuts without speaking. Marith lay down in the shade. Jax took a small wooden whistle from his pocket and began to play a soft, rather melancholy tune that echoed beautifully off the canyon walls. Florin quietly whittled a stick with a small knife. Borrel tried not to stare at the Eldar.

"How long will we stay here, Lexyl?" Marith asked finally.

"Until the sun is three fingers above Portal Rock." Lexyl indicated a massive block of rusty sandstone that towered above the western rim of the canyon.

"Where will you take us?"

"To Arandy."

"Is it far?"

Lexyl answered absently, "We'll be there tomorrow." A flash of movement on the horizon had caught her attention. Intently, she stared towards the north over the griprock. Were others following these strangers? Amber eyes narrowed in concentration. There again: a shimmer of gold amid the red and buff of the desert.

Lexyl sighed and settled back against the rock. She smiled down at the strangers, who were looking at her with worried expressions, having noticed her frown.

"Blessings of the cat god," Lexyl said to reassure them. "It's just a lion."

Marith sat up. "A lion?"

The others looked unsettled as well. "Sure. It's a blessing to see one and survive," Lexyl smiled.

"Do you worry about them when you're out here all alone?" Borrel asked.

"What makes you think I'm alone?" She was, of course, but she did not want to disclose more than she had to.

Borrel shrugged and smiled again.

Marith resumed her questioning: "What will happen when we get to Arandy?"

"The Eldar Council will decide."

Jax sighed and put away his instrument. "I hate councils."

Florin frowned at him. "Councils, tunnels, mountains: What don't you hate?"

"The sea."

Marith ignored this exchange and continued questioning Lexyl. "What does the Eldar Council usually do with...visitors?"

"I don't know. We haven't had any in several hundred years."

Borrel tossed the empty water skin towards Lexyl, but it hit the invisible barrier and dropped back onto the rock near the nyad.

Lexyl's amber eyes narrowed behind her dark glasses. "You didn't think I was that stupid, did you? If the rings weren't solid, I'd have disarmed you."

"If you could," grumbled Florin.

Lexyl replied with a disarming smile.

Borrel nodded in admiration.

Florin watched Jax gaze moodily at their captor. "So Jax, why do you hate councils?"

"Bad experiences in my youth." He thought of the hours of interrogations, the humiliating punishments, the unreasoning prejudice he had suffered at the collective hands of the Kordish royal council during his years of fostering.

"Well, I'm glad you found us, Lexyl," Borrel said. "I'd rather take our chances with a council of people than the inhuman expanse of the desert."

Lexyl lowered her dark glasses to stare into the brown eyes of the nyad Dragon. "The desert is generous."

Her words made strange sense to Borrel.

As blue shadows began to lengthen from beneath the cliffs, Lexyl rose and stretched. Without a word to her captives, she strode across the rock to the small watcher's shelter where she had lived for the last seven days. Eamon would soon be here to relieve her. Usually she was reluctant to leave her solitary home on the desert to return to the pressures and confines of Arandy, but this time she waited for Eamon with little patience. She could hardly wait to see what the Eldar Council and the law-bound chieftess would say to strangers in the Redland maze. Deftly she tidied up the small shelter, stuffed her sleeping sack, books, food and last water skin into her pack. When she returned to the strangers, she found that they too had resettled their packs and were ready to move out.

But Eamon was late. The sun was merely two fingers above Portal Rock before she heard the nest of ravens scream in the canyon.

Briefly, she instructed the strangers in desert travel. They were to walk only in her footprints, stay on the rock and off the sand as much as possible, go single file. As they began to move, the encircling blue bands of magic floated along with them.

Eamon's mouth fell in wonder when he saw Lexyl approaching him as he came up the track from Canyon Nkai. His gaze darted from Lexyl to her captives and back again. "Magic!" he hissed with fear and distaste.

"Visitors," Lexyl corrected.

"But, my lady—"

"But what? They're strangers; they're here; my magic is a much easier way of containing them than rope."

"I suppose the Eldar Council will decide about that," Eamon sniffed.

"I suppose so."

The new watcher turned his amber eyes to the north and stared at the wilderness, refusing to look at Lexyl, her captives, or the blue bands of magic that shimmered in the twilight.

Halfway down the narrow, nearly invisible path along the canyon wall, Lexyl turned abruptly to Jax who followed her. "I don't much care for councils either."

Jax's wolf grin grew slowly. "That's most reassuring, my lady."

The shadows were thickening quickly by the time they reached the bottom of the canyon. Lexyl let them have only a short drink of water before rushing them on. The way-camp was not far, but the ground was uneven, and the strangers were already tired from their days of climbing in and out of canyon after canyon.

Finally, Lexyl asked Borrel to create a light so his companions could see their way over the rocks, branches, and through the thick streamside brush. While picking their way gingerly across the brittle branches of a beaver dam, Marith asked why they could not camp where they were.

"The goddess demands we respect her desert," Lexyl explained, shocked by the idea.

"I'm a druid, Lexyl. I respect the goddess, but we've had a long day."

Lexyl peered at the old woman, who was only a pale shadow by Borrel's amber magic. "Every time we step in the sand, we upset the goddess's balance in the desert. It takes years for even one footprint to be effaced."

"Unless there's a flash flood," Borrel noted.

"Such floods are rare. Campsites are especially damaging to the desert, with their fire pits, and sanitary pits. That's why we camp only in certain areas that are more hardy and better suited for the needs of people."

"That's a lovely sentiment," Jax replied. "But how much farther do you expect us to go tonight?"

"Another hour maybe."

With no more than a couple of sighs, the four travelers stumbled on.

Once at the way-camp, Lexyl stretched the blue bands to encompass the grass-covered beach along the water's edge and the stone shelter that crouched under some willows along an embankment. Borrel walked into the shelter feeling the caress of Lexyl's magic that had enhanced and embellished the hut. Like the stone of the cliffs, it was warm and red, but not large enough for all of them.

"We can sleep out here," Borrel offered.

Lexyl considered him for a moment then shook her head. "The desert nights are lovely this time of year, but I would like to keep you contained."

Both Jax and Borrel braced themselves for the cross-magic they expected would come when Lexyl raised her hands. But the red rock moved and took shape without causing either of them any discomfort.

"Interesting," Borrel said, sitting on the grass and watching.

"Isn't it?" Jax asked softly, watching Lexyl gather twigs. "Clearly her magic doesn't affect us. I wonder if the reverse would be true."

He gestured to Lexyl's small collection of kindling. "Do you want me to light that for you?"

She stood back and nodded with a small grin.

Jax focused his magic on the sticks, and soon a small bright fire flicked orange fingers around a small pot. She winked at him, and he knew she'd been just as curious to see if his magic would cross hers.

Lexyl brewed a spicy broth made with greens she picked along the stream. Florin watched her steadily, absorbing these aspects of desert survival.

"Wow!" Borrel wiped sweat from his brow. "Hot! Really good, but really hot!"

"We're sorry we have nothing to share with you, Lexyl," Marith said softly. "We ran out of food two days ago."

"I thought as much, by the look of you."

The next day, with the autumn sun burning upon the canyon rim, they tramped deeper into the Eldar Maze, out of Nkai Canyon, over some more griprock hills, and eventually descending into another, larger canyon. Around them rose sheer walls of red rock, striped by vertical streaks of black and buff. Arandy sat tucked under massive, overarching cliffs.

A collection of elegant buildings, some as high as five stories, lined the eastern walls of the canyon. Covered with glittering tiles of blue, green, gold and white, the buildings sparkled among the red rock like jewels. Delicate statues and figures carved out of soft sandstone or the gnarled wood of hardy desert trees decorated courtyards and niches in various buildings.

A stream flowed from a spring at the base of the eastern wall into a wash filled with grass and trees, which had turned yellow and orange with the shorter days of autumn. On the sheer canyon wall opposite the village, huge murals depicted strange scenes of cities destroyed and rebuilt, moonlit rites to the goddess, and seasons of growth and decay. Further down, the canyon widened into culti-vated terraces. The music of fountains echoed off the walls of can-yon and building alike as drops sprayed into tile basins and curving brooks, which then flowed into the larger stream in the center of the canyon.

The amber-eyed inhabitants of Arandy stopped and stared as Lexyl led her captives to the largest, most intricately carved and beautifully tiled building. Inside, the palace was even more ornate. Geometric patterns of glossy tile lined the floors and more pieces of glazed ceramic formed gleaming, fanciful mosaics on the walls. Silk-covered cushions lay piled in secluded corners and near windows.

Lexyl let her fingers linger upon the welcome tile on the lin-tel, placed there by the Mystics who built the place. The blue rings flashed, and both Borrel and Jax sensed the ancient weave that had called these walls and roofs, streets, and fountains to rise out of the ruddy cliffs.

Once inside, Lexyl pulled several varicolored ribbons that hung by the door, and soon two tall footmen and one small servant arrived in the foyer to stare in awe at the strangers and in apprehension at Lexyl.

"I am sorry I cannot offer you a bath, or more substantial food at the moment." Lexyl handed her pack to the page. She led them all down a short hallway to a windowless sitting room lit by three lan-terns of carved crystal that hung from the ceiling. Fruit and water stood on a delicate table against one wall, and more cushions lay enticingly about the floor.

"Help yourself to the fruit and water here. More will be brought if you wish. The footmen can help you if you need anything else."

Jax watched his companions marvel at the luxury of the room and remembered how he used to take such comforts and beauty for granted. He turned back to Lexyl. "How long will we be here?"

She removed her straw hat and unwound the blue scarf from its brim. "Not long. The council will soon be seated."

With that, she took a deep breath and Jax could feel the workings of her magic. The blue bands snapped and shimmered as they expanded to allow the captives access to most of the room. The footmen swore in surprise, while the page trembled mutely.

Shooting a glance of disgust at the other Eldars, Lexyl left the room, followed warily by the page.

"What a place." Florin carefully poured water from a crystal pitcher into silver goblets.

"Very civilized considering we're in the middle of an uncharted wilderness." Jax bit into a second pear.

"I think it's beautiful," Borrel said. "Everything here is beautiful."

26

"The Eldar Council will see you now." The piping voice of a little boy awoke them. Exchanging wary glances, they gathered their wits and rose from the soft cushions. As they followed the boy from the room, Lexyl's blue rings constricted and moved along with them. The two footmen followed, watching the magical bands more than the strangers.

"This Lexyl is really skilled," Borrel again noted with admiration.

"So you've informed us," Florin snapped.

The boy led them down the corridor, up a flight of stairs, and down another wide passageway to a set of intricately carved double doors. He knocked once then threw them wide. "Lady Lexyl's captives, your Majesty."

Wide windows along the western wall let in the last of the twilight. Crystal lanterns hung from the ceiling, and pure white candles gleamed on a long low marble-topped table behind which sat five people, including Lexyl, still in her ruddy watcher's clothes, her blue scarf now knotted around her neck. Silhouetted by the windows stood a tall, thin man in the robes of a priest or druid. A small gray cat, with eyes as sentient and amber as Lexyl's sat in her lap and watched the prisoners intently.

"Please kneel." The boy indicated a long thin cushion on the floor some distance from the table. Only Jax hesitated. Marith tugged his trousers imperatively until he settled down beside her.

"You can dismiss the footmen, Chieftess," Lexyl said to the woman seated next to her. The chieftess did not look at Lexyl but continued to consider the strangers impassively. Although she was dressed regally in a loose white robe with thick gold and blue trim and wore her hair pulled back into a headdress set with vivid purple and blue iridescent feathers, the chieftess' features were a mirror-image of Lexyl's. Six or maybe seven years older than Lexyl, the chieftess shared her amber eyes, fringed with the same long, bronze-tipped lashes, and when she spoke her voice carried the same tones and inflections.

"Thank you, sister, for using your magic to bring us these visitors, but I think the footmen will be sufficient to watch them for now."

"Two of them have the dragons' magic." Lexyl shrugged. "But if you wish me to release them...."

The chieftess snapped an impatient glance at Lexyl while the other three council members shifted uneasily and glared at the captives. Like Lexyl, they each wore a colored scarf tied ceremoniously around their shoulders. Matched with Lexyl's blue one, Jax realized that these scarves, yellow, black, and green, represented some sort of official rank.

"Which ones have the dragons' magic?" The priest moved from the windows to stand behind the chieftess' chair.

"The two men."

"Kill them immediately," decreed the priest.

At this Jax sat down more comfortably on the cushion, pretending not to watch as the seated members of the council glanced warily at the tall priest.

"Jax!" Marith hissed.

He looked at her out of glinting sea-blue eyes. "If I'm going to be executed, I'd like to spend my last few minutes in some comfort."

Taking Jax's cue, Borrel also moved to sit.

The page stepped forward tentatively. "You *must* kneel in the presence of the Eldar Council."

"Oh?" Jax cocked an eyebrow. "I didn't realize the Eldar Council was present. We haven't been introduced."

Even Borrel gaped at Jax's boldness.

With a graceful motion, the chieftess rose from her chair, and the other council members followed her example. Jax rose as well.

"I am Eleeza St. Clare, Chieftess of Arandy and Speaker for All Eldars. These with me represent the four Eldar Collectives and the goddess. Together we form the Eldar Council. Since you have come unbidden into the Eldar Maze, your lives are in our hands."

Jax executed an elegant bow and looked into the chieftess' amber eyes. "We are travelers from the Hantland on our way to Dishroc, and we humbly entreat your mercy."

The chieftess sat down, allowing the rest of her council to resume their seats as well, although the priest continued to hover behind their chairs. Lexyl again settled the cat onto her lap. Borrel shivered as the animal's sentient eyes bore into his own.

"Chieftess, allow me to introduce these strangers." Lexyl gave their names from Jax on the left to Borrel on the right.

With an ear-splitting yowl, the cat jumped onto the table, arching his back and hissing. Lexyl sat up, staring intently into space.

"Lexyl?" The chieftess frowned at her sister, then at the travelers, then back at Lexyl.

Suddenly the blue bands of magic sputtered and flared and began to hum. Lexyl fell back into her chair, eyes wide, gasping for air.

"Stop it!" The chieftess grabbed her sister's shoulders. No response. "Seize them!" She motioned the footmen towards the strangers, but the flashing bands of magic kept the men away.

Inside the glowing ring, Borrel moaned in agony and collapsed. Jax hunched himself against the waves of pain as vomit rose in his throat and his lungs constricted. Miserably, he once again recognized the visceral reaction to major cross-magic.

Unaware of the chieftess hovering over her, Lexyl smiled at something that only she could see. Borrel groaned again and Florin bent to him, calling his name.

"What is going on?" shouted the man in the black scarf.

"Big magic," Jax choked from the floor. "Powerful magic."

Lexyl screamed and went limp. The blue rings exploded into the room and dissipated. Borrel writhed and finally fainted. Jax cringed, as knives seemed to run in his blood.

Then it was over. The cat jumped to Lexyl's inert body and nudged her slack cheek. Florin shook Borrel, who lay unconscious, gasping painfully for air. Trembling, Jax wiped tears from his eyes.

Someone pounded at the door. "Chieftess! Chieftess!"

Grimly the chieftess rose and fired off commands. "Take the outlanders to the old cellar and guard them closely." The door flew open and panic filled the room.

No longer inhibited by Lexyl's Mystic, the footmen hauled Marith and Jax to their feet then hefted Borrel's body. Florin clung to her twin's hand. Jax's head swam as he blindly followed Marith through the palace corridors, down several series of staircases and into a small dark room. The men dropped Borrel on some empty sacks and left, bolting the door behind them, leaving the travelers in the dark.

"Sweet goddess, Jax." Marith groped towards Borrel in the darkness. "What was that all about?"

"Cross-magic," he answered hoarsely. "Like when the Weaver died, only worse. Much worse."

"Mother, help Borrel." Florin had settled her twin onto the sacks and held his head in her lap. They could all hear the rattle in his lungs.

"There's little I can do for cross-magic here in the dark. I don't have my pack. Jax, can you make a light?"

He shook his head. "I can make some of the sacks burn, probably, but the smoke won't help Borrel's lungs."

"Try a small fire, just for a moment, so I can look at him."

Jax took one of the sacks and placed it between his outstretched legs. He tried to ignore the dark memories of Oblek's pit and pull up a bit of fire, but nothing happened. "Damn." After a few steadying breaths, he tried again. This time the sacking roared into flame.

"Goddess, Jax! You'll incinerate us." Marith shrank back from the fire. Immediately Jax killed it.

"Can't you just make a small flame?" Florin demanded impatiently.

"I don't have control right now."

"Well, *try*."

Again he took several deep breaths. Again the sack exploded into a wall of flame.

"Sweet Goddess!"

He pulled back his power, plunging them once more into a smoke-filled darkness.

"I have a better idea." He stood up and went to the door. "Hey!" He pounded on the wood. "Hey, can we have a light in here?"

Silence.

"Hey!" He pounded some more. "We need to see to our friend. Can't you give us some light?"

"No."

"Look, he's cross-magicked, and—."

"NO!"

"Dragons fry you, then." He stumbled back to where Marith and Florin sat with Borrel.

"Here." Marith ripped a small corner of sacking. "Light just this small piece."

The torn fabric caught quickly and burned brightly.

"Perfect." Marith handed him the rest of the sack. "Keep lighting little bits, and I'll see what I can do for Borrel."

Jax did as he was told, burning two, then three, then four small pieces one at a time.

"He's breathing more easily," Marith announced.

"But the rest of us are going to suffocate." Jax noted the thickening haze that floated in the shadows of the ceiling. The tightness in his own lungs had more to do with the closeness of the dark walls.

Florin had been watching her twin intently. "I think it's Jax's force that eases Borrel's breathing."

"That could be." Marith coughed in the smoke.

With a bang, the cellar door swung open, flooding the little room with light. Jax's seventh rag fire went out abruptly.

"What are you trying to do?" the guard demanded. "Set the whole palace afire?"

"We asked for a light."

The guard and his three companions frowned at the small pile of blackened sacking at Jax's feet.

"Give over your flint."

Jax spread his empty hands. "Don't use it."

"Well, how are you making the fire?"

"Dragon force."

All four Eldar faces solidified into grim masks of censure. Without a word, they gathered the remaining sacking, even pulling it from under Borrel. As the door clanged shut and the darkness returned, the travelers heard the bolts lock into place.

"Just as well," Jax sighed. "Working the force was beginning to ache."

"I really think it helped Borrel," Florin repeated.

"There's nothing left for me to work it on now."

"Do you have your dragonpipe?" Florin asked. "I know how music, especially dragon music, eases him when he's upset. Maybe it would help now."

Jax shook his head in the dark. "The pipe is in my pack, wherever that is."

After a few minutes of silence, Jax spoke softly. "I used to sing. When I was locked up in... in the mines. I didn't have a dragonpipe. If you want...."

"Yes!" Marith crowed. "Florin move aside." The druid grabbed for Jax's hand in the darkness. "Come over here and hold him like Florin was doing. And sing. I'm sure the music will ease him."

Jax took Florin's place, holding the unconscious nyad's head and shoulders to his chest. Florin curled up against Borrel's stomach, and Marith settled in at Jax's back.

Softly and a little roughly Jax sang the First Tune in Islish.

"I didn't know you spoke Islish," Florin said.

Jax just sang a few more Islish songs. But the smoky room and the cross-magic were affecting him too. His throat soon grew dry.

"Damn," Jax breathed, as the silent dark closed around him.

"What's the matter?" Florin mumbled.

Jax wiggled, stretching his legs and breathing raggedly. "I do not like small dark places."

"You're not alone now." Marith put an arm around him.

He shuddered. "I'm not sure that makes it any better."

"Sure it does. Close your eyes and you won't know it's dark."

He did so, mostly to humor her. Sleep soon dragged him into a kind of peace.

Marith listened to his breathing, and to Borrel's ragged gasps. Florin, she knew, didn't sleep either.

"Jax?" Borrel's voice was soft, hoarse. "Jax, let go of me." The nyad sat up, disentangling himself from Jax's arms.

"Borrel!" Florin sat up and flung her arms around her brother, accidentally knocking Jax on the chin.

Marith stretched. "How do you feel?"

"Like I've been crushed by a ton of rocks. Where are we?"

"In a cellar."

"Why?"

"The Eldars didn't know what was going on. Jax said it was cross-magic."

"He's right."

"So why were you affected more than Jax?"

"Because my force is stronger."

"Lucky you."

"I don't understand."

"The more magic one has, the more one is susceptible to cross-magic."

"I still don't get it," Florin complained. "Lexyl's Mystic hadn't bothered either of you at all then all of a sudden everything went crazy."

"It wasn't Lexyl," Jax said.

Borrel elaborated. "It was someone at Castle Caledra, I think. Somehow his Mystic got tangled up with Lexyl's weave and when that happened, Jax and I got cross-magicked, and then..." He paused, shuddering. "And then something went terribly wrong."

Far above the dark cellar, Lexyl sat in her bathtub shakily washing off the dirt from her seven days of watch duty, hoping that the resounding ache within her magic would wash away too. She had only awakened an hour ago, after being unconscious for nearly a full night and day. The Chieftess Eleeza sat on the rim of the tub, watching her sister bathe with a mixture of relief and distrust.

"You're sure you're fine?"

"I will be."

"And those two Dragons didn't cause the problem?"

"No," Lexyl dunked her face. "Someone at Castle Caledra attempted to master the Mystic. I felt him start his spell and re-wove mine to be out of his way. But something went wrong." She shuddered. "The whole fabric of magic started to unravel. Someone else stepped in, I don't know who or how, but my weaving got tangled up then, and when that mysterious power withdrew, the mastery weave imploded...exploded. By the Cat God, you don't want to mess up a spell like that."

"Do you have to blaspheme?"

"You swear by your deities; I'll swear by mine."

Eleeza stood and strode to the window, which overlooked the afternoon glitter of Arandy from four stories up. Lexyl soaped her short hair. "Why don't you come pour the rinse water for me?"

The chieftess came back to the tub and slowly poured warm water from a ceramic pitcher. When Lexyl stood, Eleeza handed her a towel.

On the bed, the small gray cat stretched then resettled himself, staring at Eleeza with those cognizant eyes. Unsettled, the chieftess turned back to her sister. "So, your captives had nothing to do with it."

"Nothing at all."

"The two Dragons sure took the whole thing badly."

"What did they do?"

"The nyad passed out in agony and the saucy one nearly vomited on the floor. When the shamans reported that various people around Arandy had also collapsed, I thought that the strangers must be the cause."

Lexyl smiled slyly in the mirror. "Those other Eldars who collapsed, they all have Mystic, don't they?"

"How can you make such nasty accusations? You don't even know who they are."

"It isn't nasty to have magic, Eleeza. Besides, I know already who suffered." She listed names while Eleeza's frown deepened. "Any Mystic anywhere in the Knownlands was probably knocked unconscious when the mastery weave failed. Just because most Eldars choose to ignore the power in their veins doesn't mean that it's not there or that I can't sense it."

"I can see why our ancestors distrusted people with Mystic. You know more than you should."

"Poppycock. Our ancestors didn't distrust Mystic at all. In fact—" Lexyl cut herself short. Even though she was the council representative for Arandy, even though she was the sister and the heir to the Speaker for All Eldars, the ancient scrolls were still forbidden, and Eleeza would never understand why Lexyl had read them.

She took a breath, picked up a comb, and began ripping at the tangles in her wet hair. "We only suppose that our revered ancestors despised magic because of the warning about dragons on the mural over there." She gestured with her comb to the window that faced west towards the vast, art-covered canyon wall. "What really happened was that fewer and fewer Eldars were born with any Mystic, much less any real power."

"Until you," Eleeza sneered. "We've covered this ground before."

"Until our uncle Valdik."

"Who went off on a hare-brained journey to this legendary Castle Caledra that you talk about and was never heard from again. And no, Lexyl, I am still not going to let you go."

"I need to go there, E'eza. My magic requires training. It's dangerous otherwise. I could end up doing something as damaging as the person who failed the mastery spell last night. That kind of accident comes from a lack of training."

"Then just don't play with Mystic."

"That," Lexyl pulled a white and blue tunic over her head, "is not an option."

"Your options are getting narrower. Especially when you go flaunting your powers with little tricks like those blue rings."

"Mystic isn't bad. The Eldar People need to relearn that. Now, what did you do with the strangers? Has the nyad recovered from the cross-magic?"

Eleeza shrugged. "I had them locked in a cellar and forbade anyone to see them. Although the guards reported that they were trying to make a fire with some old sacks, and that insolent one said he was using Dragon force to do so."

"You locked them in the dark? In the cellar? That nyad was in much worse shape than I."

The chieftess glared at her sister. "How were we to know that the whole ordeal wasn't the nyad's fault?"

"You probably haven't fed them either." Lexyl scooped up the cat and left the room.

Eleeza followed. "Why feed them if I'm just going to execute them?"

"I'd at least like to know more about them first," Lexyl snapped. "This is the first contact we've had from the rest of the Knownlands in two hundred years. Aren't you a little curious about what goes on outside the Redland maze?"

"Not at all."

"Typical."

"Don't get sassy with me, Lex."

Lexyl swirled halfway down a stairwell to stare up at her sister. "Don't treat me like a child."

"You're only—"

"Thirty-one blessed years old, E'eza. Thirty-one! I may be your heir and your only surviving family, but I must live my own life."

"And the maze isn't big enough for you."

"Exactly." Lexyl ducked through a narrow hall and into the kitchen where she collected three pears and a glass of cactus juice for herself and scraped some leftover lizard meat into a dish for the cat.

Eleeza leaned against a wall, watching the cat eat.

Lexyl waited a moment then asked: "So, can we let the outlanders out of the cellar? Maybe give them some food?"

"Shaman Ashande blames them for the sudden 'illnesses.'"

"You're the chieftess, tell the people the truth."

Eleeza snorted. "That someone working magic from a mythical location is responsible? I'm not sure I believe it myself."

"Whatever the people believe, you won't act on their superstitions and prejudices. That's why you're the chieftess *and* the speaker. Because you can see to the truth and act accordingly."

"Flattery, Lexyl? That's unlike you."

"So maybe it's not flattery." She bit into a pear and ate, watching as the chieftess considered her responsibilities and options.

"Fine." Eleeza pushed herself away from the wall and sent a kitchen servant to fetch the head guard. "I'll let them eat and rest until tonight. But then I want to have a long talk with them about this disruptive magic, and more importantly, why they're here at all."

"See if you can find out why that Jax has a different accent."

Eleeza considered Lexyl with a sly smile. "He is interesting that one, isn't he?"

Lexyl nodded. "Somehow he seems more ragged than the rest of them, yet he has this authority—no that's too strong a word for it."

Another woman entered the kitchen and planted a kiss on the chieftess' cheek. "Are you talking about a man?"

Lexyl smirked. "Jealous, Prina?"

"Should I be?"

"No," Lexyl said, with some resignation.

Prina watched the younger woman eat her pear then turned to the chieftess. "She's talked you out of executing the foreigners, hasn't she?"

"She's talked me into reconsidering it."

"Hum," Prina grumbled. "I told you she'd take a fancy to one of them. I bet it's the one with the smart mouth."

Eleeza turned to her sister. "You usually favor the impudent ones."

Lexyl shook her head, her short hair swinging. Quite clearly the cat purred, "Borrel."

Eleeza's skin crawled with goose bumps.

"Sweet goddess!" Prina swore gruffly.

But Lexyl just laughed.

Florin paced back and forth in the darkness. The others, slumped out of her way against the cellar wall, could not see her, but they could hear the frustration in her footsteps. They were long through talking. Borrel's breath still rattled in his chest, and Jax's claustrophobia was not improved by the feeling that he'd drunk too much syrupy Tarron wine. Marith was lost in her silent self-recriminations for getting them into this mess.

Without warning the door swung open. Lexyl stood silhouetted for a moment before stepping into the room, followed by a servant with a lamp. "How are you?"

Jax glanced at his friends in the feeble light. "About like we look."

Lexyl knelt at Borrel's side and took his hand. "The chieftess told me you had been cross-magicked. Are you better now?"

"Better than I was." He squeezed her hand.

"Did the council decide to execute us?" Florin asked harshly.

"No," Lexyl rose. "Nothing has been decided. But I convinced the chieftess to let you out of here. Follow me, please."

Florin helped Borrel to his feet. Jax noted the concern in Lexyl's amber eyes. The Eldar led them slowly back through the palace to a room filled with low couches. A table set with food and tea awaited them. Their packs sat by one wall.

"Please eat. When you've finished, baths will be arranged. The chieftess will come speak with you later."

"Thank you, Lexyl." Marith smiled tiredly.

Again, the travelers heard the clicking of metal locks as the bolt slid to behind Lexyl, but here, in this well-lit, brightly furnished room, the sound was much less oppressive. Attenuated by days of near starvation in the desert and the dark hours of incarceration, they approached the food-laden table gratefully.

Marith poured a dark fragrant beverage into tiny cups and Florin cut fruit, while Jax and Borrel plopped onto one of the sofas. Neither of them had recovered enough from the cross-magic to want much food. Borrel took a few sips of water. Jax nibbled at some strange yellow bread and held his cup without drinking. He surveyed the room, noting a second doorway, the thin window slits that let in the bright desert sunlight, and the wall lined with elaborate paintings and one blue glass mirror. Something about the mirror's setting and the carved panels around it triggered old memories. In an ancient wing of the palace at Kree, an observation room sat hidden behind just such a piece of blue glass.

On the other side of that mirror, the chieftess watched Jax cock his eyebrow at the glass. Through a grating disguised in the carved panels, she over-heard their conversations. Lexyl entered silently to watch beside her sister.

"Jax, you have to eat more than a corner of bread." Marith handed him a slice of pear. He placed it in his saucer.

"My stomach isn't up to it."

"We don't know when they'll feed us again."

He shrugged. "If that's the case, then it won't matter."

"I don't think they'll execute us." Borrel's voice was rough and gravelly.

Marith sighed heavily. "I must tell you that I am terribly sorry for getting us all in this fix. If I hadn't got this crazy idea about Dishroc, none of this would have happened."

"No, Mother." Florin sipped her black beverage and gagged. "Yuck! That's bitter."

"The Nomads call it keffa," Jax said. "It's a potent stimulant."

"If you can stand the taste," Florin grumbled.

Borrel took another drink of water. "This isn't your fault, Marith. Florin and I wanted to come, even knowing that there were some dangers involved."

Jax watched the steam rise off his untouched keffa.

"I'm sorry, Jax," Marith repeated.

He set the demitasse back on the table. "I know you are." He gave her a small smile to hide his sorrow at the idea of dying here, so far from the sea, his bones bleaching under the harsh sun.

When Florin had finally finished eating, they heard the bolt at the door and watched as a team of silent servants brought four tubs and filled them with warm water. Jax again cast a speculative glance at the blue glass mirror then with a shrug he dropped his filthy clothes and stepped into the water.

"Four separate baths must be a real luxury here in the desert," Marith speculated as she sank into her own tub.

With a towel wrapped around his waist and his hair a tangled wet rope down his back, Jax watched Borrel dig into his back to find his razor.

"Maybe I'll shave too." Jax scratched his own whiskers and glanced again at the blue mirror. "To honor the gift of the water."

Marith smiled gently.

Soon after they were dressed in loose robes the color of sandstone, Lexyl returned, followed by the chieftess and six guards. Jax rose and bowed to the Speaker of All Eldars. Borrel, Florin, and Marith copied him clumsily.

The chieftess settled herself in a chair. "Please be seated."

It was Lexyl who began the questioning. "First of all, Jax, we were wondering why you have a different accent."

"I speak the Landish of Kordon."

For a while Lexyl pressed for more information on where they came from and how they had become lost and how they had eventually stumbled upon her watcher's perch. These questions led on to others about the nature of their journey. Lexyl sent a page off to find a map while Marith and Florin explained their movements. When the map arrived, Chieftess Eleeza leaned forward to watch as Marith traced the course of their travels.

Jax and Borrel said nothing during all of this.

Eventually the chieftess sat back again in her chair, considering the four strangers. "And you, Jax. Why are you a part of all this."

"I am Marith's slave." He flipped the collar at his neck.

Eleeza frowned, puzzled. "I don't know that word. What is a slave?"

Lexyl explained, and the chieftess' expression grew stony. She glared at Marith. "How can you presume to own a person?"

Marith shot an angry glare at Jax. "We do not condone the practice of slavery, Chieftess," she explained. "But my son happened to see Jax at the slave auction in The Hant. We needed an assistant and my son felt that he could take Jax away from the abuses of the trolls and solve our problems all at the same time. He will work for us for a time then we can set him free."

Eleeza frowned at Marith then addressed Jax. "You don't seem like a servant."

"That's an understatement," Marith snapped. "We don't consider him a slave, my lady. He is just one of us."

Lexyl, watching Jax, realized that his own feelings about this were somewhat more complicated.

"I cannot believe that this practice—slavery—exists any place where the goddess is worshiped," the chieftess said, her voice stern.

"It's those Hantish trolls," Jax said mildly, without looking at his companions.

"Nevertheless, it proves that our Eldar ancestors were wise to isolate us from the rest of the Knownlands." She cast a significant glance at Lexyl.

A thousand more questions raced through Lexyl's mind, but the point now was to convince Eleeza to let the travelers go on their way, and more importantly, to allow her to go with them. From long years of experience, she knew that this would best be accomplished by speaking with the chieftess alone.

At a nod, the pages gathered with the guards and took the four strangers to suites of bedrooms. When they had gone, Lexyl picked up some of the fruit they had left and settled back into her chair, munching thoughtfully.

"There's more to that half-islish fellow than he wants to reveal," Eleeza mused. "He knew we were watching behind the glass. He knows how to bow, how to speak. I'd bet mother's amber rings that he was manor-born. But this slave business, it's horrible."

"Yes, you can see the noble in him, once he got cleaned up," Lexyl said absently, considering how to address this problem. She knew that the slavery issue would be most dangerous to her cause. Predictably, Eleeza warmed to this theme.

"I am somewhat afraid to let them go, Lex. What if they return to the Hantland with tales about Arandy? What if trolls come here looking for more slaves?"

"We're a long way from the Hantland."

"And who's to say what other wretched customs and goddess-forsaken practices have developed in the outer lands in all these years since the dragons came and went."

"Perhaps they even vilify people who happen to be born with magic in their blood."

"We have the responsibility to guard the Eldar Maze."

"But if they disappear here, don't you suppose that someone might come looking for them?"

The chieftess frowned.

Lexyl pressed her advantage. "Sure, they might talk about the Eldar Maze when they get back to this Hilsen Vale place, but most people probably won't believe them. Just like most Eldars don't believe in Castle Caledra." She paused, gauging her timing by the expression on Eleeza's face. "I'll lead them through the Maze to Roadsend."

"Absolutely not! It's a two-month journey there and back."

"But I'm the only person in Arandy who's been there more than once."

"You just want another look at those goddess-damned ruins," the chieftess accused bitterly.

"It's not the ruins I'm interested in at this point. If you won't let me leave the Rocredlands, then my only chance to understand my magic comes from these outlanders."

"They only have the dragons' magic."

"True, but there is something about them, both of them. The fact that they suffered cross-magic only when an outside force entered my spell is curious, E'eza. I have to wonder why my Mystic alone doesn't bother them."

"You're probably not powerful enough."

"Poppycock," said the cat.

"Oh, get on with you!" Eleeza shooed Lexyl and the cat away from her, "before your cat's big mouth gets you charged with harming the collective."

"Only to be exiled into the desert? I already spend most of my time out there." Lexyl scooped up her cat and left the room.

Alone, the Speaker of All Eldars rose and strolled to the thin window. She had no concrete arguments that she could articulate. But just as she sensed instinctively that there was something more to that tousle-haired Jax with his perceptive blue eyes, she also felt in her bones that this visitation from the outside world had consequences that went far beyond Lexyl's confident imaginings.

27

Far away from Arandy, beyond the maze of canyons, across the savanna, over the mountains and beyond the wind-blown Barling Narrows, Castle Caledra perched like a brooding bird atop the cliffs of Sageham Isle. The westering sun poured light into the great chambers where bands of Sagehamites bustled about rows and rows of cots.

On each bed a Mystic sat or lay in varying degrees of recovery from the terrible effects of a mastery attempt gone wrong. The lads and lasses brought broth or tea, fluffed pillows, and comforted the stricken as best they could.

Atop a turret, in a round room with a panoramic view of the choppy sea and wind-blown island, Klaris and Professor Lellyn sat sipping tea. Although neither of them had suffered the coma, Klaris could not stop reliving the horror.

She had been in the great hall, chatting with an exceptionally handsome Bricks and Mortar novice, only ten years her senior, when she felt the first magical tendrils of Emmil Rohan's invocation.

"Professor!" Klaris dropped the novice's hand and turned to call down the dining hall to the Tower Tutor.

The old woman sat at a small table by the great fire. Slowly she stood and met Klaris's gaze. No one else could yet feel the delicate openings of Emmil's mastery attempt. The handsome novice, along with the other Mystic students in the hall, stared at the two women.

"He's not ready," Klaris announced with a certainty that might have offended the older woman. But rather than begrudge the princess her gifts, Lellyn had always relished them.

With a magical leap, Emmil opened wide his spell. At last the other magicians in the castle, indeed all the other Mystics in the Knownlands, could now see or sense the seething fabric of magic. Far away to the south and east, Lexyl's cat jumped with a shriek onto the council's table.

At first Klaris, like the other Mystics on Sageham and elsewhere, abandoned herself to the wild outpouring of Emmil's power. Then she saw the hole in his weaving.

Emmil had attempted to master the Mystic without knowing his Secret. The Mystic held a Secret for each would-be Weaver. No one could become Weaver without this essential key. The Secret was different for each candidate, and no one could ever predict when or even if a candidate would receive this final revelation.

"No! No," Klaris called softly. "The stairways, Emmil. Look to the stairways."

No one in the room knew what Klaris meant, but they felt the trembling in Emmil's weave as something began to go wrong.

Instinctively, Klaris drew on her own magic and moved to repair the hole in Emmil's fabric.

Unlike Klaris, Professor Lellyn could not see into Emmil's weaving, but she knew that the princess was moving in to help the failing spell, and that was supposed to be impossible. Few magicians would even be able to call up their magic while someone attempted to master the Mystic. How could young Klaris see into Emmil's own mastery attempt, the most powerful and personal of all Mystic spells?

Lellyn did not know, but she engaged her own considerable and wily resources to intercept the princess.

"I can help him," Klaris said calmly.

"You must not."

"But this is going to be a disaster." Klaris paused in her weaving, which brought Emmil's weave to a grinding halt as well. Far away in Arandy, Lexyl's spell lost its integrity and became entangled with Emmil's.

"It *is* a disaster, Klaris. And a tragedy," Lellyn said softly as the weaving process stopped dead.

Klaris held the power in fine balance for a moment. She began to tremble with the effort. "Help me, Professor. What can I do?"

Lellyn knew that Emmil had made a fatal mistake, and that everyone with any magic across the Knownlands was about to suffer for it. She had warned him often enough. The surging Mystic pounded against her like the blasts of a hurricane, and she wondered how Klaris was managing to maintain any control at all. If the girl held on much longer, she might damage herself. "Let him go, Klaris. Shield yourself and let him go."

"But..." Klaris swayed as she adjusted her grip on the invisible threads of magic. "But...."

With a gasp of horror, Klaris felt Emmil wrench his spell free of her. Without her support, Emmil's weave flew to shreds and his cry echoed throughout the castle. In Arandy, Lexyl screamed as her spell exploded.

Klaris, Professor Lellyn and the four other tower-tested Mystics (at home in their own countries) protected themselves from the impact. Every other Mystic in the Knownlands lost consciousness, their magic temporarily blasted into oblivion.

Now, a day later, Klaris could not erase the ghastly image of Emmil's immolated remains. She stared out the window. She did not hear the sound of someone slowly climbing the long stairs.

The grizzled head of the Oracle's priest appeared, followed by the rest of him.

"Whew. It's quite a climb up here."

"It is," Lellyn smiled and poured the man a steaming cup of tea.

Klaris turned her haunted green eyes to the priest. He was an old Barian with no magic, but he had tended to the spiritual needs of two generations of Mystics. Their needs had been great lately.

"Thank you for coming, Father Mallix." Klaris placed her untouched tea back on the table.

The priest smiled gently. "You should not feel guilty, Klaris."

"I saw his error; I could have saved him. I knew his Secret."

"But his Secret is not your own, my lady. If you had woven his mastery for him, you both would have been bound by his limitations. Your Secret will reveal much more power than his ever could have."

Klaris stared at the man and marveled that someone without any magic at all could understand so much about the Mystic, even if he was one of the Oracle's chosen. An undulating wave of remorse swamped her. It was more than the fact that she might have saved Emmil. She knew that he had attempted to master the Mystic, had pushed his boundaries, because he was threatened by her own rising power.

She looked down at her hands. "He wanted to be Weaver. And he knew that I want it too."

"Yes." Lellyn finished her tea. "He did want to be Weaver, and he knew you had surpassed him in your studies and were waiting for your Secret. He knew what he was doing. Emmil had been here a long time, but not everyone with great power gets to be a Weaver."

Klaris knew that the old woman was speaking about herself. Lellyn had been at Castle Caledra when a young Feilor made his first weave to gain the Dock and Portal entrance. Although they had never spoken of it openly, Klaris knew that Lellyn held every bit as much power as Feilor had.

Lellyn went on: "Emmil's ambition caused him to make a foolish and fatal decision."

Father Mallix nodded. "It's not your fault, Klaris."

"Ah, but it is. If I weren't here waiting for my Secret, he would have taken the time to finish his studies and wait for his own."

Lellyn shook her head slowly. "You know it takes more than magical strength to become Weaver. I don't think that Emmil would have had all that was necessary."

Klaris stared at the old woman. As usual, she heard the multiple meanings that the old professor intended. Again, the image of Emmil's charred remains flashed through Klaris's thoughts. She had seen the results of spells gone awry before, but none had ever misfired with such terrible results.

"Professor, I'm scared. Seeing Emmil like that. I don't know that I'll... that I can..."

The Tower Professor and the Oracle's priest exchanged a glance. Both of them were old enough to be Klaris's grandparents. Both of them had known the last three Weavers, but neither had ever seen the kind of horror that Emmil had brought on himself.

Klaris saw Lellyn make a small nod then look down at her wrinkled hands.

"It's our fault, Klaris," Father Mallix said gently. "We never should have let Emmil into the castle."

"Why not?'"

"He didn't pass his soul test," Mallix answered. "It was a close thing, but he didn't pass. Still, his magic was so clearly deep and potentially powerful."

"But the soul test trumps everything, I thought." Klaris shook her head.

"It's supposed to," Lellyn admitted. "But we just don't see very many applicants with great power anymore. So, when Emmil arrived, we—it was Weaver Bizzelworth then—decided we should take him on anyway."

Klaris stared from one old face to the other.

After a moment Lellyn met her eyes. "It was clearly a mistake. Mallix and I, and Feilor too, have known for years that Emmil did not possess the soul strength needed for his Mystic."

Klaris remembered that Emmil's jealousy was responsible for leaving the Barian Prince Javix with the trolls and wondered what other malignant actions his lack of strength had strewn about the Knownlands.

"It was our mistake, Klaris," Mallix repeated. "Not yours."

A terrible thought sent shivers through Klaris's veins, but she lifted her head and asked her question anyway. "I know there was debate among you about accepting me to study here. Did I also fail my soul test?"

Lellyn, seeing the fear in Klaris's face and knowing the courage this question had taken, rose and came to give the girl a hug. "You passed your soul test, Klaris. And asking that question shows you would pass it again. Our fears for you were due to the conflicting responsibilities that you might face due to your royal birth."

Relieved, Klaris hugged Lellyn back, her green eyes glittering with determination. "We're all subject to our circumstances," she noted.

"Indeed."

"Oh, sweet goddess," Mallix swore gently. The old Barian was looking out the window at the autumn-tossed sea. A flotilla of Barian wing-ships had come up over the horizon, trailing white wakes through the blue waves. Mallix recognized the pennants on the largest ship. "It's the sealord," he said. "He's coming here."

Lellyn stood up. "The castle's a mess. We're all a mess. We're in no shape to receive the sealord."

"I'll go down to him," Klaris said. "I'll see what he wants."

Mallix and Lellyn descended the stairs together more slowly. "If we're going to host the sealord, we'd better help the lads move everyone out of the hall," Lellyn muttered.

Mallix shook his head with a wry, rather sad smile. "I wouldn't trouble yourself, Professor. I think the sealord is here just for Klaris."

Wrapped in a thick green cloak, Klaris stood on the small dock in the harbor and watched a ship's launch roll and pitch in the heavy seas as it made its way toward her. She could see that the sealord was not on board.

Ambassador Grisham stepped from the boat to the dock and bowed low to the princess. She smiled at his familiar, friendly face and spoke in her native Islish. "Hello Ambassador. Welcome to Sageham."

"Thank you, your Highness."

"What can we do for you here?"

"Sealord Bryx invites you to join him for dinner aboard the *Drixa*, my lady."

"Ah," Klaris was puzzled. "Wouldn't he rather come up to the castle?"

The old Barian cleared his throat. "The sealord prefers to stay on board his ship at the moment, my lady."

Klaris read the look in Grisham's slanted, sea-blue eyes and remembered how the sealord hated small boats in heavy seas. "Of course," she said, understanding. "I'll come."

Grisham offered her his hand as she stepped down into the rocking boat, but she did not take it. The Farsouthians, like the Barians, and the other islish races, loved boats: all except, Bryx, of course. Klaris wrapped her cloak around herself against the spray and thought about the young sealord.

She had met Bryx several times over the last few years as she stopped at Haven on her travels between Sageham and her home on Farsouth. The sealord had always been more than courteous to her, and while part of her was flattered, part of her pitied him. He was so obviously out of place among the sea-loving Barians.

He did not come onto the rolling deck of the giant wing-ship to great her, but when she arrived in his cabin, he smiled warmly and took her hand. "Thank you so much for coming, Princess Klaris. It's wonderful to see you."

She smiled back and took the offered seat. "Thank you, your Majesty."

Bryx sat close to her on the small sofa. "You know I don't have any magic, but I understand that something terrible happened here yesterday."

She nodded. "It was terrible. A man attempted to master the Mystic and failed."

"But you are well," Bryx's light blue Kordish eyes surveyed Klaris's body with so slow relish.

"I am fine, my lord. Thank you. But most people with Mystic in their blood will take some time to recover."

Bryx reached out for her hand. "I am so glad you were not harmed, Klaris."

She considered their two hands. "My lord, did you get my letter regarding your brother?"

"I did. That's why I've come, actually. I've just been to The Hant, trying to find the scoundrel."

"Scoundrel?"

"Aye. He committed treason against Kordon, you know. The loss of the Kordish markets has been devastating to the Barian economy."

"Well," Klaris extracted her hand from Bryx. "When I saw him, your brother was in pretty devastating circumstances, too."

"Tell me about that."

Klaris related the story of how they had come upon the troll and his slave that stormy afternoon on the Vrillbridge Road. "I didn't realize until we were back at the iron mines who he was. He doesn't look like you, you know."

"No, he doesn't."

"He asked me to help him then, and I tried to buy him, but the trolls hauled him away." Her voice became a little taut. "As I told you in my letter, my companions forbade me from trying to help him. They feared reprisals from the trolls if I interfered." She looked up at Bryx. "I'm so sorry."

Bryx nodded. He stood up and poured Jezellian sherry into two delicate crystal glasses. He handed one to Klaris and resumed his seat a little closer to her. "We could not come immediately to investigate your suspicions. But I did speak to the mine boss at the Hanter Iron Mines myself. He told me they sold Jax for bait."

"But he's not dead," Klaris said firmly.

"Princess Klaris, do you know what the trolls do with bait?"

"I do, my lord. But I have scried for your brother, and while I can't exactly see him, I do not believe that he is dead."

"But if he were bait...."

"Perhaps he wasn't." Klaris sat up. "Perhaps someone else saved him."

"But then where is he now?" Bryx mused.

Klaris stood up and walked to the back of the cabin to look out the large windows at the heaving sea. "This Javix of yours is such a puzzle."

Bryx emptied his glass and rose to pour himself some more. "He's a damned nuisance, Jax is."

"You call him Jax?"

"He hated the name Javix when he was little. Never mind, no less than three very illustrious sealords have borne the name before him."

Klaris turned away from the waves and considered the bitterness in the sealord's voice. Magicless, he was not aware of the small way the Mystic curled around him, just as it had seemed to swirl around Javix. So much power, political and magical, roiled around the younger Sharkin. She remembered him reeling away from the troll's club, his appeal to her for help, and came to a decision.

"My lord, are you returning to Baria?"

"Yes."

"Would you be willing to take me with you? I would like to visit the Oracle."

"Oh." Bryx looked down into the amber liquid in the small crystal glass. "You know I went to the Oracle when Jax first disappeared."

"And what did they say?"

"Nothing helpful. They couldn't find Jax and didn't know where we should look."

"So the Oracle can't find him in a scry either?"

"No."

Klaris watched as Bryx poured her more sherry. She looked up into his round eyes, so unusual in an islish face. "Still, the magic calls out for him. I want to know why."

"But he has Dragon force."

"I know," she answered. "As I said, he is a puzzle."

"He's a pain in my ass," Bryx grumbled, then smiled. "But I will be honored, my lady, to have you sail with us to Baria."

28

Sealord Bryx held the reins of Klaris's horse and watched her curtsey to the gray figure of the Oracle. They were the same size, the small gray Oracle and the feline princess. He supposed he couldn't blame the Oracle for coming at once to see her. They hadn't made *her* wait and look into *her* heart before showing her the temple. But then, Princess Klaris hadn't faced the trials that had broken and re-broken his own heart.

That heart thumped with pleasure as he watched her walk into the temple with the Oracle. He loved the way she moved, the way her dress swirled around her hips and the way the sunlight gilded the wild curls of her hair.

He had never met a woman like Klaris de Farsouth, other than the Queen of Farsouth herself. Here was a person who could stand on the deck of the *Drixa* and chat with the lieutenant, without the fear or seasickness that would immobilize a landish person. Here was someone who could ride a horse, her movements so fluid and centered that they set him to thinking of other activities.

He took a deep breath and turned to ride back to where his people had set up a pavilion with food for him while he waited for Klaris to end her meeting. He glanced at a movement off in the rubble of the Ruins of Nec. A small figure with green hair seemed to be systematically evaluating each fallen block, pausing now and then to write something in a notebook. The sealord shook his head. An organized sprite would be such a paradox as to be an oxymoron. It must be some other type of creature, although that green hair was hard to mistake.

Dismounting, he called for a glass of wine and resumed his happier considerations of the lovely Klaris de Farsouth. He could never marry her, of course. Her Mystic was so powerful that the Oracle would never permit her to hand-fast with a sealord. The goddess' *Rede and Rote* forbade a union that concentrated too much power in too few hands. In fact, Bryx remembered an unpleasant history test that had included questions about a situation where the Oracle had prohibited the heir of Phlyx from marrying the heir of Ayx, or maybe it was the heir of Callisto. Bryx had always felt it was unfair to expect him to learn all the history of Baria as well as all the history of Kordon.

But he didn't need a hand-fasting ceremony to enjoy Klaris. He could entertain her. He could ride with her. He could slip the dress off her shoulders....

Klaris sipped her tea with growing consternation.

"There was something here, just a few hundred years ago, surely." The Oracle was bent over, its head deep inside a red lacquered cabinet. They reemerged with a handful of flattened scrolls. "Someone should probably take better care of these," they mumbled trying to roll one out flat. The material fell apart in flakes.

"May I help you?" Klaris rose from her chair and held out her hands. The Oracle handed her four rolls of parchment. She reseated herself. "What exactly are we looking for?" she asked, gently unfolding one of the scrolls.

"Something about someone who can't be seen. Oh, damn. This one's falling apart too."

"Perhaps we should do this over a table so we can catch the pieces."

"That's very clever, my girl." The gray eyes rose to hers. "You're involved in this too. If you're the Weaver."

"I'm not, Oracle. Not yet."

The Oracle waved their hand and a small table appeared between the two of them. Gently they opened the scrolls.

Klaris read the flowing script that crawled across the page. It was ancient Landish. She translated it in her head then looked up at the Oracle. "Oracle, I don't mean to be disrespectful, but this is an inventory of a wine cellar."

"Hum?" The Oracle pulled the parchment to their own side of the table. "So it is. So it is. We were wondering where that list had got to."

"I hope someone drank the wine. It would have all spoiled by now," Klaris said dryly, unrolling her next scroll.

The other papers contained chronicles or records of more critical importance, and while a couple of them mentioned a Weaver, none made mention of someone invisible to magic.

Klaris had moved to stare out the window, while still surreptitiously watching the Oracle, who continued to look through drawers and decorative boxes and even under the cushions of a small sofa, muttering a fragment of a verse.

"....*a some such thing that can't be found...something else upon the ground*? How does it go?"

Suddenly Klaris's head snapped up and she gasped. Powerful Dragon force ripped through her. She pulled the shreds of her Mystic inward around herself, frantically trying to shield herself from the cross-magic.

A red cloud swirled in the middle of the room. The Oracle put down the crumpled papers and turned to face the person who coalesced out of the smoke.

"Oracle," a thin man with a gray goatee bowed deeply.

"Highlord," the Oracle said. "You might have let us know you were coming. As you can see, we are hosting a very powerful Mystic here."

"My apologies!" The Dragon Highlord cast a stricken glance at the shimmering green ball that was Klaris. "Let me adjust."

Klaris felt the Highlord pull his own magic in as tightly as her own. Slowly, she let her weave drop a bit so that they could look at one another.

"But you are a child!" The Highlord's dark eyes stared at her.

Klaris curtseyed. "Not quite, Highlord. I am Klaris de Farsouth."

"Yes, yes, I know!" He smiled widely. "You have so much power, my lady. We've known of you for years, but I had forgotten that you were so young."

"Have a seat, Raggar," the Oracle said as a priest entered with more tea. "And you, Klaris, come away from the wall. You won't get cross-magic now."

The Highlord waved away the offered tea. "I am sorry, Oracle. I should have inquired if I could visit, but to tell you the truth, I was so startled by something last night that I felt I must come to you as soon as possible."

Klaris's lungs still ached from the first impact of the Highlord's arrival. Gingerly, she took a deep breath and coughed.

"Yes, well, look what your impatience did to the Weaver," the Oracle snapped.

"Weaver?" The Highlord frowned.

"Not yet," she whispered.

"Time, time, time." The Oracle grumbled. "Everyone is running out of it, but young Klaris here has to learn patience. Perhaps you should too, Raggar."

"I don't think patience is what I need." Raggar turned his brown eyes to the Oracle. "I need answers. We saw a vision last night at Dragonsholm, during a dance for the novices. Dragons, Oracle, real ones. Huge, red, green, black, writhing out of our fire, into our dance. I've never seen such a thing. They attacked us, engulfed us in flame." He paused and shuddered. "No one was harmed, thank the goddess, but we were all singed and still carry the reek of sulfur in our nostrils."

"Are they still there? There on Jezel?" Klaris asked.

"No, we killed the ceremonial fire and they disappeared. But I tell you, we are all terrified to light such a fire again."

Both Klaris and Raggar looked at the Oracle who was pouring more tea. Finally, they looked up. "You know, of course, that Dragon force is new in the Knownlands."

"It's not new," Raggar protested. "It's been here nearly a thousand years."

The Oracle snorted. "When this Oracle was made there was Fairy and Mystic only. The repudiated magic of Axterre had finally imploded itself, but there was no power called *Dragon*, not as you know it now."

Raggar nodded. "Of course, Oracle. We know that people only began to have Dragon force in their veins after the dragon interregnum."

The Oracle nodded. "So you see, not much is known about it."

"What could such a vision mean?" Raggar's voice indicated that he had already found an unsettling answer to his own question.

"You tell us, Highlord." The Oracle's voice was implacable.

The man rose. He looked at Klaris, his eyes stricken. "They are coming back."

"No," Klaris whispered. Just today she had ridden through the Ruins of Nec with the sealord. Just today she had felt the dragons' residual power that still lingered among the broken buildings of the city the great beasts had destroyed.

"Already?" the Oracle frowned. "Is it time already?"

Klaris and the Highlord exchanged a glance. The Highlord spoke. "What do you mean, Oracle?"

In the light blazing through the windows, the wizened Oracle looked down at their hands that looked like a couple of ancient apples in its lap. "I remember fire and fear... Yes." They looked up into Klaris's green eyes and quoted:

"Oracle, speak the Mother's truth

Dragons come with claw and tooth

Your purpose for one thousand years

Is to remember fire and tears."

"You were here when the dragons came?" Klaris asked softly.

"This Oracle banished them, you know."

"No, I didn't know."

"Neither did I," said Raggar.

The Oracle sighed. "It was a long time ago. 900 years, or something like that."

"Why are you supposed to remember fire and fear, Oracle?" Klaris asked.

"Goddess, but you are full of questions," snapped the Oracle. "Can't you just pick one?"

"I can," Raggar said, with shaky determination. "Are they coming back? The real dragons, I mean. Are they coming again to the Knownlands?"

"They always do."

"What?" Klaris breathed. "They *always* do?"

"Every thousand years."

"Sweet goddess." The Highlord shivered. "The horror of it...."

The Oracle stood up. "Listen, my children. It doesn't have to be horrible. It was terrible last time because the last Oracle died too soon. It died at Axterre."

"I thought Axterre was a myth," Raggar said.

"Where'd you get that silly idea? You should both go study your Axterran history. Now, where did that damned scroll get to?"

Both Klaris and the Highlord recognized a dismissal. They stood up and each made deep obeisance to the Oracle, but the small gray creature was already leaving them, mumbling to themself again. *"Some such thing that can't be found. Like this scroll...."*

29

Marith stood at the window watching the first rays of sunlight spill over the rim of the canyon. She had searched in vain through the predawn twilight for someone performing the ritual sun salutations. Servants warmed water, cooks baked, farmers walked towards their day of labor, but nowhere could she find a priest, priestess, or druid calling souls to find their center and honor the new day.

Finally, she had returned to their sitting room and breathed herself through pose and stretch until she found her own sense of openness and oneness.

Jax padded barefoot in from the adjoining bedroom. He went to the low table where servants had just left a coffee pot, fruit, and some of the cooks' fresh-baked buns.

"Keffa, Marith?"

She shook her head. "I don't care to be so jittery."

"There's no tea, but here's some juice."

Jax brought her a small glass of pink liquid then sat and enjoyed his own breakfast. The nyad twins appeared soon after. Marith remained silent at the window.

Jax sipped his keffa and leaned back in his chair, watching the old druid.

Finally, she left the window and sat with the others, eating a bit of pear. Finding Jax's blue gaze upon her, she smiled sadly. "Even those silly Herders held ceremonies each morning," she explained. "I wonder why the Eldars don't."

"Good morning!" Lexyl swung through the door followed by her ever-present cat.

Borrel thought her smile was as radiant as the new day.

"The chieftess would like you to meet once more with the Eldar Council, but she has privately agreed to let me lead you through the Maze to Roadsend. From there you can follow the Nomad Caravansary to Dishroc."

"Thank the goddess!" Marith felt relief blossom through her.

But their ordeal was not quite over. The Eldar Council, and especially Shaman Ashande, grilled them with interminable questions from mid-morning to well into the afternoon. Marith finally admitted in exasperation that a shopping trip to Dishroc was indeed a ludicrous undertaking, and she herself was not sure why it had seemed so important or so feasible back in the Vale. This admission allowed the council to smugly grant the travelers passage through the Eldar Maze. With no visible reluctance, the chieftess announced that her sister would be their guide. The council had also directed plenty of sharp questions at Lexyl.

Given the freedom to roam the town, Jax strolled through the streets paved with flat red stone. Marith took her questions to the Eldar Shamans. Borrel went back to bed, still fatigued from the cross-magic. Florin cornered Lexyl and went with her to discuss methods of survival in the desert wilderness. Alone, Jax sat on the rim of a tiled fountain and dipped his hands into the cool water.

He listened to the tinkling song of the fountain and after a while he took his dragonpipe from his pocket and began to play a tune around the music of the fountain.

Eleeza had watched his movements from a window high in her palace. The sound of his pipe carried up to her and touched something in her heart. She listened as the shadows stretched across the canyon floor and began to climb the wall on the opposite side. When he finally stopped, she descended the stairs to join him.

"You play beautifully."

Jax stood respectfully as she approached. "Thank you, your Majesty."

"May I see your flute?"

He handed her the small wooden instrument. "It's called a drag-onpipe, Chieftess. Anyone with bit of force can play it."

"Hum." She returned the pipe quickly. "Magic."

"Music."

"I play our canyon flute and I don't have any magic at all."

Jax smiled slowly. "I think all music is a kind of magic, my lady."

Eleeza stared at him for a moment. "You play dangerous games, don't you?"

He shook his head. "I don't play. I'm just a pawn."

She reached out and touched the slave collar around his neck. It was warm. "How long have you been a slave?"

"Four years."

"So you weren't born to it?"

"No."

"I didn't think so." For a moment she considered the self-assurance in his blue eyes. "Why don't you run away?"

He looked down to the water. "I have no place to go."

The chieftess paused. "Marith seems to care for you like a child of her own."

"Aye."

She heard the burden in his answer but didn't understand where it came from. "Walk with me, Jax. I told Lexyl that you must have been manor-born. Were you?"

"Manner-born? That's an old-fashioned way of putting it. But, yes." He followed the chieftess along a path paved in flat red rocks that led up the canyon wall.

"Then you'll understand what I have to ask you. Lexyl is my heir. Our family has held the Speakership of Arandy for over six hundred years. But more than that, she is my closest relative, my only family. When she's gone, I miss her dreadfully."

"It seems that she spends a great deal of time away from Arandy."

"She does, because of this magic business. We Eldars haven't had any powerful magicians in so long that we've grown unused to them. Lexyl's power is foreign to us, and frightening."

"It shouldn't be foreign to you, my lady; she is one of you."

"She is, but then she isn't. She can do these things that set her apart. And she knows things.... Even though we've known her all of her life, many people are uncomfortable with her, with the obvious fact that she's different."

"Everyone is different is some way."

"But Lexyl's differences are dangerous." They came up out of the canyon onto the flat rimrock. The big blue mountain that Jax and his companions had used as a landmark for days now rose directly to the east. He could see windows formed of redrock arches and slopes covered with trees and rocky scree. A thin strand of green smoke climbed up from the side of the mountain.

"There's a fire up there," Jax said, wondering.

"Caveharts," Eleeza said cryptically.

"Cavehearts?"

"The people of the caves," she explained. "All the landish folk of the Knownlands came out of the caves on that mountain, you know."

"I didn't know."

"Where did you think people came from?"

"Islish people sailed from places far to the West. My tutors in Kordon said the landish folk came from somewhere to the east."

"I don't know about the islish, but this is The East." She waved her hand toward the mountain. "Most landish people migrated to other lands, but a very small group refused to leave the caves. We occasionally have contact with them. They have no writing, no architecture, no magic. And they've had no Keller now for the last fifteen years, or so."

"What's a Keller?"

"Ruler. That smoke is a sign they've finally selected a new Keller."

"They elect their ruler?"

"No. They have a series of challenges, physical and mental." She paused to shrug. "This is what Lexyl tells me. She's the only Eldar to have spoken to the Caveharts in generations. She was up there a few years ago." Eleeza paused and considered the disappearing smoke. "Curiously enough, Lex told me that a nyad was attempting the Kellar Challenge."

"There are nyads up there, too?"

"I really don't know. Lexyl, as you may have gathered, travels her own strange paths. That brings me to what I want to ask you, Jax. Will you look after her out there? Make sure she doesn't dawdle along the way."

"Me?" Jax turned away from the mountain and looked at Eleeza in surprise. "Look after Lexyl? I don't know anything about survival in the desert."

"It's not the desert that worries me. There are certain places out there that we Eldars consider forbidden. I think you'll recognize them. But Lexyl, she makes her own rules about these things. If something should happen to her, I don't know what I'd do."

Jax felt the familiar despair that none of his relatives seemed to care in such a way for him.

The chieftess asked again: "Will you watch her?"

"Yes, ma'am," he conceded. "But how will I know if she's doing something you consider forbidden or dangerous?"

"You knew about the cross-magic the other night. I trust you'll know when she does something she shouldn't."

"Maybe you should trust her, ma'am."

The chieftess shook her head. "Lexyl takes unnecessary risks. I'm afraid she might overstep the limits of her, her Mystic."

"Then why don't you send her to Castle Caledra for training?"

Eleeza looked into his strangely shaped blue eyes. "Does such a place truly exist?"

"It does."

"About ten years ago our Uncle Valdik left the Redlands to go to this Caledra place. He never came back. Lexyl finally admitted to me that she thinks he's dead, but we don't know how or why."

"It is a long way to Sageham Isle from here," Jax noted.

"Exactly. And neither I nor the Eldar people can afford to lose Lexyl."

"You love her."

"Of course, I do."

"Of course." Jax turned away and changed the subject. "What do you call this mountain?"

Eleeza considered him for a moment before answering. "Dragon Perch." She turned her eyes to gaze at the mountain, which glowed in the setting sun above the shadowed desert.

"That's a frightful name."

"The beasts landed there when they came, but Lexyl once told me that it was called Dragon Perch even before the dragons came all those years ago."

A few soft clouds wreathed the peak of the mountain. While Eleeza and Jax watched, the setting sun tinted the clouds pink, empurpled the shadowy forest slopes, and reddened the redrock walls of the canyonlands that led up to the mountain.

"Beautiful," Jax whispered, awed.

Eleeza smiled. "It is a beautiful place to live, which is why it's so hard to understand why Lexyl wants to leave."

Jax turned to follow the chieftess back down to Arandy. He thought of all the people who loved the Vale, which he had hated; he thought of how Bryx hated Baria and its boats, which he himself loved. "One person's paradise can be another person's prison."

"Perhaps," Eleeza said. "But I expect you understand that we all have our duties. It's up to us to decide if they imprison or empower us."

Twilight glowed through the canyon by the time they returned to the fountain.

"I don't like letting Lexyl go with you," Eleeza admitted. "But you won't find your way out of here alone, and frankly, she's a danger to herself here. Look after her for me, will you?"

He bowed. "It will be my honor to serve you, Chieftess."

Eleeza strode off purposefully, and Jax slumped against the fountain rim. Imprisoned by duties. He felt his anger rise around him like a wall. He twisted the slave collar around his neck. He had promised Doc that he would care for Marith, and now he had given a similar promise to the chieftess. The inequity of the slave being asked to care for the leaders of the expedition seemed to trouble only him.

The four travelers gathered again in the room with the low couches where a table of dinner was brought to them. The unfamiliar food raged with spice. Jax, who had enjoyed the fiery foods of other southern lands like Jezel and Farsouth, ate with wary pleasure. Marith and Florin, their tongues and lips stinging, chose to eat the fruit and bread. Borrel laughed as sweat poured from his brow and swallowed yet another mouthful of the hot stuff. The burning made him feel more alive.

Early the next morning Marith rose to run through a solitary and abbreviated sun salutation. She'd roused the others and gotten them fed and dressed so that long before the sun climbed above the canyon rim, they were moving down the shadowed cobbles. They wore lightweight Eldar clothes, loose fitting and colored the same ruddy brown as the canyon walls.

The chieftess joined them in the dark street before the palace, presenting them with a small goat-like pack animal called a lakema. Its soft wide hooves gave it traction on the rock and in the sand, and it only rarely needed water. With grateful thanks and many unsophisticated bows, the four said goodbye to the Speaker of All Eldars.

One final time Eleeza caught Jax's eye. "Thank you, Jax," she whispered.

He gave her the one-handed Barian salute then followed his companions down the streets and onto the track that led down the canyon.

For a week they followed Lexyl through the labyrinth of canyons. Florin could not figure out how the Eldar found her way, since one canyon looked just like the last to the nyad. Borrel asked if Lexyl used her magic to find the springs that she conveniently located each evening, but she snorted at the suggestion, saying that no one needed magic for such a simple thing. Still, it took more than a week before Florin even began to get a feel for how she did it.

Late one afternoon, Lexyl spotted a rare prickly gray bush growing up a small cliff. "Forath!" She grinned at Borrel, who clambered up the canyon behind her. "What fun!"

"Fun? What fun?" Jax demanded breathlessly, as he arrived at the ledge where Borrel stood in a patch of shade. Together they watched the Eldar climb the vertical wall and grab a handful of brambly twigs.

"What is she doing?" Marith joined the other two.

"She said something like, *formath*."

"Forath," Lexyl clarified, jumping back down among the travelers, waving the spindly sticks at them playfully. "Tonight we'll have a forath vision quest."

"Getting to Dishroc is enough of a quest for me," Jax announced.

"Forath..." Marith resettled her pack, trying to remember if she had heard of the stuff before.

Lexyl started off again, tucking the weed into her belt. As usual Borrel followed at her heels. "What's a vision quest, Lex?"

"It used to be a rigorous journey into one's own soul, accomplished through an extreme and rigorous journey of the body. Our shamans used to do them regularly. Now, no one does them in real or meaningful ways. We cheat and use forath."

"How is that cheating?" Intrigued, Jax came along right behind Borrel.

Lexyl glanced over her shoulder at him. "While the herb does give us visions, they lack meaning because we haven't worked for them."

"Visions?" Marith puffed.

"And we never remember them clearly."

"Is this forath hallucinogenic?"

Lexyl flashed the druid a sunny grin. "Absolutely."

"What's hallucin—whatever?" Florin, bringing up the rear with the lakema, was unable to hear much of the conversation.

"Something that makes you see things that may not really exist," Marith explained.

"Sounds like fun." Borrel again set off right behind Lexyl.

Florin watched her brother follow the Eldar closely. As they went ahead, she could hear their voices echoing off the Redrock canyon walls. Florin did not need any of Lexyl's weed to envision what was clearly on Borrel's mind.

That night, Lexyl had them set camp on the rim of a canyon, much to Jax's relief.

"It's better to be near the sky for our visions," Lexyl explained. "And there's no moon tonight. I prefer to smoke my forath by starlight."

Marith stirred a small pot of Lexyl's spicy green soup. "Why don't people go on real vision quests anymore?"

"The forath is much easier."

"But if you can't remember what your vision was, then what's the point?"

"An issue I've raised myself." Lexyl dug deep in the nether reaches of her pack. "I'm considered a rather dangerous freethinker in Arandy because I use the forath for simple recreational purposes. But I am also the only Eldar to have gone on a true, five-day vision quest in probably three or four hundred years."

"Why did you do that?" Jax stretched his tired shoulders.

"Eleeza says I have an obdurate, maybe morbid, fascination with ancient history."

"What did you see in your vision quest?" Florin broke a round loaf of yellow bread into five portions.

Lexyl, delving deep into her pack, did not answer immediately. She finally sat up, holding a small ceramic instrument and wearing a grin that could have come off the face of her little gray cat. "It's difficult to share the content of a true vision quest. I learned many, many things, but it would take me more than five days to tell you all of them."

"What's that?" Jax nodded towards the purple ceramic in her hand.

"A forath pipe."

"It doesn't look like any pipe I've ever seen." Marith picked up the pipe and admired its loops, curves, and twists.

"It's an ancient thing," Again the cat-like smile. "You don't want to know where I got it."

"All of this makes me uncomfortable," Florin noted. "I don't want to smoke your funny weed from that odd pipe and see who-knows-what kind of odd-ball things."

Lexyl shrugged and drank her soup. "You don't have to, Florin, but I'll tell you that we Eldars cherish the forath. We bless the goddess every time we find it, because when the smoke is in us, we feel so serene, so at-one with the world. Maybe it doesn't matter that people use it as a shortcut."

For a while no one spoke as they finished their dinner with bits of sweet pink dried cactus fruit. Lexyl crumbled the forath's tiny leaves into the bowl of the pipe and lit it with a glowing stick from the fire.

Inhaling deeply, she smiled at the faces of her four companions, glowing in the last light from the sunset. "Take the smoke deep into your lungs and hold it as long as you can."

She passed the pipe to Borrel, who coughed at first and had to have a second try. When Jax passed the pipe to Florin, she shrugged and sucked the thin, sweet smoke into her body.

Three times the pipe went around the circle before Lexyl decided that was probably sufficient for novices. She tapped the ashes from the pipe into the fire. The forath smoke lazed around them on the still air like sacred incense.

Borrel pulled out his dragonpipe and began to play. Jax found his own pipe and joined in. The song blended and harmonized with its own echo, bouncing off the canyon walls and climbing upward toward the freedom of the sky.

As the last note sighed into silence, Marith giggled.

Jax lay back on the rock and watched stars pop one by two out of the deepening blue sky.

Lexyl smiled at Borrel. "I love to hear you play your flute."

"I love you," Borrel answered softly, intently.

"Do you, now?"

Borrel had never felt such uncontrollable desire in his whole life. He had been increasingly attracted to Lexyl since he first felt the caress of her magic imprisoning them. Now he could almost see the blood pumping through her veins, almost hear the hum of her magic rubbing against his own, almost smell the warmth of her skin.

Lexyl felt the nyad's eyes bore into her soul. "Borrel and I are going for a walk." She rose, grabbing her bedroll in one hand, the nyad in the other.

"Goddess be with you!" Marith crowed and lay back giggling again.

Jax watched the two of them go, noting ironically that he was watching Lexyl, just as Eleeza had asked him to: watching her live by her own rules. Settling himself more comfortably on the rock, he stared at the sky, feeling the sun-warmed earth at his back, and the campfire tingling his toes. Just as Lexyl had predicted, he saw the unity of the desert's earth and fire with the water and air that had always seemed so central, so essential to his life.

"Jax?" Florin rolled next to him.

"Humm?"

"Jax, why don't we go for a walk too?"

Jax sat up and glanced off to the rocky shadows. "I don't think Borrel and Lexyl need our company."

"I don't mean to join them." Florin bounced to her feet and nearly dislocated Jax's shoulder hauling him up beside her.

"Hey. Ow."

With Marith's laughter echoing in their ears, Florin dragged Jax off behind a jumble of boulders and pushed him back to the sandstone.

"Sweet goddess, Florin, what are you doing?"

"You don't really have to ask, do you?"

Left alone beside the fire, Marith felt peace settle into her heart and soul for the first time since they had fled Stede. Despite their reassurances and their final luck in finding Lexyl, Marith knew she was responsible for getting all of them here. She felt the burden of that most heavily when she watched Jax walk along in his place in their line, silent with his own thoughts. He had come here at her bidding, and she felt responsible for getting him home again. Only where his home might be wasn't clear.

She looked beyond the fire, out over a canyon carved by a river that no longer ran, and saw the whole, the unity of the universe. The peace of the goddess flooded through her, like it did when she officiated at a sabbat back in the Vale. Hours she sat there, watching the stars revolve across the sky. Finally, she slept, thinking that there was much to be said for this forath weed.

Borrel woke Lexyl three times before dawn, so fierce was the call of the goddess in his veins. Florin woke Jax twice. As a result of all this nocturnal activity, only Marith greeted the sunrise with any vigor. Slowly, they gathered around the fire and drank their morning tea, trying to ignore stiff muscles and scraped knees.

Lexyl cleared her throat and glanced around at the travelers. "So, Mother Marith, I guess we should note that forath is also an aphrodisiac to nyads."

"No, it's not." Florin lounged against a rock, grinning saucily. "We're always like that."

Since no one seemed over-anxious to shoulder their packs and move out, Jax took a water skin off to a boulder for a quick wash. Florin followed him there and tackled him one last time.

"You are fabulous!" Jax laughed, "but insatiable."

Florin resolutely satisfied them both.

For another fortnight they walked through the Maze. Florin finally got Lexyl to explain her method of navigation, how she followed one canyon then moved on to another. Marith pestered the Eldar with endless questions about the various desert plants. In the evening around the campfire, Jax and Borrel resumed their pipe duets, both of them enjoying the acoustic effects of the Redrock canyon walls. And later each night, Jax watched without comment as Lexyl and Borrel went off by themselves. They were answering the call of the goddess. What harm could come from that? He was relieved that Florin did, in fact, seem to have gotten enough of him.

After several days of following a small creek through a deep canyon, they suddenly emerged into a vast plain. Far to the south a distant line of rimrock rose to meet the sky, but in the flat, wide valley between, an unwholesome haze seethed gently in the heat.

Marith remarked: "By the way, today is Samhain. We'll have to do something tonight to honor the new year."

"Today is Samhain?" Lexyl turned in alarm.

"Yes."

"Damn." The Eldar stopped and stared off onto the plain.

"What's the matter?" Borrel touched her shoulder.

"We don't want to be anywhere near here on Samhain. I'd lost track of the days."

"But what's the problem?"

"The ruins."

Jax followed the Eldar's gaze. Far out on the flat expanse he could see dim shapes through the haze. "The ruins of what?"

"Axterre."

"Axterre?" Jax gaped. "You're joking."

"Not at all."

"You can explain any time," Florin snapped.

"Not now." Lexyl reached her decision. "Let's make a dash for it."

Resolutely, the Eldar stepped from the sheltering canyon onto the plain. The others could only follow, holding their questions in wary silence. Before long, broken shards of rock distinguished themselves from the haze. Wide passages, littered with rubble and twisted metal, lay with geometric precision between the broken buildings. Empty windows, black holes in the sides of gray stone buildings, gaped like eye sockets in an ancient skull.

Something icy ran down Jax's spine as he followed Marith. The shadows moved and slipped, and something seemed to be moaning just out of hearing.

"Dragons," he breathed. "This place aches."

"My magic aches," Borrel answered. "Something terrible happened here."

"Indeed, it did." Lexyl said sharply. "Don't stop, Borrel. Samhain is no time to dally in this place."

Jax noted that Lexyl had more sense than Eleeza gave her credit for.

Silently, quickly, they passed along the ruined avenues under the shadows of the crumbling buildings. Gradually, Jax realized that by comparison the desert fairly hummed with the sound of life: buzzing insects, chirping birds, shrieking ravens. No birds or bugs existed here. The only sound was the shuffle of their own feet and the tense rhythm of their own breath. The sun beat through the haze.

This city had been larger and better built than any Jax had seen elsewhere in the Knownlands. He could easily imagine these wide boulevards full of elegant people. But now there was nothing but silence, the memory of pain, and a deep abiding anger.

After a couple of hours, they descended a twisting street and came to the bank of the river. Water foamed around the fallen blocks of a ruined bridge.

Lexyl pulled off her pack and looked around nervously. "I've never been here on Samhain before. The unhappy spirit of this place is especially raw today."

All of the travelers gazed uneasily at the dust-filled streets around them.

"So how do we cross this river?" Florin asked.

"Let's put our packs on the lakema." Lexyl began adjusting straps on the animal's back. "The river won't be deep at this time of—."

"Sweet goddess!" Marith shrieked.

A gray figure, its edges ragged, floated towards them like a cloud shadow in the silent sunlight. With it came the odor of rot and sulfur.

The group stepped closer to one another.

"Lexyl," Jax said, "Can you use magic to banish that thing?"

She shook her head. "I've sensed the ghosts but never seen them, not like this."

Jax glanced down at the druid at his side. "How about an exorcism, Marith?"

She cleared her throat. "In the name of the Holy Mother, be gone!" The words echoed back from the ruined buildings and with the echo came a cold laugh.

The shadow came closer. A wisp reached forward, like an arm, towards Jax. "Paradox?"

"Paradox?" Jax repeated the word in Ancient, vocabulary lessons coming back to him, even as he gagged on the odor of death, his heart impaled by the ghost's anger and fear.

"Paradox," the whisper came again, clearer. "I see you *now*. Too late."

Jax looked to his friends. All of them stared wide-eyed. Only he and Lexyl understood the old language.

"Too late." Again, the gray wisp rose towards him. Pinned by his friends all around him, Jax couldn't move away. The shadow touched his chest.

Images flooded his mind: These streets filled with screaming people, running, crying, howling. The air was black, but spikes of red flame rose from the river and the buildings. Backlit by the roaring flames, a squat round tower crouched near the river. Gray-clad priests and priestesses rushed from the tower, as panicked as the rest of the population. Jax smelled the acrid smoke in the back of his throat and his heart pounded in terror.

Alone, one last figure, small and wrinkled, raised its arms. Jax knew somehow that this was the Oracle, entreating the goddess for mercy. But there was no mercy, and the Oracle exploded in flame. Grief ripped through him like lightening.

With a choking cry, Jax fell to his knees.

"Too late!" The ghost pushed forward, swathing him in a gray fog.

"No!" Marith swept her hands through the shadow. "By the earth the air the fire and the water, you GO!"

The gray shadow rose up.

At the same moment, both Borrel and Lexyl called upon their different magics and pushed against the ghost. "Be gone!"

The shadow suddenly fell apart like a puff of smoke and dispersed in the still air.

Marith bent to Jax, who sat shivering in the dust of the ruined road, his arms rapped around himself.

"Jax?"

"Sweet goddess." It was almost a sob. "Sweet goddess, Marith." He looked up at her, his eyes dark and haunted.

"Let's get out of here," Florin snapped. She threw the rest of their packs onto the lakema. Lexyl and Marith held tightly to the little animal as they carefully waded through the brown water. Borrel and Florin, on either side of the trembling Jax, shared a worried glance.

On the far shore they unloaded the extra bags from the lakema, while gritty brown grime from the stinking river dripped from their clothes.

"Jax?" Florin handed him his pack. "Are you alright?"

"No." He still shivered uncontrollably. "Let's get out of here."

Without stopping to eat, they hurried through more stands of wrecked blocks and tumbled towers. By sunset they had reached the wall of cliff on the southern edge of the plain, but even then, Lexyl kept them moving. Borrel again made a light so they could push several more miles into a narrow canyon and up onto a rocky plateau, putting the ruins far behind them.

Lexyl finally allowed them to stop in a canyon cove, where a hanging garden and a small spring dripped down one wall. Exhausted, they threw down their packs.

Jax walked to the pool and knelt to splash his face and head. Marith came up behind him. "What was that all about?"

His hands covered his face and he shook his head.

Marith put a hand on his shoulder. He glanced up at her and when he spoke, his voice was uneven. "That was the ghost of the Oracle."

She gasped.

"I saw.... I saw the destruction, the fire," he paused and put his hands over his ears. "Goddess, I *heard* it...."

"I heard the ghost say *too late, too late*," Lexyl said, quoting the Oracle's words in Ancient. She had come to fill the pot with water.

Jax cringed. "Don't!"

"You understand Ancient?" Lexyl frowned at him.

"I understand more than I want to." He shuddered.

"Come back to the light, son." Marith tugged his arm. She spoke over her shoulder to Lexyl. "Do you have any lemongrass? I have garlic and peppermint..."

Within a few moments, the druid had brewed a foul tisane and pressed the mug into Jax's hands. "Gulp it down, son. It will banish the ghost."

He sipped and choked. "This is awful."

"It's meant to be."

He gagged it down but was soon retching it back up. Marith helped him to a bush far from camp. "Let it out, Jax. All of it."

He did.

Once again beside the fire, Marith got him a blanket and some peppermint tea. He still shivered in fits, but he felt better and ate a bit of biscuit.

The others took bowls of soup from Lexyl and ate in ravenous silence.

Florin wiped her bowl clean and looked at the fire-lit faces of her friends. "Can someone please explain what happened today?"

"Those were the ruins of Axterre." Lexyl poured tea into her mug. "I guess we shouldn't have tried to cross them when the veils between the worlds are so thin."

"Ghosts." Jax swallowed the last of his biscuit. "Ghosts and fairies and Axterre. I used to think that these things were just myths, just stories for kids."

"What *is* the story?" Florin demanded.

Jax pulled his blanket around his shoulders. "There was an old minstrel lay," He paused and thought for a moment then sang:

"Far away to south and east
There the dragons came to feast
Confuluence of sea and air:
Cornerstone of old Auxerre."

The others stared at him with various expressions of interest or aggravation.

Florin tapped her spoon against her tin bowl. "Sweet goddess, Jax. Where do you come up with this stuff?"

Lexyl encouraged him. "And you know the Ancient of Axterre."

"I know Ancient. I hadn't realized it was the language of Axterre."

"So this ancient city—"

"Empire."

"Existed before the dragons came to the Knownlands?" Borrel moved to join Lexyl inside her blanket.

"Long before," she told them. "And it far outlasted any other recorded civilization in the Knownlands."

"What happened to it?" Marith gave up on performing more than a perfunctory Samhain prayer and settled into her own blankets. "Did dragons attack it?"

Jax answered: "No, the dragons destroyed the Nekkian Empire on Baria. But the ruins there aren't haunted. They don't have the sense of agony or anger or horror...."

"Dragons, Jax." Florin stared at him. "You've been to other places like that?"

"I've never been any place like that. But the ruins of Nec are on Baria. They're just sad, not tainted, haunted..." he could not continue.

"There was so much anguish there," Borrel said quietly. "And betrayal, almost."

"But it wasn't dragons that got them?" Florin asked.

Lexyl answered. "The Axterrans destroyed themselves."

More lines of the minstrel lay came into Jax's mind: "*Acidic flames fell from the sky/ Those below prayed to die....*" He stopped, and closed his eyes, but the ghost's horrific flame-lit illustration of the ancient rhyme waited there. He threw off his blanket and stomped around the fire for a minute.

"Let it go, son," Marith said softly.

Watching Jax pace, Lexyl spoke quietly. "The Axterrans had a strange kind of magic, and while it could do miraculous things, it had queer and fatal side effects. First, it fouled the river and killed the fish. The Axterrans had to learn to eat other things. Then somehow it fouled the sky too, with a thick smoky haze. At that time, the land here was covered with forests and grasslands, but they cut down the trees and the grasses died, and the desert grew up from the south."

"This must have taken many years." Marith noted.

"It did, which is why so few of the Axterrans realized what was happening."

"Until it was too late." Marith frowned. "Didn't they celebrate the goddess? Didn't their druids warn them? Or the Oracle?"

"Their own magics were so powerful, they began to think that the goddess was just a myth, and who needs to abide by the principles of a myth?"

"Fire came down from the sky?" Florin looked up at the clear stars overhead.

"And the city, the heart of the largest empire the Knownlands has ever seen, was destroyed," Lexyl finished.

"No survivors?" Borrel asked.

Jax, still pacing, sang the final verse:

"With souls disfigured by their pride,
Flesh scorched and scarred they went to hide,
Snarling, gnashing: none that wept,
To live like beasts upon the steppes."

Florin sat up. "Are you saying that the monsters, who now roam the Hantish steppes, are the descendants of the Axterran people?"

"That's hideous!" Marith gasped. "Hideous!"

Lexyl nodded. "Axterre illuminates the dark face of the goddess. It's a Samhain story if ever there was one."

Borrel shifted closer to Lexyl and saw something in her face. "There were other survivors, weren't there, Lex?"

"There were. Although most Eldars don't know it, and wouldn't like it if they did, we are descended from the handful of Axterrans who fled the city before the final disaster. They followed a seer who felt the Axterran Oracle and their priests had betrayed the goddess. That's why the Eldar people have shamans now, and why we tend to be rather fanatical in our respect for goddess and her desert."

"So, what's this 'cat god' you refer to?" Marith asked.

She shrugged. "It's some kind of deity, maybe a face of the goddess. The Axterrans tried to suppress knowledge of it, and I seem to have a personal crusade to unveil such suppressions, even if no one else cares."

"Or if they exile you for it?" Jax asked.

She met his gaze then, her smile crafty. "No one likes the prophet of doom."

"Doom?" Florin snapped. "Sweet Goddess, what are you talking about?"

"Nothing, Florin." Lexyl soothed. "Nothing."

But Florin, confused and unsettled, turned her frustration on Jax. "And you, you understood what that ghost said to you? How do you know songs about a mythic place no one ever heard of? How do you know how to speak some goddess-forsaken ancient language?"

"I like to be a wise ass in as many languages as possible," Jax answered shortly.

"Stop it, you two," Borrel interrupted. "We're all unsettled by that place and finding out that the lines between truth and myth aren't all that clear."

Florin lay back in her quilt, looking up at the stars. "But the goddess is something more than a myth, isn't she?"

"Maybe. Maybe not," Marith answered quietly.

With that thought to color their dreams, the others tried to sleep through the night of the dead.

Jax continued to pace around the camp until exhaustion finally forced him to sit. But even then, he refused to close his eyes.

Despite the flippant answer he'd given Florin, Jax had learned Ancient because he was always curious about the motivations and realities of people from the past, and he wanted to read their thoughts in the original language. Also, he could study Ancient in both Kordon and Baria, whereas so much of his other schooling was specific to the country, and he was always struggling to keep up with his peers who didn't have to spend half the year away.

Watching the crescent moon slowly drop to the high cliff walls above him, he remembered playing that minstrel lay for Tallyn. He remembered the Fairy Queen's comment about "stupid" Axterran Oracles. He gagged again and had to stand up and take deep breaths.

What, he wondered, did it mean that the hallowed language of Mystic and many venerable texts had come from a place that had so violently destroyed itself?

31

In the fringed shade of a pinyon pine, Jax munched Eldar hard-cake and stared at the horizon, shimmering and yellow. Lexyl sauntered over with a water skin and sat down. Marith, Borrel, and Florin all dozed in the shade of a shallow cave. Despite the season, the sun still burned hotter here than at Midsummer in the Vale. Lexyl assured them that such heat was normal here and was actually cool by comparison to the full force of the desert summers.

Jax took the offered water skin and washed down the dry hardcake.

"On a clear day, you can see the tents of Roadsend from here." Lexyl took off her hat, shook out her hair then replaced the hat.

"Where is it?"

She pointed. "There's too much dust in the air today. It gets this way when big caravans come in or leave."

He turned to look at her. "You'll be leaving us soon."

She nodded.

"Thank you, Lexyl. I don't like to think what would have happened to us without you."

"The desert is generous."

"In a stingy sort of way."

"Oh no, Jax. It brought you to me and me to you and forced us together for these weeks. I've had the chance to learn about the world beyond the maze, and you've had the chance to venture into and out of the labyrinth."

"Will you leave the maze, now that you know a little more about what's out there?"

"Probably not. No matter what I may or may not know, Eleeza thinks she needs me here."

"You're important to her."

"Don't you start, too. She's my only family, but she's suffocating me—she and our damned superstitious Eldar People."

"At least they care for you, Lexyl. That's more than some of us can say about our families."

Lexyl took off her blue tinted glasses and polished them thoughtfully, intrigued by the bitterness in his voice. "Your family doesn't care about you?"

"*My* family sold me to the trolls."

"Why? Did they need the money?"

"I have no idea why."

"Are you going to go back to ask them?"

Slowly a humorless grin grew across his face, then he chuckled and was soon laughing hysterically.

Lexyl watched perplexed.

"Shut up, Jax," Florin demanded sleepily from the cave.

Eventually his laughter wore itself out. He took a long drink of water and pushed his hands through his sweat-tangled hair. "Sweet goddess, Lexyl. What an idea!"

"It didn't seem so funny."

"It isn't, really. But the thought of approaching my grandmother: *Excuse me, your Majesty, but...*" Again, he burst out laughing.

"Pretty formal with your grandmother, aren't you?"

"The Dowager Queen of Kordon is not an informal woman."

"The Dowager Queen of Kordon is your grandmother?"

Realizing what he had said snapped Jax back to his senses. He shrugged and glanced to his sleeping friends.

"By the cat god!" Lexyl stared, considering him in a different light. "Well, that explains a few things."

"Mother Marith, the others, they don't know," he said softly, wondering why it still seemed important to retain his anonymity.

"Didn't they guess? You are the most autocratic servant I've ever seen."

"No. People see what they expect to see. A slave is a slave. And I'm not autocratic."

She gave him a pointed look. "But you are friends with these people, especially Marith. She treats you like a child of her own."

"I haven't told them because it doesn't matter. I can't go back to Javix Sharkin, Prince of Baria and Kordon. He doesn't exist anymore."

"You don't think?"

"Lexyl, look at me. I'm sitting here in the dirt with a slave collar around my neck. I'm so far from...home."

Lexyl sat for a few minutes listening to the noontime buzz of occasional desert insects. "I can see that it would be difficult to be a noble but act like a slave."

"A paradox." He whispered, still unnerved by the memory of the ghost's gravelly voice.

The bitterness in his voice wove together with something she had read recently in the forbidden scrolls. For a fraction of a moment she hesitated to share this outlawed information, but knowledge was something Lexyl valued above most everything else: "Before their magic corrupted them, the ancient Axterrans believed that there's no such thing as absolute opposites. Everything is part of the same whole. Terms of opposition actually describe relationships rather than differences. After all, you can't understand dark without light; you don't know true joy without having tasted sorrow."

"But you can know true sorrow without having tasted joy."

"Don't be smart. I'm trying to share something with you. I have contradictions within me too, Jax. We all have. But rather than seeing conflict, I try to accept them as part of my whole."

"Prince and slave?"

"Magician and Speaker's Heir."

"Does it work?"

"Not always." She conceded succinctly, offering him some more dried fruit. "But at least it's something to go on."

"And I'm going on nothing right now."

They ate the fruit slowly. The dark wings of a raven rose in circles out over the distance.

Finally, Lexyl spoke. "Ever since that ghost called you paradox, there's been a line of poetry going through my head."

"I would prefer to forget about those ruins and the ghost."

"This poem, like most of my information, is from the ancient scrolls of Axterre. It's forbidden to read them, so I don't usually tell people the source of my information."

"Why are you telling me?"

"I think somehow you need to know this."

Lexyl began to chant softly in Ancient Axterran. Jax felt as if the ghost again engulfed him.

"A Paradox who can't be found.

The Mother stirs and shakes the ground.

Oceans rise to touch the trees,

And bring a ruler to his knees."

Lexyl's amber eyes caught the sea blue ones. "I wrote it out for you." She placed a scrap of parchment in his hand. "I think you should keep it."

He looked down, and as he slowly translated the ancient verse, it seemed to etch itself unpleasantly into his soul.

"Why?"

"You know already," she whispered. "And the ghost knew, too. You're one paradox after another."

"I'm one sorry mess."

Neither Lexyl nor Jax heard Florin come behind them. "Boo," she said.

Jax jumped. Lexyl bit her tongue.

"Sweet goddess, Florin," Jax snapped.

The nyad laughed. "I'm finally learning how to move in this treeless land."

"We have a tree right here." Lexyl plucked at a branch.

"One tree does not a forest make."

Lexyl stood up. "If you sleepyheads are ready to wake up, we might as well move along."

Marith sat up and stretched. Borrel came over to join Lexyl. He smiled at her, and once again her heart snagged on him. She reached out for his hand. "Let's go, then."

In the shade, Jax and Florin watched them go. Florin turned to gather the lakema's rope, muttering: "That girl's going to break his foolish heart."

"I think her heart's in danger, too." Jax stood up, folding the parchment carefully into his pocket.

They made camp that night in sight of the wash that would lead them down into Roadsend. Lexyl refused to go into town with them, saying that the less the Nomads knew about the Eldar People, the happier and safer the Eldars felt.

Marith, Florin, and Jax sipped Lexyl's spicy broth with heavy melancholy that evening. Borrel could not eat at all. Before the sun had set, he and Lexyl had taken their blankets and gone off together. Neither of them slept that night.

When the late autumn sun finally rose, it illuminated an ocher desert of low, rubble-strewn hills. Florin led the way down the sandy bottom. The Redland maze glowed behind them in the morning light. Borrel kept glancing over his shoulder at the solitary figure, who stood on the last low escarpment, watching them until the dry wash bent, and they were gone.

With tears in her heart, Lexyl slowly ambled north. Darkfest snows draped the Redrock canyons in frosty lace. Before she reached the tiled halls of Arandy, Lexyl realized with amazement that she was pregnant. Without any hand-fasting ceremony, without any chance of seeing the baby's father again, it hardly seemed possible. She made her solitary way across the desert, marveling that the goddess would bless her so.

After all the excitement of the journey across a continent, Dishroc turned out to be a disappointment. Mud-brick buildings crouched under blue tiled roofs as if beaten into submission by the merciless sun. Jax sat on a narrow bench in front of their small inn, awed by the heat. Darkfest, the winter solstice, was just two days away, but the heavy desert air still clung to him. Even in the shade, sweat dripped down his back.

But it was not just the heat that made Dishroc so unbearable. The Nomads proved to be a shifty bunch of merchants, who seemed to promise one thing but deliver something entirely different. Marith originally hoped to trade northern herbs and crystals for Nomad medicines, but most of her stores washed away with Ol' Pol and their tent. Forced to use money to get what she wanted, Marith decided to angle for information rather than goods. Talk was cheap, and the druid had to save her coins for the long road back to the Vale.

The problem, from Jax's point of view, was that gleaning information from old Nomad druids took even longer than haggling price over a handful of exotic spices. He and Florin took turns accompanying Marith on her errands, but both were bored into stupefaction by the long-winded Nomad druids. Jax gained a new appreciation for Marith's passion for her craft as he watched her listen to these Nomads for hours.

Poor Borrel seemed to have left his sense of humor with his heart back in the Eldar Maze. Silently he tromped along with the others through Roadsend and along the Nomad Caravansary to Dishroc. He did not eat; he did not sleep. Florin worried, but she had been through loss herself and trusted her twin to pull himself together eventually. In the meantime, however, they all missed Borrel's wry conversation.

The weather changed dramatically on Darkfest. A sandy wind blew low clouds from the west. Nothing fell from them, but the wind bit. They all felt more comfortable celebrating the sun's rebirth when it was not quite the menacing specter in the sky that it had been. The sharp contrast from heat to cold gave both Marith and Florin a nasty chill. In fact, Marith felt so poorly that she sent Jax to watch the Nomads' Darkfest celebration.

Jax coaxed Borrel into going with him, and together the two watched the Nomads' torch-lit dancing to the sun god. Compared to Darkfest dances in Baria and Hilsen Vale, the Nomad ritual appeared subdued and mournful.

It was over quickly. The crowd dispersed, while solemn drums pounded slowly.

"I wonder what they're like on Samhain," Borrel muttered, as he walked beside Jax down a dusty, twisting lane.

Jax glanced at his friend. This was more than he had heard from Borrel in days. "I suppose the sun is a tyrant here."

"And you wouldn't necessarily want to celebrate a tyrant's birth."

"No." Jax stumbled on something in the road. "Dragons! What a goddess-forsaken place this is. I can't believe what we went through to get here."

They ambled past one of the town's ubiquitous trash heaps, reeking sourly into the night wind.

"I'm glad we came," Borrel said gently. "I would never have met Lexyl."

"Never have had your heart broken."

Borrel slowed. The open doorway of a tiny wine shop cast warm candlelight onto the dark wind. "Let's go have a glass."

Jax followed the nyad inside. A grinning barkeep poured ruby wine into small round glasses.

"To the Darkfest," the barman said.

"To the sun." Borrel raised his glass.

"To the sun."

The wine tasted as dry and dusty as the Nomad Range itself. Jax loved it. In Baria, Nomad Red was a rare, expensive delicacy.

"Yuck." Borrel made a face, but he drank off his glass. The barman poured another.

"Have you never had your heart broken, Jax?"

"I have."

"And did you regret it? Did you swear never to love again?"

Jax shrugged.

Borrel went on. "If Mam Marith hadn't wanted to come here, if we hadn't been run out of Stede, if we hadn't lost our way, I would never have met her. So many lucky chances."

"That's a funny idea of luck you have."

"But it was luck. It led me to Lexyl."

Jax frowned into his wine glass. The slave pens and the Fever had brought him Jolira. But he could not, would not, view anything about slavery as good. If Jolira was a positive force in his life, it was despite the slave pens, despite the trolls and the Duke of Midipex and the Dowager who had sold him. Still, Borrel's insistent logic tumbled things around in his mind. If he had never been a slave, he would never have met Jolira, would never have known Mother Marith, never have ended up in a dragon-blasted hole in the dragon-blasted desert getting drunk with a lovelorn nyad.

A paradox, indeed. He emptied another glass of wine, feeling more and more confused about the lines between the good and the bad things in life and disliking the way Lexyl's damn poem kept running through his mind.

A fat round moon lit their way as they stumbled and crashed back to their inn. The innkeeper had locked the front door and bellowed at the two latecomers for rousing him on Darkfest. The longest night of the year, he told them loudly, was a night for a good long sleep. Marith and Florin grumbled at them too, but both women felt so sick that they could not raise much fuss.

The next morning, all four travelers awoke feeling wretched. Two with heavy head colds, and two with pounding hangovers. They sat in the dim tavern room sipping milk-thickened keffa, holding their heads, and picking at a Nomad breakfast of flat bread and honey.

"Marith?" Borrel asked softly. "Remember after we'd passed the ruins of Axterre, you said that maybe the goddess isn't real?"

"Yes."

"What did you mean?"

"Well," she paused to wipe her nose. "We use the idea of the goddess and her tales and rituals to find the divine in this world, to find it in ourselves, and to feel a connection to something greater than ourselves."

Florin grumbled over her keffa. "But she does exist, right? She hears our prayers."

"Florin," Marith reached out for the nyad's thin, brown hand. "I feel the goddess in me when I make a connection with something outside myself, but whether or not she exists outside of me isn't the point. The point is that I feel the connection. I live as if the goddess exists, so maybe she does."

Jax leaned back in his chair. "Will she go away if we ignore her?"

"Do you think she left Ohe or Axterre?"

Borrel sipped his keffa, understanding. "We have to live as if we believe."

"Believe what?" Jax asked, grumpy with his headache.

"Whatever you need to, son." Marith looked deep into the creamy liquid in her cup. "Believe whatever you need to."

Jax saw again the anguished faces of the dying Axterrans and remembered the desolate despair of his fellows in the slave pens. He let the legs of his chair thump back to the floor and winced with the impact to his hangover. "The problem is I don't like what I believe."

"Marith?" Jax glanced down at the old woman at his side, trudging through the dusty street.

"What is it, son?" she sniffled.

"Why do you keep calling me that? Don't you realize that it...it hurts?"

Marith stopped dead in her tracks and frowned up at him. "Obviously it hurts you. I keep saying it so you will figure out why."

"Why? I know why."

"Do you?"

"Because you *own* me, Marith. A son is not a possession. A son is someone you—." He choked to a stop.

"Someone you love," she said simply. "Someone you worry about and care for."

"You do?"

She smiled at him sadly. "You must have lost your own mother very young."

"Yes," he whispered. "I killed her."

Marith reached out and hugged him. "You didn't kill her."

He pulled himself free. "My birth killed her. Obviously, there was no intention on my part, but it doesn't matter what we intend, or who we are. What matters is what we do, right?"

She didn't answer. She sniffled and began walking back to the inn, wishing fervently for a hot cup of honey and lemon.

"Marith," he began again.

"What is it, son."

"You are merciless."

"In the way of all mothers."

"If I can pay you back your fifty silvers, will you release me?"

"Are you ready to go?"

"I think I should go back to Baria."

"Baria?"

"Lexyl gave me a piece of poem. It's worrying at me. There's a line in it..."

They rounded a corner and walked up to their inn. Marith stopped before the door. "So, you are ready to go home?"

He shrugged. "I'm not sure I am ready, and I'm not sure if it's home, but I am afraid for my brother. I'd like to make sure he's alright."

"A younger brother?"

"Older."

"And this poem of Lexyl's is causing your concern?"

He nodded. "I can probably get you money when we get to Kordon. I have friends there."

She waved her hand. "Forget the money, son."

He groaned and followed her into the shadows of the inn.

Three days later they left Dishroc, following an empty road to the east. Gradually the soaring barrier of the snow-covered Targheight Mountains rose above the western horizon. Snow had drifted down into the last Nomad encampment where they traded their lakema for a heavy Nomad-woven tent. With practiced ease, Borrel used his magic to weave snowshoes for all of them and they made good headway through the white drifts as they climbed higher and higher into the mountains. Winter in the Targheights might be rough, but it was mild compared to the Hantish climate. Florin relaxed visibly as they entered forests of dark pines, the first forests they'd seen since leaving Ily. She found ways through and around the stony peaks as easily as if she had spent her life there.

Jax watched his companions, amazed at their adeptness in the winter wastes. They built snow caves at night, placing the tent inside, found snow-buried berries to supplement their trail rations, and studiously avoided the dangers of avalanche paths. By Candlemas they were descending into Kordon.

The rolling hills and dales of eastern Kordon lay calm and quiet under their winter blanket of snow. The four travelers tramped along on their snowshoes, seeing no one other than the occasional hare or chipmunk.

Marith's cold, lingering on since Dishroc, came down more heavily as the trail flattened out and the air grew heavier. By the time they arrived at the tiny village of Keilor's Outpost, her fever was rising and her cough was thickening.

Because Marith felt so poorly, it was Jax who spoke to the innkeeper about beds and food.

The man looked the half-isle up and down, noting the odd, worn clothes and crisp accent. "We have a room for you, milord," he said finally. "But your creatures must stay in the barn."

"Creatures?"

"Those two," he gestured at the nyads without looking at them.

Jax ran a hand over his face. There were no other inns in this little village. He remembered the casual, maddening injustice of the Kordish sense of superiority and their inveterate prejudice towards anything not fully Kordish.

Marith coughed. Jax fixed the innkeeper with hard, sea blue eyes. "You will give us all a room. And dinner."

The innkeeper's eyes narrowed, but he bowed to authority. "Very well, milord."

"Milord?" Borrel laughed uneasily.

The innkeeper brushed past the nyad to lead them to the room, muttering, "Walks like a lord, talks like a lord, probably is a lord."

The room was small with only three beds and one shuttered window. Marith immediately rolled into one bed and fell asleep.

"Are you a lord, Jax?" Borrel dumped his pack on the floor next to Florin's.

"You didn't notice? Let's go get some food."

Throughout the meal, the barmaids and innkeeper continued to address Jax as 'milord' or 'sir.' It sounded so right to Jax to hear Kordish voices using such terms toward him, and he easily responded with the appropriate niceties.

At first Borrel laughed and Florin scowled, but as they realized how naturally Jax accepted the deference of the Kordish, they both became silent with their questions.

Despite everyone's respect for Jax, none of the Kordish seemed at all interested in the nyads. Over the three days that they rested at Keilor's Outpost, both Borrel and Florin became increasingly frustrated with the Kordish habit of ignoring them. People pretended not to understand the nyads' Hantish accent or simply acted as if the nyads were not there at all.

"Have I become invisible, Jax?" Borrel replaced his empty mug on the table, as once again the barmaid had walked past, ignoring it.

"You do seem a little faint around the edges." Jax drained the last of his lager and waved his mug at the tavern keeper. The man immediately sent the barmaid round with a fresh, frothy pitcher and a polite, "Here you are, milord."

Florin leaned forward to pour the golden ale into their mugs. "This place is all upside down. The slave is 'milord,' and the free folk are invisible."

Jax took a long drink from his mug. "My personal paradoxes are starting to rub off on you."

Florin frowned. "What's a paradox?"

Jax pushed his chair back. "I'm going up to bed."

Borrel watched him go. "Jax is a paradox."

"I still don't understand." Florin swallowed half her pint.

Borrel turned to her. "No one in the Vale called him 'milord.'"

"No. We don't usually 'milord' a slave."

"Exactly."

After three days, Marith said she felt well enough to continue on towards Rippsgate. They all ate a last huge breakfast of eggs, sausage, and potatoes. Jax tingled with excitement. In a few days he'd be at Rippsgate, capitol of the Rippsmarch, and home to his foster brother, Lord Foby Kora.

Marith rested by the fire while Borrel and Florin packed the last of their things and Jax went to settle the bill.

"Are you a half-isle, milord?" The innkeeper tried, unsuccessfully, not to stare at Jax's pointed ears.

"I am also half Kordish." Jax snapped.

"We used to have a couple of half-islish princes."

"They were fully royal, though, weren't they?" Jax noted.

"Sure. Yeah. I guess. They never came through here."

Jax could not stop himself from asking: "What happened to them?"

"Well, the one committed some kind of treason."

"Treason?"

"Aye, milord. He'll face a traitor's death when they find him."

"Prince Bryx committed treason?" Jax said the words without realizing he was speaking aloud. Had his brother done something drastic to rescue him, after all?

"T'weren't the one called Bryx, I don't think," the innkeeper mused. "T'was the younger one. Him that fostered with young Lord Foby."

"Oh." It took some effort to keep his voice level. "What exactly did he do?"

The innkeeper pushed Jax's change across the sticky bar top. "I don't know, milord. But he vanished and the king declared him a traitor. I tell you, I'd go all the way to Kree to see that execution. I'd take my kid, too."

Jax pocketed the coins. A traitor's death took three days.

"You don't look so good, Jax." Florin frowned as he joined the others by the fire. "Are you getting Marith's 'flu?"

Jax just shook his head. Along with the others, he wrapped himself in his cloak and headed out into the cold winter morning.

Although he had never seen a traitor executed, his history tutors at Kree had described with gory relish the details of a traitor's death. On the first day the traitor received two hundred lashes and their eyelids were cut off. The second day, both feet and hands would be hacked off with dull axes. If the miscreant survived until the third day, they were disemboweled and burned alive.

But how could anyone suspect him of treason? He'd been a Knight of Kordon and one of the crown princess's closest friends. What had Midipex done or said that would make the Kordish royal council convict him of treason, without even giving him a chance to speak for himself?

"You're awfully quiet back there, Jax," Marith said hoarsely.

"I can't go to Rippsgate with you."

"Why not?" Florin asked.

"I'm in big trouble here."

Florin snorted. "But everyone treats you like a lord here."

"How can you be in trouble, Jax?" Marith paused, coughing. "You haven't been here in, what, four years?"

"I didn't leave under the best circumstances."

"I thought your family sold you."

"That's part of it."

Marith stopped. "You know, son, if you want people to understand you or sympathize with you, or even to help you, you might want to actually explain things to them."

Jax looked at his companions standing in the sparkling snow. They stared back at him. "Marith." He stopped, took a deep breath and started again. "As I keep saying, I am not your son. My mother was Princess Valla of Kordon and my father was Sealord Rax VII. I am Javix Sharkin, Prince of Baria and Vice Admiral of the Barian Fleet, also Prince of Kordon, Viscount Norbay."

Marith sank down to sit on her haunches. "Is that all?"

"Why didn't you tell us before?" Florin demanded.

"What difference would it have made?"

"Marith and Doc would have freed you, surely."

"Why?"

"Because you're a prince!"

"And a prince can't be a slave? Only common people can be slaves?"

Florin opened her mouth to reply but realized that she had no answer.

"That explains a lot." Borrel stared at Jax. "You're royal. That's why you don't have much magic, and that's why you know so much political geography, and why you walk the way you walk."

"But why can't you go to Rippsgate?' Florin asked. "If you're a prince here maybe they'll put us up in a castle."

"They think I'm a traitor. I've been to Rippsgate. I fostered with the earl's son. If I'm recognized, they'll arrest me and...."

"And?" prompted Borrel.

"And a traitor's death takes three days."

"Dragons." Florin frowned. "What did you do?"

"Apparently I vanished at a bad time."

"How'd you manage that?"

"It wasn't something I managed at all. For goddess's sake, you all know what happened to me. You know where I'd been before Doc bought me."

"I don't think any of us really know you," Florin said.

Jax extended his hand to Marith and pulled her to her feet. "Come on. It's too cold to stand here talking."

Jax let Borrel and Florin move ahead. They moved faster on their long legs than Marith could manage. He could hear the twins talking, but not their words, as he stayed behind to walk more slowly with

Marith, who didn't talk, saving her breath for the effort of trudging through the snow.

The wind began to blow large white clouds from the west. Soon snow swirled around them, driven into their mouths and noses by the screaming wind. They made a quick camp, but snow still sifted into the tent and dusted their sleeping quilts.

Borrel made a small bright fire to warm their supper.

Jax had felt Marith's eyes on him all afternoon. Now, as the tent shook and bent in the blizzard, he sat down next to her. "I'm sorry I didn't tell you sooner."

She blew her nose. "Why didn't you?"

"I couldn't when Doc bought me. I had thought Klaris de Farsouth would save me. When she didn't, I was humiliated to find myself still enslaved. And you know how hard I tried to hate you."

She reached out and took his hand. He was startled by the heat of her fingers.

"I'm only a village druid, with nary a drop of royal blood or magic in my veins, but I can do what your magical princess could not."

They all looked at her.

"I can free you." She paused to cough. "Borrel, can you use your magic to remove that collar?"

The nyad's smile flashed in the dark of the tent. "With pleasure."

Jax felt the familiar rush as Borrel called his magic. He heated sections of the collar carefully, and finally, with a slice of his knife, cut through the ring; a twist and it was off. The nyad handed the cooling metal to Jax. "You want to keep it?"

"No." He opened the door of the tent and threw the thing into the snowy darkness.

Marith coughed again, softly.

He turned back to her. "I won't be able to borrow fifty silvers from my erstwhile friends in Rippsgate now."

"I told you to forget the money."

Florin began to hand bowls of stew to each of them. "I guess all of us will have to avoid Rippsgate," she said.

"True," Jax agreed. "If you're caught with me, you'll share my grisly fate, and I would not have that."

For the first time, his companions recognized the inherent sense of authority in his tone for what it was and where it came from.

"Maybe we can go to Bly," he went on, oblivious to his friends' silent revelations. "We can see if the Barians will take me back or if they have bloody plans to me too."

"Sweet goddess, Jax, uh, my lord," Florin shook her head.

"Just Jax, Florin." He rolled himself into his blankets.

Borrel dimmed the fire. Marith coughed.

After a while Jax propped himself up on one elbow and looked across the dark tent to the old druid. He could see her eyes glitter in the warm glow from Borrel's small fire.

"Thank you, Marith."

"You're welcome, son."

The blizzard kept them pinned inside their tent for the next two days. Marith's fever returned with a vengeance, and by the time the storm abated, she was too weak to walk. With grim efficiency, Florin fashioned a sling from a blanket and two saplings. As they trudged through the snow-covered countryside, Jax realized that she needed to get out of this cold wind, and that she needed a druid.

But this was a wild and empty corner of Kordon. Dark forests climbed the steep eastern slopes of the Targheights. He knew that Rippsgate was the only town for miles around. As Marith's fever rose, Jax watched his options fade as their footprints disappeared under new snow behind them.

"I thought we weren't going to Rippsgate!" Florin's voice was unusually shrill.

"We aren't. You are," Jax snapped.

"But..."

"Look, Marith can't stay outside any longer. She needs a druid.'
He shook snow off the blanket covering the old woman. "You and
Borrel take her into the town. Find the druid and get Marith healed."

"And you?"

"I'll go around outside the town walls, cross the river at a ford
about a mile up from the Rippbridge."

"But it's freezing."

Jax's return gaze was just as chilly. "I will wait for you on the
Ilyian side of the river. You'll find me in a stand of trees near the
ford." Jax had ridden all over this countryside with Foby in their days
as foster brothers.

Borrel sorted through their packs, pulling out the tent, the pots,
and the thickest quilts. "Take these, then."

Jax strapped the additional gear onto his pack. He took all the
coins from his pockets and handed them to Borrel.

The two nyads lifted Marith between them. For a moment, Jax
gazed at her face then he turned and disappeared into a swirl of
snow.

Spurred by the wet wheeze of Marith's breathing, the nyads hurried through the vast gray stone portal and into the walled city of
Rippsgate.

Wrapped in his cloak and all the quilts, Jax's fingers were still numb with cold. He dared not risk a fire, for fear his smoke would bring the border guards that the earl kept to discourage smugglers. He knew that they would think nothing of venturing into Ily to catch a criminal. Too cold to even play his dragonpipe, he lay cursing the frost that should be breaking this late in the winter, as one day, then two, passed slowly.

Footsteps crunched in the snow. He sat up, reaching for his knife. Gray dawn light filtered through the woven patterns of the tent.

"Jax?" Borrel's voice came softly through the cold air.

He leapt from the tent. "What is it?"

"We can't get a druid." Borrel's voice was tinged with panic, and his eyes rimmed with fatigue. "We've tried everything we can think of, but those people just don't see us. It's like we're not there at all."

"Marith?"

"She's dying, Jax."

"Dragons." His breath billowed into the icy morning. He thought of Doc, back in the Vale and fingered the wooden dragonpipe still in his pocket.

Without another word, he set about striking the tent. Borrel helped. Together they crossed the Rippbridge back into Kordon. "She's up at the castle," Borrel said softly as they walked through the town gate.

Jax stopped and turned to face the nyad. "The castle? Why?"

"The druid is one of the earl's daughters. We've been loitering at the gatehouse, begging to be heard."

"I'll be recognized at the castle, Borrel."

"Tell me what else to do, then." Borrel begged.

Jax pulled his hood closer over his distinctive islish ears. "Can't you use your magic, start a fire or something to get their attention?"

"We tried that. We tried everything. I started fires; they just stomped them out. We threw money at them; they let it roll to the ground. We shouted; they walked on by. We even put her on the top step at the door to the castle. Everyone just walked around her. It's unbelievable."

"Dragons fry them," Jax swore, then more softly: "Dragons fry me."

He turned and looked back the way they had come. He could see the Rippbridge through the town gate, and beyond that the snow-laden trees of Ily. There was freedom. His very, very new freedom.

Jax squared his shoulders. Bryx would have to take care of himself. It would be over in three days; all his damned paradoxes and dichotomies would be resolved after three more difficult days.

Borrel watched him looking across to Ily. He realized that Jax was facing a terrible choice. After a moment Jax turned away from the bridge and strode towards the castle. The nyad followed, his heart aching.

At the gatehouse, Florin had rigged a tarp where she and Marith sheltered in the windblown warmth of one of Borrel's magical fires.

"Thank the goddess," Florin breathed.

Jax knelt next to Marith and took her hand. Waves of heat came off her fevered body. Each breath wheezed wetly from her labored lungs.

"Hold on, Mam." He bent and placed a kiss on her cheek.

Rising, he wrapped his scarf around his face and pulled his hood down low. There wasn't anything he could do to disguise the islish slant of his eyes. "Take care of her," he said and left.

Marith stirred on the cot. "Jax?"

"He's gone to get you a druid," Florin answered, surprised by the tears on Marith's hot cheeks.

The old woman coughed heavily. "He finally called me *Mam*."

Jax walked into the castle courtyard, searching for a footman or a kitchen servant. With a sudden thunder of hooves, three laughing nobles burst from the stable yard and pounded towards the gate, their cheeks flushed from the crisp air and their exuberance. Four beautiful hounds leaped beside the horses. Jax stepped back, averting his face.

One of the dogs stopped at Jax, wagging her tail. He reached down to pet her fine head, recognizing her as Foby's favorite dog, Shaloh. She was a little gray around her muzzle now, but her tail wagged in the same familiar circular rhythm.

The lead rider courteously reined in his mount. "Hello!"

Jax knew that voice and whom he would see when he looked up. He shook his head and motioned for the nobles to ride on.

But something about this strange vagabond had caught Lord Foby's attention. And Shaloh was wagging her tail as if he were some long-lost friend. "Can we help you, my man?"

"I need a druid, sir," Jax spoke in his best imitation of the broad Hantish accent, his face still averted. He heard one of the riders dismount and caught the swish of a skirt out of the corner of his eye.

"I am the druid here." The voice of Thessaly Kora, Foby's younger sister, came closer with her footsteps. "Are you hurt?" she asked.

He shook his head and gestured towards the gatehouse. "My...A friend of mine is at your gatehouse. She's a druid as well."

"Where are you from?" Foby leaned forward in his saddle trying to get a better look at the ragged stranger. The dog continued to wag her tail.

"Up in the Hantland, sir."

"Don't you know to look at my Lord Foby when you speak to him?" the third rider said shrilly.

"Aye, fellow, look at me."

Given no choice, Jax looked up into the familiar blue eyes of his foster brother.

Foby froze, but only for a moment. He turned to his sister, who was calling for grooms to take her horse and maids to bring her druid's bag. "Will you take this fellow's friend to the infirmary?" he asked in a rather choked voice.

"Yes, of course." Thessaly looked at her brother in surprise, then back to the stranger, who was pulling his scarf close around his face.

"Thank you, my lady," the stranger said softly and turned to leave the courtyard.

"Stop, you!" The third rider nudged her horse between him and the gate. "Guards! Guards! I believe we've found one of the smugglers."

"No, my lady," Jax said quickly, still looking down. "We are just travelers from the Hantland."

"Millicen," Foby kept his voice bland. "Let him be. A smuggler would hardly walk into the earl's castle...."

"Let him pull off his hood then, and we'll see who he is," Millicen said firmly. "Guards!"

By now, four men in the earl's livery stood glaring at the stranger.

"Let him be," Foby repeated. "He's Hantish. You can tell by his accent."

"Smugglers killed my brother, Lord Foby," Millicen answered grimly. "I'm not inclined to let any of them go unpunished." She dropped from her horse in one fluid movement and ripped the hood back from Jax's head.

"I'm no smuggler, Lady Millicen," Jax said in his own voice, smiling slowly, wolfishly. "I believe you've caught a bigger fish."

Millicen's ice-blue eyes narrowed. She grabbed the fellow's scruffy cloak and pulled it aside. She frowned at the pink and black scar where the tattooed sigil of his birthright had been. "You can't hide who you are, my lord." She stepped back, then raised her voice to the grooms standing by. "Seize him! It's the traitor! The traitor Prince Javix!"

The grooms rushed him, their fists active. The hounds barked. Jax lost his scarf and heard a sword sing from its sheath. "I yield!" he shouted. Still the rough hands shoved him to his knees in the slushy mud. "I yield, damn you!"

Foby whistled to his dogs, who came to heel more quickly than the grooms. "Enough!" his voice carried over the ruckus. "He yields!"

"Stand clear!" Jax recognized the voice of Earl Kora. "Stand clear! I want to see him." The guards' fists subsided, but they pinned his arms behind his back. One held a knife to his throat. Blood dripped into his eye. He shook his hair off his face.

The Earl of the Rippsmarch stood on the castle steps looking down at him.

"I yield," Jax panted, shoving to his feet. "But I will not kneel."

"Well, that's somewhat typical." The earl came down the steps and looked into the face of the no-longer-missing prince. He noted the scar where the birthright sigil had been. With that long hair and strange ruddy clothing, he did look like one of the ruffians who skulked along the borders. But Oklan Kora had seen a great deal of this prince who had fostered with his son, and the expression in those strange blue eyes was recognizable.

"Hello, your Highness," Earl Kora said at last. "I hadn't planned on an execution this week."

"No need to inconvenience yourself, your Grace." The knife at his throat nicked his skin and a small dribble of blood ran hot down his neck.

"I suppose we might put it off a day or two. Give the country folk a chance to come in to town for the spectacle."

Foby pushed aside the groom with the knife and wiped at the blood with his handkerchief. "We know you were a slave."

"You do?"

Foby nodded. "We traced you to Hilsen Vale. Tallyn and I spoke to the druid fellow, Doc, who bought you from the trolls. Seems he had no idea who you were."

"No, they didn't know. It's Doc's mother who is sick."

"This is the woman who took you off to the Nomad Range somewhere?"

"Yes."

Foby stared into those familiar, islish eyes. "Why did you come back here?"

"I had to come for Mother Marith. You people wouldn't hear the nyads."

"But why come back to Kordon?

Jax understood the question now. "I didn't know I'd been accused of treason."

"Not just accused, my lord, convicted," said the earl succinctly. He turned back towards the castle. "Let's go inside where we can be warm while we deal with this. Bring his Highness to my solarium, but stop poking holes in him for a few minutes. And someone please fetch Lady Dayne."

The grooms, now aided by some of the earl's footmen, sheathed their knives, but they never released their grip on Jax as they led him up a flight of stairs and down a long corridor. The glass-roofed solariam was delightfully warm, scented by two potted lemon trees and enlivened by the music of a small fountain. A light desk faced a collection of comfortable chairs and low tables set with vases of unseasonable blooms.

Lady Dayne, the earl's oldest daughter and his heir, entered followed by people bringing hot tea. The guards bound Jax's wrists together and took both of his sheathed knives.

"Your Highness." Lady Dayne curtseyed shallowly to Jax. Goddess, but those eyes of his were as beautiful as ever.

Foby poured tea for his father, his sister and himself. "Would you like some tea, Jax?" he asked.

Jax just raised his bound wrists. Foby placed his own teacup into Jax's hands.

Brewed in the Kordish style and sweetened with Farsouthian sugar, the taste of the tea flooded Jax with memories. He closed his eyes for a moment.

"Well, my lord," said the earl. "Since we're serving you tea, with sugar no less," he glowered at his son, "you might as well sit down. We'd better get a rider off to Kodill and Tallyn. Do you want to go, Foby?"

"No."

The earl turned to one of the footmen. "Please fetch my niece, Ellica."

Young Ellica must have been waiting in the corridor outside the solarium because the footman returned almost as soon as she had left. Jax remembered Foby's cousin as a saucy kid of thirteen or so. Taller now, she sketched a minimal curtsy and stared with frank curiosity at Jax.

"Ellica, you may remember Prince Javix," the earl said. "Ride to Kree as fast as the post horses will go. Tell King Kodill and Princess Tallyn that we've found Jax Sharkin."

"Yes, my lord."

"And what?" Foby demanded. "Do you want to tell them that we've executed him?"

The earl sipped his tea and gazed thoughtfully at Jax. "I sat on the council that convicted you, Prince Jax, and I am duty-bound to carry out the sentence."

"But surely you'll wait until Tallyn or the king get here?" Foby stood up.

"The prince has already been convicted and sentenced," Dayne noted. "We don't have the authority to ignore a decree of the royal council."

Foby snorted. "Jax is a Prince of the Blood. That has to count for something."

Dayne shook her head. "Remember your law, Foby. A traitor convicted by the royal council has no right of appeal. The king alone can grant a reprieve or a pardon, but we all know how unwilling Kodill is to overrule the council in any matter."

"What am I supposed to have done?" Jax asked.

The earl pulled on his chin, considering the ragged prince. "You stole state secrets, my lord. The Duke of Midipex found your accomplice—some woman. The royal council convicted you of high treason."

"And you believe I would do such a thing?"

The earl shrugged. "I didn't want to believe that you would. But the coincidence of your disappearance and the loss of the treasury documents was damning."

Jax placed his teacup back on its saucer with a clatter. He had come to them as a child, worked his sorry ass off to achieve their damned knighthood, sworn fealty to their king for goddess's sake, but when push came to shove he was only *half* Kordish, and he was the one they blamed. "So, I was convicted on circumstantial evidence?"

"Yes, but convicted all the same."

Lady Dayne watched him smile mirthlessly as he turned to Foby.

"Would you loan me a few sovereigns, Foby? I'd like to pay Mother Marith back."

"I already left gold with that Doc fellow in the Vale," Foby answered.

"That was a poor investment," Lady Dayne said to her brother. "My lord Jax's story is as improbable as his ability to repay the loan."

Jax laughed. "Indeed, Lady Dayne. It took a number of beatings before I truly believed it myself."

"But how?" Foby asked. "We still don't know how you ended up a slave in the first place."

Jax took a moment to count the number of people gathered in the solarium: too many to hear the whole truth. "I was abducted from Castle Kree. By a woman named Felona."

"Abducted?" The earl sneered. "You suggest that someone snuck into Castle Kree and snatched a Prince of the Blood from the heart of Kordish power?"

"Indeed," Lady Dayne shook her head in disbelief. "That would be...."

"Treason," Jax finished. "Surely the Duke of Midipex as Lord Chancellor should view such a crime as an attempt against the state."

"Listen, my lord, *you* are the one under sentence of treason," the earl growled, resuming his chair.

"But I am not guilty."

"Dragons," Foby swore.

Jax looked at his friend, but he spoke to the earl. "Your Grace, please don't let this accusation against me affect my companions."

"It's a *conviction*, my lord." Dayne clarified.

"Fine." Jax snapped. "But Mother Marith and the nyad twins have no part in any of this. They did not know who I was... who I am."

"How could they not know?" Lady Thessaly joined them in the room, shedding her cloak.

"I didn't tell them."

"But wasn't it obvious? You bear a sigil." Dayne, an aristocrat down to the tips of her toes, recognized long generations of breeding in Jax's mannerisms, looks, and speech, despite his simple clothes and disheveled hair.

"People see what they expect to see. When Doc bought me, I looked quite authentic."

"You still do." Thessaly's druid-trained eyes swept him from head to foot, noting the leanness of his body, sculpted by meager food and physical labor, and the way he ignored his new wounds and the ropes around his wrists. She pushed aside the shirt to view the scar where his birthright sigil had been. "Someone tried to burn this off."

"Felona," Jax said moving away from Thessaly's questing fingers, "sold me to the trolls in The Hant."

"Felona?" Foby repeated. "But Midipex's guards captured her. They said she was your accomplice and was looking to the Barians for succor when she killed herself."

Jax smiled slowly. "Killed *herself*?"

"Yes. Threw herself off the Cliffs of Rockheart to avoid a traitor's death."

"Very clever."

Foby turned away from the familiar wolfish grin on Jax's face and looked out the window, remembering the executions Midipex had initiated as a result of Felona's suicide. All of the dead had been members of his own household, as were the guards executed for attacking Doc in Hilsen Vale. Why would the duke execute his own people unless he was sure they were guilty of collusion?

"Tallyn and I visited the Hantland where it seems you were, as you say, enslaved," Foby said. "Is there anyone who can corroborate your story about how you ended up with the trolls? Someone with more political weight than a couple of foreign druids?"

Bound and bloody, Jax knew he couldn't accuse the dowager, any more than he could name the Lord Chancellor of Kordon as the mastermind. He would be in mortal danger once Midipex found out he was alive and so would anyone who believed his story. An open accusation here in this room full of footmen and the earl's family would be dismissed as fantastical and desperate. Midipex would laugh it off.

He needed a more subtle approach. Perhaps he could plant some seeds of doubt and hope that they'd grow fast enough to convince the earl or Foby or Dayne to stop the execution.

"That's a question the Lord Chancellor should be asking," Jax answered. "Midipex surely realized that Felona needed an accomplice within the highest Kordish circles."

The earl frowned at him. "Truly? You were truly enslaved by the trolls?"

"Klaris de Farsouth saw me there."

"The Farsouthian Princess?" Lady Dayne frowned. "What was she doing among trolls?"

"She studies on Sageham. An overtroll and I were shipwrecked on the southern shore of Hanter Lake. Klaris was with a group of Mystics out there doing some kind of magical training. She recognized me, eventually."

"Why didn't she get you away from the troll?"

"I wish I knew."

Foby poured more tea. "Doc's husband mentioned something about this Klaris trying to find you."

Earl Kora grumbled. "Sageham's a long way off. Without Barian ships coming and going, I don't know how we would reach her in either Farsouth or Sageham."

"What do you mean there's no Barian shipping?" Jax caught himself, as Lexyl's poem again echoed in his head.

"We closed the Gates of Griffe because your accomplice, Felona, was working with the Barians," the earl explained.

"That's why Farsouthian sugar is such a luxury these days," Foby smirked.

Jax thought of fat Barian merchant ships with empty holds or worse, holds full of goods that could not be sold. He turned to Thessaly and more immediate problems. "How is Mother Marith?"

The young druid shook her head. "Not well. She should have had had medical attention days ago."

"We tried," Jax said, his eyes hard. "Borrel and Florin did everything they could think of to get your attention for two days."

"The nyad creatures?" Lady Dayne shivered in distaste. "I hope someone put them in the barn, or better yet, outside the town walls."

"They're in the barns," Thessaly said softly, catching the anger on Jax's face. "The grooms put them all in the barns, including the old Hantish druid."

"What?" Jax jumped to his feet. "Are you going to care for her at all? She's a druid, a mother. And Borrel and Florin are fine, dedicated people," he snapped. "They all deserve better than your goddess-damned barns."

"They're not people," Dayne said. "Technically."

Jax turned to Foby. "You asked me why I came back to Kordon, Lord Foby. I have been in the depths of the Hantland for four years. I had no idea that you people had convicted me of treason without any evidence. I had no idea that you had closed your ports, which will devastate Baria. But I did learn a few things over the past four years. I learned that nobility isn't only found among nobles. I learned to take care of those who need help, no matter who they are. That's why I came here today. I know what a traitor's death is. But I owe everything to Mother Marith."

The footmen, alarmed by the violence in the prince's voice, grabbed him. He shrugged to free himself and his thin shirt tore. Thessaly caught sight of the scars across his back.

"Stop!" She ordered. "Stop. Let me look at this."

The footmen pulled Jax's head back by his long hair and the cold knife again pressed against his throat. Thessaly came around to look at his back. "Sweet goddess," she whispered, pushing back the shreds of his shirt. "Sweet goddess, my lord."

"Sweet goddess, indeed," Jax said with gritty sarcasm. "Don't pretend to worship her light and bounty when all you can see is the beauty of your own reflection."

"That's enough, your Highness," Earl Kora snapped. He turned at last to his niece who had watched the entire conversation with rapt blue eyes. "We will prepare for a traitor's death. Ellica, ride to Kree and tell the king that we will begin the execution of Javix Sharkin in a fortnight, to give his Majesty time to get here, if he wishes."

"Father," Foby began, but the earl cut him off, motioning to the guards: "Get him out of here," Kora ordered.

Ungently, the guards hauled Prince Javix Sharkin down the stairs, across the courtyard, and down more stairs into a dark tunnel that wound below the castle. Here they replaced the ropes around his wrists with a pair of heavy iron fetters. Water dripped somewhere in the dark. Small cells opened off the tunnel. Someone groaned hoarsely from behind a heavy door.

They deposited him in a windowless cell and slammed the door.

Jax pulled against the chains, pacing angrily back and forth kicking the rank straw. "Dragons fry you all!" He shouted to the walls. "Dragons fry every last one of you!"

34

Eventually his anger dissipated into the cold darkness. He sat, with his back to the stone wall, his bound hands looped over his knees, listening to the vermin rustle in the straw.

He refused to let his mind recall the terrors of Oblek's pit in the iron mines, telling himself this was a solid Kordish dungeon. He worried about Marith and Borrel and Florin. He thought of Bryx trying to hold the Barian people together in the face of losing their most productive trade routes. He put his head on his knees, despairing that no matter what he did, people seemed to suffer.

Somehow the brief taste of Kordish tea had opened the gates of memory to his childhood in Kordon. He let those memories distract him from the darkness surrounding him and his future.

Memories: Falling off horse after horse, as he learned to ride, insofar as he learned at all. Foby's patient, but largely wasted, explanations of what horses or dogs or cats were thinking. The Barians didn't have pets, and Jax couldn't really make himself care about animals, when his own miseries were so apparent.

Memories: Sweat and dust and frustration day after day on the practice ground at Kree, a Kordish broadsword heavy and impossible to wield in his right hand. Tallyn's dedication to teaching him how to use the weapon, when everyone else, including Captain Karric, had given up on him; wanting to succeed for her sake, and finally doing so.

Memories: Finding the ancient scroll of Kordish Chronicles describing the political machinations that went into the founding of the Kingdom of Kordon as it now existed; the smell of ink and old parchment as he and Tallyn worked for hours over the translations from Old Country Landish and argued about the ethics of what their many-times-great-grandmother had done to craft a kingdom out of a bunch of unruly and disparate principalities.

Memories: The sweep of Cheshir's pale hair over her creamy skin: Cheshir, one day a skinny accomplice in stealing pastries from the palace kitchens, and then becoming more luscious than even the richest cream puff. Memories of how their crimes had progressed from thieving sweets to snitching certain graphic texts from the royal library with prurient intent.

Memories: Foby explaining straight-faced to the royal council how Prince Jax was merely demonstrating some aspect of advanced mathematics and not, in fact, attempting to drown the crown princess by taking her out in a boat. Foby saying to a purple-faced tutor that *obviously* Jax's essay was intended as satire and did not suggest that the Kordish might actually be xenophobic. Foby teasing him for his first ill-fated attempts to lure women to his bed. Foby rolling his eyes when he and Tallyn would argue some semantic point of political theory. Foby watching Tallyn go off with that clown Carden Yemmel, Lord of Traik.

Now all of them would stand in the crowd with their pale Kordish eyes to watch him slowly die. Dragons fry them all; he wouldn't make it easy for them. He knew he would need something to hold on to. Something to give him strength to withstand....

Finally, he hoisted an even older memory:

Sealord Rax looked across a littered desk at a small Jax.

"Nanny tells me you're not going to do your fostering in Kordon." Rax said.

"That's right, your Majesty."

Sealord Rax sighed, glanced again at his papers, and then forced himself to focus on his six-year-old son. "You are going, Jax. Bryx loves it. You will too."

"No, sir. I want to stay Barian."

"You want to stay on Baria."

The boy shook his head, the blond hair so striking among all the dark-headed Barians. "I don't want to be Kordish."

Rax pushed back his chair. "Come here, son." He took the boy upon his lap. "I know you don't want to go. But you are half Kordish, and you know that I promised your mother that I would make sure your brother and you were raised with Kordish customs as well as Barian."

Jax fidgeted. He could see where this was going.

"You will leave for Kree with Ambassador Grisham in four days. I'll be there ahead of you to introduce you to the king, and the little princess. You'll like them."

"I don't want to go!"

"I know that. But you're a Sharkin, Jax. Sharkins don't just do what they want to do. They do what they must do. You go on to Kree; you stand up tall and show them that Jax Sharkin does what he must. Make me proud of you."

So Jax had choked back his tears, although a few leaked out when Nanny crushed him to her soft bosom as she said goodbye. He enjoyed the journey across the sea to Kordon on the lord admiral's wingship, but when he had to put on the strange Kordish clothes and hard boots, his courage began to fail him.

His anxiety worsened when they sailed into Keffin Harbor and realized that the sealord's ship wasn't there as planned. Later, they learned that a storm had delayed the sealord, but now Jax had to face his Kordish relatives for the first time with only Ambassador Grisham at his side.

"Chin up, your Highness," Grisham squeezed his shoulder reassuringly as they waited to be announced to the king and his court.

"My toes hurt."

The massive door swung open. Horns blared, and Jax walked up a long room lined with strange light-skinned faces with eyes the color of shallow water and pale hair, like his own.

At the end of the room, a man sat on a throne, a beautiful young queen to his right, and a beautiful old queen to his left. A small girl with clear eyes peeked from behind the young queen's chair.

As he'd been taught, Jax clicked the hard heels of his new boots and bowed in the Kordish fashion.

The king said something, but Jax didn't understand the Landish language.

Ambassador Grisham bowed and spoke in response.

The beautiful older woman rose from her chair. Little Jax watched her sweep toward him, frozen by the look of hatred on her lovely face.

She slapped him hard across the mouth. His cry was lost in the wave of gasps from the courtiers.

Then the young queen was there, lifting him up in her arms and carrying him from the room, away from Grisham. No one did anything about his stinging face.

The young queen introduced him to the little clear-eyed girl, his cousin the Crown Princess Tallyn, and to the other two children in his foster class: Lord Foby of Rippfell and Lady Cheshir of Deepford.

Unable to understand or speak the language, he held his burning cheek and blinked through tears. A large dog bounded up to the group. Jax was rooted in fear, but Foby tackled the beast and rolled with it, laughing.

Karric, as Captain of the King's guard, was in charge of all the young fosterlings, overseeing all aspects of their training to be the future rulers of the kingdom. She and her staff prepared them for the knighthood and taught them everything from economics and history to dancing and table manners. She had taken in many new fosterlings over the years, and even though this Barian Prince didn't speak Landish, she knew that most children were homesick on their first days. She suggested that the foster class all go to the stables to meet their new horses. Because Prince Bryx had taken so keenly to his horse, Karric didn't know that Barians didn't ride. A groom lifted little Jax up onto a great bay mare, who promptly and uncharacteristically bucked him right off.

He heard his arm crack as he landed, and he screamed.

People came running. His foster-mates and even the big dog crowded around. Everyone was yelling at him, but he could not understand a word they said.

He wanted Nanny desperately, but he heard Rax's voice in his head. *Make me proud of you, son.*

The dog licked the tears from his face, which still hurt. "I am Javix Sharkin," he said to them all "Prince of Baria. I don't like your mean ladies and your big animals."

No one understood his Islish.

"What's he saying?" Tallyn demanded.

The adults were busy splinting the broken arm and fussing about the horse. It was Foby who seemed to understand Jax's distress and wrapped him in a sweet, friendly hug.

Two days later when Rax arrived, he summoned Jax onto his flagship and, in front of his officers and the lord admiral, he asked Jax to tell his story.

"Well done, son," he said finally. "You've showed the strength of a Sharkin here. I can't believe they put you up on a horse. And as for that damned Dowager Stylla: she's never forgiven us for taking Valla away from her."

Glowing with pride, Jax went back to his fostering. He'd clung to it when they held him down to tattoo the sigil under his collarbone, and he remembered it every time some trick of language or custom humiliated him.

In the dark of the dungeon, Jax remembered that glow. Shifting in the straw, he felt the dragonpipe in his pocket. He pulled it out and played a series of bold Barian tunes.

But as time wore on, the glow of pride and courage seeped away into the darkness. His neck itched where the knife had cut him. He wondered where, by the goddess, Foby was. Couldn't his foster brother get him out of this damn hole?

Jax had sat in dark places before, and he had been taken beyond the limits of his own strength by Oblek and even by Marith. He was not at all confident he could withstand the agonies of a traitor's death without humiliating himself yet again.

"He won't ever confess, Father." Foby's voice was bleak in contrast to the glorious sunny day.

"The confession is a formality." The earl shifted in his saddle, as they rode side by side along the track back towards Rippsgate.

"But you know he didn't do it!"

"I agree that it's unlikely," the earl answered coldly. "So, I'm prepared to force the confession out of him."

"Why?" Foby pulled his horse to a halt. The pack of hounds sat, tongues lolling.

The earl turned and looked at his son, with compassion in his pale blue eyes. "Foby, I must uphold the ruling of the royal council and the decree of the king."

"But the ruling is wrong."

"At this point, that doesn't matter."

"Justice always matters!"

The earl took off his hat and ran his fingers through his thinning white hair. "Son, we cannot let a convicted traitor live. And I am warning you, we will have a confession out of him."

Foby shook his head.

"We will." The voice was implacable. "I have already discussed this with your sisters. You must not interfere, Foby, for your own safety."

"My *safety*?"

"You've admitted yourself that Princess Tallyn has been curt and suspicious since you returned from the Hantland last autumn."

"Not with me."

"And there's Midipex to consider too." The earl ran his gloved fingers through his horse's mane. "I do wonder why he didn't look further into Prince Jax's disappearance. Especially after we realized that the Barian's didn't have him."

Foby recognized an opening. "Right. If Jax didn't take the Treasury Documents, then who did?"

The earl of Rippsmarch turned to his son. "The next few days will be ugly and difficult for all of us. At least Tallyn will be here when the blood begins to flow. I hope that helps you." This last was said so softly that Foby barely heard it over the roaring in his head.

The earl turned his horse and rode with a straight back through the sunlight, striped by the shadow bars cast by the leafless trees.

Foby watched him go, admiring, and at the same time damning, his father for his strength.

35

The light that seeped through the small peephole in the top of his door grew slowly brighter. He looked up, squinting, as the door slammed open. As usual, he saw the gleam of drawn swords.

"Don't ye move, milord," the guard growled. Another took his slop bucket and dropped a new one. A woman set down a small plate of food and a battered metal cup. Without any further discussion, they left. He heard the bolt slide to and then the clink as the lock was snapped closed.

He rubbed his bound hands over his face. Dirty. Just like in the mines. The fetters clanked as he stood up and went to the food. The usual: stale bread and rind of meat. The wine in the battered cup was the rich red table wine of the Rippsmarch. Even a bit old and oxidized, it was delicious.

Warmed by the wine, he tried to forget his remaining hunger by playing his dragonpipe for a while. He had lost count of how long he'd been in this dark hole. At first he'd tried to mark the time by keeping track of when they fed him, but sometimes it seemed to be twice a day and other times only once, so his marks soon lost all meaning.

He played and tried to harmonize with his own echo, until, as usual, the fellow in the cell across the passage began to bellow for him to stop that goddess-damned ear-splitting noise, my goddess-damned lord.

Goddess damned, he played one last tune in memory of Doc then pocketed the small instrument. He rolled onto his side and closed his eyes.

The cell door crashed open. "Stand up, milord. It's time for yer confession."

Jax blinked against the light. "I have nothing to confess."

"Oh, of course ye don't, milord." A second guard grabbed his arm and hauled him to his feet. "Let's go."

Half prodded, half dragged, he stumbled into the courtyard and felt the afternoon sun warm his cold skin, even as his heart froze at the scene before him.

A large platform of wide wooden planks rose above the heads of a jeering crowd. Three nooses hung expectantly from a beam. Behind this a lone whipping post rose like an accusing finger, be-ringed with dangling manacles. Several other beams and levers stood ready for bloodier activities. A muscular executioner cracked a whip loudly to cheers from the crowd.

The earl, his three grown children, and the lords and ladies of the Rippsmarch stood on another dais under a canopy embroidered with the leaping stag symbol of the Marcher lords.

The guards pushed Jax up onto the gruesome stage and forced him to his knees. The crowd shouted and screamed. Jax's thoughts spun. Was the execution to start now? The guards had talked about a confession....

The earl lifted his hands and the crowd fell silent to listen.

"The execution of the traitor, Prince Javix Sharkin, will begin at noon tomorrow."

The crowd roared and the earl had to wait before he could continue. Jax felt his mind grow still. Noon tomorrow. He looked to the clear blue sky above the gray castle walls and grasped for his courage.

The earl was still speaking: "Before the execution begins, we give the traitor the opportunity to confess and go to his death with honesty."

Jax snorted and pushed himself to his feet. Gripping the chains of the fetters, he shouldered the guards aside. He knew he didn't look much of a prince, dirty and bloodied as he was, but he was damned if they'd treat him like a common villain. His voice was firm and elegant when he spoke.

"I have always been honest with you, my lord Oklan. I confirm that I am no traitor."

The crowd grumbled, and the earl grimaced.

More guards now pulled three miserable figures onto the execution platform.

"No!" Jax shouted. "No! Dragons fry you!"

Florin, Borrel, and Marith, each tightly bound, were shoved into place beneath the three dangling nooses. He could see bruises and scabs on both Florin and Borrel. A Dragon stood close beside Borrel as well, and Jax felt her magic holding Borrel's power in a vice. He didn't want to look at Marith, and when he did his heart began to bleed.

She appeared to have recovered from her pneumonia, but her face was gray, dirt exaggerating her wrinkles. She stood beneath the noose just a few feet away from him.

"Goddess, Marith," he choked. "Goddess, I am so sorry."

"We're all sorry, Jax," Florin snapped.

Marith's eyes were sad and her voice low. "There was nothing you could do."

The earl had again raised his hands to quiet the crowd. "Now, Prince Jax, perhaps you will make a confession."

He turned toward the dais slowly. "To save Mother Marith and Florin and Borrel?"

The earl shrugged.

Jax let his gaze run across Foby's face then out to the crowd. "I confess that I have traveled with Mother Marith and the Starrish twins. I confess that I did not tell them that I was a prince in Kordon and Baria, and so they did not know."

Lady Dayne spoke dryly. "That's not exactly the answer we were looking for, my lord."

"It's the truth."

"Well, it won't save your friends."

"What will?"

"Your *full* confession, my lord."

"This makes no sense. If I lie to you and say I committed some kind of treason, then you free my friends, but if I speak the truth and maintain my innocence—all of our innocence—you'll execute the lot of us."

The earl nodded. Foby turned his face away.

Jax looked back to Marith. Tears were running down her cheeks.

"No," she whispered. "Don't do it, son." Her tears came faster as she watched the wolfish smile spread across his face.

"It won't change my fate, Mam. I'm happy to get you out of this mess."

The crowd watched as the prince took a step toward them. When he spoke, his voice rang with sincerity. "I confess that I learned to honor my place as a prince of Kordon, but today you've made me ashamed of my Kordish blood. You may have it back. I confess to whatever crimes you'd like to blame on me."

The crowd went wild. Small stones bounced off of him, stinging and bruising. He saw Marith and the nyads removed from the platform. The guards again forced him to his knees.

"At noon tomorrow then," the earl's voice boomed across the courtyard. "At noon tomorrow the execution of the traitor will begin."

He had not expected to sleep. All too well he knew that by this time tomorrow he'd be in a kind of sheer physical anguish that made sleep nearly impossible. He wanted to enjoy being whole for as long as he could. And he did feel whole for the first time since he'd been dragged out of Kordon all those years ago. Oddly comforted, he relaxed into the dirty straw and slipped into sleep.

A strange tickle awoke him. At first he thought it was another rat nosing at his belly.

Then came a breath of cold air and the pungent scent of lavender. He sat up.

"Hush," said a shrouded figure. Jax felt magic flare and the fetters opened. The figure placed them quietly on the ground then rose, pulling Jax to his feet.

He stood unsteadily.

"Come," whispered the figure. Something dropped into the straw at Jax's feet, and a cool hand grasped his own and dragged him out of the cell and into the tunnel.

The figure led Jax deeper into the tunnel, down a flight of stairs, across a wet, slippery stone floor and out through a small hole that they both had to crawl through. From somewhere up in the main castle, a dog barked. Once outside in the crisp winter night, Jax finally paused.

"Stop. Who are you? Where are we going?"

The moon was barely a sliver, but compared to the darkness of the dungeon, the night seemed quite bright to Jax. The gray-cloaked figure drew back her hood. "I'm Juna, a Priestess of the Oracle, your Highness. You've been summoned."

"That's convenient. Did you tell the earl?"

"No."

"Then how did you get to me? How did you get past the guards?"

Juna's smile flashed in the pale moonlight. "The Oracle has many resources, my lord."

Jax realized that the tickle in his stomach must be a response to the Oracle's magic. It felt a lot like fairy magic. "What about Marith, Florin, and Borrel. Are they coming too?"

"No." Juna pulled her hood back over her dark hair. "Just you, my lord. And we must be off now, before the guards find you missing."

Jax shivered, his torn shirt flapping in the cold night air. "Wait. I can't leave them here."

"You have been summoned, Prince Javix; you must come."

"No." Jax stepped away from the priestess. "If I disappear, they'll be blamed. They were nearly executed already.'"

"I left a token of the Oracle for the earl to find," Juna said patiently. She watched Jax look back up at the dark mass of the castle wall. He wrapped his arms around himself, obviously freezing. His worn shirt would have been far too thin for a frigid night like this even had it been whole. Juna snapped her fingers quietly. Silently, two more gray-cloaked figures slipped from the snowy woods. One tossed a similar, thick gray cloak around the prince's shoulders.

He turned back. "Listen, if you could get me out of there, you can get Mother Marith too."

Juna took a deep breath. "Your Highness, the Oracle needs you and they need you now. Surely you know that the Oracle only rarely requires the services of people other than its priests and priestesses, like me and my fellows here."

Jax nodded, counting four of them now surrounding him. He had been taught all this, and people on Baria still spoke of a young girl who had been summoned back when his grandmother was the seaqueen.

"So," Juna continued. "While I understand your concern for Mother Marith and the Starrish twins, you have to answer to the Oracle's higher call."

"A higher call? Do you know what Marith did for me? I can't leave her here like this."

"You do indeed owe her a great deal, my lord." Juna nodded. "But others can help her here. Princess Tallyn will arrive in the morning. But only Javix Sharkin can fulfill the Oracle's mission. You must have faith."

"Faith?" He demanded roughly. "Faith? Do you know what I've seen? Do you know where I've been?"

Juna nodded. "You have been in the darkness for a long time, my lord. Come away now. Come away with us to the Oracle. We will use force if necessary."

Jax looked at Juna for several long minutes. He could feel her magic joining with the others to form a net around him. He had no more choice here than when Felona and the Duke of Midipex had abducted him from Kree all those years ago. At least no one was coming at him with burning knives now.

"Fine."

"You are free now, my lord," Juna said, with no apparent irony.

"Freedom comes only in death."

Two more gray-cloaked people appeared from the trees, leading seven small, winged horses. The animals were so white that they gleamed in the thin moonlight. Jax had seen the Oracle's herd of pegusi grazing on the green sweeps of pasture on the Head, the southernmost point of the Barian Island. He had even seen them fly in graceful circles around the stone ring that marked the Oracle's temple there. But he had never seen them up close. Even in the dark, their beauty was intense.

Jax watched the priests and priestesses leap onto the backs of the horses. He felt the tickle in his stomach turn into a tingling kind of melody.

The horses wore no saddles or bridles. The other riders bent low over the horses' necks and held on to the flowing white manes.

Jax glanced one more time back up at the dark walls of the earl's castle.

"Marith will understand, my lord." Juna said quietly. "She would not want to watch you face a traitor's death."

Jax looked back to the priestess, remembering the tears on Marith's face. "Why is the Oracle summoning me?"

"They will tell you when we get there. Please mount up, my lord." She motioned to one of the beautiful creatures, who stood looking at Jax with its large, clear eyes.

"Horses don't like me." Jax did not like the prospect of riding bareback on a horse that could fly high above the trees.

"The pegasi are different."

Jax grabbed the horse's mane and swung himself up onto its back. He fully expected to be thrown immediately back into the dirt, but the horse just stood there and the singing tingling in his belly moved up into his heart.

"How does the horse know where I want to go?" he asked Juna.

"She listens to your heart."

Jax thought about his heart that seemed to pine for so many different and disparate places and people, most of them lost or closed to him. But maybe the Oracle would know something about Lexyl's haunting poem. He would ask them about the fairy queen's cryptic complaints too.

Juna's horse extended its wings. "Are you ready, Prince Javix?"

"I am ready."

The pegasi leaped to a gallop, spread their wings, and rose into the starry sky.

The earl awoke to horns blaring in alarm. His mistress grumbled. "Oklan, make them stop that horrid racket."

As the earl pushed back the bed curtains, his chamberlain ran into the room. "The traitor is gone, your Grace!" He held out the earl's fur-lined dressing gown. "His cell was found empty this morning. Except...Well, your Grace, come see."

The earl slipped his boots onto his bare feet and cinched his robe as he strode downstairs to the dungeon. He sniffed at the dark, rancid cell, frowning. Well, no one would be able to say he had made the lad too comfortable.

"We found this here in the straw, your Grace." The captain of the guards pointed.

The earl bent and retrieved a gleaming silver medallion. Crescent moons rose on one side, while a strange rune decorated the reverse. "The Oracle," whispered the earl, recognizing the symbols.

Had the prince brought this thing with him? As he marched back upstairs, he fired orders to the chamberlain. "Find Prince Jax's friends and lock them up, but see what they know, first. Keep me posted on the search parties. And send me Thessaly. Maybe she knows what this medallion means."

The chamberlain eventually found Lady Thessaly with Mother Marith in a chilly room in the back of the infirmary. The old woman was gray with worry. Thessaly, grim faced, sat on the edge of Marith's bed. Each held a steaming cup of morning tea.

Grooms brought the two nyads from their beds down the hall.

"Do you know where he is?" the chamberlain demanded.

"Where who is?" asked Borrel.

"Jax," croaked Marith, her voice still rough in the mornings. "They say Jax escaped last night."

"Really?" Florin could not suppress her smile.

"Really," snapped the chamberlain. "We will find him, and you will tell us what you know."

"We don't know anything," Borrel said. "How could we?"

"Take them to the dungeon." The chamberlain motioned to a phalanx of guards. "Maybe a few days with the rats will loosen their tongues."

"Mother Marith can't go the dungeon," Thessaly intervened. "She can be guarded here."

"I'm sorry, my lady. The earl's orders were quite specific. And he wishes to see you immediately."

"Very well." Thessaly rose with a concerned glance at Marith. "I'll do what I can."

Marith swung her thin legs out of the bed. Two guards came up and grasped each of her arms roughly.

"That's not necessary," Thessaly snapped. "Be gentle with Mother Marith. That's an order!" She glared at the guards who nodded a subdued, "Yes, my lady."

She found her father eating a piece of toast in front of the fire in the great hall, while he listened to reports from the various riders who had gone out looking for the prince.

"There were no tracks near the castle, my lord," one of the riders explained. "The bloodhounds couldn't find any scent."

"Thank you." The earl dismissed the rider and turned to his youngest.

"Father, you can't put Mother Marith in the dungeon. She's not well enough to survive the cold and damp."

"I must lock them all up, Thess. I'll be accused of treason if I don't. Here." He flipped something round and gleaming at his daughter. "What do you make of this?"

Thessaly caught the medallion and looked it over. "It's a token of the Oracle."

"It was found in Jax's cell this morning."

Thessaly frowned. "I wonder what it means."

"So do I."

"Your Grace! Your Grace!" Footmen came shouting into the hall. "Riders, milord! From the south. It looks like Princess Tallyn."

"Ah," grumbled the earl. "Just in time."

Tallyn arrived on a steaming horse with six lords and ladies-in-waiting riding with her. The earl and his family welcomed the princess in the courtyard. Foby followed his bow with a warm embrace and an intimate kiss. The earl waited impatiently and finally snapped. "Foby, let go of her Highness and let her come inside for some tea and toast."

"No thank you, your Grace." Tallyn's smile for the earl was tense. "Has the execution begun?"

"Eh, no, your Highness."

"Good. I want to see him first."

The earl took a deep breath. "He's not here, my lady."

Tallyn froze, her clear blue eyes hardened.

The earl continued quickly. "His cell was empty this morning. We found this there." He handed the princess the Oracle's medallion.

She looked down at it, flipped it over, and then returned her gaze to the earl. "I guess I'll have that tea, then."

Once settled into the earl's solarium, Tallyn sipped her tea, her eyes still cold.

"So, he's disappeared again?"

"Apparently so, your Highness," Dayne said. "We forced a confession out of him yesterday, as formality dictates. The guards then took him back to the dungeon and locked him in. This morning, his cell was completely empty."

"He confessed?"

"Yes." The earl looked into his teacup.

"He did it to save his friends," Foby snapped. "It wasn't pretty."

"What friends?" Tallyn held out her empty cup.

"Mother Marith, the Hantish druid he came here with, and the two nyads." Lady Thessaly poured the steaming tea.

"Maybe we'll have to execute them after all," the earl said, unable to keep the regret out of his voice.

Tallyn sat up. "You mean he didn't take them with him?"

"No."

"Well, let's have them up here and talk to them, then."

Within several minutes Borrel, Florin, and Marith found themselves facing the earl, his three children, and a tall blond-haired woman, with eyes so pale they almost seemed colorless. The earl introduced Jax's companions to Tallyn.

Tallyn said nothing, but just looked at the three strangers. The old woman had a happy face, despite the evident weakness left by her illness. The princess had never seen any nyads. Masking her distaste, she watched the two of them bow awkwardly to her, noting the wariness in their eyes.

She turned her gaze back to the old woman. "We met your son, Doc, and Father Adgar in Hilsen Vale last autumn. I am afraid that one of our men wounded Doc, but we are assured that he has recovered."

Marith sat up. "Doc was wounded? How? Why?"

"Those are some very good questions, Mother." Tallyn took another sip of tea, noting its sweetness. Where, she wondered was the earl getting Farsouthian sugar? But she spoke again to Marith. "Now, the earl tells me that you don't know where Prince Jax has gone either."

"That's right, eh, your Grace." Marith said.

"It's your Highness the first time, then my lady after that," Tallyn corrected absently. She sat back in her chair, her colorless eyes considering the druid and the two silent nyads.

Marith spoke slowly. "You know, my lady, he spoke of you."

"He did?"

She nodded. "At the time I didn't realize that the cousin Tallyn he talked about was the Crown Princess of Kordon, but he told me stories of when you two were children together. He missed you."

"I missed him, too." Tallyn took a deep breath.

"But you believe he is a traitor, my lady?" Marith frowned at her. 'You people have planned a very grisly death for the poor lad."

"I am aware of the details, Mother." Tallyn said, rising. She held out the Oracle's medallion. "Have you seen this before?"

Marith reached out to take it, turning it over. "No," she shook her head.

"It wasn't something Jax had on him when he came here?"

Marith looked at Borrel, who shook his head, and Florin, who shrugged. "I've never seen it, and I don't know where he would have picked up something like this, certainly not without us knowing about it."

"Might he have had it with him when your son bought him?"

Marith shook her head. "My lady, when Jax came to us in the Vale he had nothing. Nothing but a sense of who he was. I fear we even took that from him."

She looked at the medallion for a moment then handed it back to Tallyn.

"So," Foby cleared his throat in the silence. "So, this medallion must have been left by whoever helped Jax get away."

Marith smiled at the earl. "Maybe the Oracle didn't want you to execute him."

36

Even exiled as they were to the outer fringes of life at Rippsgate Keep, Marith and the nyads could sense the tension when the king arrived later that afternoon. They watched the procession of courtiers, knights, servants, and supply carts filter through the gate and pool in confusion in the courtyard.

"You must not blame yourself, Lord Oklan," a red-robed lord said to the earl as he straightened from his bow before the king.

"The half-islish traitor is devious and his supporters well hidden...." Marith could hear no more as the great lords entered the castle, but she saw Lord Foby's shoulders stiffen, and thought that Tallyn's smile seemed a little fixed.

"Who is that red lord?" she asked a passing groom.

"Him's the Duke of Midipex," the groom said, pulling a mud-spattered horse off towards the stable.

Marith didn't know why, but that name raised goose bumps on her arm.

Late that night, under the deep quilts of Foby's bed, Tallyn pulled his arms around her. "Midipex," she murmured.

"But why?"

"Maybe he's protecting someone else."

Foby adjusted the dog that was trying to settle in between him and Tallyn. "The dowager?"

"Maybe."

After a few moments Foby spoke softly. "Midipex always seemed to dislike both Jax and Prince Bryx. Remember the time he tried to get them both excluded from the knighthood trials?"

"That's right," Tallyn agreed. "He tried to get Prince Bryx disqualified, but Captain Karric stood up to him."

"And the sealord, as I recall."

Tallyn smiled into the dark, remembering the bold figure of Sealord Rax sweeping into the throne room, growling in his accented Landish and subduing Midipex with some force of personality that Tallyn hadn't really understood as a teenager. She understood it now.

She listened to Foby's gentle breathing and felt the dog wriggle back between the two of them. Tallyn could count a number of times that Midipex had used his position as Lord Chancellor to express open skepticism about the Barians. She wondered what motivated his long-standing distrust of all Barians and his dislike of the two half-islish princes in particular. Was he covering for the dowager, whose own hatred was well understood? Or maybe he wished to remove the Barian princes from the succession because without them, Midipex's bloodline was closest to the throne.

Breakfast the next day was served in the Great Hall. King Kodill lounged in a comfortable chair planning a hunting trip for the afternoon with the earl's huntress. Truth be told, Kodill had enjoyed his ride across his thawing kingdom and he was rather pleased to find the traitor gone and the execution cancelled. He never enjoyed watching people die the way his mother did. Now that he was here, he'd spend a few days feasting at Rippsmarch's expense and hunting his private game.

At the other end of the table, he noticed that Tallyn and Midipex and Rippsmarch were having some kind of conversation about young Jax's wild Hantish friends, but he couldn't really hear and he didn't really want to. Purposefully, he attacked another crunchy piece of toast.

"Of course, you are right, your Grace," Tallyn was saying. "We are well within our rights to execute Jax's accomplices at any time."

Midipex smiled and turned to the earl. "You've built such a nice structure, Oklan, and the people will be expecting the spectacle. Why don't you just hang them all today?"

Rippsmarch grimaced. "I gave Prince Jax my word."

Midipex looked surprised. "What could you possibly have said to bind yourself to a traitor?"

"I forced him to confess, Thorag.

Midipex leaned forward. "Did he say something to make you think he isn't guilty?"

The earl met Midipex's pale stare. "It's clear that our prince was enslaved. I'd like to know how a Prince of the Blood ended up in such a terrible situation."

Midipex nodded. "Indeed, indeed. That is an unforgivable crime against Kordon itself. If it's true." He paused and sipped some tea. "But if all that is true, then why did he confess?"

"Because we threatened to execute his friends." The earl answered. "He confessed to save their lives, so I can't execute them."

The lord chancellor appeared to think about this for a few minutes. At last he spoke, his fluty voice full of admiration. "Lord Oklan, you are the most honorable man I know. Only you would expect to keep your word to someone who confessed to treason and then escaped from your own dungeon."

Earl Kora shook his head. "My word is a reflection of me. It has nothing to do with the other party."

Midipex's voice acquired a bite: "Maybe escape isn't the right word."

"I have a solution, my lords." Tallyn's voice was like a soothing balm. "We have seen that Prince Jax cares deeply for his companions, this druid Marith and the two nyads."

Foby started to speak, but Tallyn handed him the cat that had been in her lap. She continued: "It is possible that Jax did not wish to leave his friends behind when the Oracle, or whoever it was, snuck him out of here. I believe that he may try to come back for them, especially if he knows that we are keeping them."

The lord chancellor leaned back in his chair, a gleam in his pale blue eyes. "Very clever, my princess. A plan worthy of a monarch."

"Then you agree, my lord?"

"Yes. Yes, I do. But they must be kept under close watch."

"I shall have Captain Karric see to that," Tallyn said, rising.

The lords and Lady Dayne stood respectfully. "Thank you, my lady," Rippsmarch said, taking the cat from Foby.

Jax clung to the windblown mane of the winged horse as it flew through the darkness over the rolling Kordish countryside. Moonlight flashed silver on the dark water of the River Ripp below them. The sun rose as they flew over the bare brown branches of the Darkwood Forest. At noon, they were flying over fallow fields, relinquishing the last patches of snow to the late winter sun. They did not pause for rest or food. Jax listened to the singing in his heart and felt the powerful beat of the pegasus' wings soothe and sustain him.

Sometime the next night they flew off the edge of the mainland and out over the wrinkled blanket of the moonlit sea. Jax sniffed the salty sea breeze and recognized that another Rising was in the offing. Could it really be only one year since he had been shipwrecked with Oblek in Hanter Lake?

The winged horse shook his head, as if he could understand the black terror that still engulfed Jax when he remembered hoping to drown in that sulfuric water. One year since Klaris had failed to save him. One year since Doc and Marith did.

Now, as the Island of Baria slowly climbed above the horizon, he sat up a little straighter to get a better view. The sun rising from behind him caught the island and it sparkled like a diamond set in

Barian Blue velvet. Jax's heart soared along with his steed as the familiar scent of Barian pine reached him. A handful of fishing boats dotted the blue water in the distance, their triangular sails full of sun and wind.

He smiled into the cold, clear air. He was not free. He had nothing but a wooden dragonpipe and a scrap of poetry in his pocket. But he was Jax Sharkin, and he was coming home.

Acknowledgements

I'm grateful to the many friends and family who have read this story, sometimes more than once, and made it so much better: Bill Stearns, Cathy Calhoun Damon, Warren Fox, Robbie Fox. Kristen Gould Case, Mark Menlove, Andy Cier, Joe Totten, Lisa Cilva Ward, Karri Dell Hayes, Susan Morris, Asha Rehnberg, Evan Gregory, Gloria Rice, Willoughby Staley and David Staley. I am deeply indebted to my cousin Valerie for introducing me to Starhawk and non-patriarchal religion. Starhawk continues to work in this space and can be found on Instagram. Adrian Fox Staley manages my online presence at *CAFoxBooks.com*. Check it out for information on when the next two books in the trilogy are ready to read. I wouldn't be able to share the story without the amazing support and talent of Katie Mullaly at Surrogate Press and Michelle Rayner of Cosmic Design. Any errors in the text are entirely my own.

About the Author

C.A. Fox has taught skiing, sold books, encouraged critical think-ing among college students, and raised two free thinking kids, not always with appreciation for their independent thoughts. Home is a place that requires high-elevation modifications for baking and the expectation that it may snow on any day of the year. Like the fictional poet, Featherfetch, Fox casts nets of words to catch the downy bits out of the wind. Visit *CAFoxBooks.com* for more information and follow on Facebook, *@Paradox Trilogy*.